THE BROTHERS CARBURI

Petrie Harbouri

BLOOMSBURY

First published 2001

Copyright © 2001 by Petrie Harbouri

The moral right of the author has been asserted

Bloomsbury Publishing Plc, 38 Soho Square, London WID 3HB

A CIP catalogue record for this book
is available from the British Library

ISBN 0 7475 5342 4

Typeset in Great Britain by Hewer Text Ltd, Edinburgh
Printed in Great Britain by Clays Limited, St Ives plc

For Spyros, Valliano's great-great-grandson, with love.
But also of course for my siblings, Kate, Richard,
Charlotte and Tom.

O F   T H E many people who have helped me with this book I should particularly like to thank Virgilio Giormani and Cecilia Ghetti for information on Marco and Marino Carburi, John Jefferis for guidance on engineering matters and – most of all – Anastasios Charbouris for entrusting to me a treasure trove of Carburi family letters and documents. From these threads have I woven my fiction.

1

F OR MARINO everything began and ended in Argostoli. The birth was much as these things usually are, women moving purposefully in a shuttered room; the mother was fit and strong (although the delivery was a difficult one) so that it would never have crossed anyone's mind to call on a doctor's assistance, even had such a man-midwife been available. Thus the only male presence was that of the new-born infant – held up, red and wet and screaming, for admiration, for affirmation. A second healthy son is after all an achievement. The funeral, by contrast, fifty-three years later, was attended only by men. His brothers were all far off in distant lands, his only son already dead and buried; thus it was brother-in-law and nephews and neighbours who stood bare-headed and tight-lipped in the sharp light of an April afternoon, shocked certainly, grieving possibly, at any rate crossing themselves with dry-eyed dignity. By the time they rowed back to town across the water a stiff breeze had arisen so that the sea was suddenly choppy. In the burial ground the shadows of the cypress trees were lengthening.

With the passing of the years the gravestone acquired a weathered and lichen-encrusted patina so that the name inscribed on it became illegible; it no longer stood upright but leaned at an angle, then in the earthquake fell and broke into three pieces. In due course the authorities tidied up the graveyard and removed the rubble and fragments of broken stone. Later still someone decided to beautify the place and planted shrubs. On the now unmarked grave a mock-orange bush henceforth flourished, scenting the air each April with its fugitive, tender fragrance: *Philadelphus* is its Latin name.

When I searched for Marino's grave I could not find it, not guessing then that his mortal remains must lie beneath that plant of brotherly love.

It is often said – though no one can prove it – that at the moment of death a fleeting series of pictures flashes through the mind: images of the life that is ending. Marino died so long ago and the scenes of his life flicker so faintly now that many of them are almost unapprehendable. Yet there are a few fragmented images which from time to time emerge. Let us then start with one such picture.

Brown boys swimming perhaps, naked and lissom, in the familiar waters of what they call 'the lake'. (Once again it is a segregated scene: no girls are present for swimming is not an activity suitable for the female sex.) Two or three of the boys are pubescent although most are at the earlier stage where they are growing so fast that their thin, straight legs seem too long for their shrimp-like bodies. A few are even younger, however, and still possess something of infantile plumpness; their chubby limbs and rounded cheeks make their mothers feel anxiously protective, with the result that older brothers are admonished to take care of them. It is probably just as well that the mothers do not see how the little ones are usually left to themselves to splash at the water's edge while their elders race each other or dive from the slippery gun-wales of an abandoned, half-submerged boat or on occasion balance there perilously, legs apart, and have serious peeing contests. Salt water children, island children, whose lake is in reality the long and narrow inlet of sea on which Argostoli is situated.

Giovanni Battista, the oldest of the company, usually

known as Giovambattista or (to his family) Giambattista, is already adolescent: a serious boy who swims by himself but takes his mother's instructions to heart. His two small brothers are thus cuffed and kept in order or roughly comforted if a scraped knee or face blurred with snot and tears seems to require it. 'The thing about scraped knees,' he tells Marino, 'is that they mend by themselves.' These words are said with such assurance that his brother stops howling instantly. 'You'd better wash it in the sea. And wipe your nose.' This being done, Marino runs back to the other children and joins in their game once more while Giovambattista ponders the why and the how of the way things mend by themselves. As they make their way home he gets out the knife that he carries in his pocket and carefully cuts the tip of the little finger of his left hand, on the pad just below the nail. His brothers who have turned round and are watching are impressed by this display of virility and are silent as the red blood wells up and drips from Giovambattista's hand, nor do they say a word later as their mother wonders how it could have happened and fusses and calls for warm water and linen to bind his finger. Although the cut does of course mend, it turns septic first so that the finger swells and throbs painfully. Giovambattista watches its progress and squeezes the pus from the wound with curiosity. 'Does it hurt, Yanni?' asks Marco solicitously, to which he answers, 'Yes.' He washes it in the sea. After the cut has healed he is interested to note that he has no sensation in the tip of his finger. There is a small but perceptible scar.

On another occasion, several years later when he comes to Venice to visit his younger brothers at the school of the Patriarchate, Giovambattista takes a precocious Marino aside and points out firmly, 'The only thing to be said about married women is that if you make them pregnant it's not

3

too catastrophic.' What is implied is, 'If you must.' But this of course is when they are both older, when Giovambattista is studying at Bologna and thus not able to keep an eye on them. Whether he has ever made anyone pregnant his brothers do not know; Marino and Marco have both speculated privately about this and other related matters but are too loyal to say anything, even to each other. Marino immediately passes this brotherly advice on to Marco, and Marco in turn (rather late in the day, on a visit home) to Paolo who is the baby of the family.

It seems we have not one but two images: the happy children playing in the sea and the loving, loyal, protective bonds of brotherhood.

The order in which you are born into your family is one of those things over which you have no control. I was about to say 'like the colour of your hair' – but of course hair may be dyed a different colour from that which God intended, or indeed may be powdered daily. The children's father neither powdered his hair nor wore a wig, which fact caused his eldest son occasional moments of embarrassed misery (no shame more cringing than that felt by the child whose parent refuses to conform); however, since their father's hair went prematurely silver, by the time the younger children were growing up 'it didn't show too much' (these, I think, were Paolo's words).

Not only was Giovambattista the eldest but for a long time it looked as if he would be the only child, for in spite of regular and strenuous efforts on the part of his father and many prayers on the part of his mother almost seven years went by after his birth without even the suspicion of another pregnancy. The concentrated, undiluted weight of every single parental expectation is a heavy burden to grow up with and this perhaps explains why Giovambattista was always a quiet and solemn child. His figure was tall and slender, his hair light brown and his eyes grey-green ('stone-coloured' said the only person who was ever moved by them). Marino and Marco, born little more than a year apart as if the one birth had unleashed the other, were by contrast sturdy and dark-haired and brown-eyed and capable of unruliness. Paolo, whose colouring was also fairish, was born when Giovambattista was eighteen.

(On the whole people's dates of birth and ages are a matter of plain record which can be checked. Where confusion arises the reasons are sometimes straightforward: the lingering ambiguity about Marco's year of birth, for example, is due quite simply to the fact that he was a winter baby who came into the world around the turn of the year – thus, depending on whether you follow the Old or the New Calendar, you might consider him to have been born in December of one year or in January of the next. Regardless of when the younger boys were born, however, Giovambattista grew up knowing that they were in his charge. 'You must look after your brothers,' was a lesson learned early.)

And then there was Maria, five years older than Paolo. 'Your sister will be your responsibility until she is properly married,' was something that all four of the boys knew by heart. However, girls neither rode nor fished nor swam, nor indeed were they sent away to school in Venice, and thus the bonds that bound the brothers never quite included her.

Not, of course, that there were not sometimes currents of jealousy.

'It might be mine, but then again it might be Marco's,' explained Marino about the dark-haired, dark-eyed baby that the girl held on her hip at the window as they passed by. (A touch of studiedly casual bravado here.) 'She's married, so it's quite all right,' he hastened to add, noticing an expression of disapproval on Giovambattista's face.

'You should be ashamed of yourselves.'

'Why? She was willing, she wanted to, anyway you yourself said it was safer if they were married . . .' ('Her husband's dark too,' he might have added except that he was in fact feeling rather proud of himself and didn't want to think of this possibility.)

'It's disgusting, it's like incest.'

'Ioánnis Vaptistís is becoming very moral,' Marino told Marco later that night, using his elder brother's formal Greek name in mockery.

'Oh, he's just being a hypocrite,' said Marco comfortably, 'no one's moral in this country.'

Marco was easygoing and equable. Marino couldn't quite allow himself to admit the uncomfortable suspicion that she might have liked Marco better.

Giovambattista, who (taking his fraternal responsibilities seriously) was once more visiting them and who knew quite well that he had never fathered a child, lay in bed alone feeling odd and uncomfortable pangs of envy at his brothers' cheerful first philanderings, which sensation he attributed tentatively to some slight disorder of the stomach.

(I have no wish to invade Giovambattista's privacy and shall thus try in what I write to respect some of his secrets: his dignity – always a vulnerable spot – was precious to him and, like most people, he hated being laughed at.)

'I do not like sleeping with anyone else,' Giovambattista had announced at the age of thirteen in the days when they all still lived at home. Possibly thoughts occasioned by Maria's birth had something to do with this new feeling. In spite of the fact that such a desire to be alone seemed a strange

6

conceit, his mother, whose favourite he was, allowed him to move into a small cell-like room at the back of the house. Marino and Marco continued to share a room; indeed, until Giovambattista moved out they had in fact shared a bed. ('You kicked me.' 'No I didn't. You farted.' 'No I didn't.' 'Yes you did . . .' etcetera.)

'They both snore,' said Giovambattista, in an attempt to explain the inexplicable. (As a matter of fact this was not untrue just then, since it was winter and both younger boys were suffering from a heavy cold.)

'My brothers are like little animals,' he thought to himself and loved them with irritated tenderness. Nevertheless he was glad to sleep alone.

Italy is the place where people are not moral; Italy is the place where people are chic and sophisticated; Italy has always been the promised land. It is from Venice that the artists come who perform in the theatre at Argostoli (even if the children have never seen them), from Venice that travelling magicians come, that fashions come, that – if you think about it – conversation comes (for on an island of two small towns and a rugged hinterland where everyone knows everyone else the arrival of a ship from the metropolis invariably brings something new to talk about). It is of course from Venice too that the Governor and the soldiers come, though this perhaps has always been taken for granted.

When Giovambattista arrived home in order to escort his brothers to the Patriarchal Seminary in Venice it was thus natural that both younger boys should feel proud at the thought of moving into a grown-up world.

It is true that Marco cried a little when the ship sailed out of the bay into the open sea, but then he was not yet quite ten. Marino said nothing but simply went and stood very close to him; at night he put his protective, eleven-year-old arms around his brother and they slept in each other's warmth, cuddled together under a blanket, while Giovambattista tried to read by the dim light of a swaying lamp.

'He didn't mean to and he couldn't help it,' Marino declared the next day, trying to forestall what they both feared might be Giambattista's wrath. To Marco he had said comfortingly, '*Capita a tutti di farsela addosso* – Everybody wets themselves sometimes.'

Italian is of course the language in which civilised people express their thoughts and feelings.

Marino and Marco had agreed that it was stylish to have a name that was effectively the same in both Greek and Italian; they and Maria were the only ones who did, Giovambattista being known in Greek as Yanni (for his full name was rather a mouthful) and Paolo as Pavlo. Their Greek names, however, were not in general usage after they reached a certain age. Greek is a language for lullabies and baby talk.

As a matter of fact it was also the language their parents occasionally lapsed into between themselves when alone in the marital bedchamber, although in public – at least certainly in front of the children – they invariably spoke Italian. Their mother had a pronounced Greek accent; she called her eldest son 'Tzambattista' and said 'tsembalo' instead of 'cembalo' (though actually she played it much better than Maria was ever to do).

And Greek is the language of the church: a sonorous Greek, quite different from everyday speech. None of the brothers was a great churchgoer. Of necessity Giovambattista and Marco later became well used to attending Latin masses, yet both would have agreed if they'd thought about it that the familiar cadences of the great Orthodox liturgies have a deeper power to move, a limpidity through which one may glimpse the essence of things. A wedding ceremony doesn't really seem quite complete without the long-known words – even if, as Maria was to point out tartly, they hadn't apparently done Paolo much good. (Whether these words did any good in the case of Marino's second marriage was something that no one wanted to think of.) Giovambattista and Marco both learnt to cross themselves the wrong way round, although in moments of stress they reverted to the proper way, the Greek way, from right to left.

Then there is another underlying image, existing on a level beyond language, which is that of the marsh. This is a powerful and abiding image, for Marino's triumph and later his death had to do with marshes. If Marino is remembered at all today in his native land it is by the unofficial name still given to an empty, lonely place: Carburi's marsh.

When they were children the marsh they knew best was the low-lying damp land at the end of their 'lake' where they were forbidden to go, but of course did. Mosquitoes bred in the brackish pools among the reeds; this perhaps was why it was generally held to be an unhealthy place, if not downright evil. Most people with business on the other side of the bay thus preferred to row across rather than ride or walk the long way round. (Funerals were always conducted in this manner: a little flotilla, the coffin in one boat, the mourners following in others, the sad creak of rowlocks.)

The marsh was a curiously silent place – not that there were no sounds of frogs or birds or insects, merely that in some strange way these sounds served only to emphasise the underlying quietness rather than fill it. In the marsh the children instinctively spoke in hushed tones.

When Giovambattista occasionally dreamed of the marsh, it was always absolutely silent. He never told anyone that at the beginning abroad is sometimes a lonely place to be.

Much later, he heard frogs croaking in France; everyone else complained that the noise kept them awake but Giovambattista, now called Jean-Baptiste, was suddenly made happy by them one summer night, as if sound and colour were flooding into the place inhabited by the silent dreams. This was one of the rare occasions when Giovambattista was not sleeping alone. 'It is a little-known fact that frogs everywhere always croak in Greek,' he told his companion, who, however, merely said something rude in French and pulled the bedcovers over their faces in an attempt to muffle the sound.

In the cold lands to the east were other marshes, silent and austere. Marino, now called the Chevalier Alexandre de Lascaris, told his children that marshes are fertile places but their attention wandered, they were not really very interested. He was in any case speaking to them in Italian, a language which they still associated with the schoolroom. He switched to French and told them about his childhood marsh, about the lake, about swimming: 'One day I'll teach you to swim,' he promised his son. (One day I'll teach you Greek.) They liked such stories better, although the strange, far-off, sunny world of their father's youth never seemed entirely real to them. Marino took the boy's small mittened left hand; 'Look,' he said, 'it's like your mitten. The big bay is this bit with your four fingers in it, and the narrow bay that we used to call our lake is your thumb, and the marsh is just here, right at the tip of your thumb' (kissing it).

Their nurse, to whom Giorgio and Sofia chattered volubly in Russian, was at first puzzled that a man should wish to spend so much time with his children, but in the end comfortably supposed it must have something to do with him being a foreigner.

Later on Marino preferred to put all such conversations

firmly out of mind. So much so, in fact, that he refused to describe the island in any detail to his second wife, merely telling her, 'You'll see when we get there.' She had already learnt by then that *mon petit marin* was not a name to which he responded happily.

But to go back: in that sunlit past his younger siblings – or three of them anyway, Paolo being barely two months old – were impressed when Giovambattista came back on his first visit home. He had a russet-coloured riding coat which seemed to them to be of extreme elegance, scrupulously clean hands and cuffs, and no trace of the provincial in his accent; he prescribed a purgative for Marco and a plaster for their father's rheumatism, even if he was still only a fledgling physician. Both remedies appeared to work.

Several young ladies approaching marriageable age were also impressed. Two or three sets of parents began to consider that the eldest Carburi boy might not after all be such a bad match. Giovambattista kept his thoughts to himself, flirted a little (coolly and competently, perhaps practising the bedside manner) and left again for Bologna as soon as Paolo's baptism was accomplished, his heart quite intact, with Marino and Marco under his strict but brotherly wing.

The need to study and pursue a profession is first and foremost dictated by simple economics. If all four sons have four children apiece, then quite clearly the parcels of land that this third generation will inherit will be minuscule, not enough to live on. For the land, like the paternal house, like the title later on, is inherited by all the children: thanks to Marco the brothers all came to be Counts, as indeed would their sons be, but these putative sons must live on something – this much is obvious. It is of course sensible to supplement your inheritance and your professional earnings by marrying a girl with an attractive dowry (cash doesn't go amiss, but land is best). Of the four brothers it was only Paolo who was in a hurry to get married, although the dowry he received with his bride was not quite what his parents had hoped for. However, by marrying at the age of nineteen and settling down to beget children, Paolo spared his family the expense of sending him to university in Italy.

All the same, such expense is a worthwhile investment. Never overtly stated is a further consideration: if the brothers look set to do well and be successful, restoring the family fortunes, then this, as well as her dowry, will somehow help their sister make a good marriage.

'Until she marries, Maria is your . . .'

'She's our responsibility. We know. We've heard it before. And we can't even think of getting married until she's safely wedded and bedded.'

This, although no doubt true, was indiscreet and is certainly not the way for an eleven-year-old to speak to his parent; Marino was quite understandably thrashed for insolence. (In this respect, Paolo was lucky to be younger than Maria: by the time he was of an age to think of marriage his sister was already settled.)

'It's just as well we've only got one sister,' commented Marco in the privacy of their room, tactfully refraining from commiserating on the thrashing and blowing out the candle with a certain delicacy (for wounded dignity shows less in the dark).

A couple of months later Marino received an even more serious beating. His crime – removing his mother's padded and boned linen corset from the washing line where it had been hung to air – might have been considered merely naughty (he was after all still quite a few months from his twelfth birthday) yet somehow seemed to smack of unwholesomeness. Everyone had jumped to conclusions when the missing piece of female underwear was found secreted beneath his bedclothes, with the result that no one actually bothered to ask him what he'd wanted with it. Perhaps because he felt humiliated when murmurs overheard through an open window made him suddenly realise what they thought, deeply shamed that something very simple and scientific should have been so misinterpreted, Marino was unable to explain; this was one of the rare occasions on which he did not tell Marco what had been in his mind. These two brothers, closest in age, were of course entirely familiar with each other's bodies (not long before they'd had a serious conversation about their future in Italy while Marco was sitting on the chamber pot) and to some extent were aware of each other's thoughts and imaginings, yet on this particular occasion Marco didn't feel able to ask.

It was after this incident that Marino first went to Lixouri, casually embarking on one of the caiques that regularly crossed the water with provisions for the smaller town, then spending the rest of the day nursing his injured feelings in the marshlands of Livadi that lay by the sea to the north of it. He had intended staying there all night, sleeping under the stars on the narrow, flat beach, but it was only April, by twilight he was becoming distinctly chilly, his defiance was deflated and he felt lonely and hungry and a bit scared: thus he was more glad than he wanted to admit when a fisherman who knew him by sight offered him a passage home.

The marsh as calming refuge, perhaps: a world outside time.

Marino was spared any punishment for his truancy, probably because everyone was so relieved to have him back safe and sound. All the same, 'It is just as well,' admitted his parents to one another, 'that Giambattista will be arriving soon.' The seminary of the Patriarchate, suggested and arranged by their eldest son, seemed an increasingly good idea.

Not being a boy much given to solitude (and in any case having a brother more or less the same age meant that he was rarely alone), Marino could not easily put into words his sense of the lonely, fertile power of the marsh: 'It's a sort of empty place,' was all he told Marco, and gave him a curious shell that he'd found on the beach – possibly by way of making amends for his uncommunicativeness.

'I'm cold,' he said later that night as he lay in bed, not knowing how else to describe the way he felt.

'Come in with me then,' offered Marco, and moved over to make room.

Doing well and being successful: this is not simply a question of personal satisfaction or indeed of financial security. There are words which one may never examine consciously but which nonetheless underpin all those nebulous assumptions about the directions that life should take. For the Carburi brothers two such words were 'honour' and 'family', closely intertwined. Here another image comes into play – although in this case it might more properly be called a myth; all the children were by turns entertained, terrified and awed by the stories recounted of their forebear Stamatis, killed by the Turks, and of his brave and heroic widow who fled with her children to the island and thus enabled the family to continue. 'Killed by the Turks' is an emotive phrase which allows much scope for the imagination: a cruel, bearded, turbanned face, a flashing scimitar, a bright spurt of noble blood . . . Since myths have their own dimensions, no one ever considered the possibility that this death was other than glorious, that Stamatis's life might have ended in slow agony – dark blood and stinking entrails and an awful, animal moaning – after he was hit in the belly by splintering shards from a cannon ball, or indeed that the torch had perhaps been put to the cannon by a frightened eighteen-year-old whose own belly was beset by griping pains and whose rather too sparse beard caused him much shame. At any rate, the boys grew up with a powerful, unspoken sense that something was owed to an ancestor like Stamatis.

It is conceivable that Marco's juvenile combinations of saltpetre, sulphur and other ingredients (one of his rare thrashings at the seminary was for scaring a servant out of his wits by a loud explosion behind the latrines), as well as his later painstaking and meticulous researches concerning artillery, had something to do with echoes of these childhood stories.

However this may be, the fact is that behind them, to the East, lay the past, while in front, to the West, lay the future. In the middle, in a sort of eternal present, lay the island of Cephalonia and the small town of Argostoli on its narrow inlet of sea. Home is always the centre of the world.

2

WITH HINDSIGHT, one of the things that the Carburi brothers appear to have been doing when they left
home to study in Italy was making the first few tentative
steps into becoming middle class. This idea would have
seemed incomprehensible to them, however, or – if they
had grasped its meaning – would have shocked them.

No one in the family ever thought for a moment that
Giovambattista would be anything other than successful.
No one doubted that he would find his true place in circles
more exalted than those which Argostoli could offer. His
younger brothers loved him loyally without thinking too
much about it, admired him; even when quailing occasionally in the face of his disapproval all agreed that Giambattista had great style. Perhaps – although no one ever quite
defined it – this had something to do with the poise and self-
possession which had set him apart ever since childhood. If
there was a slight aloofness, a certain inner coolness, this
only added savour to the kind of charm that comes from the
combination of good looks – but not exaggeratedly good
looks – and courteous manners. His mother was deeply
proud of him. He in turn loved his mother unreservedly,
while for his brothers he felt an enduring yet sometimes
fretful affection. What Marino, Marco and later Paolo all
took completely for granted was that Giovambattista would
in due course help further their own careers.
     It is widely held that behind successful sons lies a deter-
mined mother. This may or may not be true; what is certainly

true is that most of her children were a little afraid of Caterina Carburi (although naturally none would have dared admit it). Only Giovambattista obscurely felt that his achievements and triumphs were laid at her feet in tribute rather than as placatory offerings – but then he had always been her special son. 'You have the soul of a peasant,' she once remarked scathingly to Marino, who never quite forgot the feeling of not being considered good enough to meet her standards. Children have no means of knowing why some are loved less than others; as he smarted under this wound to his juvenile pride, Marino naturally had no idea of his mother's extremely private theory as to why her second son was less amenable than the others. (It had to do with the circumstances of his conception. She was not in the least surprised that he came into the world the wrong way round, feet first.)

Less secret but equally deeply held was Caterina's conviction that her sons would not only bring her honour but would at the same time repair the family's somewhat threadbare financial situation – the Carburis, as it happened, being rather less affluent than many of their friends and neighbours. A rumour later arose that the family had once lived by selling vegetables in the market of Argostoli, this story apparently originating from 'a gentleman by the name of Saint Sauveur,' as Maria chose to describe him, with an infinitesimal little frown of disdain that came straight from their mother. Saint Sauveur was at the time Consul General in Corfu of the newly born French Republic: Giovambattista, who had known him in France, had a fair idea of the reasons for this spite but not the slightest wish to speak of the matter, with the result that everyone found such a gratuitously unpleasant piece of slander quite inexplicable. Luckily Caterina was by then no longer alive to be outraged by it, for she herself came from Corfu – a much smarter, more lively place than Argostoli, as she told them – and would no doubt have been doubly upset at the idea that such stories were circulating there.

But to go back: it is always the eldest brother who paves the way. When Giovambattista's future began to be discussed, neither of his parents questioned the idea that a professional career of some sort should be pursued or indeed considered that it had anything whatsoever to do with his intrinsic status, money or no money. And if Giovambattista had held out for medicine rather than, say, law, this was not so much from any sense of vocation – for healing the sick, for relieving suffering – as from pure, disinterested curiosity, coupled perhaps with a youthful desire to distinguish himself, to converse as an equal with those whom he revered as Men of Science.

'He is a great man of science,' he told Marino severely. 'Through meticulous and patient observation he has arrived at an understanding of the relations between plants.' This statement was made during a conversation that took place not long after Marino's arrival in Bologna, when the elder brother was attempting to persuade the younger to curtail his social life (under which heading, naturally, was also included his sexual life) and apply himself to his studies with more diligence. As Giovambattista pointed out, it was Marino himself who had insisted on mathematics rather than following his parents' wishes and studying law.

'When you are old,' reflected Marino, 'you can afford to be patient.' It was not quite clear, even to himself, whether this thought referred to the Swedish scholar or to Giovambattista (whose twenty-sixth birthday was approaching: however, as Marco had once pointed out, their brother had without doubt been forty years old from the moment of his birth). What he said – with great seriousness – was, 'You're right of course, Giambattista.'

He had long since learnt that if you agree wholeheartedly with your brother's remonstrations it somehow takes the wind out of his sails; Giovambattista had never fully understood why conversations with Marino often left him feeling faintly dissatisfied. Various other nautical images now came to Marino's mind, leading him to laugh and say, 'What I really ought to have been is a captain, sailing the seas.'

'That's what you always wanted to be when you were small' (remembered with a smile: Giovambattista had no means of knowing that Marino's private imagery for the various stages of seduction involved such terms as 'coming alongside', 'hoving to,' 'grappling' and finally – with luck – 'boarding').

Smiles and shared memories generate warmth. Thus when a little later the brothers parted company for the evening the scolding was forgotten and the fraternal hug in which Marino enveloped Giambattista was as affectionate as usual.

For although they lodged together the fact is that their comings and goings did not necessarily coincide so very often, so that their evenings tended to be spent apart. It had been taken for granted by everyone that Marino would live with Giovambattista. ('He will keep an eye on him,' said Caterina to herself, sitting straight-backed at her desk and frowning slightly, as she took up her pen and wrote, 'My dearest son, your guidance and advice will, I know, be of inestimable value to him.') If Marino's arrival from Venice meant that Giovambattista was obliged to move from the rooms where he had been so comfortably settled for the past couple of years, this was done ungrudgingly; whether there might perhaps have been arrangements in his life which he preferred to keep from his brother's eyes no one ever thought to wonder.

However, what Giovambattista was at this time mainly involved with were ideas of classification and the painstaking, meticulous observation that this entails. If, after all, you are

19

able to register minute similarities or dissimilarities between things, this enables you to perceive relationships – which in turn allows some kind of order to be established. When he acquired Giorgio Baglivi's treatise on the Practice of Medicine (bought at a bargain price from an impoverished fellow student: Giovambattista was always careful with his money, scrupulously entering all his expenses in a neat account book), he began reading in a fairly neutral frame of mind, then became progressively more engaged, excited even, so that he sat up until past three in the morning, burning candle after candle, straining his eyes to read. The elegant simplicity of the idea that just as the truths of the universe are to be uncovered by mathematics, so also by mathematical enquiries one may come to know the workings of the body filled him with such extraordinary happiness that he had not the least desire to sleep. 'In making a history of any disease,' he noted, 'four things are most especially necessary: firstly the infinite acquisition of particular observations. Secondly, an arrangement of them. Thirdly, their maturation and consideration. Fourthly, at last, the extraction from them of precepts and general axioms.'

Giovambattista had always found beauty in order. He disregarded the stench and the misery of the hospital, looked at its patients with coolly mathematical grey-green eyes, pondered the idea that the disorders of the flesh are exactly what this word implies: an aberration from order, a falsification of true proportions. To establish what the proportions should be, what is the degree of aberration in each disease, you must observe, observe, observe. Only thus, by infinite pains, can you arrive at some proper understanding of nature.

As these ideas developed he spoke of them to his brother and was rewarded for once by a thoughtful response: 'Yes – balance and counter-balance perhaps, Giambattista, or measuring and calculating the angles right. "Give me a place to stand and I could move the world" was what someone once said,' Marino added as his mind strayed from the mathematics of medicine into a broader contemplation of poise and counterpoise. (There are people who seem to possess an innate sense of how to make things work: Marino was one of them, which is why it was always the practical applications of mathematics which interested him most, rather than the pure science.)

There is no doubt that it is important to measure effects accurately rather than jumping to conclusions about causes. Nothing should be taken for granted; 'But is this true?' Giovambattista noted in the margin of one book, and 'Yes' (heavily underlined) in another. He drew up a scheme of matters to be enquired into, starting with 'diagnostics, prognostics, various sorts of causes'. At first he arranged these in a column on the page, but soon came to see that branches and subdivisions were necessary. Thus, 'the non-naturals' (the patient's habit of body) covered diet, exercise, air, sleeping and wakefulness, repletion and inanition, and – an afterthought – what he called 'the passions of the mind'; 'the symptoms' could be constant or inconstant, 'the remedies used' successful or not, and 'the outcome' happy or fatal. An orderly perception of these particulars, followed by mature digestion and reflection, will allow one to form conclusions on the workings of the body.

A later notebook had its pages divided into three columns of varying widths. The first, headed *Causes*, was the narrowest since it had necessarily to remain rather empty for the time being. The second, headed *Symptomata or Manifestations*, was the broadest and was rapidly filled with detailed notes (in increasingly small writing so as not to waste space). The final column, headed *Treatment*, was gradually filled in, although Giovambattista began to wonder whether perhaps it needed subheadings, *Proven* and *Provisional*, for example. Parallel to this notebook was another in which the diseases reported in the first book were grouped into tentative classes.

'Taxonomy' is a word that may fill the soul with deep, calm satisfaction. It is of course a Greek word whose significance Giovambattista understood very well; 'classification' is what most of his colleagues took it to mean, yet he knew that the true essence of the word is quite simply 'the law of ordering'. Law and order and the laws by which things are ordered: these are what make sense of the universe.

It was now that Giovambattista began corresponding with a colleague in Montpellier. His correspondent wrote, 'There is no doubt that it is beyond the ability of any single physician to amass alone the observations required to draw just conclusions as to the causes of disease. What is needed is the painstaking collection and free sharing of such material among men of science throughout the world,' and signed himself '*Votre confrère.*' As he sat up late with his notebooks Giovambattista was thus tasting the chaste joys of confraternity and of ever widening horizons.

Needless to say, there are of course some bodily disorders whose immediate causes you do not have to seek far to find: the passions of the flesh, if indiscreetly indulged in, are just as disruptive to health as the passions of the mind. 'You must abstain completely until your symptoms recede,' he told a slightly frightened Marino after a silent and careful examination followed by a few dry questions, and prescribed small doses of mercury as well as regular bathing of the affected part in salt water (Giovambattista had long believed in the therapeutic virtues of salt). Self-control is an admirable quality. 'To what extent,' he later wondered in his notebook, 'is it the excessive use of any particular member which leads to an imbalance in the organisation of the body, such that the subject's health is impaired?'

Both brothers wrote to Marco at about this time. Giovambattista wrote at length of the pleasures of natural science and added a certain amount of detailed and sensible advice on how to behave in a new life and a new city (for Marco, always absolutely clear about what he wanted, had held firm in favour of studying medicine at Padua instead of joining his brothers in Bologna). Marino's letter was a rather more hasty scrawl: 'Gio:Batta: is cutting up corpses and seems as happy as can be, while I'm not doing too badly, except that I'm a little bit in love and a little bit in debt (only don't tell anyone about this) and sigh into my pillow – which because of an unfortunate ailment is necessarily a lonely one at the moment,' he said, among other things.

Marco wrote regularly to both his elder brothers. All three wrote brief, polite letters to their father and longer, more descriptive letters to their mother. Marino, whose letters were not so very frequent, usually described places and buildings and – with some censorship – people whom he met; Marco and Giovambattista tended to write more of their daily lives, of their interests and preoccupations. None of them wrote to Paolo as yet, considering him still to be a child: it is sometimes hard to be the youngest of a large family. It is also not always easy to be the oldest, especially if you are burdened with a sense of responsibility: Giovambattista's letters home regularly contained reports on his brothers' health and progress as well as his own. 'Marino will in time do very well,' he reassured his parents more than once. (No one ever worried about Marco.)

The parcels that arrived from home contained currants, quince jelly and honey, their mother firm in her belief that nowhere in the world is there any honey to match that of Cephalonia. When one winter her physician son mentioned that he was troubled by a persistent cough, she took advantage of a cousin's departure to Venice to dispatch a large bag of chamomile, gathered earlier that year on the hillsides and dried carefully; she feared the worst, begged him to keep warm and to let her know as soon as possible of his condition. Giovambattista had been dosing himself with another specific but drank copious infusions of this maternal remedy and felt better. (The sweet, pale-gold, evocative fragrance of home is in any case always comforting.) He had also bound his thin chest tightly with a length of warm flannel and rubbed it, morning and night, with an embrocation of his own devising made from mustard seed pounded with dried red peppers in a small quantity of olive oil. He examined his bodily secretions, noted a slight cloudiness of the urine, spat into a handkerchief and scrutinised his expectorate dispassionately.

'*Carissima Signora Madre*,' he wrote, 'rest assured that my health is good and that there is no sign of any consumption. I blame myself for alarming you – such was far from being my intention – my symptoms, already abating, were merely brought on by the fatigue of the journey and the miasmas of Padua.' (He and Marino had been to visit Marco.) He ended, 'I kiss your dear hands with the utmost respect,' and signed himself, 'Your most affectionate son, Gio:Batta:' (their customary written abbreviation of his name). Unless it so happens that a friend or neighbour will be travelling and is kind enough to carry with him anything you may wish to send, letters can take many weeks to arrive: this is the nature of correspondence. By the time his letter reached Argostoli, Giovambattista was indeed fully recovered.

Countless women with wayward lovers know the longing anticipation with which letters are awaited, the restlessness and irritability of weeks or months when none arrive, the secret joy of days when they do. Caterina had never in her life had a lover yet was familiar with these feelings; when she received letters from her sons – and particularly from her eldest son – the glow of happiness made her footsteps lighter and her back straighter for days at a time. Such letters were shared with no one, although of course occasional passages might be read out loud; after many perusals they were carefully refolded and stored under lock and key in her private cabinet: a secret treasure perhaps.

Needless to say, there are many matters about which sons do not write to their mothers.

It is perhaps worth noting that in Padua Giovambattista had insisted on staying at an inn, whereas Marino stayed with Marco and once more shared his bed. Before settling to sleep they had, quite unselfconsciously, kissed each other good-night: this was what they had always done as children – a sketchy sign of the cross and a formal peck on the cheek. 'Lie still and don't kick,' warned Marco. Earlier, as they lay and gossiped by candlelight, Marino had reported their elder brother's strictures on the importance of avoiding excess and the dangers of wasting precious essences: 'He says that at our age not more than two ejaculations a week are what is indicated, and that at his age one will be fine' (a tone of incredulity). After a moment's silent consideration Marco had replied loyally, 'Well, I'm sure Giambattista's right.' A further pause as he reflected. 'But then he always did err on the side of caution, didn't he? I dare say we could multiply his figures a bit to arrive at a truer answer.'

'Giambattista is *secretive*,' was what Marino was thinking, not so loyally, after they'd snuffed out the light. Their elder brother's amorous life remained a mystery to both of them, his pleasures – if any – unknown: 'Probably self-applied' was the verdict Marino reached, followed by the subversively mirth-provoking, 'if not self-inflicted.' He thought of sharing this disrespectful idea but decided he'd better not, and thus simply turned over and settled his back comfortably against Marco's.

Marino returned to Bologna in rude good health (at least as far as his lungs were concerned), though Giovambattista was already beginning to feel a soreness of the throat and a tightness of the chest.

'Contiguity is a great breeding-ground of disease,' he wrote in his notebook. Contiguity with one's own brother clearly doesn't count.

Family relationships with their complex networks of affection or lack of it are among the things that you can take for granted. If letters are addressed to their recipients by title of kinship rather than by name – 'My dearest brother-in-law,' 'cousin,' 'nephew' or whatever – this simply defines and affirms the web of ties into which you are born and which remains among the steadiest certainties in life. When the brothers wrote to one another they invariably used the same comfortable form, opening their letters with '*Mio carissimo fratello*' and closing them with '*Vostro affettuosissimo fratello*' followed by the signature. Blood is thicker than water. We do not choose our siblings but simply love them because they are ours. Even if we cease loving them, if letters suddenly commence with an ominous, curt '*Mio fratello*', our brothers still belong to us.

It is thus entirely comprehensible that the brother who makes the most money will help the others. Giovambattista knew this without thinking of it.

Of course, people also sometimes acquire family roles as well as family relationships: the good child, the sensible child, the difficult child (or the serious one, the clever one, the unreliable one), such labels being so easily accepted that they are rarely examined. Only Marino perhaps touched on them when he told Stephanie, 'Oh, I've always been the black sheep.'

No one ever imagined that Marino would make any money worth speaking of.

3

IN A period of deep depression many years later Giovambattista was to sit in his house in Paris and write to his sister, 'Of all those who go to seek their fortunes abroad there is hardly one who does not die in penury without ten *sous* to rub together, regardless of his probity or talent. Believe me, I have lived this life and know.' And later in the same letter, 'There is no security for any of us save in the possession of land in Cephalonia.'

The fact is that none of the brothers thought of himself as Greek. To all of them – even to Marco who left the island at the age of nine, who settled down in Padua and lived out his life there – the only place called home was Cephalonia. At first sight – especially in the case of Giovambattista and Marco, neither of whom ever returned – this usage might seem akin to that strange one whereby, for example, in a later century Australians and New Zealanders who had rarely if ever set foot in England still referred to it as 'Home' . . . On second thoughts, though, I think the feeling went deeper; the Greeks have a word, *nostalgia*, which was born from the aching longing of those uprooted for the lost, distant homeland of their birth. Someone he had offended once referred disparagingly to Marco as '*cefaloniotto*', and although all the brothers would have been outraged at the insulting tone of this none of them would have denied the land of their birth: throughout their lives, all went on thinking of themselves exclusively as 'Cephalonian'. When Giovambattista, writing in French to his sister, used the word *patrie* and spoke of their father and grandfather, what he was expressing, I think, was the need for that sense of belonging which only their native island could give.

Patrie, patria, patrída: home in any language is firmly labelled in paternal terms: the fatherland. And yet the marriage of mountain and sea that made up Marino's mental landscape felt feminine rather than masculine, although it was not until he was approaching fifty and decided to return home to Cephalonia that this image moved into his conscious mind, that he began to be aware of a strange small ache in his heart for the starry nights of summer and the lie of the dark hills across the narrow bay. 'When the moon rises, the hills in the lower range stay black, but the mountains above them become ashen grey,' he told Stephanie as they lay in bed, caressing the curve of her hip lazily and reflecting that a landscape is known in something of the same unthinking way as the contours of a familiar body. (Stephanie's body was becoming familiar.) This was almost the only thing he told her about the land of his birth; it didn't, however, help her to form much of a picture of it.

Marco, suddenly recollecting, told his wife, 'I cried when I left the island, though it was such a long time ago that I can't really remember why.' And, 'We ought to go back one day.'

But all these are feelings of the kind that tend to catch up with one in later life. At the beginning, the opposite of 'home' was not 'exile' but something more optimistic.

Giovambattista's undoubted probity and talents were rewarded when at the age of twenty-eight he was appointed Professor of the Practice of Medicine at the university of Turin. This of course meant that he would no longer be able to keep such a close and critical eye on the development of his brothers – and perhaps mixed with their congratulations was a slight and unadmitted sense of relief. For the truth is that Giovambattista was at this period much exercised in his

28

mind about Marino's and Marco's tendency to a rackety lifestyle. 'A man is known by the company he keeps,' had been a recent reprimand to the one brother, and to the other, on a visit to Padua, 'A little more fastidiousness in your dress would not go amiss.'

Giovambattista was scrupulous in the arrangement of his attire. It had occurred to Marino that he might possibly be a tiny bit vain, but this seemed an allowable failing – indeed, the fact that any fault at all could be detected in their elder brother was somehow endearing rather than diminishing. Giovambattista wore sober and decent subfusc in, for example, the anatomy theatre, yet had a taste for figured velvets and fine silks for the evening. His linen – chemises and drawers and nightshirts and stockings – was laundered rather more often than most people's; wherever he travelled one of his first cares was to find a good laundress. As a matter of fact – since no one could have predicted the unfortunate way things were to turn out – when some time later he heard from one of his correspondents in Venice that Marino was involved in an amour with a woman whose occupation was the expert starching and ironing of linen, Giovambattista gave a small, resigned mental shrug of the shoulders and thought to himself philosophically, 'I dare say my brother's chemises at least will be in better condition.' Now, however, as he prepared to leave for Turin, he had a coat and waistcoat made of pale sea-green silk (the colour that was later to be called *eau de Nil*) and in a letter to his mother described the elaborate self-coloured embroidery that decorated the cuffs and lapels and front of the coat. 'Always go for quality,' he advised Marino, lovingly fingering the bolt of heavy silk from which these garments were to be made, 'even if it *is* more expensive.' And, 'Avoid too extreme contrasts of colour – they invariably look tawdry.'

Marino (rather more vain of his body than of his clothes)

was touched by this human side to Giovambattista and thus took in good part, with only a preliminary gulp and a brief, minor quailing, the stern fraternal inquisition as to his debts which followed. 'The thing about Giambattista,' as Marco said, 'is that somehow you don't dare lie to him.' 'There are times when you really wish you could, though,' commented Marino.

Sea-green, sage-green, the grey-green of olive leaves: these were the colours that Giovambattista liked best. He had once dreamed that he possessed a library where all the volumes, catalogued and cross-catalogued and neatly ranged on orderly shelves, were bound in the smoothest and finest pale grey-green calf. A sense of pride and pleasure lingered with him for a little while after waking, although of course the dream was soon forgotten – as dreams must be. His books were actually bound in good quality, tobacco-coloured leather, with his monogram in gold at the base of the spine.

The move to Turin involved the careful and orderly packing not only of clothes but also of these books and of what the brothers called 'Giambattista's collection'. Clothes were folded flat and laid in a portmanteau secured with straps; for his shells and mineral specimens and the two cases of mounted lepidoptera wooden crates were required, as well as plentiful quantities of straw and rags in which to wrap the more fragile objects.

Marino sat and watched as Giovambattista supervised this packing, irritating his elder brother intensely each time he removed from its nest of straw a curiosity that had suddenly caught his eye or leant forward and picked out a book that had just been laid in its crate, only to leaf idly through the pages and then put it back in the wrong place. Marino also had the habit of humming some tune or other, which made it hard for

Giovambattista to concentrate. In spite of all this the packing was finally achieved and the crates numbered and labelled.

Before leaving, the elder brother settled the younger's debts. When they bade each other farewell Giovambattista kissed Marino on both cheeks; Marino wrote to Marco that evening, 'I promise you, my eyes filled with tears.'

What neither of the younger brothers knew was that, after much thought, Giovambattista had asked three of his friends to keep as close an eye as possible on Marino and Marco and to pass on any information which they felt Giovambattista ought to know. Since he trusted all three implicitly (and particularly Giacomo Stellini who indeed had been largely instrumental in bringing about his appointment in Turin), Giovambattista thus set out on his journey westwards with an easy conscience. What might to other eyes look like some kind of spy system was in fact based on a simple piece of reasoning: if you are not aware when your brothers are going seriously astray, how will you be able to help them?

Serious going astray, of course, means more than the occasional indulgence in the delights of female flesh, although it is worrying if money – or at any rate too much money – is spent on such pursuits. Having shared lodgings with Marino for a couple of years, Giovambattista had learned to turn a more or less blind eye to late returnings, to sporadic nocturnal absences and even from time to time to smothered laughter and a rhythmic creaking of the bed in the room next door to his own. On the whole he made no comment. Once, however, after watching from his window the departure of Marino's bedfellow, he had remarked rather frostily as his brother entered the room, 'That woman, whom I believe I have seen before, looks very much like a prostitute.'

'Quite correct,' replied Marino, 'that's exactly what she is, and an extremely nice one too.'

31

It is not really very appropriate or *convenable* to bring a whore back to your lodgings. Giovambattista decided, however, to begin the necessary admonitions on a practical level; he thus asked steadily, 'How much did you pay her to stay all night?'

Given the current state of Marino's finances this was an uncomfortable question.

'Not more than I can afford.'

His brother looked as if he wasn't going to let this evasive answer pass, whereupon Marino added, 'The thing is, it's good for me, Giambattista. It helps me concentrate. Stops me getting headaches.'

This was a stroke of genius for the physician was immediately deflected: 'You never told me that you get headaches . . .'

'Well, I don't so far – but then, you see, I might if I didn't.'

Giovambattista said no more. Nevertheless, he mulled this idea over and wondered for a moment about the throbbing ache in the temples that occasionally oppressed him in the later hours of the evening, which disturbance he had always attributed to eye strain caused by too much reading in too dim a light.

It is curious how the same words can be used to express both hatred and love. 'Bitch . . . *whore* . . .' shouted Marino some years later when he got into what Giovambattista referred to as 'trouble'; yet later still, when his hair was streaked with silver, the name he called Stephanie was 'My little whore', repeating the words in affectionate Greek whose sense she had no difficulty at all in understanding: '*mikró mou poutanáki*'. She had said, without quite meaning to, 'You know, you wouldn't marry me if you were sensible because I suppose you could say what I am is more or less a whore.' 'Ah, but I've never been sensible,' he answered: this was an image of himself that he had always rather liked, although Marco, who knew him well, had long ago pronounced robustly, 'You're perfectly sensible really' – brothers sometimes having a knack of puncturing one's vanities. All the same, in early days this image had more than once caused Giovambattista to tremble.

Giovambattista himself was of course never likely to get into trouble, was invariably sensible and reaped the rewards of this virtue. Turin was without doubt a move upwards in terms of career, a move westwards in terms of geography, as well as being in both senses a move further away from home. But perhaps for these brothers home could be said by definition to be a place where one is not: an absence, a private, well-guarded little empty space existing only in the mind.

For the citizens of the Most Serene Republic, anything further east than their own lagoon is the Orient, the Levant. The Orient is a place where people are not quite serious or responsible or sensible. (That derogatory word 'cefaloniotto' may have something to do with these connotations.) Possibly beneath their apparent assimilation of civilised standards people from these parts are more impetuous and emotional, just as beneath the appearance of health they may be carrying strange and unwelcome diseases – which is why those arriving by sea from the east are very wisely placed in quarantine for a certain period.

Giovambattista certainly never gave the impression of being particularly impulsive, but then he might be seen as the exception that proved the rule. Cool critical assessment in any case sits better with a physician than hasty impetuosity. The road leading westwards towards Turin passed through low-lying, insalubrious, damp and marshy lands along the course of the great river; for several days Giovambattista suffered from a fever with shivering and headache, but judged it advisable to press on with the journey rather than to stop in some uncomfortable inn. And in this he was probably right, for Turin was a healthier place in which at last to rest and recover.

Turin as a matter of fact was also the place where in due course he finally lost his virginity – technically speaking, that is to say, for none of his various amorous encounters had hitherto involved the penetration of another human being – although neither his brothers nor his friends nor anyone else ever learned anything of the extraordinary happiness that this occasioned. (There were a great many well-guarded places in Giovambattista's mind.) To his mother he wrote of the king, of the court, of the university, of the decent and serious atmosphere that prevailed; 'I believe I shall be very content here and may live at no great expense,' he told her.

Letters from Cephalonia took longer to reach Turin than they did Padua or Bologna but, by way of compensation, letters to and from Montpellier were transmitted more rapidly. Giovambattista's scientific correspondence was steadily increasing. To François Boissier de Sauvages in Montpellier he wrote in elaborately polite disagreement with his colleague's manner of classifying the febrile diseases; to his revered namesake in Padua, Giovanni Battista Morgagni, he sent details of some interesting autopsy findings. In what he considered his rough notebook he observed, 'The fevers, hectic, purulent or intermittent, differ widely in their signs, indications and outcome,' and put down his pen as he mused on the increasingly widespread idea that fever might be simply a manifestation of disease rather than a disease itself, and on how this might or might not be demonstrated by examination of the organs *post mortem*.

*   *   *

'You have a fever in the blood,' said Stephanie much, much later.

'It is because I am from the south,' answered Marino, who had never considered that he came from the east – this to him meaning Ottoman territories. 'Southern people are always of an ardent temperament' (forgetting for a moment his elder brother). Stephanie found that she liked this ardour, which is perhaps why she was not too shocked when some time later he told her about the trouble which had been the reason for his hurried departure from Venice and for his adoption of a name not his own, adding as if in justification, 'After all, it's in the nature of meridional men to be passionate.'

(For Marino the word 'passionate' carried not only the strictly sexual connotations that we might give it today but also meant 'hot-tempered', 'hasty', 'jealous', 'prone to violent reactions'.)

'How old were you?' asked Stephanie, contemplating his greying hair and compact, still muscular body.

'Twenty-nine. Well, thirty really. Old enough to have more self-control, I suppose you might say.'

This, however, was not what Stephanie said.

Stephanie had told Marino that she was thirty-three; Marino – who had a good eye for many things, including women's bodies – knew perfectly well that she was older but let the statement pass without comment. Something about this small lie amused and touched him, although he did not bother to analyse quite what or why. It was only when they had set off on the long journey back to his island and were spending the night itching in a miserable inn in the mountains that he had said, 'Stephanie, now that we are man and wife and are sharing each other's fleas quite lawfully, won't you tell me how old you really are?' And she had paused for a moment, thought of saying 'Thirty-six,' then, gaining sudden confidence from the darkness, admitted, 'Well, forty actually.'

'Birds of a feather flock together,' Giovambattista might have said, looking down his patrician nose in disapproval: the woman who claims to be younger than she is, the man who has for years gone under an assumed name – people whose messy lives are woven with greater or smaller pretences and fictions. And perhaps there was indeed some element of like recognising like in the amused tenderness that Marino felt for Stephanie.

Giovambattista had long been comfortable in the knowledge that his approval was important for his brothers. He wrote back promptly and encouragingly when Marco, aged twenty-four, sent him a draft of his first work intended for publication. This paper, entitled *A Letter on a Species of Marine Insect*, had been written during Marco's thirty days' quarantine at the *lazzaretto* following a visit home – a surprisingly prudent and diligent use of the enforced idleness which made Giovambattista feel that, when once settled, this brother might after all prove to be a kindred spirit. He thus refrained from scolding too much at the fact that it was written in Italian, merely pointing out that Latin is a more appropriate language for scholarly work. Scientific papers in the form of letters must be addressed to some illustrious person and the choice of recipient should not be made rashly; the question of future patronage and support needs to be taken into account. 'I would recommend,' wrote Giovambattista, 'that you address it to the Procurator Marco Foscarini.' Marco followed this advice gratefully.

'My dearest brother,' he had written to Marino, proudly enclosing a copy of his paper, 'I know you will remember this gelatinous creature from those long-gone, happy, heedless hours we spent in the waters of our native land' (his 'marine insect' was in fact a jellyfish). 'I have put myself into the hands of Gio:Batta: as regards the possibility of publishing it and am awaiting his answer impatiently, as you can imagine.'

It is not of course possible to admit that a dismissive or scathing letter would be a grave blow: self-esteem is more easily reinforced if Giambattista finds your work acceptable. Marino understood this without any need for it to be said and wrote back loyally, 'He'd have to be a raving lunatic not to like it.'

A copy of the paper was also sent in due course to Argostoli. Caterina, to tell the truth, did not actually read all of it but put it away in her cabinet with a small half-smile of satisfaction; during the next few weeks, however, she was more than once heard by friends and neighbours to speak of the seriousness and steadiness of her first and third sons in a manner that suggested slight boasting. About her second son she said nothing. Her fourth son, now aged fifteen, was by this time getting a little weary of these paragons constantly held up for his emulation and felt a certain sneaking admiration for the apparent refusal of Marino – whose visit home the previous year had not gone entirely smoothly – to fit the expected pattern.

Shortly after Marco received his degree in medicine, two letters reached Turin which on first reading ruffled Giovambattista's feelings slightly. '*Mio carissimo fratello*,' wrote Marco, 'after much thought I am quite clear in my mind that I do not desire to pursue a medical career and join that profession of which you yourself are so distinguished an ornament. My true inclination lies along a path which is indeed parallel to your own and, dare I say it, equally honourable – I have in other words decided that the science which I wish to pursue is that of chemistry.' (These phrases had taken Marco rather a long time to compose.)

Father Giacomo Stellini – valued friend of Giovambattista

and former tutor of Marco's friend Anzolo Emo – wrote, '*Mio caro amico*, I have spoken at length with the younger of your two brothers and find his mind made up as to the calling he intends to follow, of which, he tells me, he has already written to you. I do not think that you should feel any trepidation about this decision: the young man is undoubtedly able and likely to do well in his chosen field. The weaknesses which have caused you concern are such as frequently characterise extreme youth and will, God willing, very shortly be overcome.' (These youthful faults were, among other things, levity, obstinacy, an unwillingness to listen to advice and a slight touch of arrogance.)

There does not seem much cause for discomfort here, yet Giovambattista had recently been enjoying the delightful promise of affinity and indeed ever since Marco began studying medicine had been planning possible career moves for him; he thus felt an instant of chagrin at all these projects come to nought. This sort of brief, faint disruption to the smooth, predictable functioning of life is often perceived as a twinge of discomfort somewhere in the region of the stomach: Giovambattista attributed it to wind and decided on a small dose of a mild carminative. After sipping a glass of peppermint water and reflecting on the matter for a short while he felt better. He replied to Marco's announcement with measured fraternal encouragement and support, as well as with a reminder that seriousness and consistency are of the very highest importance in any branch of science.

To Marino Marco had said, 'Doctoring is all very well but chemistry is the nobler art if one wants to *know*.'

'Know what?'

'How things work, I suppose.' (Either Marco was not being particularly articulate or this was a sort of shorthand which his brother understood.)

Marino, having just spent a good hour enthralling Marco's

landlady's children with various simple but effective working models of the kind that he enjoyed making, as well as with conjuring tricks, thought of asking, 'What about mathematics and mechanics?' but didn't feel like getting into a brotherly argument or spoiling Marco's happy relief at the fact that Giovambattista did not disapprove. He thus merely laughed and said, 'We'll leave the doctoring to Giambattista then,' after which they went out to dine and amuse themselves in ways of which their elder brother would certainly not have approved.

This turned out to be the last occasion on which – in a sort of cheerful re-enactment of their adolescence – they shared a woman. Feeling that in some way the evening was Marco's celebration, Marino generously offered, 'You can go first if you want' (in the past Marino himself, being the elder, had always automatically had priority).

'No, no,' said Marco, 'it's quite all right, I don't mind being second.' A couple of hours later, back in his lodging once more, he admitted calmly, 'Actually, I've always liked it when you make them nice and slippery first.'

The thought crossed Marino's mind that Marco generally knew what he wanted.

Some people know what they want and find their path in life without much trouble; for others it is less easy. What no one approved of at all was the fact that after completing his mathematical studies Marino apparently saw no need to seek any kind of career or earn any money. He expected his family to recognise that he was making very great efforts to live within the income supplied to him from home and to understand that it was by no means always possible to succeed in doing so. At this stage in his life he found that writing letters to Cephalonia required an increasingly uncomfortable effort, so that he tended to put off doing so; somehow he also dreaded his mother's replies.

'His influence on your brother Marco when they are together is not an entirely happy one,' wrote Giacomo Stellini to Giovambattista, 'and it is thus perhaps just as well that he has recently settled in Venice.' Giovambattista refrained from passing this verdict on to Caterina, although it is not clear whether this was out of some loyalty to his brothers or was merely due to a desire not to distress his mother with matters about which she could do nothing. Needless to say, he wrote regularly to Marino with much advice and many exhortations to make some use of the talents which God had given him. From Marino's point of view these periodic reproaches were only to be expected, reassuring even in their predictability; after all, an elder brother who did not chide and scold would almost certainly be demonstrating lack of love. Approval would of course be best of all, but then Marino had long since got used to being disapproved of; and anyway lack of approval – even when occasionally accompanied by a fretful inability to let well alone – is infinitely more comfortable than chilly indifference.

A bird's-eye view back through time would show us the three brothers in their different cities at this period: Marino living a life of idleness in Venice; Marco now in Bologna whither he had followed Iacopo Bartolomeo Beccari, the beloved professor of chemistry whose favourite pupil he was; Giovambattista established in Turin instructing pupils of his own and elucidating the workings of the human body. From time to time the two younger brothers managed to meet; letters between the three of them regularly criss-crossed Italy. This pattern seemed to all as if it would continue indefinitely. Far from home they might be, yet the land they had become accustomed to living in was a comfortable and familiar place. None ever thought in a language other than Italian.

4

THERE IS really no need to beat about the bush, so I may as well say straight out that what necessitated Marino's speedy departure from Venice in the early hours of a July morning was the fact that he had put his strong brown hands around a woman's slender white neck and gripped and squeezed, so that the anger in her eyes turned to terror, she choked and clawed at him desperately but ineffectually, then went limp and died. The simple name for this act is murder and to commit it in the Republic of Venice, as elsewhere, is to lay yourself open to the full force of the law.

Marino made his way to Trieste. When the Senate has offered a reward for your capture 'alive or dead', a busy seaport just outside Venetian territory is probably the best place in which to lie low. The days followed one after the other, the sun rose and set, Marino's body continued with its normal animal rhythms: he went to bed and slept, hungered and thirsted, ate and defecated as if nothing out of the way had happened. In fact it rather surprised him that his appetite and digestion were so good and that he slept so well, since the deep and usually dreamless slumber into which he fell each night was invariably followed on waking by instant wretchedness as reality impinged once more: a chilly sense of a page having been turned irrevocably, a door shut for what seemed as if it must be for ever.

He found himself quite unable to tell his parents what had happened; after several attempts and much wasted paper he gave up. He had, however, written at once to Marco, making great efforts to be discreet and signing himself for the first time 'Alexander Lascaris', this name having arrived at the tip of his pen of its own accord as he realised that his own signature would be dangerous; he had carefully started the letter with 'My dearest friend', not 'My dearest brother' (Marco would anyway recognise his writing). Sitting at the end of the common table in the waterfront inn where he'd found a cheap room, he shielded the page from indiscreet eyes with his arm and wrote: 'A certain accomplished starcher and gofferer of frills with whom I was intimately acquainted is unfortunately no more. I myself am now deeply worried about my own state of health and would be grateful if you could *with the utmost haste*' (heavily underlined) 'consult that excellent physician whom we both know so well and seek his advice as to the remedies and manner of proceeding that will best help me avoid a fatal outcome to my troubles.' Marino was rather pleased with the opacity of this, yet could not stop himself spoiling the effect a bit by adding a desperate post-script after the new signature: 'I beg you to help me.' Logically speaking, it would of course have made more sense to save time by writing directly to Giambattista, yet somehow this didn't seem very easy; possibly, too, Marino felt that Marco would put in a good word for him. At any rate, having dispatched this plea he waited anxiously.

If your brothers will not help you, then no one will.

It is noticeable that Marino thought of his mistress's death as 'something that happened' rather than 'something I did' – a means perhaps of wriggling out from under the guilt which might otherwise have overwhelmed him. In the moments when he was unable to prevent various awful images from seeping surreptitiously into his mind, he succeeded in dismissing them by means of categorical statement-thoughts along the lines of 'She got what was coming to her,' or even the primitive 'It served her right.' ('Serves you right' had

always been among the litany of childhood exchanges between Marino and Marco. Occasionally, before they left
home for school in Venice, it had been said in defiant Greek
rather than Italian: *Kalá na páthis* – this intimate second
person singular, however, having in any language long since
been superseded by politer forms.)

The only dream that came to Marino in Trieste went back
to these distant days: he and Marco had been happily
occupied poking around in the marsh, then looked at the
position of the sun in the sky, realised it must be nearly time
for dinner and set off home together, for some reason
holding hands. Dreams are strange visitations with their
own odd distortions: in actuality, as far as Marino recalled,
even when very small they had never walked hand in hand.

The hardest of all realisations in that exile is truly beginning. Since the penalty that awaits you in Venice is decap-
itation 'between the two columns of San Marco' you can
clearly never go home again, for home lies in Venetian
territory. If you have to flee to distant lands it is very possible
that you may never see your brothers again. What makes
these things even more terrible is that they have come about
entirely through your own doing.

Giovambattista wrote in slightly stiff Greek when he told his
father what Marino had done, no doubt thinking that the use
of this language was more discreet. His parents' surprise at
the uncustomary alphabet was dispelled as soon as they read
the content of his letter, just as his mother understood
instantly why her son had addressed it solely to his father:
on a matter of such seriousness it is fitting that the head of
the family should receive the first formal intimation.

(If I have made little mention of their father, Demetrio, this
is because he never figured as prominently as their mother in
his sons' imagination.)

Needless to say, both parents were appalled. 'Your son is a fool,' said Caterina, which was very possibly true. 'You brought him up soft and spoiled him,' was what Demetrio thought but refrained from saying – and this was quite certainly not true at all. When your child commits a crime so heinous that he is pursued by the forces of the law it is no doubt easiest to consider that your spouse must be to blame for any fault in his character; however this may be, both parents duly gave thanks to God for the swift and cool efficiency with which Giambattista seemed to have dealt with the problem.

Who, to his great credit, had responded to his brother's cry for help without once saying, 'If you're in trouble now you're only getting your just deserts,' or 'It serves you right,' or 'I told you so,' or 'As you've made your bed, so you must lie on it,' or any other of those unpleasant little phrases people tend to use when events prove that their distrust of the other person was entirely justified. What Marino read when he tore open the impatiently awaited letter from Turin was a series of detailed instructions in Giovambattista's tiny and illegible handwriting about where to go (Vienna), how to get there, whom to contact there, where to apply for money if, as he rightly supposed, Marino was short of cash for the journey. ('Do not attempt to raise money or secure a loan anywhere else in Trieste. I believe this man to be trustworthy and you may give him my name as surety, but you should leave as soon as you have seen him, without any further delay.') The letter ended with a recommendation that Marino should pray for God's forgiveness, which since Giambattista had never shown any signs of being unduly pious was slightly surprising but under the circumstances remarkably mild and forbearing.

Marco wrote, 'You are an utter, utter fool.' However, he ended his letter with, 'I shall miss you. I embrace you lovingly,' which was very comforting.

What everyone, including Marino himself, felt was that he

had disgraced the family name. Giovambattista made arrangements to repay the money borrowed in Trieste, hesitated slightly as to how to enter this sum into his account book, then smiled grimly as his pen formed the words 'For necessary family expenses.' For sparing us all the shame of having a brother arrested and executed for murder, he thought.

For helping my brother; for providing a place of refuge where they will not hunt him. Giovambattista woke, sweating and distressed, from a dream in which a pack of lean and silent hounds pursued a hare through the fir trees on the slopes of Cephalonia's highest mountain. 'There are certainly hares on the island,' he said to himself, dismissive of such empty imaginings, 'though equally certainly I have never heard of anyone there keeping a pack of hounds.' But of course the trouble with foolish dreams – as he had often had cause to think – is that you have no control over them.

Nor indeed do you have any control over the urge of the stomach to eject tainted food. A ragoût of hare eaten a few days later, shortly after Marino set off for Vienna, led to serious vomiting – although no one else who ate it was affected – so that Giovambattista resolved to avoid such dishes and stick to a plainer diet.

Needless to say, the contacts in Austria who sprang immediately to Giovambattista's mind were men of science. But contacts know other contacts, the Dutch physician van Swieten was well liked at the Viennese court, favours may be sought and granted: Giovambattista was trying to think ahead. As a matter of fact, upon receipt of Marino's letter (which Marco had forwarded), he had for a brief space considered whether there were any important favours to be called in or whether a sum of money spent in the right quarter might not sort the matter out; however, ten minutes' careful reflection told him that the offence was too serious for either of these possibilities to be of any use. He thus sat up late and composed a couple of letters to colleagues in Vienna, as well as the instructions that Marino awaited with such agony. If it did not cross Giovambattista's mind to refuse to help, this may well have been because of that desperately scrawled postscript: memories of a small brother's swaggering bravado in times long past, attempting with only partial success to conceal the fact that he was scared.

Of course the advice that Giovambattista had given Marino could, strictly speaking, be considered as the aiding and abetting of a criminal. His friends, however, when some time later he cautiously admitted his part in his brother's escape from justice, understood that he could not have acted otherwise; 'He is my flesh and blood,' explained Giovambattista, 'he turned to me for help.' And, 'I have been like a father to him.' This was the first time that he had voiced such a thought; at night, when alone, he was troubled by the idea of having somehow failed in this paternal role, of having been too lenient, of not curbing various dangerous tendencies in his brother while there was still time. 'Am I my brother's keeper?' was a question which Giovambattista would have answered in the affirmative without a moment's thought. 'Spare the rod and spoil the child' was also a sentiment he would have understood. But then, 'Giambattista's bark is definitely worse than his bite,' as Marco had once pronounced.

Giovambattista concluded his nocturnal reflections (turning restlessly in his solitary bed) with the acknowledgment that he had always known he would one day be called upon to deal with some dreadful misdemeanour. In spite of priding himself on being a severe rationalist, his last thought before sleeping was something like, 'It was written in the stars.'

It was to be hoped at least that Marino was suitably chastened.

*   *   *

46

Repentance and regrets and remorse are none of them very pleasant states of mind, which may be why little light falls on Marino during his time in Austria. Perhaps the darkness is simply that of depression and despondence. This condition is what all three brothers called 'low spirits'; all would have agreed that there is nothing whatsoever to be done about such a state except live through it as best one may.

'My dearest son,' wrote Caterina to Giovambattista one winter evening, as the candles flickered and threw strange shadows on to the garlands of the painted wooden ceiling, 'our hearts are gladdened by your continuing successes. Nevertheless your father has been sorely grieved at the anxieties so thoughtlessly brought upon us by your brother's behaviour, with the result that he has been much vexed these past months by a very great lassitude and a shortness of breath which have so far proved obstinate.' Caterina attached less importance to the death of a woman – unknown to her in any case and assuredly indiscreet – than to the embarrassment and distress that it caused her family. 'We have had no word from your brother Marino, who does not deign to answer the letters we have sent.'

Much of Giovambattista's reply was taken up with complicated family financial matters (not all of Maria's dowry had yet been paid) and congratulations on the pregnancy of Paolo's wife, Aretousa – as well, naturally, as medical advice for his father; he thus made no mention of Marino, and his mother did not apparently notice this discreet silence.

The fact is that Marino had never received the most recent of Caterina's lengthy missives and thus had not had to summon up the courage to read its six closely written pages of criticism and reproach or to force himself to pen some kind of answer. It is unthinkable to say to yourself, 'My heart sinks when I see my mother's handwriting,' but life is certainly more comfortable when you don't see it too often.

'How could you? How could you descend to such a bestial level, how could you so shame us?' were among the questions his mother asked insistently.

'But why?' asked Stephanie. 'Why did you do it?' (No one had ever bothered to ask this simple question before.)
    'She was cheating on me,' replied Marino.
    'Do you always kill women who cheat on you?'
    'Not usually. Though I'd prefer it if you didn't.' He added slowly, never having thought about it until now, 'The truth is, I don't really know what made me do it.'

An awful rending pain in your chest is a perfectly understandable response to the realisation that what you thought was yours alone is in fact shared with someone else: the *hortus conclusus* as public park perhaps. 'You bitch,' shouted Marino as he slapped her, 'you filthy whore' – these impoverished epithets stemming from the appalling feeling of something private having been sullied and besmirched: quite intolerable that someone else should lie in the wonderful grip of those strong, soap-scented arms, should push back the tendrils of dark hair made curly by the steam of her ironing and bite that delicious ear, should run crude hands over that shapely instep, should have any knowledge of the things that made her eyes close and her breathing quicken.
    Conceivably matters might have stopped here – an ugly, jealous scene, slaps and bruises and an arm cruelly twisted, followed by a slammed door and angry footsteps receding down the street – if the woman had only been able to resist the temptation to goad. 'What ever made you think you were so marvellous?' she mocked.
    Marino never quite knew or remembered what among the many things his mistress had said had stung him so sharply that it led him to strangle her (for such a loss of control, such a

blind, passionate surge of violence surely indicates a sting piercing to the very depths of the soul, over and above the common kind of jealousy). He did of course recollect some of the wounding words and as it happened later repeated to Stephanie a couple of uncomplimentary phrases referring to his penis. There is an extraordinary happiness in realising that what once hurt no longer matters the slightest bit to you, so that you can laugh about it with someone else: Stephanie, whose manners occasionally tended to be robust, lapsing from the quiet tones that are generally held to be polite, roared with laughter and said, 'What rubbish.'

What Marino did not tell Stephanie, however, was that the hairiness and clumsiness of his hands had also been criticised – this being one of the things which had not hurt so very much and which he had forgotten. There's no doubt that people become angry when they are defensive (confronted with a faithlessness that is manifestly impossible to deny) and when angry they are given to exaggerate; the backs of Marino's hands were certainly hairy, yet whatever he touched was invariably handled adroitly and competently so that the accusation of clumsiness was very unfair.

The other thing Marino never had any memory of at all was the nasty little comment that he had the body and soul of a peasant.

Some years before this terrible event, when Marino had gone back to the island for a few months' stay at the age of twenty-five and Caterina saw him as an adult for the first time, she had noted his hairiness and attributed it to the unsuitably animal position which her husband had demanded on what she had always assumed was the night of his conception – not something that a husband generally requires of his wife but those were still the days before Demetrio felt he had enough children, when he still satisfied his desires largely in the marriage bed. (Subsequently he found himself a nice, quiet woman who was compliant in such matters and thereafter slackened in his marital attentions.) Most people, however, considered that Marino was a fine figure of a man, even if not as tall as his three brothers. If some of his behaviour was a trifle unconventional – like making coins or handkerchiefs appear and disappear in improbable places, to the delight of a rabble of children, or stripping off his clothes and swimming in the sea just as if he were still ten years old (though at least he had the grace to keep his drawers on) – those who remembered him as a child merely shook their heads and smiled.

'Watch out a mermaid doesn't get you,' mocked the men down by the shore.

'Why don't you try it?' he responded, ignoring the ribald laughter, but none of them considered this a good idea in spite of the fact that most had swum as children.

After someone spotted Paolo swimming with Marino one afternoon, their sister Maria pointed out that he was no longer a child and warned him that of course Marino had always done exactly what he wanted but that on the whole if one wished to fit in it was better not to act too differently from everyone else. Elder sisters, like elder brothers, may appoint themselves guardian to a younger sibling; Maria, who in any case had always been possessed of remarkable common sense, had begun to appropriate this role after the birth of her first child.

Caterina said crisply, 'People will talk,' and then, when no contrition appeared to be forthcoming, 'You will become *swarthy* if you stay in the sun like that with no clothes on.'

Marino bowed his head respectfully but said nothing; the following day he got a boatman to take him over to Lixouri, where he stayed for a couple of weeks. Echoes of a juvenile running away maybe, or simply an attempt at discretion, although various stories inevitably reached Argostoli.

Perhaps when 'home' is a place which has long existed only in your mind the actuality of it is bound to be disappointing. It may well be that Marino's flight to Lixouri was spurred by the desire to find that sense of homecoming into a world of peace and happiness which had somehow eluded him in the parental house. While in Lixouri he walked over to the marshes of Livadi a couple of times and did indeed feel better – another eccentricity, this walking, but Marino had long since assured Giambattista that without physical exercise his health went to pieces (which the physician put down to a restlessness of spirit).

'My dearest son,' wrote his mother to Giovambattista with teeth determinedly gritted, 'the arrival of your brother has been a source of great happiness to us all. There is no joy like that with which a parent greets the much-loved child so long absent from home.' She then proceeded to fill two pages with an account of Marino's failings great and small: he lies abed until all hours of the day, he expects his father's servant to come and shave him whenever he chooses to get up, he behaves indiscreetly (by this she meant the swimming), he consorts with vulgar people, he spends too much time playing cards (for ridiculously large sums of money), he is a bad influence on his younger brother (in other words Paolo), the presents he brought from Italy were meagre in the extreme, he hadn't bothered to remember that they would have liked sugar as well as coffee. She omitted to mention what she suspected (rightly) to be the case, namely that he was also wasting his money at a house of ill repute. She ended her letter with the statement that her happiness would be complete if a suitable bride with a decent dowry were to be found for Marino in Argostoli so that, since he seemed incapable of making any career, he could settle down and live the life of a gentleman in the parental home.

Giovambattista was not in the habit of questioning his

mother's sentiments; he agreed that marriage might indeed be good for Marino and went to some lengths to arrange with one of his friends for twelve pounds of sugar to be sent on the next ship sailing from Venice to Cephalonia.

'I am not thinking of marriage quite yet, sir,' declared Marino to his father with as much firmness as he could muster.

The time was to come, however, when he was to say to the man he hoped would be his father-in-law, 'It was a youthful crime of passion of which I have repented long and hard.' Since it was impossible to avoid all mention of his past, repentance seemed the best note to strike. And this policy paid off, it appears: his 'indiscretion' (Marino's other euphemism) did not apparently render him ineligible, so that in due course the marriage took place. This was in St Petersburg, whither Marino moved after Vienna.

To Stephanie he said, much later, 'I had to tell him my real name. I wasn't at all sure her family would let me marry her.'

St Petersburg on its damp and marshy banks is a long, long way from the lagoon of Venice and an even longer way from home.

If anything is written in the stars it is perhaps that brothers born of the same parents will nevertheless inevitably be different people: different bundles of inherited characteristics, different layers of acquired habits and accumulated experiences.

A sad and lonely idea occurring to Marino towards the end of his life was that possibly in spite of everything Marco had always really had more in common with Giambattista. Stephanie was the only person to whom he had ever tried to express all the fleeting thoughts that passed through his mind: 'Maybe it was because I made my life so far away, maybe it is just that their paths diverged less,' he mused, weighing this idea tentatively. Then: 'Maybe you and I were fated to converge,' he told her. This was a less lonely thought.

5

W HEN GIOVAMBATTISTA received Marino's first
letter from Austria he was getting dressed in order to
go the palace, standing in front of the looking-glass in
stockings, breeches and chemise while his servant proffered
a discreetly sumptuous waistcoat of embroidered snuff-
coloured velvet. Giovambattista made the boy wait while
he slit open the seal and unfolded and read the letter without
any change of expression, then put on both waistcoat and
coat, called for his wig, arranged the frills of his cuffs to his
satisfaction, and for some reason placed the single page in his
pocket instead of locking it in his bureau. Thus Marino's
letter lay close against his body all evening as he inclined his
head respectfully and conversed with the king. This very
likely meant that he was pleased by what Marino had written
at the end of the letter (although he might just as easily have
been faintly exasperated by his brother's tendency to overdo
things).

What Marino had written was: 'I am filled with deep
regret, my dearest brother, for the pain which I know my
follies have caused you. Equally profound is my gratitude for
the tender and fatherly care which you have ever shown me
and which I am resolved to merit better in future. I kiss your
hands with humble and penitent fraternal respect, your most
affectionate brother, Alexandre de Lascaris.'

On second thoughts, it was probably the single word
'fatherly' that touched some secret chord in Giovambattista's
heart.

No doubt Giovambattista noted the particle and the

gallicisation of the name; no doubt he was also aware that there's not much point using an assumed name if in every second sentence you make your blood relationship with the recipient of your letter crystal clear. In fact, once well out of Venetian territory there was no real reason why Marino should not have reverted to his true name – except, of course, for the consideration that it was probably wiser for his family not to appear too obviously to be in correspondence with him.

All the same, 'It seems that "Marino Carburi" is not good enough for him these days,' sniffed Caterina.

What did not occur to anyone was that when your life has fallen to pieces so that you suddenly find yourself in a strange place where an unfamiliar language is spoken, bereft of friends and family, the horrid sense of having to start over again is somehow eased by the adoption of a new persona. If Marino chose to give himself a rather grand name, this seems fairly forgivable, especially since his elder brother's colleagues were not much to his taste so that he spent his first few weeks in Vienna in rather miserable solitude with nothing but his fantasies for company.

'Alexander' is a self-enhancing name, a whistling-in-the-dark name, when you are feeling confused and inadequate, a fantasy name whose origins are not too hard to fathom: Marino's knowledge of history was sketchy but Alexander the Great as mythical hero had once filled both his and Marco's imaginations, with his horse and his army and that valiant, manly conquest of dastardly and effete Persians. (It is perhaps not so very surprising that Marino had always envisaged these Persians as brandishing scimitars, turbanned and bearded – though in some strange way effeminate nonetheless.) And 'Lascaris' is a stately name, an old, old Byzantine name. Unless you have extreme delusions of grandeur and claim to have been born in the purple, calling yourself 'Porphyrogenitus', then 'Lascaris' is about the most dignified name that you could choose.

Striking perhaps that both these names looked eastwards rather than westwards – to past rather than future – although no one apparently noticed this.

Just as no one, of course, was at all amazed that Giovambattista was so well received at the court of Turin. Nor should anyone have been in the least surprised that he continued to have his scapegrace brother's welfare in mind or that, after a little more careful thought, he used his increasing prestige in the highest circles (as well as a certain amount of hard-earned money) to gain for Marino a commission in the Empress's corps of engineers. These things are not always easy to arrange at a distance: perhaps it was that first letter nestling close against his heart for a whole evening that somehow made him persevere. To Marino he wrote sternly, 'This is the utmost that I can do for you. My greatest hope is that you will now apply yourself to make the most of this opportunity that I have been at very great pains to secure for you.' And, slightly more kindly, 'I have no doubts as to your talent and ability.'

Needless to say, by now Marino had written more than once; all his letters, including that first expression of penitence, were safely bestowed in the pigeon-holed bureau of Giovambattista's own designing in which the eldest brother kept his correspondence neatly filed. (Giovambattista always emptied his pockets before undressing and had his clothes aired and if need be pressed before being put away.)

'He got his servant to put a damp cloth to my coat and breeches and press them before he would let me go out,' said Marco, describing his recent visit to Turin.

Giovambattista's servants were remarkable for their youth and good looks. None ever seemed to stay with him for any very great length of time: 'I dare say he's a hard master,' had been one of Marino's early thoughts on the subject. However, as each boy left an equally attractive one would appear to take his place. Now Marino expressed a new and daringly subversive thought to Marco: 'Do you suppose that Giambattista . . .' (a pause as he rejected the first rather crude term that had come to mind), 'I mean, do you think he actually *beds* his servants?'

Marco – who had also occasionally had irreverent thoughts about Giambattista, although not quite of this kind – did not pretend to be shocked but considered the idea carefully in the light of his recent stay in their brother's household. Then, 'No,' he pronounced stoutly, 'I am quite, quite sure he doesn't.' (In this, as it happened, Marco was perfectly correct.) 'Giambattista's always liked having nice things round him – could you really imagine him with servants who were wall-eyed or smelly or old and lazy or something?'

'*Always go for quality*,' said Marino seriously in perfect imitation of their brother's voice, and both laughed.

It may have been because of this relaxed laughter, this happy, comfortable sense of mutual understanding, that Marino found himself able to say, 'I'm not really in the mood just at the moment,' when Marco said, 'Apropos . . .' and suggested going in search of some female company to round off the evening. Instead they went out drinking (in moderation, for Marco had to leave early the next day) and Marino introduced his brother to the dubious pleasures of beer.

'It seems a pretty pointless kind of drink, if you ask me,' commented Marco, who had been obliged to withdraw into a side-street to relieve himself as they made their way back to Marino's lodging. 'I doubt if I'd ever really take to it.'

'Me neither,' agreed Marino.

This meeting took place in Vienna. The Austrian capital was not in fact on Marco's itinerary but a brief detour to see his brother was impossible to resist, even if imprudent; he thus worked out an elaborate pretext and left his companions to wait for him in Salzburg. This he did not intend to tell the family until a long time later, knowing quite well that Giambattista would not approve.

Giambattista might also not have approved of the way Marco slipped the (admittedly not very large) cost of this little incognito trip to Vienna in among his general travelling expenses. Marco didn't give a second thought to the small subterfuge; he felt happily affluent and had in any case recently reported back to Venice that reliable draughtsmen were proving more expensive than foreseen and that palms required greasing if unrestricted access to mines and furnaces was to be guaranteed. When he had passed through Turin on the first stage of his journey – the mines of Piedmont being the first he was due to visit – his elder brother had reminded him of the importance of keeping accurate accounts of all monies disbursed, and Marco, with a comfortable sense of cheerful virtue, had since assured him in more than one letter that this was being done.

He also assured his brother that his bowels were in good fettle in spite of the sometimes unpalatable food and told him of the extraordinarily high prevalence of goitre that he had observed in some of the Austrian villages through which they'd passed, knowing that this information would interest Giambattista.

For the truth is that just when Marino's star seemed to be foundering, Marco's was rising. The age of twenty-eight was apparently as auspicious for the third brother as it had been for the eldest: congratulations from Turin were warm when the newly established chair of Experimental Chemistry at

Padua was given to Marco. Ill-natured tongues remarked that of course it was far more economical to appoint a youthful newcomer who would not expect the salary which his olders and betters might demand; this sort of thought did not occur to Marino who, when they next met (this was before he disgraced himself), hugged his brother with vicarious pride and said, 'They couldn't have made a better choice if they'd tried for fifty years.'

'I would have been too old by then,' Marco pointed out drily.

The dedication of the *Marine Insect* letter to the Procurator of San Marco and the happy hours spent in the Emo house had clearly paid off: both Marco Foscarini and Alvise Emo, father of Marco's friend Anzolo, used their influence in favour of Marco's appointment. This was noted with some satisfaction by Giovambattista. Nevertheless, to one of his friends he wrote: 'My brother Marco is still young in years and – I would be guilty of an untruth were I to claim otherwise – continues from time to time to show an unbecoming levity. I am not convinced that he has paid due attention to the need to improve his Latin and fear that, without steady application, he will have difficulty lecturing in this language. However, there is no doubt that his engagement in the pursuit of scientific knowledge is ardent and I thus hope and believe that he will deserve the honour and justify the faith which his friends have shown in him.' To his family he was more positive: 'My brother's new position reflects well on all of us,' he told Caterina among other things, and, 'I am confident that he will in due course make a name for himself.' The largest part of the letter, however, had to do with financial affairs, the fact that Giovambattista had until now been the only son earning any money having endowed him with a certain authority to speak on such matters. He and his mother understood each other perfectly.

*   *   *

58

Marco's salary was 1,500 Venetian *lire* per annum. This is something over two hundred ducats. As he pointed out to his mother, it was a respectable but not over-generous amount; what he was trying to hint – but didn't dare say outright – was that money from home would still be extremely useful. 'Nonsense,' thought Caterina to herself, frowning as she read between the lines, 'he is unmarried and can perfectly well learn to live on his salary.'

However, before Marco had time to receive her letter to this effect, before he had time to start worrying about brushing up his Latin and preparing his first courses, he found himself setting off on extensive travels in possession of official authorisation to spend more than ten times his professorial salary – in other words, what seemed to him the enormous sum of two hundred ducats per month.

'My elder brother was envious of him,' Marino later told Stephanie, which of course might have been the truth. On the other hand, when Marino made this pronouncement he was deeply angry with Giovambattista and thus may very well have been doing him an injustice; if their elder brother was somewhat cool in his response to the news that Marco had been entrusted with a mission of such importance, it could simply have been because he felt anxious about the very great responsibilities involved.

What this mission was is easily stated: the Venetian government, worried by the low yields from its mines, was sending Marco on something politely called a tour of inspection of foreign mines (no one, it goes without saying, ever mentioned the word 'espionage'). Once more, Marco's web of friendships was standing him in good stead: 'Why not send young Carburi?' someone – I think it was Alvise Emo – suggested, and so it was decided.

*　　*　　*

Travelling is not something that anyone in his right mind would undertake for pleasure. Giovambattista was later to travel fairly regularly between Paris and Venice – one of the most perilous of journeys, since it involves confiding your life to the rough but luckily sure-footed porters who carry you over precipitous and slippery mountain paths where neither horse nor carriage can pass. Even when no longer young he set out each time undaunted, yet his letters written on the road to friends and family frequently made mention of poor food and fatigue and discomfort and expense. Nevertheless, Marco was excited by the prospect of seeing foreign lands, although he took pains to appear blasé and offhand about it. (Marino was not deceived.)

There is of course a difference between travelling on business and travelling into outlawed exile. When the two brothers sat in a warm, fuggy room one winter night and drank beer together, only Marino was in some way aware of this; the bitter liquid seemed at each sip to reiterate the loss of a whole world of sunlight and laughter and familiar tastes and sounds. However, such feelings are much better not admitted, so that he agreed, apparently cheerfully enough, with Marco's verdict on the uncouth drink.

As they said goodbye the following morning Marco embraced him and Marino found himself saying, 'God keep you.' (Faintly surprising, these words, since they were not the sort of thing the brothers usually said to one another.) Marino stood in the chilly grey light of morning and watched until the diligence disappeared round a bend in the road, then abruptly turned on his heel and kicked out at a mongrel dog which was suddenly under his feet. This action was also somewhat uncharacteristic: Marino generally had good relations with dogs and children.

Perhaps if partings are invariably full of sadness it is because the future is so uncertain and the tricks which fate may play so pitiless. The worst thing about seeing your brother off like this is the lack of ceremony; amid the hustle and bustle, the securing of a place, the bestowing of luggage (although on this occasion Marco was travelling light), there are things that somehow don't manage to get said. It occurs to me that Marino's pious wish may have been a bungled attempt to say something that had never previously needed to be articulated.

Marco's last words before leaving – securely tethered in practical considerations – were, 'Don't forget, Giambattista doesn't need to know I've been here.'

Later, one of the things that Marino understood and sympathised with in Russia was the ceremony of departure: those few collected moments spent sitting in stillness and silence that mark each leaving.

When Marino and Marco speculated disloyally about their brother's relations with his servants, what did not occur to either of them was something that most servants – including Giovambattista's – know instinctively without putting into words, namely that irreverent thoughts are a great means of redressing the balance between authority and obedience.

Marino was at any rate right in one thing: it is perfectly true that Giovambattista was an exigent master who expected to be obeyed. His demands – although sometimes excessive – were usually met promptly, however, since not to do so was to invite a chilly sarcasm; he was, into the bargain, not easily hoodwinked. His most unreasonable stipulation was that anyone in his employ should, at least once a week, strip naked and wash from top to toe – in summer this was all very well but in winter there was sometimes a temptation to shirk the task. On one memorable occasion he had sent a youth whose ablutions he judged to have been inadequate back to wash again, had himself mounted the narrow stairs up to the attic (a thing unheard of) and had stood in the doorway, silent and impassive, watching as clothes were removed, a basin filled with cold water and a thin, shivering, resentful body hastily scrubbed with a piece of rag kept for this purpose. The boy's thoughts that Sunday morning were both irreverent and profane and are best not repeated. He made a very rude sign indeed behind his master's back.

On the other hand, Giovambattista invariably remembered his servants' name-days with a small gift of money and had once tenderly nursed with his own hands a boy called Piero when he lay sick for almost a month (though dismissing him as soon as he was fully recovered).

His servants were in turn correct in their assessment that Giovambattista was not easy to deceive; as it happens he had a pretty shrewd idea that Marco might attempt to visit Marino. He preferred to ask no questions, however, and applied himself to the daily business of examining the sick with his customary steadiness of purpose. At night, alone with his books and his correspondence, he was from time to time distracted by fretfulness at the thought that to be seen to consort with their fugitive brother would be damaging to Marco's prospects. Among Giovambattista's favourite words of disapprobation were 'rackety' and 'harum-scarum': 'consort with' was a verb he tended to use for any association between the people thus described.

A great many physicians do not want to admit the simple truth that illnesses will frequently either resolve by themselves or end in death, regardless of any intervention and no matter what steadiness of purpose may be shown. (Life ends in death, after all.) There are indeed different views as to what a physician should be doing: wrestling with obdurate diseases and overpowering them with an armamentarium – a good word, this – of powerful medicines, or tinkering: a massive assault by the heavy artillery or repeated swift attacks by the light cavalry.

Giovambattista inclined to the latter approach: 'It is preferable,' he taught, 'to start with very small dosages of the remedies that lie at our disposition, then increase them incrementally according to whether or not the patient shows any response. A large dose may do more harm than good; a careful observation of the effects of a smaller dose may teach us whether or not to continue.' (Marco was not far wrong when he characterised their eldest brother as cautious). He had also come to favour restraint in the letting of blood, having noticed by self-experimentation that excessive fatigue may follow the loss of too much blood, this fatigue weakening the patient rather more often than it weakens the disease. There is no doubt a great inner satisfaction in applying the clean, sharp blade to the vein in one's own left arm – Giovambattista was right-handed – and seeing the red blood flow, but an even greater satisfaction is to be had from knowing when to stop, from a sense of just proportions, from self-control.

When he dispatched to his mother a carefully wrapped package containing the powerful medicine that comes from the foxglove plant, Giovambattista thus included detailed instructions on exactly how much of it his father should take (in gradually increasing quantities), ending with a stern warning, written in a slightly larger and clearer hand than usual and emphatically underlined: '*Do not on any account exceed these dosages.*' He also recommended infusions twice daily of nettle or dandelion – 'or whatever herb you may lay hands on which will provoke a frequent passing of water' (he was not quite sure what might be available in Cephalonia) – as well as the avoidance of any great excitement or disturbance of mind.

It is always extremely useful having a physician in the family.

Giovambattista had had a certain amount of success treating dropsy, which is what his father appeared to be suffering from, in this manner. Nevertheless, as he pointed out to his students, there are some cases which remain obstinately unresponsive to the regimen of digitalis and diuresis; this was a problem which he had long been turning in his mind. When one morning he held up his hand imperatively to halt the caress of the well-honed blade over his cheeks and chin and throat, called for pen and ink to be brought, reached for his notebook and jotted down a new idea, the sudden clarity of perception may have had something to do with thoughts of his father (it is a heavy responsibility to treat one's progenitor from a distance), although of course those daily minutes of intimacy and trust and quiet under the skilled hands of the servant who shaved him were always conducive to reflection. The idea that he wished to record without delay was this:

'It may be that differences in response are simply due to the idiosyncrasies of each patient. Yet might it not be possible that, though the manifestations be similar, the origins of oedematous disease may prove as dissimilar as those of the fevers? Might it not be that an understanding of cause would lead to an ability on the part of the physician to discriminate and discern the existence of different diseases? If this were so, then there is no doubt that the remedies prescribed would also differ.'

A couple of weeks later he expanded this idea to a colleague in Leiden. By then, however, a letter from Argostoli forwarded by a cousin visiting Venice had informed him of some improvement in his father's condition.

Marino, who was fully aware that he was considered responsible for his father's poor state of health, went through a period of not writing much to anyone: even his letters to Marco were rather cursory. Of course, this may have had something to do with the fact that he was involved in what is called 'finding his feet' in a world for the first time separate from that of his brothers; 'finding one's feet', it seems to me, is something like feeling for solid rock in a quagmire.

Indeed, as the months passed Marino had gradually come to feel less of the chilliness of being on his own; after all, a new beginning also means a slate wiped clean, which in turn means that you can recreate yourself. He was starting to learn a little German – enough anyway for the daily business of ordering food and dealing with servants. Most of his communication with his fellow humans, however, was in heavily accented and at this stage not entirely fluent French. This language (and the persona that went with it) pleased him: another aspect of life that belonged solely to him and could be shaped any way he wished. Whenever he found himself at a loss for a word he unhesitatingly substituted a gallicised version of an Italian one; this gave his conversation an apparently cosmopolitan style and character of its own. 'French and Italian,' he was heard to declare one night when slightly inebriated, 'are the civilised tongues.'

Marco, by contrast, felt no need to get to grips with strange and difficult languages. With what seemed like unlimited funds at his disposal, he was paying lordly sums for interpreters to accompany him on his travels through Bohemia and Hungary.

When in Vienna Marco told him that they could all now rightfully claim the title of Count, Marino was gratified yet made no immediate use of it, having already awarded himself another title: his fellow-officers in Austria knew him as the French-speaking Chevalier de Lascaris.

6

T HE ARMY has always been a suitable place to which
younger brothers may be consigned (if you live in a
society where only the eldest inherits the family property) or
ne'er-do-wells and black sheep sent to make their fortune as
best they can. It is also a place where fellow-officers may
drink and play cards together in a sort of comfortable
camaraderie. And it is a place which provides an organised
context for those whose bent is for making things work but
who are otherwise rather lazy. The first of these points never
occurred to Giovambattista when he attempted to find some
solution to the vexed question of his brother's future; in their
case the rules of primogeniture did not apply, all siblings
being held in Cephalonia to belong equally to the family and
thus in due course sharing the paternal inheritance. Drinking
and gaming were occupational hazards, as well of course as
vices which might very well be indulged in anywhere. (In
what concerned the former he was possibly taking a pessi-
mistic view; Marino was not, as it happened, given to any
particularly heavy use of alcohol and only resorted to serious
drinking later, at the very nadir of his life. As regards
gambling, the least said the better; certainly life in Maria
Theresa's army was unlikely to make things worse.) All in
all, Giovambattista felt that he'd probably made the best
choice possible in the circumstances. His conscience was thus
easy as he described in his account book a largish expense as
'For the settlement of M.' The fact that he drew a line under
this entry was perhaps purely coincidental.

The next entry of any importance read 'Monies paid to

Marco for the restoring of the family title'. This was preceded by such everyday items as 'For laundry', 'For senna of Aleppo', 'For a pair of silver buckles', and was followed by 'For syrup of figs', 'For a present for Nicola on the occasion of his name-day', 'For the binding of two folio volumes', and so forth. No lines were drawn between any of these entries.

No matter where life takes you, your first loyalties must always be to your family. And 'family' and 'house' are at a certain unthinking level interchangeable; what these words conjured up for all the Carburi brothers was an island, a small town within that island, an ancestral house in that quarter of the small town known – as was customary – by the family name: the *Carburata*. If Giovambattista invariably referred to it as the dominical house rather than the paternal house (which was what his brothers called it), this only goes to indicate its central position in his scheme of things. 'House' of course may also mean dynasty.

It is thus understandable that Giovambattista did not in the least disapprove when Marco first broached in a letter the possibility of claiming the title. Caterina had in any case brought them up to believe that it was rightfully theirs; their ancestor Stamatis was without doubt noble in both senses of the word when he fell, martyred by the cruel Turk. 'After all,' wrote Marco, 'how may I travel and converse on equal terms with the nobility of the countries which I shall be visiting if I myself appear to be a person of no consequence?' Needless to say, the pursuit of such a claim involves not only applications and legal paperwork – which Marco had already set in action – but also the payment of a sizeable fee; 'If you could see your way to helping, my dear brother, I have no reason to believe that there will be any impediment.' This further call on the physician's purse for once gave rise to no secret discontent or inner dissatisfaction. His health was good, as he assured Marco when he wrote back to signal his agreement, and he was at last apparently free from that costiveness which had recently been plaguing him.

In due course the title was indeed ratified. A letter was addressed with great pride to the *Nobilissimo Signor Conte Giovanni Battista Carburi.* A lovely warm feeling suffuses the soul when you know that you have achieved something which will be well received; Marco expansively signed his next letter to his mother 'Your most affectionate and re-spectful son, Count Marco Carburi' – a harmless vanity to which Caterina's reply was gratifyingly gracious.

'Stephanie, how would you like to be *Madame la Comtesse?*' Marino asked much later, in Paris, in the days when they were all older (but not necessarily wiser).

'Oh, I wouldn't settle for anything less than *Madame la Marquise,*' she answered lightly, not having understood what he was saying. She couldn't see the expression on his face because he was standing behind her with his knee pressed into the small of her thin back as he pulled the laces of her corset tight.

A brief pause. Then: 'You're far too meagre to need much lacing really, aren't you?' Adding in querulous tones, 'I must say, I do like a woman who has a bit of bottom you can get hold of, *de quoi remplir les mains d'un honnête homme . . .* I'm asking whether you'd care to go back to Cephalonia with me. What I'm talking of is marriage.'

The thought passed through her mind that he had possibly been drinking. She said, 'I'd like it,' much as one might humour a child, fully expecting that this idea would rapidly dematerialise under the chilly scrutiny of sober good sense.

But: 'I was not mocking you, I meant it,' he said a few days later.

'He is a *loyal* person,' was the strange phrase that came into her mind.

If Marino realised on the afternoon he first bedded her that Stephanie was somewhat older than the age she admitted to, he also noted dispassionately that she had certainly borne a child or children. During the following weeks he refrained from asking her about it, however, first because he wasn't in the mood to contemplate or speak of children but also because her own reticence made him think that the subject might be painful to her too. 'Think' is the wrong word, of course: it was not so much a question of conscious reflection as one of those odd flashes of sympathy in which you are suddenly attuned to the feelings of someone you barely know. Perhaps in turn it was her perception of this that made that even odder word 'loyal' come into her mind when he spoke of marriage.

Dynasties need a continuation of the generations, this much is obvious. Hence it is hardly surprising that by the time Marco completed his travels and returned to Venice in order to put his findings into practice Caterina was becoming increasingly preoccupied by the fact that none of her elder sons was yet married. Considering that they were now forty-one, thirty-four and almost thirty-three respectively, this seemed a state of affairs that required remedy. However, when a couple of very delicate hints to Giambattista produced no response, for some reason she found this high-mindedness not unsatisfactory. 'He is too selfless,' she said to herself and wrote pointed letters to both Marino and Marco, while at the same time making extremely discreet enquiries about the dowries of various young women in both Corfu and Cephalonia. 'It will be best if they marry girls from home' was an idea that she took for granted.

*   *   *

69

There is very little that can be kept secret from your family as far as your public life or career is concerned. It is after all understandable that they should be interested. (Your private life is another matter, provided of course that you conduct it discreetly.) When Giovambattista began to hear rumours that Marco's comportment on his travels and – worse – the fruits of these travels left something to be desired, he wrote several anxious letters to Venice seeking to discover exactly what had gone wrong.

'What seems to have happened,' replied one correspondent waspishly, 'is that a great deal of public money has been spent, in return for which your brother has provided a large number of elegantly penned letters and scholarly reports, as well as a substantial portfolio of beautiful plans and drawings, none of which is of the slightest use in solving the increasingly pressing problems arising from the low yield of the mines.'

Someone else was blunter: 'Your brother Marco has spent money right and left and has tended to act in a somewhat lordly manner. He has moreover shown a lack of tact or restraint commensurate with his lack of practical knowledge of mineral ores, and as a result has made enemies among those whose daily occupation has taught them more of the processes of extracting metals than he can well conceive. The furnace he has constructed is of little value.'

There are black sheep and there are golden boys: sometimes the boundaries between these categories are blurred, the one may become the other. Caterina, who gave a slight imperceptible shrug of her small, firm, silk-clad shoulders whenever Marino was thought of or mentioned, was deeply chagrined that Marco's mission was not a success, mortified that he had (as she put it) 'let us all down'. Marco had been taking the maternal directives about marriage in his stride but was thoroughly discomposed by three carping pages in which the words 'disgrace' and 'shame' and 'failure' were repeated several times. Marino could have told him that such letters are best perused once, rapidly, and then destroyed; Marco, less experienced, read and reread his mother's censure and suffered from miserable indigestion after dinner.

Rather surprisingly, it was Giovambattista who attempted to smooth things over with their mother, 'making excuses for his brother' (once more, her words). These justifications included the reasonable comments that, after all, Marco possessed no experience of mining, that he had reported back faithfully on all he had seen, and that the initial error – in any case not Marco's but that of the Council of Ten and the Deputy of Mines who had employed him – had been to imagine that what applied in Hungary or Sweden would be equally valid for the Venetian mines of Agordo. He omitted all mention of the rumours coming to his ears of Marco's extravagant behaviour.

This was especially generous if Marino's subsequent interpretation was correct and the eldest brother had indeed felt a pang of envy for his heedless junior, although if such a feeling existed it was well concealed. What is certain is that Marco's travels had taken him to Stockholm and Uppsala, where he was received by that distinguished man of science, Carl Linnaeus. It goes without saying that this introduction was helped, or maybe even brought about, by a letter from the professor of medicine – a correspondence on the importance of accurate naming had for some time been taking place between Turin and Uppsala – and that any civilities extended to the young Count could be seen in part as being shown to his elder brother: consolation of a sort, if consolation were needed. Possibly Marco's report describing bad teeth, Latin as halting as his own and a strange appearance in what he called 'outlandish Lappish garb' was not as respectful as it might have been. However this may be, Giovambattista's letters to Marco in the months following his return were noticeably sterner in tone than those to his mother: 'You have behaved quite crazily,' for example (*pazzamente* being another of his favourite words).

After consulting a couple of Piedmontese experts, he wrote once more to his mother, telling her, 'There is no doubt that my brother's Swedish smelting furnace, while cleverly constructed, has unfortunately proved unproductive due to the fact that the pyrite of Agordo contains less iron than that of Sweden.' He added, 'I cannot, however, conclude from this that all of his suggestions and proposals will necessarily be found invalid; we should perhaps bear in mind that a certain amount of resistance is always to be expected when innovations are introduced.' Giovambattista had observed this more than once in his own field of medicine. 'Nevertheless, I believe it will be as well for Marco's happiness and reputation that he should return to Padua and commence his courses as soon as may be possible.'

This fair-minded approach, leaving out all mention of extravaganzas and arrogance and tactlessness, was also a clever construction. At first sight it looks as if a certain discretion – sibling solidarity even – was manifesting itself here, although it may also be that Giovambattista preferred any rebukes to Marco to come from himself alone; if questioned he would have replied, after only the briefest of pauses, that it was surely better to spare his parents further gratuitous distress.

But with friends one may be more spontaneous. The following evening he expressed his feelings fairly openly to Antonio Vallisneri (the Professor of Natural Science under whom Marco had studied), chewing fennel seeds from a little dish beside him on the table as he wrote: 'My very dear friend, your kind letter filled me with happiness. I wish I could have embraced you in person – however, the calls on

72

me are many at present and I have thus been obliged to postpone my journey to Venice. I am doubly sorry for this since, quite apart from my great desire to converse with you once more, I cannot but feel that I could be more useful to Marco if I were able to speak to him face to face than I can be in letters. Nevertheless, I have been writing to him almost every week, both as brother and as physician, and showing him no mercy. If someone had only kept me informed of his follies I could perhaps have suggested remedies to cure him. During all his travels, however, I heard merely of the good work he was doing – not a breath of anything that could have led me to suspect such grave faults – and when at last various vague remarks began to cause me disquiet I could do nothing to put things right. I find it most unreasonable and strange that if a friend or relative is ill all will hasten to tell you of it, yet should that same person behave unsuitably and risk the loss of his reputation, which indeed is worth more than life itself, the matter is only murmured about or half-spoken and no one will inform you directly. Well, enough of this, what's done is done.'

A sigh here and a brief pause, after which Giovambattista dipped his pen in the inkwell once more and continued. 'It was almost inevitable that Marco, who despite his years has a somewhat youthful approach to life, should have been per-turbed in his judgment when suddenly transported from obscurity and lack of means to relative opulence in a wider world. My dear friend, how could he yet have learned that true richness lies in the ability to apply oneself steadfastly to a task, in the respect of the world around one and the posses-sion of a few good friends? It is natural that, after the life he has been leading, his return to Padua may well seem very tedious to him. But this aversion will vanish with hard work and that sweet sense of independence which, as you and I both know so well, is the reward of one who holds a professorial

73

position. Marco has knowledge and good qualities, he is untainted by any criminal vice, and this causes me to be hopeful that he will one day make his old friends and teachers happy – not least among them you yourself who, as everyone knows, have ever looked on him as a friend and taught him as a chosen disciple. Indeed, one of the rocks on which my hopes are founded is the continuation of the friendship which I perceive you still feel for him. I believe my brother to be deeply ashamed of the manner in which he has disappointed those who wish him well, so that he no longer dares believe in anyone's friendship. I beg you to have the generosity to allow him the benefit of your loving advice and, as you care for me, to keep me informed of his way of life and behaviour. I have made a similar request of our friend Peristiano and my beloved Father Stellini. You have my word that he will never learn that I receive news of him from you or from any of my friends. I remain your most sincere and affectionate friend, Gio:Batta: Carburi.'

Giovambattista's letters tended to be either very long or very short. This was one of the longer ones, which took him a good hour to compose in the quiet of late evening. When he finally went to bed the dyspepsia that had been troubling him earlier had disappeared, although whether this was the result of the fennel seeds absent-mindedly chewed or of the un-burdening of his worries to someone he trusted was not at all clear.

It is not possible to write, 'I feel like a whipped dog with its tail between its legs' but Marino was able to read between the lines and understood something of Marco's dejection. He did not quite know how to answer and thus contented himself with a breezy description of his own affairs followed by a reference to one of their childhood escapades. He ended, 'I miss you sorely, my dearest Marco, and embrace you tenderly. Your most affectionate brother who loves you with all his heart, Marino.' Something about all this – perhaps just the lack of censure – was comforting. Neither of them noticed that for once the signature was not 'Alexandre'.

Not everyone was cross with Marco, however. Father Atanasio Peristiano, the third of Giovambattista's close friends, remained grateful for Ulfila's Gothic translation of the Gospels which Marco had been to some trouble to acquire for the library of his monastery. Marco, who always rather enjoyed a challenge, had found a copy in Stockholm with a few pages missing, whereupon he had set out to track down these pages and had succeeded in doing so, finding them in three different cities, the expense of this search being once more borne unwittingly by the Venetian Republic; although one page was damaged and another quite badly marked, all were legible. Atanasio Peristiano wrote with some perspicacity to Giovambattista: 'Your brother has a good heart and shows a tenacity of purpose which, if properly directed, will serve him well. Do not be too harsh with the young man.' (Father Atanasio knew his friend quite well.) 'I believe that he will respond better to being ridden lightly than to too short a rein.'

'It's rather like having a collection of shells with one important example missing,' Marco had explained when he showed these pages to Marino some eighteen months earlier. 'It irks you. You feel you can't rest easy until you have completed the series.'

All the brothers had collected shells as children; Marino and later Paolo at some point lost interest, but Giovambattista and Marco had gone on refining and expanding their collections. When they left home for the first time and travelled to Venice Marco had as a matter of course taken his juvenile collection with him and had been upset and obstinate when Giovambattista commented that he would do much better to arrange it by species rather than by colour; 'I prefer it my own way,' Marco had said, instantly replacing all his shells in their box and stubbornly refusing to get them out again in their elder brother's presence.

Neither Marino nor Marco could read a word of the Gothic script, of course, but both recognised how fervidly a collector might desire it. Thinking of which, Marco searched through the capacious pockets of his *redingote* and got out two perfect petrified shells: 'I bought the one and then the very next day found the other,' he told Marino.

'Will you give them to Giambattista?'

'I don't know. I might. It depends.' (In the end Marco decided to keep them for himself.)

If Marco was a tiny bit reserved or preoccupied it may well have been simply that he was fatigued. He had come a great distance to meet Marino – although Marino, who did not appear at all tired, had also had several days of travelling. By now he had left Vienna for St Petersburg and they were meeting in a straggling, mean-looking village in Finland after a complicated exchange of letters, maps and instructions: neither of them had ever been here before. Marino had arrived first and had waited for five days, at the beginning with the impatience of happy anticipation, then with increasing anxiety and a distressing heavy feeling in his stomach.

'I thought you weren't going to come,' he told Marco, and for a moment a faint echo of something almost like accusation reverberated in the air.

'I came.'

There was a curious lack of intimacy about this first afternoon together, which is why it seemed easier to speak of the Gothic Gospels and fossils and furnaces and the strange insect-eating plants that grew in the chilly marshes – which Marino had seen but Marco had not. 'What a godforsaken place,' commented the younger brother. However, after a night spent together in a not very comfortable bed under a luckily ample feather eiderdown things improved.

'You stink,' said Marino.

'I know,' replied Marco cheerfully, 'but it's far too cold to wash or take one's clothes off properly. Anyway, you do too.'

It was the middle of spring. Marco had suggested a later meeting but Marino had demurred: 'We can't afford to delay. Once the thaw sets in it will be almost impossible to travel,' he had answered.

As a matter of fact the smell of one's brother's unwashed body is actually rather pleasant, which is probably what led both to be in a better mood in the morning and what made Marino smile and say *'Adelpháki mou.'* This Greek diminutive – 'my little brother' – contained a whole world of mocking, tender, protective affection which Marco understood perfectly well in spite of the fact that he claimed, 'It's been so long, I've forgotten all my Greek.'

'No, you haven't,' declared Marino.

And this of course was true. When a pan of water had been heated on the stove Marino shaved in silence, then offered, 'I'll shave you too, if you like.' Whereupon Marco got out of bed, grabbed a warm gown and said in Greek, using the second person singular, 'Watch out you don't cut my throat.' To which the answer, in the same language, was, 'Now what on earth would I want to do a thing like that for?'

All the same, in spite of this resumption of intimacy, not much was said in any language about Marino's exile or about the reason for it. Marco did indeed remark at one point, 'It's fairly widely known by now that you went to Vienna.' But this was merely a parenthesis in the middle of an account of his own experiences in Austria and Pomerania and Westphalia, in return for which Marino gave a rather inadequate and lifeless description of St Petersburg ('It's a sort of watery place.' 'Like Venice?' 'Well no, not quite'). Homesickness was something else about which they did not speak – but perhaps there was no need to.

For Marco had idly noted as he pushed away a half-eaten plate of salted fish, 'They seem to eat nothing but long-dead fish and tasteless roots in these parts.'

'In summer they have various sorts of berries as well,' Marino had told him judiciously and then added suddenly in quite a different tone, 'I'd sell my soul for an orange.'

Once long, long ago Marino had claimed that he didn't possess a soul, but this was something which he'd completely forgotten and of which Marco had never had any knowledge.

And after his return to Venice Marco dispatched a whole crate of oranges to his brother which miraculously survived the journey and arrived intact, none the worse for wear. Marino ate three immediately, one after the other, gloriously, greedily, messily, with the juice running down his chin, then decided to make them last and rationed himself to one a day.

When Marino and Marco parted – once more on an icy morning in an alien land – both knew that they were unlikely to meet again for many years to come, if ever. There is a pain in this which it is better to leave unmentioned; they thus simply kissed each other three times on the cheek, wished each other a safe journey and went their separate ways. Marino might have called out something like, 'Don't forget me,' but of course didn't. The words he shouted into the wind after his brother's receding figure were, 'Embrace Giambattista for me.' And Marco turned and raised his hand to show that he'd heard.

7

GIOVAMBATTISTA WAS lucky in his friends. When he wrote that happiness lies in the possession of a few good friends he was not merely mouthing sententious platitudes but was speaking of his own experience, although he had certainly never stopped to analyse quite what friendship is and equally surely never wasted much time thinking of happiness. What Giacomo Stellini, Antonio Vallisneri and Atanasio Peristiano gave him – and he them – was a warm mixture of affection, respect and tolerance. The fact that after he left for Turin (and then in due course for France) these valued gifts were exchanged almost entirely by correspondence mattered not one whit; it may even be that Giovambattista sometimes found it easier to admit to various worries on paper than he would have done in any face to face conversation. The tolerance these men shared was of the intellectual sort – a calm acceptance of those ideas or convictions held by a friend with which one does not necessarily agree – but also of small personal failings: vanity, for example, or a tendency to irritability when plans go awry. Had Giovambattista ever become involved in an open scandal his friends would certainly have been utterly astounded, yet it is possible that they would have risen to the occasion and gone on loving him. For when such friendships last many years, a lifetime even, they can properly be called a kind of love.

Leaving love aside, however, there is no doubt that most people liked Giovambattista well enough and respected him.

In Turin the king certainly did, which was why at home in Argostoli Caterina regularly received letters which made her heart glow. '*Carissima Signora Madre*,' wrote her son upon his appointment to the post of chief physician – effectively director – of the hospital of San Giovanni, 'though the work be demanding and the salary not very great (adding, to be precise, only a further three hundred *lire* per annum to my existing remuneration), there is no doubt that this is an honourable position which I shall do my utmost to fill in such a manner that my friends may have no cause to complain of me.'

In this context, the word 'friends' of course meant 'patrons', of whom at this time the most important was that single royal one, although it would be perfectly understandable if Giovambattista also had some slight wish to appear well in the eyes of his personal friends; unlike his brothers, he was at least secure in the knowledge that his mother would find no grounds for criticism. She wrote back, 'My dearest son, with what pride we received your last letter I need hardly tell you. Money is certainly mere dross compared with reputation, you are quite right in this, just as the king is right to recognise your worth by appointing you to this position. My only fear is that your labours in the hospital will prove onerous and greatly fatiguing to you: my prayer is that your patron saint for whom it is named will ever have you in his keeping.' Not long after the first income from the hospital was entered into the physician's account book, an item of expenditure was noted: 'For two pairs of gloves and lace for my mother.'

Very occasionally – not more than four or five times a year – there were small expenses for transactions of the kind that Marino was later cruelly to call 'fumblings in dark alleys' which were never entered into the account book.

*   *   *

Marco, who of course knew all his eldest brother's friends, moved in slightly different circles. As a matter of fact he was being more than a little disingenuous when he claimed to Marino that he couldn't remember a word of Greek, since he heard this language spoken from time to time in the Emo household, where visitors from the Orient were often to be met with, even if he didn't use it much himself.

When he had gone back to the island for the long visit home that each of the brothers made in turn after completing his studies, he had gone out of his way to entertain his friend Anzolo's cousin, Giacomo Nani, on whose ship Anzolo had been serving. Perhaps Marco did something to offend, however, or perhaps Cephalonian hospitality was not quite to Giacomo Nani's taste, for he it was who later made scathing and rude comments on Marco and on Cephalonians in general. It may well be that Marco was more transparent than he thought when he was asked to give a hand organising what Giacomo called his 'little museum' and they compared shell collections. To Marino Marco had written at the time: 'He believed himself to be very crafty when he proposed that we make some exchanges, took from my collection what was missing from his, and in return gave me worthless specimens of which he had duplicates. I said nothing, pretended not to notice, but, my dearest brother, you can imagine with what mirth I was laughing up my sleeve – since he was quite ignorant of the fact that what he considered rare in my collection and coveted were shells which are to be found in plenty on the shores of the southern part of the island. I thus took great pleasure in giving what he had given me to some ragamuffins playing in the dust, waited until he had left for Corfu, then set out with a mule (and an armed servant, our mother insisted on this) and collected more. I spent three or four very happy days on this expedition, I can assure you, and wished that you were with me.'

It is of course possible that Giacomo Nani may have seen Marco handing the shells from his collection to dirty children in the street: this would have been enough to ruffle anyone's feelings.

However this may be, Marco's place in the esteem of the Emo and Nani clans was unaffected, and Giacomo's brother Bernardo remained a friend and supporter.

When Marino and Marco were together, however, Marco instantly relinquished – or rather suspended – all other ties and they spent their time exclusively in each other's company.

Such things are rather hard to describe. When Marino tried one day to tell Stephanie about this sense of twinship she commented, 'Heavens, anyone would think from the way you speak that you were a bit in love with him.'

This idea would have been offensive if it were not so utterly absurd as not even to merit an answer; yet for some reason he did respond. 'You forget yourself,' he told her sharply in unusually icy tones, '*Vous vous oubliez, Madame, il s'agit de mon frère.*'

When Marino returned to St Petersburg after parting from Marco he rather carefully put all thoughts of his brother out of mind. Nevertheless, a few weeks later in one of those half-waking reveries he remembered the two petrified shells and for a moment thought they were of such perfect symmetry that they must have been the two halves of one whole – although of course, considering that they had come from different sources, this was about as foolish a fancy as one can have.

Letters take a long time to reach Russia, which means that your decisions have been made and acted upon before the various members of your family have time to express an opinion or offer advice. The move to Russia was in fact itself the first decision concerning his own life that Marino had ever made without consulting anyone. These two statements probably go some way to explaining why before too long his new acquaintances began to feel that the Chevalier de Lascaris was someone who could be counted on to solve problems methodically and with good humour; this reputation might have surprised Giovambattista, but there's not much doubt that if people take you at your own valuation, this somehow helps you to be what Marino always privately called 'trim and shipshape and well afloat.'

It is right that fellow Cephalonians should help one another; with this in mind, soon after arriving in St Petersburg Marino had paid a visit to Pyotr Ivanovich Melissino, General of the Artillery. No doubt the fact that the general's wife, Princess Dolgoruki, had a discreetly indulged taste for dark eyes and shapely legs led her to encourage her husband in his laudable desire to assist his compatriot. At any rate Marino fairly rapidly did what he referred to as 'landing on my feet'. To his family he described Pyotr Ivanovich and his brother Ivan Ivanovich as 'Piero and Giovanni Melissino from Argostoli'. They had of course recognised Marino at once: 'I had to tell them my new name,' he wrote to Marco.

'I am now attached to the Direction of the *Corps de Génie*,' he informed his mother with understandable pride some weeks later, omitting to say that a slight hiccup had occurred when he had come face to face with a gentleman who rightfully bore the name Lascaris. However, a bit of quick thinking may extricate one from embarrassment: 'Much as I would be honoured by the connection, I cannot pretend to claim any legitimate relation with Monsieur Lascaris' (a disarmingly rueful smile, an extremely polite bow and a very slight emphasis or fractional pause before the adjective, implying that unavoidable kink in the lineage which has to do with bastardy). Nevertheless, Marino found himself sweating, drank rather more than usual in the hours that followed and as he lay in bed that night was visited by the exquisitely mirth-provoking thought, 'If I'm a bastard, then my mother's a whore.' News of this little awkwardness was inevitably carried rapidly to the Empress's ears; it appeared though that she had no great objection to a plausible liar who is good at his job, and thus a certain amount of gossip ensued but no marked signs of disfavour.

As a matter of fact, being drawn to the Empress's attention in this way proved later to have done Marino an indirect service, for when General Bezkoy in the face of a certain amount of opposition favoured the Chevalier de Lascaris's proposals, at least she knew who he was talking about. ('Ah yes, that little Greek *officerik* of yours,' she said.)

Giovambattista was wrong in believing that Marco would find his return to Padua tedious but right that he would have difficulties with his Latin. Marco, however, who was a great believer in solving problems as simply as possible, did the unthinkable: after struggling through his first lecture he announced to his students that henceforth all classes would be taught in Italian (at which possibly some of them felt rather relieved), and none of the authorities ever breathed a word about this radical departure from tradition.

To Giovambattista he wrote: 'It would seem to me, my dearest brother, that if the purpose of teaching is the transmission of knowledge, then clarity is above all what is required. I do not dispute the elegance of Latin, nor the value of this language as a means of communication between scholars who do not share a common tongue, but the fact is that my pupils do share a common tongue – Italian – and I see no reason not to use it.'

Antonio Vallisneri wrote: 'My dearest friend, you and I have been accustomed to a different manner of doing things, yet I make no doubt but that your brother has put his finger on the pulse of the times. Whether we like it or not, his is probably the way of the future and teaching in the vernacular is likely to become widespread.'

Giovambattista, who had laboured long and hard over his own Latin, felt a little piqued; it is, after all, fairly human to give way to thoughts along the lines of 'If I can do it, you can.' He himself continued to lecture in Latin, however, occasionally even managing the odd joke (at which all the embryo physicians in front of him laughed politely, regardless of whether or not they understood it or found it funny).

The purpose of language, as Marino could have told his brothers when he began to learn a smattering of Russian, is communication. By now his French (which was of course the language he mostly used) was fluent, although until his dying day he retained a strong Italian accent. Of all the brothers, it was only Giovambattista who possessed the ability to perceive and reproduce the different rhythms and intonations that belong to different tongues, so that the French he spoke had a smooth, elegant flow and poise about it which Marino's more staccato version could never attain; indeed, when he visited England Giovambattista took pains to acquire two or three polite phrases which he uttered so convincingly that his interlocutors frequently did not at first realise he had no knowledge of their language. Dutch, it must be said, proved to be beyond his capacities. In the Low Countries as in England, however, Latin was extremely useful as a means of communicating with men of science. Maybe it was simply that Giovambattista had a good ear, or possibly he understood that you fit in better if you sound much like everyone else around you. It does occur to me though that this linguistic adaptability might have been a very subtle variation of the same inner need which led Marino to emerge more dramatically into the new persona of the capable and likeable Chevalier de Lascaris.

85

There are languages read as well as languages spoken: for someone who reads Greek the Russian alphabet looks approximately familiar, but although over the years Marino became able to get along reasonably well in this language, he never had much cause to read Russian. Nevertheless, among the stories that in time he told his children was that of St Cyril and St Methodius – or Kyrillos and Methodios, as he called them – who travelled from their monastery in distant Greece not only to convert the Russians to Orthodox Christianity but also to teach them to write.

'They had to make up a new alphabet,' he explained.

'But then how could people read before?' asked his son.

'They couldn't read because they couldn't write, you see,' said Marino, full of amazement and pride that Giorgio not only could read but also – just like Giambattista in the faraway, sunny past – treated whatever books came his way with a kind of ceremonious care and, without being told to do so, washed his hands before opening them.

Not so surprising, perhaps, that quite a few of Marino's stories came from Greece, considering that his wife's family, although long resident in Russia, preserved some sense of Greekness. 'We are Cephalonian,' he told his children, but 'I am Greek,' he once overheard his son tell someone seriously.

Marino's mother and sister both read French. Even though they had never had much occasion to attempt to speak the language, they could, if the need arose, certainly have managed to entertain a French-speaker with a decent amount of pleasant conversation. Nevertheless, when Marino later took his second wife to the house in the *Carburata* nothing but Italian was spoken in the drawing room or at table, in spite of the fact that he pointedly used French himself. 'Such a pity that Madame does not speak our language,' were the only French words finally offered by

Caterina, accompanied by a small, tight smile of charming regret. Stephanie smiled in return and inclined her head fractionally with a degree of controlled insolence which would have impressed him had it not been for the fact that he was too beset by feelings of impotent rage to notice.

Although Marino did not realise it when he asked for his first wife's hand in marriage, it was in the end probably his Greekness which led George Chrysosculeo to accept him as a son-in-law: some primitive notion that it is fitting for one's daughter to marry 'one of us', or – a Greek word surfacing – 'a *palikári* from our own parts.' (This is a word which conveys youthful masculinity and courage. Marino couldn't really be said to be very youthful, being on the verge of his thirty-sixth birthday, and his courage had perhaps never been put to the test, but certainly a general sense of satisfaction in life now made him feel happily masculine.) It is possible too that Pyotr Ivanovich Melissino's good word counted for something. Needless to say, the acceptance of his offer was preceded by some long and detailed conversations about his origins and parentage and finances; 'interrogations' was what Marino called them when he told Marco about it.

For it was only to Marco that he wrote of his hopes, with strict instructions to 'say nothing about it, not even to Gio: Batta:, not to *anyone*' (underlined). Marco at first found this desire for secrecy to be rather absurd then, on reflection, concluded that it would be humiliating for Marino to have to announce he'd been rejected, and so was loyally silent. As it happens, Marino's feeling was more inchoate and primitive: a sort of touching wood, a fear that if the whole family knew he desired something, then somehow the fates would conspire to blight his hopes. There was also, no doubt, an element of childish glee at the thought of announcing a *fait accompli*.

Thus to his mother in due course he wrote: 'I think you may be gladdened to learn that I was married a week ago to the daughter of Monsieur Chrysosculeo, who is the Councillor for Foreign Affairs in the Empress's realms. Her dowry is substantial and includes the house in which your affectionate son now sits and writes, and from which he kisses your hand respectfully.' The signature was as usual 'Alexandre de Lascaris'. After it was added as a sort of postscript, 'Her name is Elena and our marriage took place on her name-day.' Nothing else, it seemed to him, needed to be said. Although the letter was written in late May it did not reach Argostoli until July. Caterina commented when she next wrote to her eldest son, 'This at any rate would appear to be better than what we could have expected or hoped for.'

Marino's letter to Giovambattista was longer and more expansive and included a small pen-and-ink drawing of the church where the marriage had taken place. Accompanying the letter was a package containing four rather large and fine pieces of clear amber for his brother's collection, one of them with an insect trapped inside it. Giovambattista was pleased by this curiosity; like his mother, however, he couldn't help noting that nowhere did Marino specify exactly what his new wife's dowry consisted of, and as a result worried a little in the silent hours of the night lest Marino's boasts might be empty and all not quite what it should be. Nevertheless, he made no mention of the matter when he wrote to thank his brother for the gift, merely expressing his delight at the news of the marriage and his fond wish that it might be blessed with offspring.

On this subject Marino had already written to Marco: 'I am now doing my utmost to get my wife with child – which considering that I have hitherto always made great efforts in the opposite direction is, as you may imagine, quite wonderful.' They had long since agreed that 'stopping halfway' –

which is what they called the coitus interruptus once recommended to Marco by Giambattista – was not a very
satisfactory procedure and thus generally resorted either to
luck or to the strange devices Marino called 'engines' and
Marco 'contraptions'. If neither had, to his knowledge, sown
any crop of bastards throughout the years, this seemed a
matter of self-congratulation; it did not occur to either that
they might not be very fertile.

Perhaps in a strange way there were indeed some threads of
twinship linking the two brothers, for when Marco received
the letter in which Marino first wrote of his wish to marry
Elena Chrysosculevna he was himself entertaining similar
hopes about a certain young lady named Cecilia Barbò
Soncin. For one reason or another he felt a kind of reticence
and for a couple of months was not much inclined to tell
Marino anything about her. However, in a moment of
discouragement when negotiations looked as if they were
slowing to a halt he wrote to his brother, explaining, 'The
problem is that her father doesn't think much of me.' To
which the reply, arriving many weeks later, was: 'At least
you haven't got anything really awful to confess to him
about your past.'
    Only to Marco could Marino have made this reference; on
the whole his trouble in Venice was a subject which the
family had tacitly agreed it was infinitely preferable to pass
over without mention, just as if it had never happened.

But there were other differences too, apart from Marco's
blameless past. None of the family ever met Elena and thus
she was invariably referred to as 'Marino's wife'. Marco, by
contrast, took his wife on a visit to Cephalonia and Giovambattista met her regularly once or twice a year on his
journeys to Venice; this is probably why she was usually

referred to as 'Cecilia'. Marco always addressed his wife by her name (except in front of strangers) and throughout their marriage slept in the same bed with her. Marino only slept with his wife when he was interested in begetting children, or at any rate desirous of the activities that lead to the begetting of children, and almost invariably addressed her courteously as 'Madame'. This polite usage was, however, suspended in bed, where he called her by Greek names that she did not understand: first because her knowledge of Greek was minimal, and second because she had in any case been far too well brought up to understand some of these words in any language.

Everyone was really rather surprised that, from both the social and pecuniary points of view, Marino seemed to have made such a good marriage.

'She was a virgin,' said Stephanie (more statement than question).

This was shortly after he married her, when they were making their long, slow way south from Paris and had hour after hour for conversation.

'Yes, of course she was,' he answered.

'And did you like it?'

'Well naturally, of course I did.' He added, 'After all, one expects . . .' (He'd been about to say 'One expects one's wife to be a virgin' but suddenly realised what this sounded like and hastily emended the phrase.) 'One expects one's first wife to be a virgin.'

Stephanie, Marino's second wife, was known to the family quite simply as 'the Frenchwoman', although Giovambattista was more than once heard to use the expression '*la coquine de Marino*' – Marino's little tart.

8

A WHOLE GENERATION of physicians trained at Turin would smile in later life when, in conversation or correspondence, some colleague quoted phrases that were instantly familiar, calling to mind a tall, thin figure whose measured tones and grey-green eyes and legendary concentration on the matter in hand had always inspired a certain amount of awe. 'The three main areas of medical enquiry' – this was how his first course invariably began – 'concern the manner in which the body functions, the manner of the ills and diseases which disturb this functioning, and the manner of treatment with which the physician may attempt to combat them.' Or another dictum: 'What is first needed in each case is a scrupulous and systematic ordering of the facts: these we must observe but may also elicit by careful questioning. Only after this has been accomplished should we proceed to a consideration of the diagnosis and hence of the remedies to be applied.' Or: 'Restraint should be our watchword: hastiness of judgment kills more often than it cures,' and 'In the severely debilitated, purging, like bleeding, should be used sparingly.'

Restraint and order and system are good words.

Giovambattista had just arrived back in London from Edinburgh when he received the news of his father's death. Reticence is also a good word; he locked his mother's letter into the small chest that did duty as a desk while he was on his travels, made no mention of this personal blow to any of the distinguished gentlemen he met that day, took part in a lengthy scientific colloquy on spontaneous generation and contributed a few pertinent remarks with his usual calm courtesy. It was only when he returned to his rooms much later in the evening that he told someone.

'I shall not retire immediately,' he said to the servant who had waited up to help him remove his clothes and now proffered a warm gown, 'I shall write, I need more lights.' And when these were brought: 'I have today received the news that my father is no more.'

The servant, who had accompanied him from Turin and who in spite of being Neapolitan was a good boy, found it hard to believe that his employer could have anything as ordinary as a father but said politely, 'I am very sorry to hear it, *Signor Conte*.' Then, feeling that something more formal was necessary, 'May he rest in peace.'

You cannot very well say to a servant, 'Please don't go away, please stay for a minute.' Giovambattista's customary way when he wanted company was to call for a series of small comforts to be brought to him; now he requested in turn a shawl for his shoulders, some peppermint water for his digestion, a receptacle in which to urinate, and a rug to keep the draught from coming under the door. When all these matters had been dealt with, the boy stood gracefully waiting to learn what further needs his master might have. A feeling of tension in neck and shoulders, an incipient headache, a temptation to say, 'I would like you to stand behind me and put both your hands between my shoulder-blades and massage my back while I close my eyes and find ease.' A temptation to say unthinkable things including, 'Please stay.' What Giovambattista actually said was, 'You may go to bed now, I'll extinguish the lights myself.'

It is not easy to be sure how much grief for the loss of his father was compounded in the turmoil of feelings that distressed Giovambattista, yet there is at any rate no doubt that the death of a parent signals the end of an epoch. Caterina's letter stated, among other things, 'You, my dearest son, are henceforth the head of our family.' As he sat pondering these matters and penning careful letters to his mother and to his brothers he was certainly aware of the weight of this responsibility. Yet it is also possible that there was the faintest glinting thread of satisfaction interwoven with the sadder fibres: a sense that the mantle assumed – no matter how heavy – had always rightfully been his.

That he himself was indirectly responsible for his father's sudden departure from this life was of course something Giovambattista couldn't know and luckily never thought of – for his mother never mentioned it and indeed never made the connection, although the plain truth was that Demetrio had died as a result of an excessive dose of the medicine prescribed for him by his eldest son. After all, if a little of a remedy appears to be doing some good, a larger amount may be even better. Everyone knows, thought Caterina as she unlocked the small cabinet in which this medicine was kept, that Giambattista has always erred on the side of caution. ('Circumspection sits well with a physician,' was another of his favourite pronouncements, as well known to his family as it was to his pupils.)

Something that neither Giovambattista nor anyone else ever really thought about was the fact that Marco was probably wise when he abandoned all ideas of a medical career: the chances are that he would never have made as good a clinical physician as his elder brother since he appeared to lack the gravitas which so reassures the patient.

'Marco is given to enthusiasms,' was what Giovambattista said to himself and later wrote to one of his friends, although in this case the thought was tempered with a brotherly smile; the current enthusiasm was justifiable and could even be considered as betokening an entirely admirable appetite for work. (Marco had written happily about the setting up of his new laboratory.)

Giovambattista himself, quite apart from knowledge and skill, possessed that undefinable quality, an air of quiet authority perhaps, which makes people feel they are safe in their doctor's hands. Moreover a simple accident of fate – the fact that he was taller than most of the people around him – meant that he tended to incline his head in order to listen to the anxious recital of symptoms; the courteous respect implied by this had for some reason struck the king, among others, as a sure sign that Carburi knew what he was doing.

All this goes some way to explaining how it came about that the professor of medicine was transmogrified into court physician (to the great pride of his mother), then permitted to embark on a long voyage to northern lands, all expenses paid, in order to engage in mutually fruitful discussions with his Dutch, English and Scottish peers (to the great pride of his brothers). Needless to say, his distinguished presence in Leiden and Utrecht and London and Edinburgh could not but reflect well on the level of scientific advancement prevailing in Turin. When Giovambattista was proposed and then elected a Fellow of the Royal Society he wrote at once to his august patron, couching his letter in such terms that the king felt almost as if the honour had been paid to him personally, or at any rate to the enlightened kingdom of Piedmont and Sardinia over which he ruled. ('Tact is of extreme importance if one wishes to advance in life,' as Giovambattista had stressed to Marco in another context.) A similar letter to the king was subsequently written from Edinburgh describing further honours, followed by more detailed descriptions for the physician's mother and brothers.

Connections are also important: among the three sponsors for Giovambattista's election to the Royal Society was his old acquaintance Giovanni Battista Beccaria, professor of Experimental Physics at Turin. (The others were John Turberville Needham, with whom he had been in correspondence for some time, and Joseph François Wicardel de Fleuri: these names, however, meant nothing to his family.)

Marino felt surprisingly little at the news of Demetrio's death, although of course he made efforts to compose a suitable, formal letter of condolence to his mother; he wrote of 'filial grief' – he thought this was rather a neat phrase – and 'our excellent parent' and even of 'fond memories of home'. This letter passed muster, it would seem, for when his mother replied some time later her tone was milder than usual.

Three months earlier there may have been a trace of flippancy in Marino's initial response to the news of Giovambattista's successes in London; at any rate Marco had been suddenly sharp: 'I don't think you have fully understood what this Royal Society is or how greatly our brother has been honoured.' Marino answered promptly: 'I know, indeed I do. You mistook me, for what I wrote I meant quite seriously.' (Among his earlier comments had been, 'I can't think of anyone who deserves such distinction better than our much-loved brother Ioánnis Vaptistís.' It was probably this mocking name that made Marco feel some rebuke was called for.) Just as well, perhaps, that Marino had not shared his amusement over one of the letters from Edinburgh: when Giovambattista used English words to announce another compliment paid to him – *'honorary burgess of the City and Royal Burgh of Edinburgh'* – the improbable and incongruous image of his elegant and fastidious brother as what must presumably mean 'a Scotch bourgeois' had made Marino chuckle out loud.

Another outburst of flippancy the following year brought stern reproofs from Giovambattista, who could only assume that his brother must have been in his cups when the letter was written. After the news arrived that an earthquake – by God's mercy not so terrible as that in Lisbon – had shaken the island and had caused a certain amount of damage to the dominical house in the *Carburata*, the physician arranged with their cousin Demetrio's help for ceilings to be repaired and walls replastered, then as an afterthought sought Marino's opinion as to what else, if anything, should be done. 'Knock it down and build it again out of wood,' came the frivolous reply.

However, as regards the honours paid to Giovambattista in those northern countries, Marino had of course expressed warm (and perfectly sincere) congratulations. He had also asked whether it was true, as he had heard, that both Farinelli and Carestini were in London, and whether his brother had been to hear either of them; to these questions the answers some weeks later were, 'Yes, I believe both singers are indeed at present in London,' but, 'I have, however, been far too much occupied to go to any concerts.'

Marco's sharpness evaporated rapidly. Before long he was writing at length to Marino about his laboratory: 'You're quite right, my dearest brother, I am indeed impatient for it to be completed – I cannot tell you how well nigh impossible it is for me to teach any longer without the wherewithal to carry out experiments and demonstrations for my pupils. Gio:Batta: counsels patience, yet I doubt that he himself would be in the best of tempers were he obliged to practise his doctoring without the requisite equipment. By the time you receive this, however, I have hopes that I shall be fittingly installed. I don't know whether you remember Padua well enough to recall it, but it's the old Capodilista house in the

Contrada della Bovetta which has been leased and is being transformed into a model Chemistry school: people are always afraid of explosions, you see, which is why they were prudent and chose a building somewhat isolated from its neighbours. As you enter on the ground floor, the laboratory is on the right; it will be divided into two sections, both of which are well ventilated with all manner of openings to permit the escape of fumes. On the floor above is a fine room where I shall lecture, with a painting of Mount Olympus on the ceiling – and I hasten to add that this does not depict any of the more amorous exploits of Jove, of the kind that might prove distracting to my pupils. As for me, I should tell you that I've become very serious these days and have more or less renounced such distractions.'

As he read this, Marino reflected that – if one could judge by Giambattista – a devotion to Science did seem to have this effect on people.

Marco's description continued: 'All round this room are set fifteen cupboards capacious enough to contain not only the instruments, natural substances and reagents needed for experimentation but also the mineral collection, your contributions to which have been so gratefully received.'

(In return for oranges and for the sweet, plump raisins that tasted of sunlight, Marino had been sending his brother specimens of jasper and malachite.)

A later letter apologised for a slight hiatus in their correspondence and explained: 'I have had to prepare all the acids, bases and salts that I need by myself, for nowhere, not even in the pharmacies, may one find even an ounce of pure alkali or concentrated acid of any kind – which just goes to show how new this science is here.' And, 'Before I gave my first public course, by rectifying fuming oil of vitriol I succeeded in obtaining stellate vitriolic acid, in the form of white stars resembling snowflakes – a great satisfaction – with the whole

97

procedure taking somewhere between four and six hours.' And, 'What is most convenient, occupied as I am, is that my living quarters are in the same building as my laboratory.'

Marino, whose own living quarters were undoubtedly more elegant than Marco's, if not quite as grand as he had implied to his mother, felt a curious kind of pang when he received this letter; 'It's all so far away,' was one of the thoughts that passed through his mind, although perhaps what he really meant was not so much that Padua is far removed from St Petersburg as that Marco's apparently total engagement in his own life somehow excluded his brother. Nevertheless he replied cheerfully enough, albeit slightly vaguely when it came to any description of his own doings. For an instant there might have been some even vaguer apprehension of separations, of wedges which, driven into the tiniest of cracks, will split the hardest and most enduring of rocks; however, if such a thought existed it was soon put aside.

Oddly enough, it was only much later, when Stephanie made an unusually foolish and frivolous comment, that this image came fully formed into his mind. After a chilly reproof and a few minutes of awkwardness (she remaining silent, he in the prey of painful memories), he dismissed the whole subject of his brother from his thoughts and – one idea leading more comfortably to another – began to tell her in more detail about the Rock (in Marino's mind it always had a capital letter).

Elena – but no, let us simply call her 'Marino's wife' as everyone else in the family did . . . Marino's wife always enquired politely after his brothers when he received letters from them and from time to time wrote to her unknown mother-in-law on that distant island; these days when Marino himself wrote to Caterina his letters invariably ended with something like, 'Your daughter-in-law Elena kisses your hand, as does your respectful and most affectionate son, Alexandre de Lascaris.' When at long last a pregnancy was announced ('It wasn't for want of trying,' Marino told Marco), Caterina dispatched honey and a dozen diminutive embroidered bonnets and a gossamer-like woollen shawl – although whether this latter was intended for mother or for baby Elena wasn't sure, and when she asked Marino, thinking that it might perhaps have something to do with some Cephalonian tradition, he wasn't particularly helpful: 'Use it yourself if it pleases you, otherwise wrap our son in it.' Then: 'If you don't like it, give it to that old woman on the corner of the street' (which seemed amazingly casual and unfilial).

When your only means of communicating is by letter, this has the strange benefit of allowing you to present yourself and your life in any way you choose. If you declare yourself settled and prosperous and content in some far-off land none of your correspondents is in a position to gainsay you. Only Marco had usually been able to understand whether or not Marino was speaking the truth, but at this period he was busy and preoccupied and so took his brother's letters at their face value without giving the matter much thought. Caterina, however, who had more than once had her second son whipped for lying when he was a child, took everything he said with a very large pinch of salt and thus subjected the gifts her new daughter-in-law sent her to careful scrutiny. Nevertheless, 'They seem decent enough and of a good weight,' she told Giovambattista about a set of silver teaspoons, although a tiny filigree frame with a miniature icon of St Catherine in it was described merely as 'a pretty trinket'. ('Decent' in the vocabulary of both Giovambattista and his mother meant the opposite of 'trumpery'.) All the same, regardless of any slight embroidery of the truth,

Marino's marriage was clearly real enough and no one thought to question the pregnancy.

Which indeed was also perfectly real and which, when he learned of it, had caused in Marino an extraordinarily fierce surge of emotion compounded of happiness and pride, a sense of success and a wonderful secret feeling which if it had surfaced into verbal thought might have been expressed as something like 'That will show them.' Quite what would be shown to whom wasn't clear: in any case the only words that found their way into Marino's mind were, 'I have begotten a son.'

Which, in turn, was of course not true, although on the strength of this happy thought Marino went to Louis David Duval et Fils and borrowed a smallish sum of money. His dealings, as always, were with Madame. 'She may be old but she knows a man when she sees one,' was what Marino liked to think, imagining that if the widow Duval was obliging, this must be due in part to his virile charms. No doubt Madame Duval (who was less than twenty years older than Marino) may very well have known a man when she saw one, may have had a soft spot for this particular client and enjoyed a little mild flirtation, but what is certain is that she also had a very accurate idea of the Chrysosculeo finances and had been entrusted with the investment of part of Elena's dowry. The sum Marino succeeded in borrowing was thus slightly smaller than he had hoped for but slightly larger than he had expected.

The reason it sometimes suited Marino to borrow a little cash was that his wife managed the family accounts and he did not wish to hurt her feelings or risk annoying his father-in-law by devoting too large a part of his salary to private expenses incurred in relation to card-playing or young ladies. The reason he needed money now was that the thought of having begotten a son made him feel such an extraordinary masculine vigour that a supper *à deux* with one of these ladies (a dancer), perhaps at Ekaterinhof in a private box at Locatelli's, seemed entirely appropriate.

Giovambattista at this stage in his life was not in the habit of borrowing money (his professorial salary of three thousand *lire* being supplemented, to his mother's pride, by the generous sum of a thousand *lire* which King Charles Emmanuel had decreed the physician should receive as a kind of annual bonus or pension for the duration of his life). Had he wanted to borrow money, however, he would have disliked the idea of doing business with a woman and would have carried out the necessary transactions with a man. He would quite certainly have considered that flirtation had no place in dealings of this kind. Marino had no such feeling about the matter; conceivably the fact that both countries in whose armies he served were ruled over by powerful women may have had something to do with the fact that he was perfectly comfortable with the idea of a woman banker and money-lender. Or perhaps it was simply that he enjoyed the company of women. Marco never officially borrowed any money from anyone except his eldest brother and so for him the question didn't arise.

Let it be said, however, that although Giovambattista's business dealings were exclusively with men and his social relations to a large extent oriented towards his peers (by definition of the same gender: men of science), in his professional life he was highly popular among his female patients – from the humblest old woman in the hospital to the king of Sardinia's daughter. And here too an element of (albeit unacknowledged) flirtation entered into things: on the patients' side that curious little frisson or charge in the atmosphere which comes of being examined and palpated and questioned by a good-looking male physician, and on his side perhaps an extra pleasantness in unconscious response. I was about to call this charge 'erotic' but of course the whole point is that the medical encounter is non-erotic – or, to be more accurate, perhaps exists in the narrow, shadowy space that lies between the definitely non-erotic and the possibly erotic, so that 'flirtation' really does seem as good a word as any to describe the mood that coloured such consultations. I need hardly say that Giovambattista was invariably scrupulously correct and austerely medical in his dealings with female patients of all ranks and was quite unaware of any faintly improper feelings they might have. It also goes without saying that safeness and reassurance are what you require above all when you are indisposed; hence Giovambattista's very remoteness and untouchability paradoxically served to make him more, rather than less, attractive.

And of course it is true that if the patient desires to please her physician she is more likely to follow his instructions to the letter and comply with whatever treatment he may prescribe. When in due course (if everyone concerned is lucky) a cure is achieved, it is hardly surprising that she will feel deeply grateful and resolve that he is the only medical man worth consulting.

It had never occurred to Giovambattista that the practice of medicine is an art as well as a science.

When Marino's daughter was born the news took longer than usual to reach Giovambattista, since he was on the road from Turin to Provence in the entourage of his new royal patient. The weather was sultry and the journey uncomfortable, in spite of the fact that he was accompanied by his own two servants to look after him and minister to his needs. Giovambattista felt wretchedly out of sorts. Before they reached their destination he was overcome by shivering and began to dose himself with quinquina, of which luckily he had a good supply in his medicine chest.

From Aix-en-Provence, where he received Marino's letter, he wrote to St Petersburg congratulating his brother on the birth of this tiny female child. He did not at once dispatch a christening gift; life, as he very well knew, is all too uncertain, so that on balance it was probably best to wait and see whether the infant would survive the first few months of her life before sending an expensive present.

Marco sent a silver teething-ring immediately, so that it arrived even before Marino's daughter was baptised in the church of St Spyridion at the age of five months and given the name Sofia. 'They take good care to heat the water in the font before they take off all its clothes and plunge it in, so that the baby won't catch cold,' wrote Marino. He then proceeded to recount what he called 'an amusing story' which from the pen of a first-time father might have seemed in questionable taste: 'On the Feast of Epiphany they baptise children in the River Neva, having first made holes in the ice – they don't seem to worry about babies catching cold on this hallowed day. Not long ago the priest accidentally let an infant slip from his hands as he immersed it . . . I dare say it went straight to heaven, at any rate the priest didn't bat an eyelid but simply wiped his hands on his apron, turned round and said "*Drugoi*", which means "Give me the next one".' More seriously, Marino also noted, 'In this country for some reason they say "St Spyridion" instead of St Spyridon' (at which Marco was puzzled and thought: Has he forgotten that we do the same here too?).

Tales of St Spyridon and of how he walks through the streets of Corfu at night doing good deeds were among those dredged up from Marino's memory some years later, when

Giorgio begged, 'Tell me another story, tell me a new one . . .'

Daughters when they grow up need to be married. King Charles Emmanuel of Sardinia and Piedmont had succeeded in arranging an alliance for his daughter with the younger brother of the French king's heir and had appointed Giovambattista to serve as her personal physician and keep an eye on her health and well-being: this is why, shortly after his return from northern parts, he had now left Turin once more and was making his way to Paris via Provence.

9

I T I S one thing to travel to other countries in order to keep abreast of the latest scientific developments and meet the learned colleagues with whom you have long corresponded; it is quite another thing to move, lock, stock and barrel, to a distant city in a foreign land. No matter how much you may be gratified by being appointed to such a distinguished position (and by the generous remuneration that goes with it, more than matching the professorial salary), the fact remains that there is something rather anxious-making about packing up your possessions and setting off on a long, slow, uncomfortable journey to a new life. Anxieties very naturally give rise to thoughts of mortality; before leaving Turin Giovambattista thus made his will. This, however, was fairly straightforward and was achieved without too much agonising: he left his collection to the University of Turin, his library to the University of Padua (considering no doubt that his books would thus be accessible to Marco), tokens of remembrance to his closest friends, and 'One quarter of any monies of which I die possessed to my sister Maria, wife of Elia Corafa; in the case that my sister be no longer living at the time of my decease, I bequeath this portion to her eldest son, my nephew and namesake, Giovanni Battista Corafa. The remaining three-quarters, as well as my share of our patrimony in our native land of Cephalonia, to be divided equally between those of my three brothers who may survive me. To my brothers I also bequeath the care and succour of my aged and dearly loved mother.'

(Caterina – who was to live for almost two more decades – was what might be called spry; Marino had once said to Marco, 'She'll outlive us all,' neither needing to admit to the other the faintly sinking feeling that this prospect engendered.)

'I am no longer young,' Giovambattista wrote to Atanasio Peristiano when the quinquina had taken effect and he had recovered from the worst shivering, teeth-chattering torments of the fever. 'So many cares have been laid upon me since those heedless days when I first had the happiness of being honoured with your friendship – it is scarcely to be wondered at if they have left their mark.' Giovambattista was at this time forty-five years old. Father Atanasio, some ten years older and himself in poor health, understood his friend's low spirits and took up his pen at once to reply with warm and encouraging words.

Low spirits and a feeling of weariness may well have had some connection with the recognition that it was time to do what is usually thought of as 'settling down'. Giovambattista took a lease on a house in the rue du Faubourg Poissonnière, reflected carefully for a while, then wrote a long letter to his mother enlisting her help in the search for a wife. 'I am not young,' he told her, among other things, 'and do not require extreme beauty, although I would wish for a wife who is not marred by any very obvious physical defect. I would like good teeth, sweet breath and clear skin. The girl should be young enough and healthy enough for child-bearing. In temperament she should be docile. As to her dowry, all other things being equal I should naturally look to receiving some decent amount of property with my wife, but know, my dearest Mother, that I may safely leave this matter to your discretion. If a suitable person be found, then she could be sent to Venice, where I would marry her in the spring of next year.'

Caterina found all this perfectly reasonable and considered that any girl would be lucky to marry Giambattista.

Cecilia was perhaps luckier, for Marco loved her.

'What is she like?' asked Stephanie.

'Oh, I've never met her,' said Marino, 'Marco married her after I'd left.' He refrained from adding, 'She used to write chatty letters to my wife.' Quite clearly no pleasant letters to Stephanie were going to be forthcoming.

Cecilia had of course asked her husband what his brother Marino was like.

'Well, he's smaller than me – by about half a hand, I should say – and he's a tiny bit slimmer than me, yet not thin like Giambattista. Sort of well-proportioned really . . . He has black hair which is so thick and curly that as soon as he takes off his wig it springs up again. He's a fine-looking man,' concluded Marco loyally.

This physical description was not quite what she had wanted: 'I mean, what is he actually *like*?' she asked again.

'He's good with his hands, he always knows how to make things work,' said Marco, and with this Cecilia had to be content.

A memory of a long-gone day when tadpoles had been swallowed suddenly came to mind, yet somehow it seemed better not to mention such things. Thus after a little while Marco merely added, 'When he was ten he learnt how to tell the time from the stars.'

His wife did not immediately understand whom he meant, since by now her thoughts had moved on to other things.

'Marino eats tadpoles,' was what all the children had gone on saying throughout one whole spring and summer, with varying degrees of awe and disgust at so appalling an aberration. What was referred to was in fact a single occasion on which the marsh water in two cupped hands, containing half a dozen small black tadpoles and a frond of water-weed, was defiantly gulped down after their cousin proclaimed in a loud voice that Marino would never dare.

'Can you feel them wriggling inside you?' asked Marco anxiously when they were alone.

'Yes,' replied Marino.

Marco had once illicitly consumed a sweet cake that was covered with ants; when their sister announced this to their parents he had been walloped but also dosed with a small glass of grape spirit – 'so that the ants will get drunk and stop crawling inside your stomach.' Feeling that this remedy might also work for tadpoles, he waited until the coast was clear, then purloined a rather larger glassful for Marino and stood over him while he drank it. The following day Marco suggested scanning the contents of the chamber pot in the hope of finding evidence that the tadpoles had been safely expelled, drunk or sober, but for some reason his brother refused to allow this.

The fact is that when many years have passed since you last met the brother to whom you write so often, the picture of him that you hold in your mind may no longer correspond to the reality. Giovambattista was absent for more than two years on his travels, and after he settled in France rarely came to Venice (or Padua) more than once a year, yet meetings between him and Marco were at any rate regular enough for neither of them ever to be suddenly shocked by the small signs of ageing in the other: greying hair, for example, or a cross-hatching of fine lines round eyes and mouth or – in Marco's case – a slight tendency to *embonpoint*. Both of them, however, persisted in imagining Marino as a neatly made, dark man in his early thirties for whom time had stood still.

A man left behind, perhaps.

'I thought of you,' Marco sometimes wrote to Marino, the trigger usually being someone from the old days encountered by chance, something seen which Marco knew would have interested his brother, a scurrilous joke which would have amused him.

'I often think of you too, especially when I look at the stars,' Marino wrote back in answer to one such letter. Perhaps there was some sense of the unity of things, that Marco – if he stepped out of his laboratory and if the night was clear – would see the very same stars, although for some reason when Marino imagined his brother looking at the night sky it always seemed to be summer, the air warm and scented, the quiet, low trill of crickets in the background. He attempted to describe the extraordinary silence of winter nights in this northern land and the hugeness of the starry sky, then explained more mundanely, 'The reason I've been looking at the stars is that living conditions here are very cramped and more than a little primitive. If you thought that village where we last met was like the back of beyond, you'd shudder to see me now. This is marshland when it's not frozen, so there is no village. I'm housed in a sort of cabin built of logs which will be dismantled when we leave – well built, I should add, they make the walls double and use a kind of moss for insulating the gap in the middle – with a stove that burns night and day. But there's very little space and the place is already none too fragrant, so in the late hours when I want to relieve myself I wrap up in furs and venture outside.' And look at the chilly stars, and reflect on many things. 'I am suffering from an ache in the hip which makes these nocturnal expeditions a little arduous, so that I put them off as long as I may. What is curious and might interest you, my dearest Marco, is that your piss freezes almost instantly as it touches the ground and takes on a crystalline appearance – as another sortie in the light of morning reveals.'

To Giovambattista at about the same time Marino wrote: 'I have been feeling very unwell and am troubled by rheumatic pains in my hip and leg and a sluggishness of the bowels. The lack of any exercise is a sore trial. My diet here is monotonous and unappetising, consisting solely of salted meat, salted fish and a sort of broth made from roots. There is nothing in the way of salads or green vegetables of any kind – although in summer there would doubtless be many edible plants to gather, at the present season all that remains are a few frozen, blackened stalks of sedges. However, if the ground were soft my task would be impossible and I have therefore resigned myself to putting up with the unavoidable discomfort. My gums hurt though and I live in fear of losing all my teeth from scurvy.'

The physician replied, 'My dearest brother, what you need is lemons. I have charged Marco that he should send you some with as much haste as may be, since they are more easily come by in Padua than in Paris and certainly at very much less expense. I have myself only just returned from Venice: had I known of your need while I was there, I would have dispatched these fruits to you myself. For your bowels I recommend senna if you are able to send to St Petersburg for it – the best is from Aleppo, but that from Alexandria will serve equally well. I suggest senna since I believe you may probably be able to obtain it; another remedy would be five grains of *mercurius dulcis*, commonly called calomel, and fifteen of rhubarb, made into a bolus. If the problem is extreme, you may also find some relief from a clyster of chamomile or, should this be unavailable, of soapy water.'

110

However, by the time this letter arrived the problem had resolved itself. By the time Marco's lemons reached St Petersburg, along with another box of oranges, spring had come, the thaw had set in and Marino had returned to the city.

What Marino had been doing in a frozen marsh in Finland some twenty versts from St Petersburg (which, as he told his brothers, is about ten leagues) was making the first preparations for raising and then transporting the rock.

'I have always been too passionate a partisan of simplicity in machines to go for anything that is over-complicated,' Marino told General Bezkoy when the subject of transporting the rock first came up. He was later to repeat more or less the same words in his book – hardly surprising, since this idea reflected a deeply held creed. ('The more complex a machine is, the more likely it is that some part of it will break down,' Marino had once explained to Marco. 'It's plain logic.' He had not even attempted to describe the aesthetic aspect, for this is something that is hard to put into words: the wonderful, soul-satisfying beauty of a machine which is very simple and at the same time functions perfectly; 'I like things that *fit*,' he told Stephanie a lot later, and this was the closest he ever came to expressing it.)

The general was doubtful, as indeed was everyone else. A great many learned men maintained that the Chevalier de Lascaris's proposals were unrealistic and impractical, it was clearly impossible to raise such a mass, no one had ever done such a thing before. A great many people held it to be unnecessary in the first place: a base composed of several smaller rocks would, it was claimed, be perfectly adequate.

'I have told them,' wrote Marino, 'that it would be a grave mistake to make the base for so grand a statue out of an agglomeration of different pieces of rock somehow cobbled together with iron or copper bolts. This might look all very well at the beginning – and indeed Monsieur Falconet himself thinks it will serve the purpose. He, however, though an artist of great genius, has little idea of matters beyond his own field. For, as I tell both him and Monsieur Bezkoy, such a composite pedestal would not wear well: as surely as night follows day the bolts would become worn and eroded, rusted by the inclemencies of the weather. Repeated frosts would take their toll, cracks would first appear and then progressively widen, and before too many years had passed what once looked imposing would be reduced to a ruinous heap of stones so that the bronze horseman would risk an ignominious fall. In my view, the only solution is to place the statue securely upon a single monolith which will endure unaltered by the ravages of time and weather. Such a massive block of stone will no doubt not be easy to find, and there is much murmuring that the costs of transporting it and setting it up would be considerable. Yet – as I have been repeating several times a day – in the end it always pays to go for quality.' Marino smiled as he wrote this last sentence, for the letter was addressed to Giambattista. When it arrived in Paris, however, the physician read it carefully and approvingly without any change in his expression.

Neither Giovambattista nor Marco thought to point out that bronze bolts in a composite base would presumably last at least as long as the bronze horseman to be set atop it, nor indeed did General Bezkoy. Perhaps there was something that made Marino especially plausible and convincing in his vehemence – it did not at any rate occur to anyone that he might already have a particular rock in mind.

The idea that Marino's opinion had been sought on a matter of such importance as the base for Monsieur Falconet's statue of the great Peter was of course highly pleasing to Giovambattista. Nevertheless, when a couple of months later the news arrived that Marino's views had prevailed, that a

suitable rock had actually been found (a touch of disingenuousness here) and that Marino was now submitting a plan
for moving it, he could not help worrying lest his brother
might perhaps be unrealistic or over-confident in his own
abilities. Giovambattista slept alone in the narrow bed that
he had always preferred and just before settling to sleep
usually spent a moment or two reviewing family obligations
in his mind and deciding what, if anything, needed doing. As
a general rule it is probably better not to start thinking about
things that may lead to fretfulness or anxiety when it is time
to sleep: more than once his thoughts had caused Giovambattista to get up again, relight the candles and sit at the table
to dash off a couple more short (and illegible) notes of
instruction or advice. When subsequently Marino set to
work and letters began to arrive from that frozen Finnish
wasteland, worries about rheumatism, smallpox, constipation, fevers, scurvy and plague (not necessarily in this order)
kept the physician tossing and turning until finally he quieted
them – to some extent – by getting up and penning appropriate remedies for those ailments afflicting Marino. The
outbreak of plague, as he reassured himself more than once,
was in Moscow, a city Marino had never visited, lying at a
considerable distance from St Petersburg. If smallpox occupied the physician's thoughts, this was very probably because a correspondent in London had recently informed him
that in Turkey – surprising though it might seem – *variolation* was apparently practised: in other words, a kind of
inoculation against smallpox whereby a mild and harmless
form of the disease is induced in order to protect the patient
against its more virulent manifestations (for, as everyone
knows, those who survive smallpox never catch it again).
Even if the reports from London were true, however, this
seemed to Giovambattista an exceedingly risky procedure.

*   *   *

Giovambattista had never been a man to shirk obligations and thus on occasion visited his wife's bedroom for what he called 'marital conjunction'. After this had been accomplished he would let a brief but not indecently brief interval elapse, then would bid her good-night with unfailing courtesy and return to his own private room. In a well-ordered household these conjunctions properly take place at night: Giovambattista was thus surprised and faintly shocked when something Marco once said gave him to understand that his brother found the long, hot afternoon hours in summer an ideal time for such activities. Nevertheless, there is an extraordinary satisfaction in having a brother with whom you may converse on serious topics (and, what is more, Marco's equally serious dedication to his laboratory and teaching could not but give rise to warm feelings of affection and fraternal support), so that after a few minutes Giovambattista said to himself, 'Well, *à chacun son goût*, I suppose.' It was to be presumed that Marco, who after all had studied medicine for several years, would have the good sense not to overdo things.

The conversation on this particular occasion concerned the engendering of mammalian life – not so much the act of engendering, in spite of Marco's momentary levity, as the process involved: whether, in other words, the embryo pre-exists in the form of a minuscule homunculus contained in the male sperm, which then grows and develops in the female during gestation, or whether it is the fertilization of an undifferentiated ovum that creates the embryo.

'*Ex ovo omnia*,' quoted Marco.

Giovambattista tended to agree since the opposite view, no matter how tempting, fails to account adequately for certain undeniable facts, as for example the commonly observed truth that most offspring have characteristics of both parents. ('What is commonly believed may well prove false,' he had taught when stressing to his pupils the importance of an objective attitude in medicine; 'what is commonly observed, however, cannot be discounted – provided only that the observer be willing to suspend belief and thus avoid any hasty conclusions.') Having acquired a fine microscope in Leiden while on his travels, Giovambattista had used it to examine his own semen and, as he now told his brother, had seen for himself the animalcules therein exactly as Leeuwenhoek described them.

'*Animalculi* are not necessarily *homunculi* though,' commented Marco.

'Quite so,' said Giovambattista who was delighted with the neatness of his brother's phrase and rather thought that it clarified his own reflections on the subject.

The physician's many sources of anxiety did not happen to include those worries about sin and defilement that had so sorely beset Leeuwenhoek; he thus felt no need to enter into any elaborate mistruths or explanations about how the semen had been obtained. Both brothers were pleasantly at ease as they sat and discussed these serious matters beneath the opulent gods and goddesses of the ceiling in Marco's lecture room.

'I can't help feeling sorry for her in a way,' Cecilia had said rather daringly shortly after Giovambattista's marriage, then – when Marco was offended at the implied disrespect to his eldest brother – had hastily qualified the statement: 'I only meant that he's more than twice her age.'

Marco had described their new sister-in-law in a letter to St Petersburg: 'She's from the junior branch of the Dallaporta family, eighteen years old or thereabouts, not bad-looking, very quiet and shy, has some property in Cephalonia – somewhere near Lixouri if I'm not mistaken. I must admit I was rather taken by surprise that our brother should make up his mind to marry after so many years of blameless and monkish existence' (this latter was the adjective which Marino and Marco had long since decided fitted the case), 'but, such being his wish, our mother has at any rate made a very good choice for him.'

It was actually extremely unfair of Marco to have scolded Cecilia, for if Marino had been present they might have permitted themselves a moment of disloyalty so that he might very likely have commented, 'Poor girl . . .'

But of course there are things that you could say to someone face to face yet would never even think of writing in a letter: perhaps this is simply due to the fact that you cannot see the person you are addressing or that you cannot be sure that his will be the only eyes to read what you write, or maybe it is because you are always aware of the time that must pass before the letter will arrive (which makes you less hasty, more reflective and temperate). However this may be, when Marino was entrusted with his great undertaking Giovambattista certainly did not feel able to write to Marco of his anxieties about their brother's possible failure. He was in any case due to set off soon on the long road to Venice, having various family business transactions that needed attending to, and thus merely sent a brief note ahead of him to the effect that, God willing, he would have the pleasure of visiting Padua and seeing his brother in a month or so.

And when they met, Marco responded to his tentative expression of misgivings with calm conviction: 'If Marino says he can do it, then you may be quite sure that he will succeed.' Had he bothered to expand the thought, Marco might have said, 'If he told you that he was on the point of gaining a million roubles, you might perhaps have some doubts; if he told you that the most beautiful woman in all Russia was languishing for desire of him, you might take it

116

with a pinch of salt and simply assume that he'd got a new mistress; but if he tells you about how to solve a problem that interests him, then you can be certain that he knows what he's talking about and means every word literally.' Old loyalties perhaps prevented him from saying all this; at any rate Marco merely repeated the reassurance: 'He knows what he's doing.'

One of the things that Marino never wrote to Marco about was his love for the son born two years after Sofia. Not that he didn't speak of Giorgio, but that these mentions tended to be of the kind 'He's cutting another tooth,' or 'Giorgio wore his first breeches today,' or 'He can now read very well in French. He understands a lot of Italian but is not yet accustomed to speaking this language.' Giorgio liked stories and Marino found himself recounting the exploits of heroes and ancestors and saints and winged horses, half-remembered from some long ago time and reworked or embroidered when necessary. Giorgio listened seriously, turned these stories this way and that in his mind, then on occasion posed difficult questions.

'What language do saints talk in?' he asked his father.

'Well, St Spyridon speaks Greek, and so do St Kyrillos and St Methodios. I suspect St Giorgio does too. St Giovanni Battista and St Marco always speak Italian.' Marino suddenly wondered about this. He suggested judiciously, 'I think if you spoke Latin to them you couldn't go wrong. All saints speak Latin.' Then, noting an anxious look on the boy's face, added, 'And they don't mind if you make mistakes.' (Giorgio had just begun to learn Latin.)

A further question: 'If I met a saint, how would I address him?'

'You could just call him "Monsieur", that would be all right, but you'd have to make a very polite bow.'

When he was little Giorgio believed that his father's patron saint was called Alexandre and rode a winged horse called Bucephalus: since St Giorgio also had a horse and since saints are fearless people who can quell the wildest of beasts with a single glance, this seemed very right and proper. Such confusion was understandable but Marino did his best to straighten it out: 'My saint is really St Marino. When I am here I am called Alexandre, but when I'm at home I'm called Marino. Some people have two names, you see. Like Louis David Duval – you might call him Louis or you might call him David, but he'd still be the same person.' This sounded convincing even if it led to further questions. ('Who's Louis David Duval?' 'Someone I do business with.' Not worth trying to explain that Louis David himself has been dead some years now but that his name lives on.)

No doubt St Marino speaks every language there is. 'When I'm here I speak French but when I'm in Cephalonia I speak Italian,' Marino explained on another occasion. 'Sometimes I say things in Greek.' This conversation took place in the shipyards at Cronstadt, whither Marino had brought his son in the face of protestations from both mother and nurse. 'Sailors speak all the languages under the sun,' Giorgio's father told him and was filled with an unbearable wrench of love when a couple of minutes later the boy declared, '*Vous êtes mon marin alors*,' and then looked a tiny bit nervous in case this daring wordplay might be considered impertinent.

The fact that Elena, like Marco's wife, did not seem very apt to conceive was certainly remarkable but bothered Marino not one whit. For the truth is that after Giorgio was born he never felt the need for another child. He did indeed beget one four years later, yet when this pregnancy ended in miscarriage grieved more for his wife's sake than for his own. Later still, when Giorgio was ten, Elena conceived once more, but this child too was fated not to be born. These are the sort of things that not even Marco would ever really quite understand.

When the life in Russia was over and Marino married Stephanie he wrote defensively to Marco, 'I am not looking to have children from this marriage,' as if this would somehow make it more palatable to everyone. As if these things always depended on intention alone.

Marco had said to Cecilia (trying to focus on the bright side), 'Perhaps at least my brother will have more sons.'

But of course it is a mistake to imagine that you can simply beget one person as a substitute for another.

10

MARRIAGE, BY its nature, brings with it great changes to one's way of life. Giovambattista's establishment became more extensive, thus requiring a larger number of domestics to run it, some of whom were now of necessity women. Quite a few of them – both men and women – were French: naturally enough, one might think, although Giovambattista always maintained that Italians make more graceful and serviceable servants. He probably knew what he was talking about; he was after all a demanding and sometimes irritable employer who liked everything just so, and there's no doubt that it takes both grace and patience on the part of the servant to handle such a master equably. Or maybe it was simply that all the myriad small intimate details of life are more happily dealt with in the automatic language in which one thinks. At any rate his own personal servants were invariably Italian.

A further change had somehow come about even before his marriage: he no longer replaced his servants regularly but kept them for as long as they wished to stay, provided, that is, that they were clean in their habits and honest and gave satisfaction. This made sense for, as he said to himself, it is a pity to let them go just when you have trained them to your ways. Of course, anyone could have pointed out that this would surely have been equally true in the past, but then no one had ever presumed to question Giovambattista's arrangements so that if for so long he chose to dismiss his servants after a year or eighteen months (though often with a small present and almost always with a letter of recommendation to help them find other employment), then doubtless he had his reasons. What these reasons were he himself had never thought to consider.

To his personal servants Giovambattista always used the second person singular.

Many years later, when terror reigned in Paris and any sense of known order had ceased to apply, in the dreadful upheaval that Giovambattista always called '*les événements*', the world seemed a bleak and loveless place; his dear friends were all dead by then, and even had they been alive he could never have risked committing any of his distress to paper – which of course is also why he could write only the blandest and most innocuous letters to Marco. On a wretched January day when the news that he was grimly expecting was brought to him, he withdrew to his shuttered bedroom – he had given strict orders that all windows were to be kept barred and shuttered and all outside doors locked and bolted – and crouched miserably in his armchair in the half-dark, vomiting repeatedly into a basin until there was nothing left to vomit but only a painful retching. The swiftly descending blade that severs royal heads from bodies severs at the same time the links of ordered connectedness that make sense of life and hold chaos at bay. After a little while his servant came in, removed the basin, brought him water to drink, then stood beside him and silently, unthinkably, put his arm around his master's thin and elderly shoulders. Whereupon, instead of freezing in outrage, Giovambattista turned wordlessly and rested his head against the man's chest. For the truth is that if you do not dismiss your servants but keep them with you for many years, then a feeling develops which might almost be called love. Sometimes there are blessed moments when nothing needs to be said.

*   *   *

Marco, much earlier, had written: 'Our household is certainly a lot less grand than that of Gio:Batta: yet suits us very well. We live above the shop, I suppose you could say – which is extremely convenient when I am teaching, especially since I have made it quite clear that all my courses will be given in the first morning hour, this being the time when my pupils are most apt to concentrate.' (Marino, reading this, reflected that Marco had always tended to be an unconscionably early riser.) 'I am now teaching sixty-four lessons per year. My dearest Cecilia is luckily an excellent manager of our family finances, and I too have necessarily had to learn how to budget and plan better than I used to, for at the beginning of each August I receive, along with my salary, the sum of three hundred and ten ducats with which I must purchase all the coals and utensils and materials to be used in my laboratory during the following twelve months.' An earlier letter had explained, 'I am experimenting with various local clays and craftsmen in order to find the best manner of producing the necessary utensils here, which will be very much cheaper than importing them – with the consequence that I shall be able to spend more on the chemical substances that I require.'

As a matter of fact, once Marino started working seriously on the rock he also started rising fairly early – a great change, this, which would have amazed his elder brother. For the first time he experienced on waking each morning that sense of pleased anticipation that comes with total engagement in a task. To Giovambattista he had written, 'There is no doubt, my dearest brother, that it is a difficult challenge, yet one which I am convinced is not impossible. I am beginning to perceive how it may be done.' And to Marco, 'I wake in the mornings and dream with great clarity of all the component parts of the machine that I shall construct, then leap from my bed and spoil reams of paper with preliminary drawings.'

('Dream with great clarity' were the best words he could find to express that curious process, glimpsed before but only fully experienced now, by which the mind circles around and around a problem, deliberately ignoring the centre, until suddenly the circle is so elaborately woven that you find the central solution has appeared by itself.)

To Stephanie he said afterwards, 'Everyone believed it couldn't be done, but I did it.'

This was on their third meeting and of course she barely knew him. However, she did know, or thought she knew, that men who are not in their first youth sometimes need the encouragement of feeling successful and important; she thus murmured to him various things along the lines of 'Well done,' and 'How clever of you.'

As it happened Stephanie was experienced in the ways of men who were quite a lot older than Marino, being realistic enough to have recognised long since that when you are not exactly young yourself this is your best bet. The fact that Marino did not in the end seem to require much in the way of encouragement made a pleasant change: like a lazy Sunday after a working week, she thought.

People do not always understand drawings or verbal explanations. Marino thus made a working model in order to explain to General Bezkoy just how he intended to set about moving the rock. This occupied the better part of a month, after which he made another, much smaller model for Giorgio, in spite of the fact that everyone laughed and said, 'He's far too young to appreciate it.' Sofia, for whom no models had ever been made, said scornfully, 'He'll break it within five minutes.' However, her brother's small fingers were already careful and he did not break it.

Before making his model Marino had submitted to the

123

general a clear and succinct report (of which he had made two copies and sent them to Giovambattista and Marco). The introduction to this stated: 'The Rock in question is a parallelepiped in form, forty-two feet in length, twenty-seven in width and twenty-one in height. These dimensions, and particularly the last two, are more than adequate to permit it to be shaped to form a single block suitable for the base of the statue. It should be noted, moreover, as the peasants assured me and as I have since observed with my own eyes, that the Rock is partially submerged in the marsh wherein it rests, to a depth – as far as I have been able to ascertain – of about fifteen feet. It is cloven at one end by a slanting crack: the work of lightning, as I believe, whence must derive the name of *Grom-kamen* or 'Thunder Rock' by which it is apparently known among the local people. The extreme hardness of this monolith means that to cut it would require much time and very great expense, the saws needed would have to be especially long, like those used to cut porphyry; in my opinion such an operation would moreover be excessively hazardous. It is for this reason that I propose it be raised and transported entire.'

It was natural enough that most people should mock and tell one another that Monsieur de Lascaris's great plan was likely to meet the same ignominious fate as the new bridge over the Neva. The Admiralty was markedly disinclined to get involved. But of course it was the Empress herself who had the final word.

'Let the little pseudo-Lascaris try,' she pronounced and gave instructions that he was to be removed from all other work in order to devote himself exclusively to the attempt. Perhaps she liked a handsome man (slight of stature no doubt but neatly proportioned, with warm, treacle-coloured, lazy southern eyes), perhaps she was not averse to taking a few risks, possibly – as the name she called him implied – she remembered Marino's rapid and charming deflection of trouble with the real Monsieur Lascaris; it is more probable, however, that she had noted how the roof of the *atelier* built for Falconet had remained intact in the storm, in spite of its unusually wide span, when all around it other roofs were destroyed right and left, and recalled that it was the small, dark Greek who had designed and constructed it.

Marino had, as it happened, written with great pride to Cephalonia when in the aftermath of the storm the *atelier* was found to be undamaged; his mother, however, had assumed that this was merely boastful exaggeration and had been offhand in her reply. Marco had been more appreciative.

Giovambattista of course knew very well that his brothers were proud of him and also knew with a kind of serene dignity that they were right to be proud. He was aware too that it is fitting that the head of the family should be someone to whom the others may look up (and certainly expected from his wife a degree of reverence as well as obedience). He took it for granted that if his brothers needed medical advice they would apply to him for it – although of course if the illness required urgent treatment they would in the meantime have to consult some physician nearer at hand; to Marino he recommended James Mounsey, a Scotch gentleman whose acquaintance he had made in Edinburgh, who had now, he believed, been appointed first physician to the Empress Catherine. (Marino refrained from telling his brother that he was perfectly happy with the Greek practitioner whom his wife's family had long trusted. He did, however, announce that he had recently undergone variolation at the hands of an Englishman, a certain Dr Thomas Dimsdale, in order to protect himself against the smallpox and would have the procedure repeated on his children provided he himself survived the experience without untoward effects. It being clearly useless to question the wisdom of this decision retrospectively, Giovambattista penned a rapid reply in which curiosity as to the depth of the incision made in his brother's arm and the source of the inoculum used for once got the better of anxieties.)

It seemed entirely right and natural, though, that Marino should write to seek his elder brother's advice on his bowels or his rheumatism or on the roundworms that infested his children, or indeed should send his fellow-officer Prince Baratinsky, troubled by a tapeworm of great length, all the way from St Petersburg to Paris to be treated by Giovambattista – money being no object in this particular case and the chronic discomfort caused by the parasite no longer bearable.

As a matter of fact, shortly after his arrival in Vienna Marino had thought of writing to ask Giambattista's opinion on an unfortunate amatory problem, namely that although the desire existed the performance was lacking; that he had in the end not done so was not due to any difficulty about discussing this subject with his brother generally speaking, but was rather because the circumstances of his departure from Venice were such that he felt slightly embarrassed to mention it just at that moment. (This was also the reason why he said nothing about it to Marco when they met.) Of course before too long the matter mended by itself as so many things do: Giambattista had once, in a moment of surprising openness about his profession, said something in Latin – *aut salus aut mors* – which apparently meant 'Either you get better or you die.'

And Giovambattista in turn was full of fraternal pride when his brothers did well in life. In a sense this may be easily understood: any achievement by one brother reflects well on the whole family and is thus particularly gratifying to the head of the family. However, I rather imagine that some other feeling was involved as well; perhaps the adjective should be 'paternal' rather than 'fraternal', stemming from some half-formed thought, 'I brought them up' – and of course, this being so, if Marco and Marino distinguished themselves then what their success meant was that their elder brother had not failed in his difficult task. Possibly the physician's continuing care for the health of his brothers' bodies was on one level or another a sad admission that other aspects of their lives – their social and professional health, one might say – were beyond his control.

No doubt Marco had caused some anxieties and nocturnal soul-searchings, yet no one except Giovambattista had ever really seriously feared that he would not settle down and make a successful career. Marino, however, was different; hence the dawning realisation that, as Marco put it, *he knew what he was doing* provoked in his elder brother an extraordinary aching tenderness. Giovambattista certainly did not give any conscious thought to the parable of the Prodigal Son but it is very likely that some idea of a lost brother returning to the fold was involved. Which feeling manifested itself in a steady flow of stern letters about such matters as health and diet and moderation in all things, although before the signature, before the customary ending 'Your most affectionate brother' now came a new and unaccustomed phrase, '*Vi abbraccio con tutto il cuore*': 'I embrace you with all my heart.'

'Were you naughty when you were little?' asked Giorgio, who had somehow understood that when he was alone with his father he could ask such questions.

'Terribly. I was always getting thrashed,' replied Marino, who had never beaten his son, not even once. (To begin with Giorgio was never naughty – or at any rate not in such a way that required any chastisement over and above a few wallops in the nursery. But even if his son had committed some fearful misdeed Marino felt that he could never have beaten someone so small and pale and serious.)

'What did you do? Who thrashed you?'

'My father. I did lots of things, I learnt how to do magic.'

This Giorgio knew, since both he and Sofia had seen coins appear miraculously from their father's ear and a silk handkerchief vanish as if it had never existed, no matter how much they searched his pockets. They were perfectly aware that their mother didn't really approve, although she said nothing. As she got a little older Sofia decided to ally herself with her mother and didn't approve either, but Giorgio continued to know that Marino's magic was something special.

'Who taught you? How did you learn?'

A slight pause as Marino remembered, so that Giorgio was afraid lest he had asked too many questions and done what is called being impertinent.

'A travelling magician taught me. He came to Argostoli . . . I waited until my brother was asleep, then I climbed out of the window in the middle of the night and went and found him and asked him to teach me.'

Climbing out of the window sounds like serious naughtiness: Giorgio somehow didn't dare ask, 'Will you teach me too?' and thus stored this request in his mind for another time, asking instead, 'What is the most difficult kind of magic?'

Marino almost replied truthfully, 'Cutting someone in half and then putting them together again,' but realised just in time that, should a demonstration be demanded, Elena would draw the line at this; 'Making pigeons come out of a hat,' he said, 'we'll do it on your name-day.'

Quite why magic should have been held to be so utterly beyond the pale isn't really very clear, yet so it was. It may be that it smacks too much of mountebanks and dangerously rootless people; perhaps there is even a whiff of the unnatural about it – a perversion of what is right and normal. What is certain is that it is based upon deceit.

All the children had known without anything being said that Marino's new skills were something that must never be mentioned to adults and thus for a whole summer the secret was kept. But it was inevitable that sooner or later someone would tittle-tattle and in autumn Marino received a really major thrashing; he always suspected it was to his cousin Demetrio that he owed it. (No one likes being told that they're doing something all wrong: Marino had watched his cousin training a dog and had commented, 'The way you're doing it is stupid. If you go on beating him like that he'll obey you because he fears you, but if you teach him gently he'll obey because he loves you. The best obeying in dogs is when they love you.' Marco had secretly agreed but would never have dared say anything since their cousin was older and bigger than them.)

'I was nine years old and amazingly innocent,' he explained to Stephanie, just before they finally arrived back in Argostoli. (Actually he had been ten.) 'I hadn't a clue what he wanted. But I'd set my heart on learning so I couldn't bear to give up and go away, even though he made me feel scared. Anyway, in the end he did teach me, he gave me three lessons and nothing untoward happened, though I have to admit I felt a lot more comfortable when he moved on.'

What the man had said was, 'It'll cost you.'

To which Marino had replied, sadly and honestly, 'I'm afraid I haven't got any money.'

'Then you'll have to pay me some other way, won't you?'

This was when it began to be frightening. Marino said nothing, shifted a little, awkwardly, but stood his ground. Either the man took pity on him or (as he afterwards thought) probably decided that a well-spoken child of presumably influential parents was too risky.

'You can sell me your soul then.'

This was frightening in a different way. Marino said instantly, 'I can't do that.' Then, feeling that his chances of learning magic were dwindling rapidly, had a moment of inspiration and said as politely as he could, 'I can't do that, sir, because I haven't got a soul, you see.'

The man watched him for a moment, then said lightly, 'Well, in that case it seems we're colleagues . . . Looks as if I'll have to teach you for free, doesn't it?'

And was as good as his word, although Marino went on being uncomfortable. Which was perhaps why he never told Marco very much about this business and in fact made his brother feel hurt and left out when for the next few weeks he kept going off by himself to the marsh to practise his first three beginner's tricks.

'Later, in Venice, I found someone else to teach me some more,' he told Stephanie.

On the ship crossing to the island there was very little privacy and Stephanie rather kept him at arm's length. Marino to some extent understood the reasons for this and resigned himself to evenings spent playing cards with her. He impressed her greatly with simple tricks of the kind 'Pick a card, any card, put it back in the pack and I'll tell you which one you picked.' He invariably got it right but would never explain how he did it: 'I'm a magician, don't forget,' he laughed, and told her instead about how he had learned conjuring.

He had already described to her how the peasants who watched the moving of the rock had crossed themselves and murmured words like 'wizard'.

However, the laws that govern the way things behave have nothing to do with magic. Marino never used neat notebooks of the kind in which his elder brother recorded his ideas, but tended to jot down random thoughts on whatever piece of paper lay at hand (and everyone in the household had the strictest of orders never to touch or disturb the master's papers); this apparent casualness did not, however, mean that the thoughts were not following a logical sequence. His letters presented them in their distilled and refined form. As he constructed the scale model for General Bezkoy, for example, he told Marco: 'It is customary to use rollers or cylinders, yet this seemed impracticable to me when dealing with the enormous weight involved in this case because of the very great friction produced. What is more, if they were made of wood they would quite simply disintegrate under the weight of the Rock, and although metal cylinders of such size and diameter could perhaps be made by those who are experienced in casting cannons of great bore, the fact remains that they would be unwieldy. For even if I managed to acquire them, it would be well nigh impossible to keep them perpendicular to the direction of travel since the force applied to them would not be evenly distributed along their length so that they would start moving in all directions. I toyed with the possibility of finding some way to fix such cylinders into a parallel position but rapidly discarded this idea. What I have therefore decided upon is spherical bodies set in two fixed parallels: their weight being much smaller than that of cylinders allows more promptness of movement, and the friction produced is also very much less.'

And later: 'These small spheres or balls will move freely in a metal gutter, its sides made convex – the corners rounded off – in order to reduce friction, set along the upper surfaces of two great beams, each of which will be thirty-three feet long, fourteen inches wide and twelve inches thick. Each beam will have fifteen balls. This is the lower part of my machine, or track, along which the Rock will be moved.' (Just as Marco always spoke of 'my laboratory', so Marino invariably – and perhaps with even greater justification – spoke of 'my machine'.) 'The upper part or chassis, upon which the Rock will sit, will also consist of two parallel beams, although their dimensions are different: forty-two feet long, twenty-eight inches wide and sixteen inches thick. They will bear a metal gutter along the length of their undersides which will fit exactly on to the lower gutter containing the metal balls. Four transverse beams will connect them, of lesser thickness so that a space will exist between them and the Rock, for otherwise, if its weight rested directly upon them, they would soon bend and break. The Rock on its chassis will thus be drawn along the lower beams: of these I shall have several made so that as the chassis advances more beams may be laid in front of it.'

Various clearly labelled sketches accompanied these descriptions, so that Marco, who after all was not an engineer, should understand the beauty and the simplicity of the conception. Giovambattista received less detailed but equally regular reports. When the model was demonstrated to General Bezkoy with a weight of three thousand pounds upon it which could be moved easily on the horizontal plane 'without requiring the strength of more than one finger to pull it' (a slight and perhaps forgivable exaggeration here), Marino was jubilant. He celebrated this success privately – luckily he had some cash left over and thus did not need to pay another visit to Madame Louis David Duval – and on his return home in the late, late hours sat and wrote to both his brothers with delicious ambiguity: 'I was most satisfied.'

For some reason Marino stopped writing at all to Cephalonia during this period; what he said to himself was, 'I am far too busy.'

11

JEAN-BAPTISTE Carburi (as most people now called him), being a foreigner, was not permitted to practise medicine in France. This prohibition did not, of course, apply to the court: a foreign princess has every right to bring her own medical man with her – and if the king himself is impressed by the tall, thin, courteous Italian count (this is what everyone assumed his nationality to be) and chooses to consult him, then who may presume to question such a decision? Needless to say, on the first such occasion there was a certain amount of subdued murmuring on the part of the other royal physicians but this soon subsided since the gentleman concerned did not appear to give himself airs and in any case had always been scrupulous about maintaining good confraternal relations. There was indeed a moment when everyone present in the king's bedroom held their breath in horror at his extraordinary temerity: he requested permission to sit, called for a stool to be brought, seated himself at the bedside, asked for the royal chemise to be removed, then calmly laid his ear to the king's naked chest and tapped with his fingers and listened while his patient breathed in and breathed out obediently. Rather amazingly, the king was pleased rather than displeased with this proceeding: '*Monsieur Carburi connait très bien son métier,*' was his verdict.

On the whole, however, the princess whose care was his particular charge was healthy, although of course there were various minor ailments which he was called upon to treat and indeed several times (especially at the beginning) he had responded to a summons only to find his patient apparently perfectly well but insisting on a full and lengthy examination. It did not occur to him that the French court was perhaps a difficult place in which to make one's life and that the young lady may simply sometimes have wanted to hear a voice from home; in any case Giovambattista invariably examined his patients thoroughly – even if they seemed in good health – and understood without thinking about it that a small prescription to aid the digestion or to encourage sleep is always soothing.

One way and another Giovambattista's medical duties thus did not occupy a great deal of his time. In spite of the fact that – as he told Marco – he sometimes missed his pupils and his teaching, this arrangement suited him well enough; a large part of his days could now be devoted to expanding and cataloguing his collection and his library, and an increasing number of hours was spent in keeping up with his scientific correspondence. From time to time he saw foreign patients (no one could possibly object to this), including several Greeks and that unfortunate Russian prince whose tapeworm, when finally to his great relief he passed it intact, measured all of eight ells.

One of the things that the Carburi brothers had in common was an ability to transmit knowledge, to explain things in such a way that the explanation not only made sense but stuck in the listener's memory: they were all, in other words, good teachers. Perhaps it was simply that each was able to communicate a sense of excitement, passion even, for his subject.

'People do not understand drawings unless they have a special visual proclivity or have been trained to do so,' Marino had written to Marco before setting out for his frozen marsh. 'I have thus found it useful to break my drawings down into their several component parts, each carefully labelled, and to present them as a sequence: in this way I may explain, step by step, how the Rock will be lifted,

how my machine will work and how the many difficulties –
for example the fact that the course the Rock must follow is
not a straight one – may be overcome. What with my
drawings and my model, the general was convinced
(although I haven't yet told him of the problems that will
be encountered once we get the Rock down to the river . . .
One thing at a time – to tell you the truth, I haven't myself
quite worked out yet how to surmount these difficulties and
in any case, properly speaking, transporting the Rock by
river will be the Admiralty's job rather than mine). More to
the point, the Empress has graciously consigned the task of
raising it and bringing it to the river to my hands, so that as
soon as the ground is frozen hard I shall start work. I have
already given orders that the vegetation be cleared from the
route over which the Rock will move. I estimate that the
whole business will take at least two winter seasons.'

Marino also made simple but accurate drawings for Giorgio
and explained to him all about mass and weight and levers
and fulcrums. 'To lift something huge and heavy like my
Rock you have to use levers,' he told the boy, and, 'Once
upon a time there was a very famous mathematician who
knew everything there was to know about it. He said that
even the whole world could be lifted and moved, like a huge
giant rock, if you could only find a place to do it from that
was far enough away.'

'Could anyone?' asked his son.

'No, of course they couldn't.' And Marino explained
about theories and about how you may deduce things even
when you can't actually demonstrate them in practice, then
quoted, '*Dos mi pa sto kai tan gan kináso*,' adding, 'He was
Greek, you see, Giorgio, so he said it in Greek. It means
"Give me a place to stand and I will move the earth."'

Giorgio liked the stories of this man and of how he leapt

from his bath crying '*Eureka, Eureka*' (which Marino automatically pronounced in the Greek way, '*Evrika*', with the accent on the first syllable). 'Did he put his drawers on?' was the next question, to which Marino replied seriously, 'I don't know. I shouldn't think so.' This for some reason seemed terribly funny and occasioned delighted laughter. The end of the story was sad though. Giorgio was made a little anxious by the idea that a mathematician could be killed because people thought he was a magician and were afraid of him; 'It isn't like that any more today,' his father reassured him.

Giorgio and Sofia were properly brought up and both used the respectful second person plural when they spoke to their father (or indeed to their mother or to any other adult). He in turn, once they were past their very first infancy, tended to use the plural form to them too; when alone with Giorgio, however, he reverted to the simple, loving '*tu*' – a private custom which neither father nor son ever thought to mention to anyone else. As it happened Marino never used this singular form when he spoke in French to Elena, even if it occasionally surfaced in Greek during those bedroom murmurs that she hadn't ever understood. (Greek is a language for rumpled sheets, for desires urgent or lazy, for sharp, sudden moments of pleasure.) 'Of course I love my wife,' he would have said had anyone asked, but equally of course there are degrees and degrees of intimacy.

Stephanie, who was more forthright and liked to know what was what, asked him fairly early on in their acquaintance what these words meant. 'They all seem to begin with M,' she remarked.

'I suppose they do,' he agreed, and translated some of them for her. 'When I call you *mátia mou* it means "my eyes" – that's because eyes are precious – and *moró mou* means "my baby" and *manoúla mou* means, well, literally it means "little mother" but really it's just a way of saying "sweet-heart" . . . What have I left out? Ah, yes' (a smile), ' "my wonderful great big cunt" is what *mounára mou* means.'

Some words, however, began with P: there was *poutanáki* and *peristéri* and *poutsoglýftra* or *poutsoglyftroúla* (these two words being of Marino's own devising) and *perdhikoúla* – my little whore, my pigeon, my cock-sucking girl or its delighted diminutive, my little partridge.

There is a sense of accord which is utterly comfortable. When Marino told Stephanie about his early days in Russia, about General Melissino and his wife Princess Dolgoruki, she commented, 'There's nothing wrong with sleeping your way to where you want to be.'

'No indeed,' he replied, 'it's called being a whore.'

'My point exactly,' she said. 'That makes two of us.'

It was after this that Marino began to use the second person singular to Stephanie outside the bedroom as well as within it (though not, of course, in front of other people).

'You have stone-coloured eyes and a heart as hard as stone to match them,' said someone in Paris. What Giovambattista had said to himself was, 'I am not young,' which meant, 'These things are impossible.' The eyes that beseeched him were young and brown and full of tears.

Hard work is a great remedy for any potential hankerings after the impossible; Giovambattista gave strict instructions to his wife that he was not to be disturbed and sat up late, night after night, working on a paper on the *Taenia* or tapeworm. Since such scientific papers are better and fuller if they are not merely descriptive and theoretical but also include specific clinical material, and since he had no patients of his own on whom to experiment further with the new treatment which had proved so successful in the case of Marino's friend, he had approached various French colleagues as to the possibility of a collaboration. It is of course right and natural that men of science should work together, as he told Marco when he wrote to him of his current (professional) preoccupations.

'How disgusting,' said Cecilia when her husband read this letter aloud, wrinkling her nose in repugnance, whereupon Marco gave her a little lesson, declaring, first, that any subject, no matter how disgusting, may very properly be considered from the scientific point of view, and, second, that tapeworms, although admittedly unattractive, are among the ills that cause wretched discomfort to the human body, just as wearying as any more dramatic sickness, so that Giambattista's interest in what appeared to be an effective remedy was entirely appropriate and indeed laudable.

(Possibly Marco no longer had irreverent thoughts about Giambattista; at any rate he was quick to defend his brother if Cecilia seemed to be expressing criticism.)

The reason Marco read most of his letters out loud to his wife was that he expected her to help him in answering them; 'I am too busy,' he pleaded, and luckily she had no great objection to covering sheets and sheets for him with her neat, convent-trained handwriting. Typically, Marco wrote the first page of, for example, letters to his mother – or even a mere half-page – in rather large writing to fill the space, then passed them to Cecilia for her to complete the remaining two sides of the paper. Each sheet of paper was folded vertically in the middle to form a front, a back and two inner sides; the back bore the address of the recipient when the letter was folded once more and sealed, leaving three sides to be written on. More pages could be added if need be, but too much blank space makes letters look a bit meagre, so that Marco was extremely grateful to Cecilia for her ability to come up with enough gossip and news and affectionate sentiments to fill the sides decently. The only personal letters which he continued to find time to write by himself were those to his two elder brothers. Nevertheless, out of habit he often read Giovambattista's letters to his wife, and on occasion Marino's as well.

The reason Marco was so busy was that, apart from his regular teaching duties, he was also now charged from time to time by the Venetian government with finding solutions to various practical problems, mostly concerning artillery. No one was quite clear whether the apparent tacit agreement to forget about the fiasco of the Agordo mines was due to the influence of powerful patrons or whether – as Caterina and Marino both believed, from their separate viewpoints of Cephalonia and St Petersburg – it stemmed from a simple recognition of Marco's talents. At any rate, in Paris Marco's new status was felt by Giovambattista to be a source of great relief but at the same time of sporadic anxiety lest his solutions prove unsuccessful.

'You should have more faith in him,' Marino might perhaps have said if Giovambattista had ever shared these anxieties.

The problem Marco was trying to solve at this time had to do with the fact that each charge of gunpowder for the firing of artillery pieces was necessarily wrapped in paper; since the residue of the previous charge's wrapping, if still alight, had the dangerous tendency to cause premature firing while the cannon or musket was still being reloaded (with a resulting loss of life and limb among the unfortunate loaders), the need to produce paper of rapid and complete combustibility was clearly urgent.

'My dearest son,' wrote Caterina, 'I tremble when I think of the many dangers attendant upon such experimentation and beg that you will take care.' She also questioned the wisdom of offering his services in this way to the State without seeking any payment in return. This letter annoyed Marco; he was heard to mutter something about people who didn't know how to take care not surviving very long in any chemistry laboratory that he'd ever come across, and instructed Cecilia to tell his mother to leave him to conduct his own business as he saw fit.

What Cecilia actually wrote was, 'My dearest Mother-in-Law, your worries are entirely understandable. Indeed I confess I would share them, were it not for the fact that Marco has always been the first to stress the importance of caution in work of this nature.' She judged it better to make no mention of the lack of recompense, on which subject, as it happened, she and her husband did not quite see eye to eye.

What neither of them knew was that the Venetian Senate had already been offered, for the price of a hundred *zecchini*, the secret of the combustible paper used by the English but had decided that its very own professor of chemistry might well come up with a solution that would probably be more reliable and would certainly cost a lot less. The fact that Giacomo Nani was now one of the three Superintendents of Artillery may or may not have had something to do with the desire to pay as little as possible for whatever invention Marco might produce.

Their mother, in spite of having always assured her eldest son that honour and reputation were of infinitely more worth than mere money, felt that Marco was a fool to work for nothing. (Unguarded of him to have admitted this, one might think, and indeed he later regretted having answered her uncomfortably direct question honestly: Marino could have told him that a little goes a long way as far as information supplied to one's mother is concerned.) Possibly this discrepancy in Caterina's attitude was due to the fact that Giovambattista had always managed to combine a solid reputation with an equally solid income, or maybe some vague mention of

Marco's youthful extravagance on his travels through Europe had somehow come to her ears. What she was not of course aware of was that, after several small loans and a lengthy nocturnal reflection on Marco's seriousness of purpose, Giovambattista had decided to assist his brother with a certain sum of money each year (entered into the account book simply as 'To Marco'), this fraternal generosity being a transaction that for many years remained quite private between the two of them. Possibly this was one of the reasons why these days Marco would hear no criticism of Giambattista.

However this may be, he wrote to Marino: 'Our brother's visit was a happy one. He stayed in Padua for ten days just before leaving for Paris again and I thus had ample opportunity to converse with him and to demonstrate – with some pride, I must admit – the work on which I am currently engaged. He is still plagued regularly by the tertian fever that afflicts him and tells me that he is frequently troubled by disorders of the stomach, yet apart from this his health seems good on the whole and his spirits reasonably cheerful. He is much occupied with his books and showed me a list of the volumes that he has purchased while in Italy. We discussed, among other things, my idea of providing some elementary training in chemistry to the pharmacists of Padua in order that they may be able to prepare many of the more widely used medicines themselves; for at present such is their ignorance of chemical operations and experiments that they buy in medicines from Venice without any ability to judge their quality. Gio:Batta: approved as much as you did, I'm glad to tell you, with the result that I am encouraged to proceed and – when time permits – shall put together some definite proposal to submit to the Senate. I have at any rate given this matter more thought since I last wrote: what I envisage is a course lasting one month, during which I would make them work without interruption every single day, for as many hours as

141

they could spend, under my assiduous direction. Actually, I think that this plan will be accepted, jumped at even, for it is an idea dear to my heart and I shall thus seek no payment for my time and trouble – I need hardly tell you that our glorious Republic keeps as tight a hold on its purse-strings as a costive maiden lady on you know what and is always eager to find ways of avoiding expenditure.' (This was possibly indiscreet since it was not unheard of for letters to arrive with their seals damaged and you never knew whose eyes might not peruse them; Marco let it stand, however.) The idea of money and budgets somehow led back to thoughts of Giambattista, so that the letter ended with, 'We are fortunate indeed in having so excellent a brother.'

A sentiment with which Marino did not in the least disagree: he had just received the physician's instructions about senna and calomel. The thought that your brother cares for your health and well-being is always heart-warming.

In spite of the fact that he felt wretched, Marino's own health was in truth good enough to withstand the discomforts and dietary rigours of the frozen marsh. He did indeed lose one tooth, but this was from a painful purulent *apostemation* or abscess rather than from the scurvy he so much feared ('That's why sailors often don't have any teeth left,' he had explained to Giorgio on one of their visits to the docks). Anyway, luckily the tooth lost was at the back of his mouth so that the gap didn't show – as he wrote to Marco, who attempted to console him by pointing out that few men in their forties still possess every single tooth and that he himself had already lost three.

All the brothers would have maintained that a tendency to indigestion or intestinal problems ran in the family. Giambattista suffered worst, as everyone acknowledged; Caterina had often thought how unfair this was, considering that it was her eldest son who necessarily bore all the worries of the family on his narrow shoulders.

Marco's letter telling Marino about the medal struck in his honour never arrived in Russia. The fact that Marino sent no congratulations and that his letter the following month was brief and mainly concerned with the work in the marsh upset Marco for the better part of a week: everyone else's approval seemed almost to have lost its savour. However, even before Cecilia spoke with the voice of common sense and said, 'Well, he probably never received your news – if you come to think of it, it's a wonder anything ever gets there,' Marco had come to the same conclusion himself and thus some days later wrote again.

Had Marino been in St Petersburg he would probably have said to his wife, 'I am made a little worried by my brother's silence.' As it was, having no one at hand but a couple of junior officers sent to assist him (who mostly got in the way), two regimental drummers, a great many workmen and the few peasants who appeared as if from nowhere to watch the work in progress, he kept this thought to himself. During the brief daylight hours he was wholly absorbed by the rock; in the long evenings he played cards with one or both of the officers, wrote a bit (a day to day journal of each stage of the task, as well as letters), looked at the stars when he was obliged to venture outside, and generally retired to sleep at an extraordinarily early hour.

The truth is, of course, that you would have no means of knowing that your brother had died until long after he was buried, so that at the very moment when you are thinking of him, writing to him, sharing your thoughts, he might no longer exist, might already be turning to corruption in the grave. For although you may feel that you would know instantly the moment of his death, that some sharp pang would reverberate in your own flesh, some chilly silence maybe invade your consciousness, the chances are that this is nothing but folly and self-delusion.

When finally a letter from Marco was brought out to him, along with provisions, Marino instantly felt like celebrating. The only women in the vicinity, however, were those dumpy, bundled up, largely toothless creatures whose gender – as he later told Stephanie – is a matter of some doubt until you get very close to them, after which their powerfully rancid smell is definitely offputting. *'Je n'étais quand même pas arrivé à ce point là,'* he explained, 'And anyway, even if I had been willing to hold my nose and use my imagination to supplement the want of any obvious feminine charms, I wouldn't have fancied having one of their male counterparts come after me with an axe.'

(Stephanie possessed most of her teeth, although the front ones were slightly crooked; for some reason this small imperfection seemed to Marino to be a mark of beauty, filling him with a strange, all-encompassing tenderness. The musky, living-animal smell of her body was an unfailing delight.)

'I have been living like a monk,' he said to the young lady in St Petersburg with whom in due course he celebrated. And, *'Cela se voit, mon cher,'* was her dry comment.

To Giorgio he had written earlier, 'I sleep with my clothes on and often don't shave, so that I'm beginning to look and smell like a wild old monk.'

Needless to say, he did not write anything of these matters to Marco but instead congratulated him warmly: 'I am delighted by your news, my dearest brother, and brimming over with pride – although of course I always knew you could do anything you set your hand to.'

'The English have long had a paper of this kind,' Marco had written (for the second time), 'yet mine proved better. This is not, as you might think, a vain boast: a certain Sergeant-Major Pattison agreed to bring some specimens of the English paper to Padua so that a comparison could be made, and was generous enough not only to concede that mine was superior but indeed to write a memorandum to this effect to the Superintendents of the Artillery. In recompense for my invention the Senate then commanded that a gold medal be struck – which command, I must tell you, was carried out with such exemplary rapidity that the medal is actually in my possession as I write these words.' (Marco, basking happily in the sense of being honoured, had no idea that the cost of this token of the Republic's appreciation had been twenty-four *zecchini*, in other words just under a quarter of the amount originally demanded for the secret recipe of the English paper.) 'Some copies of the medal have also been minted in silver and in bronze. Of those in silver I have sent one to our mother in Cephalonia and another to Gio:Batta: and there is no need for me to tell you, my dearest Marino, that a third is for you. I have hesitated to send it, however, especially since my last letter apparently went astray and never came to your hands, and thus shall keep it for you, trusting that some safe means of getting it to St Petersburg will before too long be found.'

Naturally enough, Marco longed for his brother to see this medal and thus filled half of the next page with a description of it. 'So that you may know what it is like, I should tell you that one side bears the lion with the gospel of my patron saint between his paws and beneath it the words RESPUBLICA VENETA, while on the obverse it reads M. COM. CARBURIO. P. CHYMIAE ANTEC. MUNIFICENTIA SENATUS A. and the date. Beneath this inscription are two crossed cannons and a great quantity of cannon balls

145

as well as other munitions. By common admission it is a very elegant design.' At this point Marco added a small and not very good drawing.

(As a child Marco had always felt that the emblem of Venice was somehow personal to him, its saint being, after all, his own; he and Marino had assumed that the words 'Peace to thee, Marcus my Evangelist' must be spoken by God and considered it entirely appropriate that God should use the second person singular, supposing that he wanted to speak to you.)

'My brother Marco is very, very clever,' said Marino to his son some weeks later.

One of the things that the brothers had in common was a lack of any false modesty in describing to one another their successes and triumphs. Marco's happy pride seemed entirely right and proper to both Giovambattista and Marino, just as later Marino's delight when he wrote of his own achievement never struck either of the others as being excessive. When he read this letter Marino smiled, almost feeling for a second that he could hear the smile in his brother's voice.

As a matter of fact the Carburi voice was another thing that all the brothers shared: a light voice, slightly higher in pitch than one might have expected, unemphatic even when speaking of triumphs, yet with a definite colouring. In old age – at least in Giovambattista's and Marco's cases – it developed a faint creak. Marino's singing voice was a pleasant tenor; he was the only one of them who ever sang (to himself, to his children), although in the next generation both Paolo's surviving sons had the Carburi voice and both were tenors. If Giorgio had lived long enough for his voice to break it is likely that he too would have possessed this family characteristic.

12

'I HAVE ALWAYS loved my brothers,' he told her quite simply. 'It's only natural, after all.'

Stephanie had told him that she had no brothers or sisters; this seemed easier than trying to explain that she had once had a brother – who, it was to be presumed, might very probably still be alive but who had not desired any contact with her for the last twenty-two years. Twenty-two years is a long time.

'I haven't seen my brother Marco for more than fifteen years,' he said. Then laughed and added, 'When we were children we had the foolish idea that if we were ever parted each of us would only have to pick up a shell and hold it to his ear and listen to know that the other was alive and well somewhere in the world. My brother Giambattista maintained that the distant murmur when you hold a shell to your ear is nothing less than the sound of your own soul, for he refused to believe that what you hear is the sea. Which was why Marco and I thought we might hear each other's souls.'

Stephanie was well used to half-listening, paying just enough attention to produce intelligent comments or soothing assent, depending on what seemed to be required. Marino certainly appeared to want to tell her about himself – most people do – yet on occasion asked, 'Am I boring you?' and had once even said quite calmly, 'It's nice of you to pretend to be interested' (whereupon she felt rebuked and thought to herself that she'd better try a bit harder). He also appeared to want to know about her life, which was slightly annoying: you don't necessarily wish to tell an ardent middle-aged man everything about yourself yet inventing stories is sometimes a bit of an effort.

However, if you happen to be speaking truthfully, it may be that the telling of something to another person makes you suddenly recall it more clearly yourself – even if not necessarily with complete accuracy, the curious thing about memories being that you recreate and interpret them in the manner that best suits your own needs. What Giovambattista, then a serious eighteen-year-old, had actually said was, 'It is always right to seek the mechanical explanations that lie behind natural phenomena.' Followed by, 'It is very much more likely to be an echo of the pulse of your own life that you hear, Marco, rather than some mysterious marine memory of the animal which once inhabited that shell.' This conversation had taken place during the month they spent in quarantine when they first arrived in Venice on their way to school; Giovambattista had never before spent such a long period in the company of his younger brothers and was conscientiously making great efforts not only to ensure that they changed their linen regularly but also to discourage juvenile superstitions and guide their intellectual development on to a properly rational path.

'So did you ever try it?' asked Stephanie.

'No, of course not' (dismissively), 'those were just childish things.'

Later that day, continuing to reminisce, he told her, 'Giambattista always liked shells . . . I used to draw them for him sometimes.'

Probably what led Marino to remember these drawings – often neat cross-sections of spirals, made while he was still studying in Bologna – was the fact that half an hour or so earlier he had been showing Stephanie the new drawings of his machine and was now explaining to her how to make sense of cross-sections: 'Imagine slicing through something vertically with a sharp knife,' he said, and demonstrated on one of the three apples with which he had been absent-mindedly juggling.

As it happened Giovambattista had kept Marino's drawings and in Turin had had them bound into a slim volume which bore no title on the spine but which had its place in his library alongside books on shells and other marine creatures. Marco's work on the jellyfish was also among them. In the catalogue that he was preparing these works were listed respectively as 'Shell: drawings of the structure thereof, by my brother Count Marino Carburi: twenty-six drawings, named and annotated' and '*Lettera sopra una spezie di insetto marino*, by my brother Count Marco Carburi: a description of *Vellela vellela* with an account of its geographical distribution, appearance and anatomy.'

The question of how one arranges books in a library merits careful thought. What would be most pleasing to the eye would be an orderly arrangement by size – folio volumes on the lower shelves and quarto volumes above them – although unfortunately the requirements of the eye and of the mind do not coincide, so that from the scientific point of view such an arrangement would be most unscholarly and of no value. (Giovambattista occasionally felt that in a perfect world books would be of uniform size.) Clearly, what makes sense is to arrange books in sections, by subject. However, further questions then arise: do you, for example, separate your books according to what language they are written in, with different shelves for Latin, Greek, Italian and French? There is a certain neatness and logic in this, yet it does not satisfy the need for a wider view whereby content matters more than language. Moreover, what if you have a very few works in a language that you are unable to read? (Giovambattista possessed four or five books received as gifts from colleagues in Edinburgh and London.) Should they languish by themselves on an otherwise empty shelf? But would not this in itself be constantly irksome to the eye as well as wasting valuable space?

'The system which has appeared best to me, after much thought, is a classification of volumes by subject, within each section of which they are then ranged upon the shelves alphabetically, according to the name of the author,' he wrote to Marco. 'I recommend, my dearest brother, that you adopt the same method, for by so doing you will find that, once you are familiar with the classification chosen, you will be able to lay your hand instantly on any volume you may wish to study.'

To his mother Giovambattista mentioned the very strict orders he had given about the cleaning of his library: a pair of servants should work together, one of whom, wearing gloves, would remove and then replace the volumes while the other dusted; all books should be replaced the right way up and in the correct order. The gloves were important, since after all you don't want smudgy fingerprints on the warm golden-brown leather of the bindings and, unless you stand over them constantly, most people are remarkably slapdash about washing their hands with any regularity. Normally speaking, one might have expected that Giambattista's wife would have assumed responsibility for the running of the household and the supervision of servants, yet – as Caterina knew well enough – her eldest son had always had a tendency to fuss about details.

'I am very much engaged in this great task,' wrote Marino to his mother at about the same time, after a longish silence, 'and am thus not able to write as often as I would wish.' It was a little unfortunate that Giovambattista's letter, which had arrived in Argostoli ten days earlier, referred to a steady stream of letters from St Petersburg to Paris.

'Your brother Paolo is deeply grieved that he never hears

from you,' remarked Caterina in reply, 'and fears that the importance of your occupations is such that your home and your family must now seem of little significance to you. I assure him that this is most unlikely to be the case since your elder brother tells us of the trouble you are taking to keep him informed of the progress of your labours.'

This letter arrived at a bad moment: the rock, while being lifted, had slipped and settled once more into its marshy bed, presumably because the beams and blocks of stone placed beneath it at each phase of levering were not adequate to support the great weight, whereupon a nasty little knowing satisfaction prevailed in certain St Petersburg circles which gossiping tongues took care to bring to Marino's ears. This upset him more than he wanted to admit, in spite of the fact that he made great efforts to pay no attention. 'Malice and spite arise from ignorance and envy,' he told himself repeatedly, yet couldn't help feeling low. He slept badly, which made things worse, was suddenly troubled by diarrhoea (perhaps he had been taking too much senna) and by pains in his joints once more; it was now too that for the first time a bleak midnight thought forced itself into his mind: 'Not even my brothers ever really expected me to succeed in anything.'

However, a small dose of opium is a panacea – an effective remedy which soothes aches and binds bowels, as well as an encourager of deep sleep which in turn helps to banish lonely thoughts.

'*Ma très-chère femme,*' he wrote laconically a couple of days later (he persisted doggedly in putting a hyphen between '*très*' and its adjective even though Giovambattista – who had a tendency to correct people – had twice pointed out that this was an error when Marino had quoted other people's words in French to him), 'I have been feeling most unwell and am thus doubly grateful to you for the medicine which you so opportunely sent me. Work proceeds. Embrace my son for me and

151

our daughter. I kiss your hand respectfully, your most affectionate husband, Alexandre de Lascaris.' And of course work did necessarily proceed, for when you have four hundred workmen awaiting instructions you cannot allow yourself to continue too long in that state which at home they used to call 'Marino having a fit of the sulks'.

Both Caterina, when she finally received a letter from Russia, and Giovambattista felt that 'four hundred workmen' should be taken with a pinch of salt, neither of them having fully imagined the vast extent of Russia or the numberless myriads of its people and both of them finding it hard to believe that Marino could possibly be responsible for directing such an army of labourers. However, Marino was not being wildly inaccurate: the exact figure was in fact three hundred and eighty-nine.

'My first care,' he had told Giovambattista, 'was the construction of barracks for so many men and the digging of latrines. Marshes are by their nature full of unhealthy vapours to start with, and in the second place military experience has taught us how promptly fevers may spread when a great many men are encamped in close proximity, with the result that I determined to take whatever precautions seemed possible.' (Marino had been perfectly aware that, while labour was no doubt expendable, loss of life on any large scale would provide fuel for detractors and spiteful slanderers.) 'These dangers are indeed more pressing in the heat of summer than in the present icy cold, yet for safety's sake I have nevertheless had the cabin that serves as my own quarters built some little way removed from the barracks that house the men.'

Marshes may well be insalubrious; they are also, in warm climates, places of burgeoning life and rampant growth. Reeds may be cut to the ground in late summer or autumn, yet before a full year has passed they will be twice the height of a man again. If you keep very still in the marshes of Cephalonia you can almost hear the plants grow.

In the deadened silence of a winter marsh so deeply frozen that the only thing to be heard was the occasional howling of wolves, Marino dreamt of Lixouri and the marshes of Livadi: a vision of warmth and fertility and abundance and secret happiness from which he woke in much more cheerful mood. (It is quite possible that the small doses of opium he had been taking for two days were responsible not only for the fact that his bodily discomforts had abated but also for this dream.)

'It is a powerful medicine which should be used very sparingly,' wrote Giovambattista. 'You would be ill advised to resort to it for many days at a time.' This made Marino smile, since he couldn't help remembering a pronouncement of Marco's to the effect that if you watched carefully you'd see that when Giambattista took communion at Easter he only ever sipped a quarter of the spoonful that the priest offered – 'It's in case too much holiness in one go disbalances the organism, you see.' However, by the time this advice arrived all medicines had long been put aside, Marino had given orders for the broad pit that had been dug around the rock to be deepened and was now occupied from daybreak to sunset with slow and steady application of the levers.

'I am using twelve levers,' he wrote first to one brother then to the other, 'each one of which is composed of three "masts" bound together, sixty-five feet in length, and each of which is, I calculate, capable of raising a weight of two hundred thousand pounds. They are manipulated by a system of pulleys in triangular – or better, pyramidal – frames securely mounted on broad and heavy bases; "shear-legs" is the name by which these pyramids are known to engineers.' (There is doubtless a certain satisfaction to be had from impressing your brother with words that are unfamiliar to him.) 'The rope attached to the end of each lever runs through the pulley to a winch or, as I call it, capstan, once more securely anchored by a line of stakes which I had caused to be driven into the ground in good time before it froze. Each capstan requires not more than three men to work it.' (A beautiful economy of effort here, which Marino hoped Giambattista would appreciate.) 'For this position I have selected those who are not only brawny but also show some signs of intelligence. Co-ordination of movement between the teams at the capstans at all times is of prime importance in order to maintain equal tension on all twelve levers.'

And: 'Each time the levers are applied the Rock is raised by about a foot or so. Wedges of timber and stone are then placed beneath it, the bases on which my pyramids are bolted are raised commensurately by the addition of timber baulks, and the process starts again. I should tell you, my dearest brother' (this was in a letter to Marco), 'that right at the beginning a minor mishap occurred which discouraged me greatly, yet the setback was only temporary, I took appropriate measures, and all now proceeds entirely as I intended. To facilitate the action of the levers I have placed four further capstans and pulleys on the opposite side whose ropes are attached directly to the Rock, into which I have had iron rings set with lead.' A drawing accompanied this explanation to make it clearer. 'As you can see, it is really just a question of patient pushing and pulling and my Rock is steadily rising.'

When it had been raised to a point close to equilibrium Marino set up six further capstans behind the levers, with more thick ropes to secure the rock and prevent it from toppling over, until at last the day arrived when these could be gradually paid out: at this point people crossed themselves and the men working the capstans held their breath; the only sound heard was the drummers giving the rhythm. For a moment the rock seemed to totter, free at last from the marsh, then was lowered till it came to rest on its side upon the bed prepared for it: a platform covered by a layer of moss and straw six feet thick. Marino, who until now had been directing the drummers with his hand, involuntarily closed his eyes and did not open them again until a collective gasp and the beginning of loud applause told him it was safe to do so. 'It was a critical moment,' he explained later when he came to write an account of the whole business, 'I feared lest it fall too violently and fracture as it met the ground.'

At the end of March he returned to St Petersburg, filled with pride and satisfaction, yet – something that surprised him – too exhausted to feel like celebrating immediately. 'I must be growing old,' he thought. He did not, needless to say, speak of this aspect of things to his brothers although his next letter to Giambattista mentioned in passing the very great lassitude that threatened to overwhelm him. But of course by the time the physician's sensible reply (early nights and a quiet life) reached Russia Marino had regained what he thought of as his customary vigour and had long since shown both his wife and his latest mistress how much he had missed them.

'The Rock has been dragged from its slumbers and now rests upon its new bed like some great beached leviathan,' he told Marco. The metaphor was no doubt mixed but Marco failed to notice this, just as he did not quite recognise the strength of emotion which had given rise to this unusual flight of fancy. 'The season is now too advanced to permit me to proceed with the second stage, the transportation of the Rock to the banks of the Neva, for the ground will very soon be too soft to bear such a weight – and, as you may imagine, the last thing I want is to see my Rock sink once more into the quagmire. Thus of necessity I must rest and wait until autumn has set in before I can continue my work. The final stage, and perhaps that most fraught with perils, will be the bringing of the Rock by river to

St Petersburg. Its weight and mass are such that no ship exists on which it could very well be loaded as cargo without capsizing instantly. What's more, the river is in places too shallow to permit a ship of any very great draught to navigate it. This final proceeding is supposedly the responsibility of the Admiralty, which, it is to be assumed, knows all there is to know about ships and such like – my task officially ends when I have brought the Rock to the river.' Marino paused for a moment at this point, then confided: 'Nevertheless, my dearest Marco, the truth is that I have grave doubts as to whether there is anyone but myself capable of accomplishing this difficult undertaking. I have not of course breathed a word on the subject to General Bezkoy or to anyone else, yet am already considering how best it may be done: it seems to me that my Rock could be floated on a barge secured between two ships – although a great many details (such as how to keep the barge intact when the Rock is placed on it) are still unclear to me.'

The drawing included in this letter showed two fully rigged ships, swallow-tail pennants furling in the breeze at each masthead, between which loomed the massive bulk of the rock. 'My brother always liked ships, he hasn't changed,' Marco commented to Cecilia when he passed the pages over for her to read, with a very understandable feeling of fraternal pride as well as a rather pleasant sense that for once – notwithstanding that touch of arrogance – his brother was showing in a better light than her own (who had just married very much beneath him).

Marco might have been amused to observe that Marino's habits had not changed either and that this lovingly drawn sketch had been made with tongue between teeth. All his life Marino tended to stick his tongue out slightly in concentration as he worked on his drawings; in the old days Marco had often teased him about it.

*   *   *

156

A liking for ships seems harmless enough and there is really nothing intrinsically disreputable about making a career in Russia, yet a certain (not necessarily unpleasant) frisson attaches itself to the idea of a man who has killed a woman with his bare hands. One does not, however, think the unthinkable, which is presumably why Cecilia occasionally allowed a trace of doubt – maybe even the faintest hint of disapproval – to pass over her face when Marino was mentioned, and had indeed pointed out to Marco with some asperity that murder cannot really be called 'a youthful scrape' and that anyway his brother hadn't been exactly young at the time. And this in turn may have something to do with the fact that, without quite realising it, Marco had gradually been coming to feel that Marino was someone for whom allowances or excuses had to be made – and thus was now feeling pleasantly vindicated.

'He's a passionate man,' he had explained, 'but not really a violent or intemperate one. I'm sure there must have been great provocation.'

To Cecilia this had sounded like special pleading.

Marino told his son in detail about the ropes and pulleys and capstans used in the raising of the rock and explained: 'Unless you are a very great genius, the truth is that the solutions you find have been lying ready all the time, waiting somewhere within your memory, so that when the moment is ripe all you have to do is call them forth and cut and trim them to fit the problem at hand.' It occurred to him from Giorgio's puzzled expression that this sort of thinking aloud perhaps wasn't very clear (although the boy was much too polite to say so); he thus added, 'When I was your age I used to hang around the quay at Argostoli watching the ships hoist their sails and load or unload their cargoes. I did the same thing later on at Venice too whenever I got a chance. And that's how it happened that when I needed to work out how to prise my Rock from its bed I already had all the answers in my mind.'

'*Vous m'avez manqué*,' Giorgio had said when his father returned to St Petersburg after the first winter in the marsh, 'I missed you' – and was immediately reprimanded by his tutor for putting his own feelings forward in a manner that was not in the least polite.

'Never mind,' Marino had told him five minutes later when they were alone, 'I knew you didn't mean to be impolite and I wasn't offended. I missed you too.'

Conversations in bed are often silly.

Marino was later to pin her down with his strong hairy arms, one lazy afternoon in Paris, and demand, 'What do you dream of?'

Stephanie, deflecting the intrusive question, laughed and said lightly, 'Oh, nothing much . . . When I was young I used to dream of getting married, girls always do.'

'Perhaps neither of us got what we dreamed of.'

This was also a question of a sort, inviting the answer, 'No, I never got married,' or 'Well, actually I *was* married once.' Stephanie, however, made no answer at all.

'When I was a child,' he continued, smiling, 'I used to dream of running away to sea.'

'So you're my sailor,' she responded, feeling on safer ground ('*Vous êtes mon marin alors*'). 'Come on then, *petit marin*.'

But this, meant as an invitation, had the opposite effect: he stopped smiling and let go of her.

'I don't think I'm really in the mood after all,' was what he said.

Sometimes silliness turns wretchedly sour.

13

MONEY LAID carefully away in a locked coffer is most satisfying; money invested in the hands of a trustworthy banker is even more so. It is not a good rule to spend all your income. It is foolish and vulgar to devote an inordinate amount of money to outward show, yet it is certainly important to be nice in your dress and not at all *bon chic* to appear to be miserly.

These were all axioms that Giovambattista had tried to instil into his brothers in their younger years, along with the importance of keeping proper accounts: shortly after his marriage he had instructed his wife, 'I would wish you to reflect carefully before each expenditure' – which perhaps was as good a way as any of summing up his views. Much soul-searching preceded his later decision that the family house in the *Carburata* should be enlarged and embellished.

It is probable that both Giovambattista and Madame Louis David Duval recognised the money-making possibilities of Marino's rock-moving feats long before he himself did. Madame Duval said nothing to anyone but followed the reports arriving from the frozen wasteland and advanced a slightly larger sum than usual to Marino when he came back to the city (fully aware of how it would probably be spent). At about the same time Giovambattista wrote to his mother, 'My brother Marino has certainly succeeded in the first stage of his mission and has accomplished what many believed impossible, namely the raising of the rock. I know you will understand me when I say it is premature to speak of such a

159

thing – indeed, my dearest Madame Mother, I would not think of mentioning the matter to anyone but yourself – yet it seems to me that, should the whole endeavour finally meet with the success which we all desire, then it is likely that the Russian Empress will reward him handsomely. Of course there is no need for me to remind you that not all royal patrons are as generous as those in whose service I have had the honour to be employed. However, should my hopes prove well-founded, then Marino's daughter may very well bring her future husband a dowry of some substance.'

The reason that the question of Sofia's dowry occupied her grandmother's and uncle's minds was quite simple: ever since information from a reliable source had reached Giovambattista in Paris as to the extent of Marino's wife's dowry (of which the greater part, if not all, would presumably in due course form Sofia's portion), he and Caterina had been delicately discussing what they called 'the plan that is dear to our hearts' – in other words, a marriage between Marino's daughter and her first cousin, Paolo's elder son Valliano. No one else, not even Paolo, had ever heard the faintest whisper of this idea.

Whether it was Paolo or Caterina who first suggested that Valliano should be sent to study in Paris rather than in Padua or Bologna is not really clear; what is certain, however, is that it never occurred to anyone, not even for a moment, that Giambattista would be unwilling to help his brother's son. 'Life in France is ten times more expensive than life in Venice, and a hundred times more so than life in Cephalonia,' the physician pointed out to Paolo with a certain acerbity, yet before too long gave orders to his wife to have a room prepared for his sixteen-year-old nephew and as he lay in bed at night debated how much spending money a young man could properly be considered to require and what sort of state his wardrobe and his linen would be in. There is no doubt at all that fashions differ between Paris and Argostoli: while there was no necessity for the boy to be dressed in the very latest mode, he should at least be *decently* clothed . . . At this point Giovambattista decided with only the briefest of pangs to forego the ordering of a suit of dove-grey figured velvet for himself until he had established exactly what outlay would be needed in order to make Valliano presentable. Anxieties about money and occasional dreadful dreams about ending up in penury were troubles to which Giovambattista continued to be prone, no matter how comfortable his income.

The thought that Marino might make some money was a new and gratifying one.

'When you are a bit older,' Marino told his son, 'maybe you might go and study in Paris.' (For a French-speaking boy this seemed a more sensible idea than Italy.) 'Your uncle would look after you.'

Giorgio thought about this a little doubtfully. 'What is it like in Paris?'

'I don't know, I haven't ever been there,' replied his father, who for some strange reason never minded admitting ignorance to his son. 'We might go together. He could look after both of us.' This image made Giorgio's uncertain expression turn to a happier smile. 'You wouldn't have to go if you didn't want to,' added Marino as a sort of casual afterthought. And a moment or two later: 'When we went away to school in Venice for the first time my brother Giambattista looked after us . . . Marco was upset and wet himself in the night even though he was nine years old. He wet me too in fact, because we were sleeping together on the ship.'

'Were you cross with him?'

'No, of course I wasn't. I knew he felt scared about going away, you see.'

'Was my uncle Giambattista cross?'

'No. We were awfully afraid he might be, but in the end he wasn't.'

This conversation took place when Giorgio was nine years old.

'Nine is a very special number,' Marino had told him on his birthday.

'Why?'

'If you multiply nine by . . .' (Marino paused to think of a difficult one) 'by seven, what do you get?'

'Sixty-three' (with only the briefest of hesitations).

'And if you add six and three, what do you get then?'

This was easy and the answer was instantaneous. 'Nine.'

'There you are, you see,' said Marino. 'You can do the same thing all the way from nine times two to nine times ten. It doesn't work for nine times eleven, but after that you can continue doing it.'

Giorgio managed to multiply nine by twelve but then admitted sadly, 'I can't do nine times thirteen in my head.'

'Yes, you can. Do nine times three first, then do nine times ten, then add them together.'

When thirteen and fourteen had been successfully dealt with Giorgio thought for a minute. 'There's another way for fifteen,' he announced. 'You could do nine times ten and divide it by two and do nine times ten again and add the numbers together.' A pause. 'Or you could do nine times five and multiply it by three.'

'Indeed you could.'

'Why doesn't it work for eleven and twenty-one and twenty-two?' asked the boy after he had slowly and carefully made his way to nine times thirty.

The easy answer is that it is because the products of these multiplications already have a nine in them. Another answer is that numbers possess an odd, unpredictable magic of their own. 'Actually it does work, but in a different way,' was what his father replied. 'Twenty-two times nine, for example' (rapid mental arithmetic here), 'is a hundred and ninety-eight. If you add one and nine and eight you get eighteen, and if you add the one and eight of eighteen you get nine again.'

'But why?' Giorgio asked again.

'No one has ever known,' said Marino.

The most interesting numbers are always those awkward ones that will not at first sight fit the pattern, that do not immediately obey the rules.

'He is small for his age, but well-formed and straight-limbed,' Marino had written to Marco a year or so earlier. 'He is of a somewhat pale complexion, never having felt the caress of that bright sun under which we grew up. *Autres temps, autres moeurs*, I suppose – by which I mean that children here do not run free in the way we used to. For much of the year it is too cold, and then when the brief summer finally arrives it is only boys of the poorer kind who swim in the river. As a matter of fact even in what is considered here to be the heat of the summer the water is really far too chilly for swimming. Between you and me, I have tried it for myself – most discreetly – on a couple of occasions, which is how I know.'

Marco reflected that his brother had probably always been a little eccentric; for one reason or another he did not read this letter to Cecilia.

Giovambattista had once declared, 'I believe marriage has proved of great benefit to my brother.' His mother had assumed that what he referred to was Marino's improved financial situation or indeed the advancement of his career, presumably brought about by his father-in-law: 'I have been appointed Director of the School of Cadets,' a letter from St Petersburg had announced, long before the rock was ever thought of, 'and hold the rank of Lieutenant Colonel,' or later, 'I am now Aide-de-Camp to General Bezkoy, who is in charge of all public buildings and construction works'. No doubt these were matters not to be despised, yet if Giovambattista had attempted to clarify the thought that lay behind his statement he might have borrowed his brother's nautical imagery and said something like, 'Marino's wife and children are a good strong anchor that keeps him secured in a safe port.' He might even have struggled to express an even more nebulous sense that the danger of exile is rootlessness, although this was not, for some reason, a worry that would have applied to Marco (and certainly not to himself): perhaps it was just that Russia is very far away, or possibly simply that some intrinsic characteristic in Marino laid him open to such dangers.

On an April day, many, many years later, when Giovambattista and Marco sat in the courtyard of the School of Chemistry in Padua – both of them well muffled up just to be on the safe side, in spite of the spring sunshine – the physician admitted, 'I have long blamed myself for not immediately attempting to find a suitable second wife for our brother when he arrived in Paris as a widower.' At which Marco quietly put his hand on Giovambattista's arm for a moment, having also been thinking of Marino.

However, when Marino returned for his second sojourn in the marsh Elena was not only alive and well but as a matter of fact secretly hoping she might at last be pregnant again (although this turned out not to be the case). Marino had accompanied his wife and children when they went for a long

164

summer visit to the Chrysosculeo country house and had found – not for the first time – that the card games played in his mother-in-law's *salon* were unexciting in the extreme and that the long light evenings tended to pass rather slowly: during the couple of weeks that he stayed he had therefore got into the habit of retiring early, and favoured his wife with more assiduous conjugal attentions than usual (before kissing them all goodbye and returning to work).

'I am now encamped on the banks of the little Neva which, I should explain, is a tributary stream of the greater Neva, at the point where my Rock will be embarked, and am occupied with the construction of a landing stage and mole,' he wrote to Giovambattista. 'I am glad to tell you that I am in excellent health and vigour, having followed your prescription for a quiet and domestic life. The result is that I have, I think, put on a little weight. I have been instructing my son in simple geometry and have taught him to play chess, for which game he shows great aptitude, confirming me in my belief that he has a good mathematical mind – had he been slightly older I might perhaps have been tempted to bring him with me so that he might learn something of engineering. However, this vicinity is not a wholesome place in summer so that, as I tell myself, at any age he is better away from it. I am plagued daily by all manner of biting insects. Nevertheless I am pleased to be at work again and hope, my dearest brother, that before too many months have passed I shall have the pleasure of telling you that my machine has proved its worth in practice: I have, as a matter of fact, remarkably few fears on this score. Praying from my heart that these lines will find you in good health, I remain your most affectionate brother . . .' The signature that followed was the compromise that Marino had arrived at for family use: a large and indecipherable flourish of initials, which might have been 'A.L.' but could just as easily have been 'M.C.'

This letter was read in Paris with anxious approval. The mentions of domesticity were naturally a relief, yet Giovambattista could not prevent various gloomy reservations from coming into his mind associated with uncrossed bridges and unhatched chickens and slips betwixt cup and lips: a feeling that, no matter what Marco said, people who display too much confidence frequently come to grief. (Naturally enough, the calm confidence of the experienced physician who knows what he is about was not included in this category.) Marino's references to the unwholesomeness of marshes and river banks were unfortunate in their timing, for as it happened his letter reached the rue du Faubourg Poissonnière when Giovambattista was still keeping to his room, having barely recovered from a fit of the shivering ague – which, as everyone knows, is a disease contracted from marshy miasmas. It was thus perfectly understandable that the physician should be distressed until late at night by the idea that even now Marino might be shivering or burning with fever and, worse, that there was nothing whatsoever that could be done about it from Paris; the feeling of listlessness and weakness which generally followed his own attacks frequently made pessimism lie like a leaden weight on Giovambattista's soul.

Since he disliked retiring to bed in the daytime, Giovambattista generally spent his periodic days of illness huddled in his armchair, wrapped in blankets and shawls, sipping an infusion of chamomile (sent regularly from Cephalonia) and attempting to read or write in the intervals between feverish dozing. Engrained habits of mind are just as persistent as old anxieties, quite apart from the fact that there is little point being a physician if you cannot make use of your own sufferings to record the progress of a disease; Giovambattista thus kept his notebook at hand, beside the small case with his monogrammed blood-letting blades and cups, and jotted down observations as to the exact timing of the stages of the illness, the timing and amount of the doses of quinquina taken, the colour and quantity of urine passed, and any other relevant information. The single word 'dreams', for example, meant the occurrence of the kind of tormenting visions which had troubled him much in his youth and which continued to visit him at such times. (Later, when he was preparing his great work on fevers, Giovambattista gave some thought to the manner in which an imbalance in the organism allows such dreams to invade the mind. However, in the end he omitted any mention of the subject, finding after mature reflection that it offered no useful ground for discussion.)

At such times, too, the whole household knew that perfect quiet was required. When Giovambattista sent his servant with a polite note to his wife informing her of his indisposition and regretting that he must thus deprive himself of the pleasure of her company for a few days, she would dutifully take pains to ensure that no slammed door or clattered dish or childish voice should disturb the silence until he emerged once more from his private rooms, pale but recovered.

'I was sorry to hear that you were troubled again by your old malady,' Marco wrote from Padua. 'I fear, my dearest brother, that, fatigued and unwell as you were, you have fallen into a state of fretfulness which is quite unwarranted. Allow me to state the matter simply: if Marino failed in his endeavour, something that personally I consider utterly unlikely, why then he would no doubt have to put up with a certain amount of criticism and adverse gossip, would return to his customary occupations at the School of Cadets and would thenceforth continue as usual.' And would possibly abstain from all amorous activities for a little while: this

Marco – who imagined he still knew quite a lot about Marino – thought but did not write. 'You need hardly fear that he will discredit the family name, Giambattista, since ours is not the name he uses. I beg you to set your mind at rest on the matter. I am fully convinced that our brother will succeed in his great enterprise, but even if he were to fail the results would be far from tragic.'

If my brother were to fail he would be most unhappy, thought Giovambattista in a moment of rare perspicacity (accompanied by the beginnings of another half-glimpsed idea: namely that an unhappy Marino meant a reckless, foolhardy, dangerous Marino.)

Marino worked for the rest of the summer on his landing stage. 'It must be of great solidity in order to remain intact in the thaw, when the river brings large blocks of ice which have a tendency to destroy everything in their path,' he told Giovambattista. 'I have thus had a palisade of piles sunk into the river bed to protect my *radier*' (this was what he called it), 'and have caused a great quantity of boulders and rocks to be placed in such a way as to form a defensive mole. At the same time I have given instructions for any remaining moss or other vegetation to be removed from the Rock's path, for gravel and fir saplings – both of which are luckily to be found at no great distance – to be mixed into the muddy surface of the ground and for more piles to be driven into the softer parts. A whole team of men is standing by awaiting the first snowfall, their duty being to sweep the snow daily from the path.'

'Strange as it may seem to you, my dearest brother' (he was writing now to Marco), 'a thick layer of snow actually protects the ground beneath it and prevents it from freezing very deeply. I am doing all I can to ensure that the ground over which the Rock will pass should freeze to a depth of at least four feet, thus forming a very hard and compacted surface which will withstand so great a weight.'

These preparations completed, Marino returned to the city to await the cold weather. With the raising of the rock the previous winter any doubts the Empress might have felt were dispelled; as a result, instructions were given to General Bezkoy and Marino found himself in the wonderful position of being able to pick and choose whatever specialised workmen he might want from among the best in the whole city.

'He's a very clever fellow from Strasbourg,' he told Giorgio, referring to the man named Figner whom he had employed to make the huge cast-iron jacks which, placed beneath the Rock and screwed or unscrewed by means of the pulleys and capstans already devised, would raise or lower it at will. ('This is how I shall raise it from its bed of moss on to my machine, and this is how I shall transfer it to my turning machine when we reach that point,' he had already informed Marco). 'Few men could have understood so well what I needed or have executed the commission so successfully, Giorgio – it was my good fortune that he came to Russia to make the armature for Monsieur Falconet's statue.'

In answer to the boy's question his father then explained what an armature is ('Like a sort of metal skeleton around which the artist builds his model') and why it is technically difficult to make such a large bronze statue of a man on a rearing horse. 'If the horse had all four hooves on the ground it would be a lot easier, you see. Sometimes they cheat and put something that everyone pretends is a convenient piece of rock or tree stump underneath a statue to support it, but Monsieur Falconet's conception is grander – he wants no pretences and his horse has to be properly rearing. It's going to rear so high that its tail will just brush against the serpent being trampled under its hind legs – at least that's what people will think when they look at it, but actually it's a clever trick, Giorgio, for you see the contact of the tail with the serpent gives it another point of support.'

'Have you seen it?'

'I've seen the preliminary model. You'll like it. The horse isn't really as fierce and wild as it looks, just very strong and brave.'

When he was younger Giorgio had been a little afraid of horses. 'He'll grow out of it,' Marino had said firmly, in the face of everyone's scoffing, and had told his son of Bucephalus who was frightened of his own shadow, of the horse that St Giorgio rode when he killed the dragon and of the bronze horses of St Marco which are the most gentle, sagacious, beautiful creatures in the whole world.

'I am not really nervous about horses any more,' Giorgio now declared carefully after a moment's pause.

'No, I thought you probably wouldn't be,' said Marino.

It is of course not possible for any great enterprise to be carried out without at least a few setbacks or problems. For one reason or another, however, Marino was less distressed by them than might have been expected. When, for example, after the advent of winter and the resumption of work in the marsh the iron balls in his machine proved too brittle and were rapidly crushed by the rock, people said cruel things about trying to move a mountain by balancing it on eggs; yet this time he managed to pay no attention and simply had new balls made from copper mixed with a small amount of tin, five inches in diameter, which remained intact and worked more or less as they should. The only slight problem was that these balls occasionally ceased moving (pressed against the side of their gutter) or clumped together (in which case their increased surface area led to increased friction), but Marino promptly placed seven men with iron rods to push them back into motion whenever necessary – two on either side of the machine and three beneath it – after which the balls fulfilled their function perfectly.

There was a sort of serenity of confidence about all this which might or might not have been reassuring to Giovambattista.

'That must have been extraordinarily dangerous for the men underneath the rock,' Stephanie was to comment later. She was beginning to find that she was actually quite interested in Marino's stories and had moreover observed that after conversations to which she contributed more than the occasional murmur he was more ardent and less prone to lapse into gloom. This ardour she had classified in her mind as 'fine as far as it goes', which meant something like 'certainly rather pleasant but I don't yet know how much money he has'. (A sensible approach to life is something you learn the hard way.)

'It's true they weren't very enthusiastic about it,' Marino replied, 'although I had thick mats like little sledges made for them to sit on and attached them to the Rock on the inside and outside of the machine so that they were drawn forward with it and didn't have to creep along bent double. And nothing awful happened to them, they all survived.' He added after a moment, 'Do you know, the thing about the whole business that in the end almost makes me feel the very greatest pride is that in all that time – two whole years – there were no accidents and not a single life lost.'

This was something he hadn't told anyone else, perhaps merely because he hadn't quite recognised his feeling about it until now; the following day he added a few lines to the same effect to article five of his book, reflecting as he wrote that a

171

woman to whom you can talk in bed just as if she were a man is really rather a rare creature.

'I am in good health,' Marino wrote from the marsh more than once to both his brothers (and once to his mother), 'and am little troubled by any of the ills that plagued me last year apart from a slight stiffness in the morning.' He himself attributed this to a less meagre and monotonous diet, barrels of pickled cabbage and beets having been brought out from the city this time, together with a larger and a smaller box from Italy containing lemons and raisins respectively. Of course, as he told Giovambattista, the fact that he was necessarily getting a lot more exercise, constantly walking backwards and forwards along the track now that the rock was on the move, was also certainly good for both his digestion and his spirits. Nevertheless, it is always better to be on the safe side: with the previous winter's miseries in mind, Marino had thus taken care to bring with him a generous supply of senna pods (for constipation), of tincture of opium (for diarrhoea or aches and pains), of salt (for bathing cuts and minor injuries: this was what Giambattista recommended) and of chamomile (for fevers if taken internally or for sore eyes if applied externally).

This latter remedy had – most surprisingly – arrived in a parcel from Cephalonia, causing Marino in due course to inform his younger brother, 'I am apparently in her good books for a change, though I have to tell you, my dearest Marco, that in spite of these tokens from our respected and much loved mother I am feeling a great deal of happiness.'

'What on earth does he mean?' asked Cecilia on reading this letter, then, since her husband did not reply at once, reread the sentence, thought about it for a moment and pronounced, 'What a dreadful thing to write.'

'It's only a joke really,' explained Marco, realising that he had perhaps been ill advised to show her this letter since other people did not always understand Marino.

There are sometimes feelings that would sound like nonsense if you attempted to put them into words. As the winter progressed Marino had an increasing sense of his rock as a living being, a sentient creature which was not merely docile or biddable but actually responsive: like a woman, for example, or a horse guided by the grip of his muscular thighs. These were more or less waking dreams belonging to those strange moments in which one surfaces from sleep, put aside as a matter of course during the daylight hours yet somehow giving rise to a more general feeling of the *fitness* of things (which is what Marino called 'happiness'). And this feeling in turn has a strange way of conferring confidence and sureness of touch – legerdemain in the literal sense of the word.

14

ROYAL ORDERS must be obeyed: the Empress of all
the Russias let it be known that she wished the rock to
arrive in St Petersburg on the 22nd of September, the
anniversary of her coronation.

'That seems perfectly possible,' Marino told General Bezkoy. 'I don't foresee any difficulties. I shall have brought my
Rock to the river bank before the thaw sets in, which leaves
several months for the Admiralty to find out how to float it
down to the city.'

The general, with other cares on his mind, did not notice
the possessive pronoun or indeed the implication that this
floating might not prove so easy; Marino preferred to say
nothing more about his doubts as to the Admiralty's com-
petence but nevertheless lay in bed during the long, dark
winter nights thinking in ever narrowing circles about how
to get the rock on to a barge.

'It weighs three million pounds, as near as I can calculate,'
he told Giorgio later. 'Archimedes would have understood
the problem.'

Marco, lying in bed in Padua with what he had described to
their elder brother as 'a fever accompanied by a painful
croup', reread Marino's recent letters and – the enforced
leisure providing a good opportunity for a reply that was
longer than usual – sought clarification of a point that had
been puzzling him. 'I have studied the dimensions of the
rock,' he wrote, 'and have noted that its width now appears
to be twenty-one feet although in an earlier letter you

described it as being twenty-seven feet – but perhaps this first figure was a mere approximation or estimate. Yet, if I have understood right, the upper part or chassis of your machine is only seventeen feet wide. I have complete confidence, my dearest brother, that you know very well what you are doing but must admit that I haven't been able to work out the reason for this shortfall of four feet. Or ten feet? I await enlightenment. I'm also curious to know what purpose the large sledges attached behind the rock serve' (Marino had sent him a sketch in which such details were lovingly drawn). He added as if in explanation, 'I have had many hours in which to contemplate this question since I am at present confined to my bed by one of those seasonal maladies that make their appearance at this time of year. Gio:Batta: worries that it may be exacerbated by the fumes attendant upon my profession; I assure him, however, that his fears are unfounded, that my laboratory is well ventilated with a hood over every single burner and that in any case half Padua is suffering from the same illness. Actually I am going on very well, making liberal use of the honey with which our much-loved mother keeps us supplied, and don't doubt that I shall be able to resume teaching immediately after the feast of Epiphany.'

In Paris and in the marshlands beyond St Petersburg Marco's brothers worried about his health. This is understandable: distance and the time that must elapse before any further news can arrive inevitably make you fear lest things might be more serious than your brother has said. If no one was anxious in Cephalonia, this was simply because Marco had unequivocally forbidden Cecilia to make any mention of his health when she wrote to his mother.

Giovambattista took advantage of the fact that a colleague was about to leave for Venice and wrote in haste, fretting about fumes; he approved of the addition of honey to – he assumed – Marco's infusions of chamomile or other febrifuge ('Honey is without doubt an emollient for the larynx') and recommended a rinsing of the throat several times a day in warm water to which much salt has been added ('The cleansing property of salt should never be overlooked' – One of the bees in my brother's bonnet, thought Marco disrespectfully), as well as the use of a croup-kettle from which to inhale soothing vapours ('You may find tincture of benzoin, commonly called friar's balsam, to be convenient and of good therapeutic effect'). Bleeding was probably not necessary; if applied, however, it should not be done more than twice and the quantity of blood let each time should be small. As an afterthought Giovambattista also sent a copy of what he called 'my account of the *Taenia*', now published, since Marco would undoubtedly find it of interest.

Marino, who had not received Marco's letter until just before Epiphany, wrote: '*Mio carissimo fratello*, I attended the service of the blessing of the waters, having returned to St Petersburg to celebrate the feast days with my wife and children – although as a matter of fact if I'm to be really accurate it's rather more a case of blessing the ice since the river is frozen to a depth of about five feet. Whichever way, the candle I lit on this occasion was accompanied by the fervent prayer that you may by now be fully recovered from your malady.' Marino thought of writing, 'I beg you to take care. Many people here have died of the croup this winter,' but decided not to, probably because to think such thoughts, let alone write them on paper, amounts to a sort of tempting of providence. Thus instead he continued, 'My heart will not be easy until I have news of your recovery. I pray you to write soon.'

A pause at this point as Marino waited for the ink to dry, after which he turned over the page and began to answer his brother's questions. 'The reason for your confusion as to the width of the Rock is very simple, my dear Marco: in the position in which it lay in its marshy bed it was twenty-seven feet wide and twenty-one feet high; in the position in which it now reposes upon my machine it is twenty-one feet wide and twenty-seven feet high. *Quod erat demonstrandum*! The reason for the discrepancy between the width of the Rock and the width of my machine is also simple: it is beneath this overhang or *saillie* of two feet on either side that I place my cast-iron jacks whenever I wish to raise or lower the Rock. And this as a matter of fact is what I have been doing these two days past, for we have reached the point where the path that the Rock must follow changes its course by something slightly less than a right angle; I have therefore raised it by means of my jacks (which are capable of supporting so great a weight that I need only twelve of them) and transferred it on to my circular or turning machine. This is a mere twelve feet in diameter, conceived in exactly the same manner as my machine proper, except that it is stronger: the beams of which it is formed have a width and thickness of eighteen inches, the bottom of the copper gutter is three and a half inches wide, and fifteen balls are used. By the day after tomorrow I believe that the turning process will have been accomplished safely, after which I shall use the jacks once more to place the Rock back on the machine and set it off on its new course. Incidentally, the purpose of the sledges about which you ask is also very easily explained: when machines of this sort are in use, they very frequently require repairs (made with either wood or iron); thus the sledges contain whatever instruments and tools and material may be necessary – they are drawn along behind the Rock in order that I may always have at hand anything I need. This is also why I have constructed a forge on top of the rock itself.'

✤   ✤   ✤

'It's a question of economy of effort,' he told Giorgio. 'I'm very lazy really.'

This puzzled his son since it did not seem true at all.

Marino had once told Marco that Russian peasants are wonderfully skilled carpenters, in spite of their lack of tools; 'Give them a saw and a hammer and they can make anything,' he had declared.

As a matter of fact, several winters previously Marino had with his own hands made a sledge for Giorgio. Elena was faintly embarrassed by this at first, feeling she'd really prefer people not to know that her husband was as adept with saw, plane, chisel and hammer as any working man or peasant, and sang or – even worse – sometimes actually whistled as he worked; however, when her father learned of it he merely laughed and commented that the Great Peter himself had been no mean carpenter, possibly reflecting drily that, as vices go, woodwork at least has certain advantages over gaming or womanising in that it does not require the spending of large sums of money.

'I like using my hands,' Marino told Stephanie some years later.

'Good,' she said, misinterpreting (something she rarely did), 'I like it too.'

The truth is that Giovambattista also liked hands. Not, I hasten to add, plump, white, manicured hands of the sort that he thought of as vicious, but workaday, willing hands, honest hands, often with callused palms and ragged nails. In his days at the hospital of San Giovanni in Turin Giovambattista had seen a great many working men with one illness or another, and had for a while kept professional notes on the bodily wear and tear induced by various kinds of manual

178

labour, on the differing types of callosity to be seen on the hands of cobblers, for example, and farmers; sailors, he had observed, have very particular calluses on their feet. On a most private level, the sight of bitten fingernails on a young, willing, working hand provoked in him both an infinite, anguished tenderness and great disturbance.

Tapeworms, of course, cut across all social boundaries. It was Giovambattista who first mentioned to the king the effectiveness of the Swiss treatment: this might at first sight seem a strange topic of conversation, but the king was feeling rather pleased with his 'Italian' physician and no doubt enjoyed the sense of being well informed and abreast of the latest medical discoveries. Giovambattista did his best to point out respectfully that this treatment could not properly speaking be called 'new' since its main ingredient – the root of the male fern – had been recognised by both Theophrastus and Dioscorides, and indeed by Avicenna, as being an anthelminthic agent, that it was rather the combination and timing of the separate parts of the treatment that were both new and indubitably effective. The king, however, dismissed this as hair-splitting. A royal wish that the subjects of the realm should benefit from the newest of cures very naturally led to an invitation to its Swiss originator to visit Paris; in due course Monsieur Turgot, the comptroller-general of the finances, and Monsieur Trudaine, the intendant of the finances, directed Monsieur Carburi and his colleagues to examine and verify the effects of the treatment and to make it public. Since Giovambattista and his friend and fellow-physician Louis Claude Cadet de Gassicourt (usually referred to in letters to Marco simply as 'Monsieur Cadet') had already been discussing the possibility of such a rational and methodical trial, this was most gratifying.

*   *   *

The cure in question had been devised by a certain Madame Nouffer of Morat in the Canton of Berne. Having in the past heard much from his brother about the manifestly dangerous practices of 'quacks, charlatans and wise women', Marco had been more than a little surprised that Giambattista should show enthusiasm for a female practitioner.

Nevertheless, 'She is a decent and sober woman,' Giovambattista had written some months earlier, after Madame Nouffer arrived in Paris. 'Her knowledge of the uses of medicines is extensive, her understanding of the doses to be applied quite sound and her demeanour simple and respectful.' (Possibly he was well able to recognise the calm confidence of someone who knows what he – or in this case she – is doing, yet there is no doubt that Madame Nouffer's manner helped gain his approval.) 'I have for some time been aware of this treatment through correspondence with Monsieur Mottet, surgeon at Morat, and have indeed applied it twice, with excellent results, as I think I have told you.' (The second patient had been one of Giovambattista's own servants.) 'Together with Messieurs Cadet, de Jussieu, de la Motte and possibly a couple of other physicians, our intention is now first to watch Madame Nouffer administer her treatment to five patients and then to record the results.'

What the book consisted of was Giovambattista's careful description of the appearance and habits of the tapeworm or solitary worm, *Taenia lata*, and of the similar parasite *Taenia cucurbitina*, as well as the symptoms that they provoke in their human host, followed by detailed case reports of the patients treated by Madame Nouffer herself and of a further five patients treated by Giovambattista and his colleagues after her departure.

What the treatment consisted of was a four-part process: the soup, given at seven or eight o'clock at night, about a quarter of an hour after which the patient should have a biscuit and a glass of white wine; the clyster, applied just before the patient retires to bed for the night (this, however, is only given if the patient has not been to stool that day or is naturally costive); the specific, given the following morning, eight or nine hours after the soup, while the patient remains in bed to avoid nausea ('It will be right for him to chew lemon or something else that is agreeable to him, or he may likewise smell vinegar, but he must be careful not to swallow anything,' wrote Giovambattista); and finally, two hours later, the purging bolus, washed down with one or two dishes of weak green tea, after which the patient should walk about in his chamber. When the bolus begins to operate, the patient should continue to take a dish of the same tea occasionally as he sits on the close-stool, until the worm is expelled. In cases where the patient has not kept down the whole bolus or is insufficiently purged by it, two to eight drams of Epsom Salt dissolved in boiling water should be given four hours later. 'It is unusual for patients who have kept down both the specific and the purging dose not to discharge the worm before dinner time,' noted Giovambattista.

The composition of the various parts of this cure was given in detail. The soup, made of a pint and a half of water, two or three ounces of good fresh butter and two ounces of bread cut in thin slices, seasoned with salt and boiled until it takes on the consistency of a *pannada*, seemed clearly to be intended as a lubricant of the intestines. The clyster was unsurprising, being made of mallow leaves boiled in water with two ounces of olive oil added after straining. The specific – the most important element, since it was this that either killed the worm outright or at any rate made it relax its hold – was prepared from two or three drams of the root of the male fern, reduced to a very fine powder, in four or six ounces of water distilled either from fern or from the flowers of the lime tree. (No cure is possible unless the worm is passed entire and intact: 'The *Taenia* or solitary worm breaks easily in coming out of the body; and if, after being broken, that end which has the head of the worm happens to return in again, this broken extremity grows and regenerates again like a plant,' noted Giovambattista.) The purgative bolus consisted of ten grains each of resin of scammony and of panacea of mercury fourteen times sublimed, and of six or seven grains of good gamboge: each of these substances was to be reduced separately to a powder and then mixed into a bolus with some conserve of hyacinth.

Marco, who as Giovambattista had rightly supposed was most interested, read this book in one session but before retiring to sleep decided that on balance it would probably be better not to show it to Cecilia: not many women are capable of looking at things in a scientific spirit. He did, however, tell her about it and quoted to her one of Giambattista's more memorable expressions of caution and understatement – 'If the purgative is too strong, it occasions too much irritation and evacuations that cannot fail to be inconvenient' – which they laughed about together in the privacy of their bed-chamber.

Stephanie, although quite untutored in the practicalities of engineering, asked one or two reasonably intelligent questions and appeared to have some grasp of the problems involved in transferring the rock on to a barge.

'The gentlemen from the Admiralty failed abysmally,' he told her. 'They constructed a barge of suitable size and allowed it to fill with water so that it would settle on the river bed – the depth of the water there is eleven feet. They loaded my Rock on to it by opening one side of the barge, for it was now at exactly the same level as the *radier* on which the Rock rested, reclosed this side and caulked it thoroughly, then started baling the water from the barge with buckets and pumps, four hundred men working as fast as they could, it must have been quite a spectacle. The only trouble was that no one had had the wit to foresee quite what would happen as the barge was emptied of water; what did happen, to everyone's discomfort, was that the weight of the Rock made the centre of the barge remain on the bottom, while the poop and prow rose, arching in a more and more exaggerated curve until the strain forced the timbers to gape open – whereupon of course more and more water flooded in.' He laughed and added, 'They spent several weeks trying to remedy the situation, but to no avail.'

'So they had to call you in to solve the problem for them.'

'So they called me in, yes. But what they wanted was for me to get the Rock safely off the barge again. The weather was becoming increasingly windy, you see, and they were afraid of losing it altogether.'

Stephanie, who had not been giving her full attention to the beginning of this account but whose imagination was struck by the idea of the curving barge, concentrated for a few moments and then tentatively offered, 'If they had put weights at both ends to balance the weight in the centre, would that have worked, or would it have prevented the barge from floating?'

'Not bad,' he answered in evident delight, 'not bad at all. In fact the barge wouldn't have floated, yet that was the very first thing I did – a sort of remedial measure, you might say.'

Marino had rather pointedly returned to the city after depositing the rock on the landing stage beside the river. If there was a feeling of anticlimax or restlessness, he never spoke of it; 'On the 22nd of September, I imagine,' he replied coolly when his mother-in-law asked when the rock would finally arrive. For some reason he wrote few and scanty

183

letters to his brothers during these months of waiting, which gave rise to nocturnal anxieties in Paris about Marino's health and a strange feeling in Padua that Marino might perhaps be in low spirits (Giovambattista expressed his worries to Marco, but Marco preferred to say nothing to anyone, not even to Cecilia). By the end of the summer Caterina for once had the most recent news – however, this was simply because Elena had written one of those periodic, dutiful letters to Cephalonia in which she reported, '*Votre fils et vos petits-enfants jouissent de la meilleure santé*' (she always wrote in French, a language with which Caterina apparently never had the slightest difficulty).

'Waiting' is indeed the best way to describe this period when life somehow seemed to be suspended. It was only to Giorgio that Marino explained, 'I am biding my time. They will need me and will send for me again.'

Giorgio would have liked to ask, 'Can I come with you?' but knew that this would never be allowed; he thus requested instead, 'When the rock arrives, can I be there to see it?'

A doubtful expression on his face, grey-green eyes full of beseeching and hope: Marino ruffled the boy's hair and said with great seriousness, 'I shall most particularly require you to be there. If you were unable to be present on the appointed day I would simply have to ask Her Majesty to change the date.'

'You couldn't do that.'

'No, I couldn't. So you'll have to be there.'

In due course the gentlemen from the Admiralty admitted defeat and the inevitable summons reached Marino. 'I am in good spirits, my dearest brother,' he announced to Marco a week later, 'and have once more been hard at work.' A brief description of the problems that had arisen followed, after which he noted, 'Clearly, what was needed was that the weight of the Rock should be distributed equally to all parts of the barge. I did not consider it necessary to withdraw the Rock from the barge (although this is what I was requested to do). My first measure was to load the poop and the prow with heavy stones, in order to force them down to the river bed once more. When this was achieved the timbers that had been gaping returned to their original form. I then used my jacks to raise the Rock six inches above its chassis, in order to put into effect the only solution which seemed to promise success: you will understand it best if I use an architectural term and name the beams I set up 'flying buttresses'. These buttress beams were fourteen in number, seven on each side, the outer ones longer and the inner ones progressively short-er, with one end fitted against the Rock and the other attached to pieces of wood fitted against the barge; to support them I placed cross-beams or struts, bolted to them with iron crosses.' A sketch was included here. 'When all this was set up, I lowered the Rock once more – with a deep breath, I must admit, dear brother, yet fairly secure in my mind that this system would function as planned and would disperse the weight throughout the length and breadth of the barge. Finally, I had the water pumped out of the barge and the heavy stones removed from poop and prow. I need hardly tell you with what delight I observed the vessel float once more, conserving its form perfectly.'

Marino wrote a similar though slightly less detailed description to Giovambattista, adding with some pride, 'The whole procedure took a mere six days – but this, of course, was because I had already conceived how it should be done.'

Once the sailors had moved the barge away from the landing stage, Marino put into effect the last part of his plan. Two ships were brought and attached to the barge with strong cables, one on either side, in order to do what he called 'relieving the barge,' providing support and protection against wind and waves. Naturally, Marino was offered a cabin on one of these ships. Equally naturally, he preferred to travel on the barge: a small, dark figure, well muffled up in a warm cloak, standing for hours on end in front of his great rock as it made its way down river through the wild and lonely marshes.

After the rock finally arrived in triumph in St Petersburg, he laughed and said lightly, 'It was my Rock, you see, Giorgio. It had been lying in its marsh for aeons, waiting patiently for me to come and fetch it.' And his son, familiar with countless fairy tales, felt that this was very probably true.

Your fate is what lies in wait for you throughout your life.

15

'My son was drowned,' he said to her. 'He was eleven years old. I loved him.'

Never having seen anyone sit so still or weep so soundlessly Stephanie was not quite sure what was the best thing to do, and thus simply took his hand in hers without saying anything and held it firmly for a while.

The children had been pinched and pale and silent, too frightened to be seasick any more. For as long as possible Marino had tried to quell his own misgivings and reassure them, though at the same time repeating voiceless prayers and wild promises to deities known and unknown. But in the end the animal instinct against being trapped, the feeling that below deck was not a place to be, became insistent: 'We'll go and look at the sky a bit,' he told them. 'We need some air.' He was making an effort to appear calm, yet as they struggled up the ladder amid the sound of creaking, straining timbers thought he felt a hurrying rat brush past his hand and could not bite back a sharp *'Dio Signore . . .'*

And then there was blackness and howling wind, a hasty sign of the cross over Sofia as he passed her to a sailor, a rope to lash Giorgio close against his own body (desperate fingers fumbling the knots: *'Kráta yerá'* he said in a language the boy didn't understand, 'Hold on to me tight'), then icy Baltic waters and a great cry for help to the All-Holy Virgin in the same language, the unthinking tongue of his earliest childhood: *'Panayiá, voíthisé mé'.*

* * *

Not even Giambattista can raise people from the dead, although Marino couldn't stop feeling that if he were only here then everything would be all right. He was kneeling amidst flotsam and seaweed, sobbing in raw, harsh gasps as he tried whatever he could think of, attempted again and again to breathe life and warmth back into the sodden, chilly, limp little body. Then simply went on kneeling, mute in the hopeless paralysis of utter loss.

Later people led him away and made him strip off his clothes in a room with a fire burning in it, made him drink some kind of aquavit. Later still – probably it was the next day – he was reunited with Sofia. When they set off once more on their journey westwards it was by road, and by then Giorgio was buried in a cold and alien land under a plain wooden cross: an everlasting exile.

Sofia never forgot that her father had handed her to an unknown sailor. Marino never ceased thinking that if he had handed Giorgio to the sailor his boy might perhaps have lived. Just three weeks after Giorgio's death, on the day that should have been a happy one, his son's name-day, Marino sought refuge from other people in what he had hoped would be the darkness of a church: it was not dark though, on the contrary was plain and bare and filled with empty whiteness – no icons, no incense, no candles (although he had half thought of lighting twenty or thirty of them for the repose of his boy's soul). In spite of the chilly nakedness of the place he sat there anyway for quite a while and cried.

He wrote to his brothers from an inn on the road, as well as managing a brief, painful note to his mother. He gave no address to which anyone could reply. In any case these letters took a long time to arrive, so that as it happened Marino and Sofia and their surviving servant reached Paris in their sombre clothes before Giovambattista had received the wretched news. And Giovambattista, usually a model of polite good manners and never very demonstrative, put his arms around his brother in front of everyone and held him close.

Looked at from a severely rational point of view, the death of Marino's son was a blow to the family. For the only other male children of the next generation bearing the name Carburi were Paolo's two, Valliano and Giovanni Battista (Maria's sons – including another Giovanni Battista – being considered to belong to her husband's family). Naturally everyone grieved, even though no one had ever set eyes on Giorgio and the only drawing of him that Marino had sent had been when he was nothing more than a babe in arms. At which age all babies look much of a muchness; what is more, everyone knew that Marino could draw buildings or machines or ships but had never been any good at faces. Mixed with their grief, however, was an understandable sense of dynastic loss. And mixed with Marino's relentless ache of desolation was a strand of feeling that would have shamed him if he'd allowed it open expression, even in his own mind; the closest he came to admitting it was when he wrote to Marco, 'I was too proud of him, I loved him too dearly' (a half-formulated feeling that what is most precious will always be taken away from you), yet could not say that among the causes of fierce pride was the fact that neither Marco nor Giovambattista had managed to beget a son.

That Giovambattista only had one daughter was perhaps not so surprising, since he had married rather late in life and – as far as anyone could see – was not of a particularly ardent temperament. That Marco too had only a single daughter, conceived suddenly after years of childlessness, seemed not just surprising but even unfair: Marino had good reason to know that Marco's appetites were perfectly normal, so that when he settled into cheerful uxoriousness with his Cecilia one might have expected him to produce a whole quiverful of equally cheerful, determined, obstinate children. But there were other feelings too which didn't bear examination. On one level or another both Marino and Sofia knew very well which of his children he would have preferred to lose, supposing that he'd been offered the choice. The result was an awkwardness, a sudden antipathy concealed as best as possible and consequent guilt on the one side and a sullenness attributed to shock and grief on the other; father and daughter were thus both relieved when what everyone considered the most sensible practical solution was found and Sofia went to live in Giovambattista's household, to continue her education in the company of her cousin Carlotta.

There is always a tormenting temptation to try to unravel the fateful sequence of events: if Elena had not died we would not have left St Petersburg; if I had not got her with child she would not have died; if I had not spoken so much about ships Giorgio would not have begged to go by sea; if I had not laughed at the story of the infant drowned during its baptism in the Neva my own child would not have been drowned; if I had never felt so much pride in my success I would not have been punished. Or (worse): the sins of the fathers are visited upon the sons unto the fourth generation; an eye for an eye and a tooth for a tooth; if I had never taken a life then his life would not have been taken from me.

None of these were thoughts that could be shared with anyone.

A series of discreet brotherly letters passed to and fro between Paris and Padua. The sober physician wrote, 'By God's great mercy Marino has suffered no lasting ill effects to his bodily health from his recent tragic experience, nor indeed has his daughter, yet our brother's spirits remain low and I fear the remedies he seeks are not such as will bring him any lasting benefit.' Marco interpreted this to mean 'whoring' – which was not far wrong although Giovambattista had also meant 'drinking too much'. (Marino was at this period a regular visitor to the establishment run by Madame Charlotte Geneviève Hecquet as well as to the rather more expensive Hôtel Montigny, in both of which places the drink was as readily available as the girls; however, whether the large sums of money he spent there bought any relief only he knew.) Marco wrote back sensibly, 'I believe that the greatest benefit to our brother will come from occupation.' Neither he nor Giovambattista, however, could think immediately what sort of occupation to suggest.

On the night of what would have been Giorgio's twelfth birthday Marino consumed a large amount of brandy and had the rest of the party roaring with laughter at his scandalous tales of St Petersburg: the child General Bezkoy had in his younger days begotten on the Empress's mother, the Empress's own tendency to fall passionately in love with a series of very beautiful if slightly louche young men and the unorthodox, not to say unnatural, means she resorted to in order to avoid any of the pregnancies which might otherwise have resulted. It was on this evening that he met Stephanie for the first time; he noted her – it would have been hard not to since, at least at the beginning of the evening, she was the only woman present – but paid no special attention to her.

At their second meeting, 'You are quite correct, Madame,' he agreed when she declared calmly, 'Monsieur le Comte, you are clearly far too drunk for there to be much point in the attempt.'

Their third meeting went better. Marino – perhaps because of that trouble in his past – had a certain sense that what was lacking in polite society was some recognised form of etiquette as regards the bedding of another man's mistress;

he had therefore taken the rather unusual step of going directly to Monsieur Pauquet and expressing his desire for an afternoon or two of Stephanie's company. A delicacy of a different kind subsequently made him refrain from telling her that the answer – slightly surprised but consummate in its urbanity – had been something along the lines of, 'By all means, my dear fellow, by all means . . . If the lady consents, that is . . . Good heavens, how very civil of you . . . *Je vous en prie, Monsieur.*'

It was, as it happened, Giovambattista who, unable to concentrate properly on the volume in his hand as he sat in his library one afternoon, suddenly found the solution.

'I have suggested to Marino that he write a detailed account of the method by which he succeeded in raising and transporting the rock,' he wrote in his next letter to Padua. 'I am fully persuaded that the work involved in the preparation of such a book may provide that employment of which, as you rightly note, our brother has so sore a need. His initial response to this idea was tepid and lacking in enthusiasm, yet I make no doubt, my dearest Marco, but that the seed has been planted in his mind since he has subsequently spoken to me again of the matter. By way of encouragement I have undertaken to provide a chemical analysis of the rock which he may include as an appendix.' Giovambattista did not feel quite able to express that other question which had been exercising him recently, namely that no matter how great one's private grief, it is somehow inappropriate – ill-bred even – to allow it to affect one's conduct. However, it is possible that Marco understood this without it having to be said, for in his reply he commented, among other things, that Marino had always tended to be extreme in his reactions (and recommended patience).

With the foundering of the ship Marino had of course lost

the chests containing not only his books but also all his papers, including his drawings. 'Then go ahead and make new drawings for the engraver to work from,' Marco wrote, reasonably enough, when Marino in due course told him about the planned book but pointed out that without illustrations it would be a poor affair.

What Marco couldn't know, and not having a son probably wasn't able to imagine, was how often Marino had shown the original drawings to Giorgio, explaining each detail of pulley and ball-bearing, with what paternal pride questions had been answered, models lovingly made and treasured, now presumably lying battered to pieces on some Baltic shore. Thus what his brothers had hoped would provide a distraction from grief became for Marino more an act of painful remembrance: a sort of hommage, if one can pay hommage to a child. Or perhaps it was a hommage to the person his son might have grown up to be, or maybe even an explanation, an apologia for Marino's own life made to this hypothetical young man. These, however, are not things that one can speak of – even to oneself – and Marco was at any rate right that occupation was a good idea. Marino drank slightly less and got to work.

When you set out to write a book the first question that arises is what language to use.

'I shall write it in French,' Marino announced to his elder brother. The fact that Stephanie did not speak Italian might have had something to do with this decision, the 'one or two afternoons' with her having by now turned into a regular arrangement. Maybe, though, it was simply that French was Giorgio's language.

'That is a wise choice,' responded Giovambattista approvingly, and set about considering which Parisian publisher he might best approach on behalf of his brother.

It is, however, neither wise nor appropriate to refer in a book of this kind to matters that are exclusively personal. 'You should not speak of these things,' Giovambattista was to protest before too long, when he was shown a draft of the preamble or introduction, then, when he read the first chapters a couple of weeks later, remonstrated in even sharper tones, 'You really must not write of your costiveness, it is not *serious.*'

'On the contrary, it was very serious, it discomfited me immensely,' Marino replied, wilfully refusing to see the point. Nevertheless, in the final version he submitted to his brother's judgment and omitted any mention of the state of his bowels, although the references to scurvy and rheumatism remained (they were, however, decently removed from the body of the text and relegated to a footnote).

The preamble too remained as originally written. Indeed, Marino's obstinacy about it gave rise to an argument that might almost have been a quarrel, except of course that such a thing would have been quite unthinkable; at any rate their disagreement caused the younger brother to declare loudly, 'I shall either write my book my own way as I see fit, Giambattista, or I shall not write it at all.' (A sudden surge of rather surprising anger on the one side: on the other an anxiety that Marino's apparent inability to listen to reason might indicate a disturbance in the balance of his mind, followed by a subsequent disturbance of the physician's own digestion to which neither fennel seeds nor peppermint water brought any relief and which led to miserable insomnia.) The subject of contention was Marino's determination to explain how he had come to be in Russia in the first place.

What he had written was this:

'The author of the present work, having been known in Russia only by the name of the Chevalier de Lascaris, finds himself under the necessity of rendering some account to the

194

public of the reasons that obliged him for so long to adopt a name other than that which appears on the title page of this book and which is that of his family. A passion, of the kind that is ever impetuous in youth but made a hundred times more tyrannical by meridional climes, led him to commit an act of violence which, although perhaps excusable on the grounds of his age, was nevertheless one which his heart must detest and which the law could not fail to pursue. The rigorous punishment which the author imposed on himself was exile – a cruel pain indeed for one who had the good fortune to be born the subject of so wise and illuminated a Republic. Moreover, in thus leaving behind him his homeland he also desired to give up a name which must have bound him to it for ever, determining to bear a borrowed name with dignity until such time as he might once more be worthy to use that transmitted to him, along with such excellent examples of blameless conduct, by his forefathers. This happy moment has now arrived.'

Marco, more tactful than Giovambattista where Marino was concerned (although neither of them understood at all why such an apologia should be needed in the first place), suggested that if this passage were to be included, then perhaps a more pronounced note of repentance might be a good idea. Marino considered this for a little while, then acquiesced and added: 'It is not without regret that the author, ready to provide his readers with an account of one of the greatest and most noble undertakings that our century has seen, must needs draw attention to himself. But if there is a time when it is permissible for the author to speak of himself, it is without doubt when he wishes to confess his faults and express a most sincere repentance for them.' And with this everyone had to be content, for Marino refused to alter a single word.

To Giorgio in the late, late hours he said, 'Please forgive me. I never meant you to have to pay for it. I would have told you about it when you were older.'

When Marino, without consulting anyone, added to his first chapter a sentence describing the loss of his original drawings in the shipwreck and the death of his son, neither Giovambattista nor Marco dared make any comment at all. 'At least,' each thought privately, 'he doesn't dwell on it.' Marino's feeling about the written word being in some ways akin to his feeling about machines, he preferred simplicity of phrasing as far as anything that mattered was concerned; he had thus stated plainly, without adornment, *'Je ne puis pas en donner les dessins; ils ont péri dans le naufrage que je fis en quittant la Russie, et dans lequel j'ai eu le malheur affreux de perdre mon fils'* – and these words 'terrible unhappiness' were no more and no less than what he meant. (It was after this chapter had been written that Marco once more robustly suggested new drawings, made from memory.)

The fact that Marino seemed to want to pass his time in what the elder brother considered slightly unsavoury company was a tiny nagging source of unease to Giovambattista during these months. Marco, when consulted as delicately as possible, said, 'Let well alone,' or words to this effect (which, incidentally, had also been his final verdict on Marino's obstinacy about the book), but all the same the feeling that your brother might in some way embarrass you or compromise your good name is not comfortable. In the end Giovambattista thus ignored Marco's advice. 'Your reputation is beyond attaint, Giambattista, nothing any of us do could possibly ever damage it,' replied Marino generously, with which the elder brother had to be content; if there was a note of defiance, he perhaps did not detect it. Certainly allowances had to be made: equally certainly it is never very easy to admit that you might love someone better at a distance than at close quarters. What Giovambattista did was to give his wife a sum of money and instruct her to have a new black gown made for Sofia, whereupon his niece thanked him prettily and he felt better.

It was probably just as well that Giovambattista never knew of the worst excesses, for, quite apart from the very real worries about his brother's health these might have engendered, there is also the undoubted fact that an uncontrolled and rackety lifestyle leads all too often to the spending of a sizeable fortune in a very short time.

This was what the physician had told his nephew Valliano more than once, adding tartly that where there is no fortune to begin with, such harum-scarum extravagance is so foolish as to cast doubts on the spender's intelligence; the boy, whose extravagances were really very minor and whose debts pathetically small, shuffled and looked at the ground and swallowed awkwardly in a manner that Marino would have recognised all too well from those long-gone Bologna days.

'Everybody wets themselves sometimes,' Marino said late one night, after a particularly excessive evening, and thought that perhaps he might have been talking to Giorgio, although on second thoughts the child was much darker and it seemed to him that he had said it in Italian, so maybe it was Marco. But these are merely foolish, drunken dreams.

Although it was certainly true that Marino had been spending largish sums of money on the pursuit of pleasures that might bring oblivion, he was not Giovambattista's brother for nothing, or at least all those serious lessons had presumably been taken to heart; thus – as he told Stephanie with apparent casualness – most of the money earned in Russia had been left in St Petersburg.

'I left it in the hands of a woman,' he said.

'You must trust her a lot then,' was her comment.

'Oh, I do, I trust her absolutely, she's as solid and un-movable as my Rock.'

'But you moved your rock.'

'True, but no one else could have.' He explained: 'She's a jeweller and money lender and she knows how to make money grow.'

(So far so good, thought Stephanie.)

Curiously enough, when Giovambattista first became aware that Marino had done what he called 'taken up with that Vautez woman, Monsieur Pauquet's concubine', he felt no forebodings but rather a sense that under the circumstances this might be no bad thing. As he told Marco, 'Given our brother's nature, it is at any rate likely to prove somewhat cheaper than regular frequentation of bordellos – whose prices here are, as far as I can gather, ten or twelves times higher than those of the equivalent institutions in Venice.'

Quite how Giambattista could have come by this infor-mation was a question that tantalised Marco for a few brief moments – some faint echo of a long outgrown irreverence perhaps – before he dismissed this train of thought firmly.

What both the physician and the professor of chemistry took entirely for granted was that Stephanie would be merely a passing interlude in their brother's life. 'He will no doubt weary of her before too long,' Giovambattista said to himself dispassionately as he lay in bed at night and pondered with impotent, irritated tenderness how best to help his brother, 'after which there will be plenty of time to think of another marriage.'

It never crossed anyone's mind that Marino would do anything as mad as marry the woman.

16

'I F GIAMBATTISTA is a little stern sometimes about women it is because he doesn't really quite understand,' Marco had once said to Marino with the tranquillity of perfect certainty. 'It's not something he can help.'

Many years later, when Giovambattista was approaching his eightieth birthday, Marco had a similar thought after a conversation in Padua about the marital misadventures of their brother Paolo. A new idea occurred to him: 'Giambattista is like the English chemist who can't see colours the way everyone else does.' However, Marino was long gone by then and Cecilia would probably require too many explanations; since there was thus no one with whom he could very well share the thought, Marco kept it to himself, having simply steered his elder brother's attention to the interesting phenomenon of blindness to colour, or 'Daltonism' as he called it, which was of course a much less fretful subject than Paolo and his wives.

In Paris Giovambattista assumed without needing to think about it (or perhaps preferring not to think too much about it) that Stephanie's charm for Marino lay entirely between her legs. 'I suppose,' he said to himself, 'that this is natural enough,' there being no doubt that a great many men – even sometimes learned men and scholars – find such charms irresistible. However, normally speaking one may expect the need for any very frequent gratification of the amative urge to wane with the passing of the years; Marino was nearly forty-nine years old when he arrived in Paris and his elder brother couldn't help hoping that fifty might prove to be the age if not of continence then at least of the beginning of some greater dignity and restraint. The belief that one's brother's experience may very well parallel one's own, although often wildly erroneous, is at least understandable: in spite of having long since come to accept as a simple, incontrovertible and sometimes uncomfortable fact the difference between Marino's undisciplined lifestyle and his own, Giovambattista nevertheless persisted in feeling that Marino's increasing absorption in his book on the rock might bode well as far as these tendencies were concerned – the creative supplanting the generative impulse perhaps. (The physician associated the writing of his own book on tapeworms with the recognition that certain things must henceforth belong to the past.) It was thus with guarded optimism that he set about preparing an account of the physical and chemical nature of his brother's rock.

No one ever questioned the idea that Giambattista was eminently qualified to write such a description, medicine being after all simply the first and foremost of the natural sciences. Marco, who in other circumstances might have been asked to carry out the chemical analysis, probably understood that Giovambattista's name would add prestige to the work; he thus contented himself by telling one brother loyally, 'You are in excellent hands' (which Marino knew) and suggesting tentatively to the other that, should a second opinion seem desirable, then Monsieur Le Sage might be a good person to consult.

'My dearest brother,' Giovambattista wrote in reply, 'I am grateful for your suggestion which, as it happens, accords entirely with my own intentions since I had already made up my mind to consult not only Monsieur Le Sage but also Monsieur Cadet, both of them naturalists of great experience and intelligence. Monsieur Palas is by ill chance not in Paris at present. My purpose is, with their assistance, to assay what may be the working of vitriol and of aqua forte upon the component parts of the rock and, further, to observe the changes which may be effected by the application of heat. Before proceeding to such tests, however, I am examining Marino closely in order to learn from him the exact condition of the rock as it was found, together with the vegetation and geology of the surrounding area.'

Giovambattista omitted to tell Marco that a slight source of irritation was the fact that Marino rose late in the mornings and was frequently otherwise engaged in the afternoons and evenings, so that these scientific cross-questionings could not follow a logical timetable but had to be fitted in randomly whenever their brother deigned to show up at the rue du Faubourg Poissonnière. Ungenerous feelings do not cohabit very comfortably with the kind of magisterial calm that befits the head of the family; Giovambattista paused for a moment, inspected a loose thread in his cuff, made an effort to be fair and continued, 'It is indeed fortunate for the work in hand that our brother possesses so excellent a memory and is able to recall with such clarity all the details I require to know.'

Needless to say, it was also fortunate that among the packages which Marino had dispatched from St Petersburg to make their slow way across Europe – to Paris, to Padua – had been samples of the rock, since those he carried with him when he left were of course lost at sea.

'You know you are drinking too much when you piss yourself without even noticing,' he told her. 'Does that disgust you?'

'Not particularly,' Stephanie replied with a certain sternness (one way of discouraging excesses in men, she had come to believe, was not to appear very impressed by them).

A crystal-clear memory may seem to its possessor more of

a curse than a blessing: 'It's in order to forget,' Marino explained.

'Does it work?' (slightly more kindly).

'No, not really.'

Stephanie made no comment, but the thought 'Well then, why bother?' hung in the atmosphere between them.

'I like her, she suits me,' is what Marino might have answered, had any neutral, unprejudiced voice asked him what he saw in Stephanie. 'I can talk to her.' If he'd thought about it a little more he might even have said, 'She makes me laugh.'

Laughter in bed was something of which Giovambattista had very little experience, apart from a strange, brief interlude one summer that was undoubtedly best forgotten.

'It is always best to be clear, to the point and as brief as may be compatible with the subject matter,' the physician had declared to both his brothers in days long gone by when he had been at pains to instruct them in the appropriate manner of writing scientific papers. Naturally this advice had been aimed mostly at Marco, from whom a scholarly career and a series of learned publications seemed more likely to be forthcoming than from Marino. Marco's publications, however, were limited to two juvenile works (this was how the elder brother thought of them), the Marine Insect letter and a short paper on a species of mustard growing in Cephalonia; his strange reluctance to put pen to paper and write the chemical treatise that everyone expected from him remained a constant disappointment to Giovambattista and 'I am far too busy' an excuse that failed to convince.

Antonio Vallisneri tried to heal the sore place in his friend's fraternal sensibilities. '*Mio caro amico*,' he wrote, 'I have read with deep sympathy your letter recently received. I can fully understand your desire to see Marco distinguish himself in print and your bitter chagrin that he has so far shown no signs of so doing, yet must remind you that, since taking up his Chair, your brother has manifested an energy and conscientiousness in his work beyond what is commonly seen. Is it not the case that the reputation of a great teacher lives on not only in the books that he may leave behind him but also – indeed, perhaps even more importantly – in the future generation of scholars who have received the foundation of their knowledge at his hands? Let us not forget, my dear Battista, that just as you and I have built upon the foundations transmitted to us by our own beloved teachers, so too will your brother's pupils; moreover, just as I feel proud to have counted Marco Carburi among my disciples, so too in days to come, when you and I have long turned to dust, other men of science will boast that the cradle in which they first drank of the milk of knowledge was the laboratory of Marco Carburi in Padua. There was a time, was there not, when we were both made anxious by your brother's youthful follies, yet with what rapidity these were cast aside once he had established his laboratory and commenced teaching. His lectures are now widely attended and his laboratory renowned throughout Europe: he himself complains that the entertainment of distinguished visitors is sometimes a sad distraction from his work.'

This statement, meant by Vallisneri to gratify and reassure his friend, did not have quite the effect intended: news of the recent visit to Marco's laboratory by the Emperor Joseph and the Archdukes Leopold, Ferdinand and Maximilian had provoked in Giovambattista the sort of annoyance that makes itself felt in indigestion and insomnia.

Vallisneri ended, 'Your brother is a great credit to you, dear friend – as I believe your own heart would tell you, could you but pause in the midst of your many occupations to listen to it.'

In the general run of things, a royal visit can only be seen as an honour. Marco had written to Marino, 'The Emperor was pleased to watch several experiments and then to grill me with the most difficult and testing questions that he could think of; luckily, however, I was able to answer all of them without hesitation and he left declaring chemistry to be one of the most interesting arts. I later heard that he had enquired as to my salary and expressed the opinion that it ought to be much greater – unfortunately, my dearest brother, I fear that the Venetian authorities are unlikely to pay much heed to this particular royal pronouncement.'

What upset Giovambattista about all this was simply the fact that the Emperor Joseph was known to have total control over all the masonic lodges in his realms and Marco, most unwisely, seemed to have been led into dabbling in such things; this, at any rate, was what Giacomo Stellini had reported, although Marco himself kept very quiet about it. Keeping quiet in itself suggests a guilty conscience. 'My brother is quite hopelessly naïve about politics,' the physician said to himself and worried about the repercussions. When he later learned that it was Anzolo Emo who had brought the Imperial party from Venice to Padua to visit the university, he fretted even more lest Marco's whole web of friendships should prove to have been dangerously subversive right from the beginning. He felt unable to disillusion his mother when she wrote with happy pride of the visit, snapped at his wife with most unusual discourtesy and suffered from prolonged and painful dyspepsia.

Marino would certainly not have disapproved of free-masonry in quite the same way as Giovambattista, yet the truth is that for one reason or another Marco had never made any mention of it to him. Perhaps this was simply due to the subtle inhibitions that letter-writing imposes, or to the fear of broken seals and hostile eyes perusing what was written (this fear, many years later, was what led Giovambattista to cease writing to his family in Italian and instead to pen letters in elegant French whose content was entirely trivial, innocent of all political comment); possibly had the two brothers met face to face the subject might have been spoken of. On the other hand it may well be that Marco's silence stemmed from some basic shift in allegiance of the kind that tends inevitably to occur when brothers are parted for so long: it is after all undeniable that people grow up at different rates and in different directions. This in turn probably had something to do with the fact that Marco felt an increasing difficulty in responding to Marino's unhappiness with anything other than brisk practicalities. However, if Marino found Marco's letters obscurely unsatisfying, failing to fill that inner ache of emptiness, he never told anyone.

Giovambattista's royal patient being indisposed and the court currently at Versailles, he was obliged to leave Paris for a few days. When his presence was required at the palace he resigned himself to a certain amount of discomfort in spite of the fact that he invariably took his personal servant with him. At the beginning the rooms allocated to his use had been small and cold, with a fireplace that smoked more often than not and a noisome public latrine situated at the foot of the staircase (never used by Giovambattista who preferred to send his man up and down the stairs with a chamber pot). Less than a year after arriving in France he had explained to Caterina, 'You cannot, my dearest Madame Mother, imagine the biting cold of this land nor the wretched misery of the constant damp. It is hardly to be wondered at that many, including my own Princess, are afflicted by an obstinate catarrhal flux of the chest – although I hasten to add that my precautions appear to be successful and that so far this winter I have escaped it.' (These precautions involved, among other things, making sure that his bed was well warmed before he retired to it each night and wearing a sort of flannel cummerbund or binding under his chemise from armpit to navel.) 'As regards the inadequacies and discomforts of my own accommodation, I have given some thought to what you suggest, yet, quite apart from the fact that I am a foreigner, do not believe that complaint in such circumstances is likely to bring any great benefit. It will be of more profit to me to conduct myself discreetly and await the fruits of developing relations.' Caterina accepted that her eldest son's judgment in such matters was unquestionably fine and accurate. And indeed after the king had called him in two or three times for a consultation matters improved and the physician was assigned a better set of rooms. Nevertheless he continued to find the palace an uncomfortable place.

Had Giovambattista not been absent from home on this later occasion it is possible that his disapproval might have discouraged Valliano from dining in the company of Marino and Stephanie and two or three other not quite suitable people (thus unknowingly blighting all his uncle's hopes of a marriage with Sofia, even though at this stage she was still unaware of Stephanie's existence).

'He's an attractive boy,' said Stephanie.

Marino, who when he arrived in Paris had met his nephew for the first time, might probably have agreed, except that various other complicated feelings got in the way; most of these were impossible to express but a little tinge of something like jealousy coloured the half-joking question, 'Do you fancy him?'

'Not especially.' (When you are on your own in life you

learn very quickly to distinguish between rose-tinted fantasy and hard, daylight reality.) She couldn't resist teasing: 'Why? If I did, would you kill me?'

Marino was instantly serious. 'No. No, I don't think I could ever do that, Stephanie.'

And perhaps Valliano was not impervious to her charms for much, much later, when Giovambattista and Marco were preparing to sue Stephanie, to reclaim the share in their family lands that Marino had foolishly left her and if possible strip her of every penny she possessed, he was the only member of the family who maintained some contact with her and tried to suggest negotiation as a better way of handling the matter. His uncles, however, put him very firmly in his place; no one ever knew that Stephanie had considered – but rejected – the possibility of encouraging the young man into closer relations.

'It is difficult,' wrote Giovambattista, methodically beginning at the beginning, 'to hear this rock spoken of without wondering of what it is composed, and why it is of so regular a shape or indeed how it came to be found in the midst of a marsh twenty or thirty leagues from the nearest mountains. My brother, who was able to transport it, did not possess the knowledge necessary for its examination. For while Nature by herself may sometimes produce an engineer, a naturalist is made only with the help of a long period of study as well as the habit of applying the senses and meditating upon the objects that properly belong to this science.'

Marino made no comment when he read this: the recent arguments about his own manner of writing had led to an awkwardness which it seemed better to hold in check rather than magnify, and in any case the habit of accepting their elder brother's authority was in spite of everything still deeply engrained. He thus vented his annoyance by writing to Marco, 'Gio:Batta: has never been willing to understand that a great deal of meditation and many years of *practical study*' (underlined) 'go into the making of an engineer. He apparently forgets moreover that, whether the engineer is produced by Nature in a prodigious act of virgin birth or begotten after vigorous insemination by the kind of study that is perhaps too rude and masculine for our brother to call it by this name, he at least practises his profession without harming a single soul, whereas the physician applies all his deep meditations to killing his patients right, left and centre.' This was unfair, first since he had recently told Stephanie with some pride, 'My brother is an excellent doctor, possibly the very best in all Europe,' and second since Giovambattista's next sentence was slightly more emollient and described Marino as having 'the disposition and the patience which render their possessor capable of minute observation.'

Marco, perhaps wisely, did not attempt to answer this complaint and forbore to point out that some at least of the contrivances of the engineer who is employed in a military capacity are surely aimed at killing as many people as possible. Instead he wrote of the subject of his own current meditations, namely what to do about the fact that a large part of the powder stocked in the arsenals of the Republic was invariably later found to be spoiled. (That the purpose of gunpowder is killing people never crossed his mind: right hands often do not bother to wonder what left hands are doing and a problem to be solved in the laboratory is simply a challenge with a beauty of its own.) He ended his letter with the words, 'It is not possible, my dearest Marino, for me to embark on the long journey to Paris and I am all too sadly aware that you may not without peril think of venturing into Venetian territory, yet – in spite of such apparently insuperable obstacles – the fondest wish of your most affectionate brother's heart is that we may before too long meet and discuss all these things in person.' Possibly Marino's small spurt of rebelliousness against Giambattista's calm assumption of superiority awoke some old, long-buried instincts of solidarity and loyalty; at any rate there was a warmth about this which had been lacking in Marco's recent letters.

To Giovambattista he wrote with careful tentativeness that, on balance, it might conceivably not be a bad idea when testing the effect of acids on the rock perhaps to carry out these experiments twice, once with the acid applied cold and once heated – provided, of course, his brother considered that this might prove useful. Giovambattista, who trusted Marco's judgment on matters of chemistry if on nothing else, followed this advice.

'The rock,' he wrote, 'is formed of a granite whose component parts are differing amounts of feldspar, mica, schorl and quartz. Its hardness is such that the workmen employed to shape it, and in particular to make entirely level the surface destined to be its base when the rock reached its final position, encountered great difficulties. Since this base was uppermost during the transportation of the rock, and in order to save valuable time, these men were set to work at once, even while the rock was being moved, and to facilitate their labours a fire of burning coals was made on it, brought to great heat by the use of two large bellows.' (Giovambattista had perhaps misunderstood the original purpose of Marino's forge.) 'The action of such heat upon the surface of the rock was at first to turn its colour white, after which small cracks formed, then blisters, and finally a vitrified substance was produced, milky and shining. This whole process required about eight hours.'

('It was a wonderful thing to see, Giorgio, my Rock on the move with a forge and bellows and a whole team of men working on top of it – stripped to the waist, most of them, although everyone else was well muffled up. Crowds of people came all the way out from the city to marvel at the spectacle. I wished you could have been there too . . .'

Elena, however, had vetoed this because of the cold and the rough conditions.)

'The crystalline parts of the rock, or quartz,' continued Giovambattista, sitting at the table in his library with his notes on all the experiments arranged in careful order at his left hand, 'were found to be harder and to be present in smaller conglomerations according as one moves from the surface of the rock to its interior. When a quantity of this quartz, two *gros* in weight and roughly crushed, was heated to the temperature at which iron may be melted in fifteen minutes, it lost all colour and turned white and opaque, with the exception of a very small part which became as transparent as water. Wishing to establish whether a longer period of heating would give a more marked degree of vitrification, I repeated the procedure; the substance, however, remained as before with no further change. The application of spirit of vitriol and of aqua forte on the quartz before it had been subjected to heating led to the formation of a very few blisters and the production of a very slight milkiness, whereas when these acids were applied after the quartz had been heated, no change at all was seen.'

He proceeded to describe the same experiments performed on the other component parts of the rock. The feldspar, he noted, when heated became white and opaque and very much more shiny than the quartz; when heated for a second time its surface took on the colour and luminosity of the best quality porcelain. Unlike porcelain, however, when struck by steel it gave off abundant sparks. Even boiling aqua forte produced no effect after the feldspar had been heated.

Valliano, chastened by some stern rebukes and possibly trying to please his uncle, asked, 'What are you seeking to find?' to which the answer was the single sharp word, 'Niente' (Giovambattista did not like being disturbed). All the same, before too long the habits of half a lifetime spent teaching reasserted themselves so that he explained carefully and more kindly, 'When you know nothing, you do not know what you are seeking. By carrying out simple experimentation you may arrive at results which may sometimes provide an indication as to what you should seek.'

Nevertheless, in this particular case the indications were few. Giovambattista ended his report, in the true spirit of scientific enquiry, with a series of questions. If, as is believed, granite is constituted of an admixture of pre-existing minerals cemented together by a 'common matter' once liquid, now solidified, then which of the component parts of this rock was the binding factor? Might it be possible that iron, which is of course of vegetable origin and hence plentiful in marshes, could be one such binding factor? ('Iron, whether as an ore to be mined or as an ingredient in the marshy mud, is so plentiful in this region that Peter the First was able to establish the foundries of Cisterbek, near Cronstadt, to supply all the needs of his army and navy,' noted Giovambattista.) Could the feldspar in the rock simply be an earlier stage in the development of the quartz? He consulted the notes of his conversations with Marino and wrote in conclusion, 'The Gulf of Finland contains many small islands on which an ash-grey granite is quarried, used among other things for the construction of the quay in St Petersburg; the lake of Ladoga furnishes a great quantity of different marbles and granites, out of which, for example, the church of Isaac is built as well as a fine mansion near the quay. It is to be hoped that Monsieur Palas, who has already contributed so greatly to the en-

211

richment of Natural History by his voyage into Siberia, will be in a position to examine this region.'

When both parts of the book were completed and the engraver was already at work on the illustrations, Giovambattista suggested that it might be a good idea if he were to correct Marino's French. Marino accepted this offer, although warning, 'If you alter anything apart from the grammar or the spelling I shall proceed no further but shall withdraw the book, Giambattista.' As it happened, however, the only points about which the elder brother felt unhappy were those which had already given rise to arguments, and – a pleasant surprise, this – Marino's French proved to be grammatically correct throughout and even in its simple way not inelegant; the only corrections needed were thus orthographical (Marino had a tendency to double consonants unnecessarily and still insisted on putting a hyphen between the word *très* and the adjective it qualified.)

In due course the manuscript entitled *Monument élevé à la Gloire de Pierre-le-Grand* (here the hyphens were added by Giovambattista) was read by some underling of the *Garde des Sceaux* and found to contain no seditious matter, after which it was published by Nyon the Elder and Stoupe, bookseller and bookseller-printer respectively. Copies were dispatched at once to Padua and to Cephalonia. Another copy was given to Stephanie who made Marino surprisingly happy when she declared, 'No one has ever given me a book before. What a lovely present!' (and apparently meant it).

Everyone knew, incidentally, that Giambattista's spelling was flawless in both French and Italian. Whereas everyone else in the family – including the boy himself – always transliterated from the Greek and wrote 'Valliano', Giambattista, a stickler for purer forms, insisted on spelling his nephew's name 'Vagliano'. It was noteworthy though that for some unfathomable reason Stephanie's name seemed to present problems for him: the first time he wrote of her to Marco he spelt it perfectly correctly – Vautez – yet in subsequent letters some months later, after Marino announced his lunatic intention of marrying her, he more than once referred to her as 'la Voté' and no one ever knew at all whether this was deliberate or whether it was just a strange slip of the pen because he was (quite understandably) upset.

However, before this dreadful prospect loomed into view Marino's book was a satisfying achievement to both brothers and their relations apparently once more amiable. The only slight cloud worrying Giovambattista was the fact that Marino seemed remarkably tardy about settling the question of his daughter's keep or handing over to his brother a suitable sum of money to cover it. The physician felt reluctant to mention this matter to Marco, simply writing, 'I fear Marino is extravagant.' To himself in the late, late hours he said, 'My purse is not bottomless.' The following day he was sharper than usual with Valliano – perhaps, however, this was merely because he was not feeling very comfortable, having just spent a fruitless hour on the mahogany chair that contained his chamber pot, so that his servant, who was intelligent and well trained, went and fetched the senna without being asked.

The other small point about the book worth noting is that, whereas Giovambattista appeared in it as '*le Comte J. B. Carburi, Médecin-Consultant du Roi, de Madame, & de Madame la Comtesse d'Artois*' et cetera, without any mention of his place of origin, Marino was described as '*le Comte Marin Carburi de Ceffalonie*' followed by his former rank and position in the Russian army.

It was at about this time that Marino told Stephanie, 'You know, if it were not impossible, what I would really like would be to go home.'

17

THERE IS a difference between home as a familiar absent place in your mind (which, however, does not have much immediate bearing on the regular, daily ins and outs of your life) and home as a distant place where you long to be, which – could you but get there – would provide a healing salve for all your wounds.

'I am too busy,' said Marco with a touch of irritation, 'and anyway, it would cost far too much'; Cecilia translated this into, 'My dearest Mother-in-Law, I cannot tell you how sorely we both regret that Marco's occupations will prevent us from allowing ourselves the pleasure of the visit to Cephalonia which we had so much hoped to make during the coming year.' This letter was written entirely by Cecilia, although at the foot of the last page Marco added, '*Carissima Signora Madre*, I kiss your hands with deep filial respect,' in the blackest of black ink which only he ever used.

Marino said nothing to anyone except (in an unguarded moment) to Stephanie.

'There is no need for ink to fade if it is properly prepared,' Marco had once told Marino, and indeed had on different occasions confided to both his elder brothers his own tried and tested recipe, specifying the exact proportions of linseed oil, turpentine and soot or lamp black to be used; neither Marino nor Giovambattista, however, had the least desire to go to all this trouble and both thus continued to purchase what Marco considered to be oak-gall ink of inferior quality. In Giovambattista's account book expenditure on writing materials – always regular – was making an increasingly frequent appearance and was invariably scrupulously specified: 'for paper' (bought by the ream), 'for ink', 'for a dozen pens', and so on.

Incidentally, if the truth is to be told, Giovambattista also kept a second account book or diary. I have hesitated to mention it since this small notebook was extremely private, its very existence being unknown even to his servants: in it were entered expenditures of a bodily kind. Some – although not many – items were underlined, a few marked with a small cross (denoting the marital bed as the place where they occurred), while most merely registered date and time. A whole series of such notebooks was to come into Marco's hands many years later, after Giovambattista's death; Marco naturally had no idea what these dates might mean, suspected that they must probably have something to do with systematic scientific research and actually found his eyes blurring with tears as he turned the pages and looked at Giambattista's tiny and illegible handwriting. This was perhaps why he felt quite unable to commit the sacrilege of burning or throwing away his brother's notes and instead had them locked in a chest and placed in the cellar, where with the passing of time the ink in which they were written faded to a paler and paler ghostly brown until one winter a sudden flood reduced them to pulp.

'My writing is much better than yours,' Marco had pronounced, coolly and objectively, when he and Marino were still at school in Venice. And this remained true: Marco's hand was a confident and decorative italic that was easily legible.

However, the notes that Marino began to make in Paris after completing his book on the Rock were of the kind where calligraphy counts less than content: personal –

though not especially private – memoranda. The content itself might seem at first sight slightly surprising, having apparently nothing to do with engineering.

'I need some introductions,' Marino told Giovambattista one autumn morning, 'perhaps you can help me,' adding that the people he wished to meet must have both practical and theoretical knowledge of agronomy.

This, if mysterious, at any rate sounded sober and perhaps meant that, in spite of the continuing liaison with Stephanie, Marino was settling down to a steadier way of life; impossible, moreover, to refuse your brother when he asks for your help – with the result that Giovambattista scribbled off two or three brief letters on Marino's behalf (one of them to a distinguished botanist at the Jardin des Plantes). He assumed that his brother's new-found interest in plants and crops was scientific, gave Marino a notebook of plain paper bound in dark-red calf on the occasion of his name-day, shortly thereafter settled Valliano's small debts with minimum fuss and felt a really rather pleasant sense of calm protectiveness. The word that came into his mind was *aegis*.

Marino's interest was focused on coffee and indigo, on cotton and sugar. Home, after all, is a place where all these things are imported in the ships whose cargoes he had long since watched being unloaded at the quay of Argostoli. After he met Etienne Bandu, recently returned from Louisiana, his notes became not only more copious but also more detailed.

Stephanie watched Marino stand by the window and juggle in silence for minutes on end with the four small metal balls that he tended to keep in the pockets of his coat, two on each side. He dropped one and swore (the language unknown to her but the general purport of the words comprehensible: actually a particularly crude phrase acquired in the barracks of St Petersburg). 'I used to be able to keep five in the air but now I'm failing to manage four,' he told her. 'I must be growing old.'

'You don't do so badly,' she said.

'It helps me concentrate when I'm thinking,' he explained. He put the balls away. 'Perhaps it annoys you – it irritates my elder brother immensely.'

These small balls were the only thing saved from the shipwreck, simply because they had happened to be in Marino's pockets at the time and had somehow miraculously remained there: they were four of the ball bearings from the model of the rock-moving machine, with which he had been trying to amuse and distract his children in the midst of the storm.

Home is of course also a place where the prestige of the family should be properly expressed. Giovambattista's decision to enlarge and improve what he called the *casa dominicale* in the *Carburata* was taken after much thought and many letters to and from his mother. Both were in perfect agreement that their efforts at embellishment should be concentrated on the first floor of the house, the drawing-room floor, where for example the old-fashioned painted wooden ceilings could be replaced with more elegant moulded plasterwork; since no one ever entered the bed-chambers above save family and servants, these could remain as they were for the time being. That Giovambattista did not consult his brothers about these plans is not so very surprising – his, after all, was the authoritative voice as regards all family matters – yet of course the expense of any alterations to the family house is something that should be borne by all. On arriving at the rue du Faubourg Poissonnière one afternoon, Marino thus found himself presented with a document drawn up by Giovambattista's man of business in Cephalonia and already bearing Paolo's and Marco's signatures.

'I hardly think all this is necessary, Giambattista. Surely my word is good enough.'

'I'd prefer you to sign it.'

A steady, uncompromising grey-green gaze: Marino took the pen which his brother had already dipped in the inkwell and now offered, and signed the paper 'Marino Carburi'. He made a large ink blot just beneath his name (which irked Giovambattista). After this document had been safely put away another sheet of paper was produced on which the expenses of Sofia's upkeep and education were itemised.

'Very well,' said Marino, and gave his brother a largish sum of money on the spot.

The reason this money had been in his pocket was that he had been intending to buy a rather extravagant present for Stephanie.

The first present that Marino had given Stephanie had been an enamelled locket which she had instantly recognised as being pretty enough but of no value. 'This is for you to wear,' he said, 'I thought it would suit you' – whereupon she thanked him with rather chilly politeness and considered to herself, 'So either he is poor or he is mean' (neither of which qualities augured well for any prolonged association with him: life is frequently disappointing). However, he then put his hand into some more secret pocket, took from it a tiny black cloth bag and added composedly, 'And this is for you to put wherever you put the things that might be useful on a rainy day.' What the bag contained was an unset diamond, of good water and of reasonable size. 'If you want to sell it, consult me first and I'll see you get a good price.' Then, tranquilly, 'And now that we have completed the formalities, Madame, will you permit me to take off my coat?'

The reason Stephanie was thinking about prolonged as-

sociations and lasting arrangements from the very first afternoon she spent with Marino was simple: her protector,
Monsieur Pauquet, was advanced in years, his children
had been scolding him with increasing frequency about
her presence in his life, and – a thought that gave rise to
considerable anxieties in the middle of the night – he would
assuredly die before too long. (Stephanie had recently been
withholding her favours as often as she dared, out of the fear
that they might prove too much for him, even if – as she later
told Marino – his demands were not so very great these days.
'It's a good way to go though,' commented Marino. 'Not for
the woman it isn't,' she replied sharply.)

The fact that Marino was not yet quite fifty and moreover
vigorous in the performance of what he called 'the genial act'
was undoubtedly agreeable, the fact that he sometimes lapsed
into silent gloom or asked extraordinarily impolite and em-
barrassing questions ('How old are you? What sort of presents did he give you?') being a small price to pay for the
pleasures he offered. 'Nothing is permanent in life,' Stephanie
told herself firmly more than once; nevertheless the most
amazing fact of all – that he appeared to want her company
and conversation on a regular basis – seemed to be one of
those unexpected blessings that you might very well go down
on your knees and thank God for.

When Marino, lying on his back with his hands behind his
head, told her that he wanted to go home to his island,
Stephanie supposed that his departure had always been
inevitable. She couldn't quite bring herself to make the
obvious suggestion, namely that his brother might perhaps
be able to help him (by which she would have meant
Giovambattista, who was undoubtedly in a position to pull
strings), and privately crossed her fingers that it might not
prove so easy to sort out Marino's difficulties with the
Venetian authorities. What she said, as lightly as possible,

219

was, 'I shall miss you when you leave.' At which he turned and faced her, watching her with a rather curious expression as he gently ran his finger from her collarbone to her pubis, lingering for a moment at the faint mark between her breasts left by her corset.

'*Mio carissimo fratello*,' Marino wrote shortly afterwards to Marco, 'I shall perhaps surprise you when I tell you of the plans that are ripening in my mind.' (The word 'plans' seemed to Marco to sound very positive.) 'I have long been thinking that our native land could very well produce and export crops other than the ubiquitous currants. In case you're saying to yourself that I know nothing of agronomy, I should add that I've recently made the acquaintance of a Frenchman who has spent much time in the New World and who has been instructing me on the manner of cultivation of various plants from those regions – for among such, I believe, are many that could well be grown at home. In short, I now want to put my ideas to the test (and hope to persuade this gentleman – *façon de parler*, as Gio:Batta: would say – to accompany me). Obviously I'd have to start on a small scale and would allow two to three years for experimentation. The only stumbling block – and it's a rather large and awkward one, I have to admit – concerns my return to Cephalonia, in that I do not yet know quite how that old trouble may be surmounted.'

'He wants to go back home,' commented Marco to Cecilia, running his hand absently through his thinning hair as he passed her this letter. In spite of being busy, he wrote the following day to both his brothers in Paris. To Marino he said among other things, 'Consult Gio:Batta: if you haven't already done so. If anyone can make things smooth for you he can.' To Giovambattista he noted, 'It is very natural that, after so many years of absence, our brother's heart should yearn for the land of our birth. I do not know to what extent the fame acquired through his feat in Russia may be held to cancel out that unfortunate episode, or at least to allow it to be buried in the past where it belongs. If you felt it to be proper, I could make some preliminary enquiries.' To which in due course the physician answered sharply, 'Do nothing and say nothing. The matter is a delicate one.'

There are some things so obvious they don't need stating. Marino was perfectly aware that he should seek his elder brother's help; he told himself that if he had put off doing so, it was simply because he was too busy investigating the conditions required for the cultivation of cotton, indigo and sugar cane (Etienne Bandu had ruled out coffee categorically, saying that it needed higher altitudes and would not do well near the sea). Nevertheless, even before receiving Marco's advice, he made his way to the rue du Faubourg Poissonnière, only to find that the king was indisposed and Giovambattista thus absent from home, so that he was shown into the *salon* instead of the library and passed a rather slow hour in the company of what he thought of as 'Giambattista's hens' – although one of them was his own daughter Sofia, whose Italian, he was glad to note, was now much more polished: 'Our brother's wife has very little conversation,' he remarked to Marco in a subsequent letter, 'though his daughter is pretty enough.' His second visit, made a week later, was more successful. Giovambattista put aside the papers on which he was working, got up and embraced Marino formally (noting that his brother had perhaps not washed so very recently), listened carefully to his ideas then asked a great many questions.

When Marino left, Giovambattista called for some chamomile tea to be brought to him – not that he was feeling ill, just that it is always soothing – and returned to work, there being no doubt that a severely methodical approach, by which each task is completed before the next is begun, enables one to achieve more in life than would any ill-disciplined butterfly-like flitting from subject to subject. (The virtues of order and consistency were as thoroughly familiar to Marino and Marco as they were to Valliano.) What he was working on was his monograph on the Nautilus. He thus set out his notes once more, indicated to his servant the exact spot at his right hand where he wished the chamomile on its silver tray to be placed, waited until the man had withdrawn, then proceeded to complete the section on the geographical distribution of this interesting mollusc. It was only much later that night, after he had written to his mother, that he began to consider how best to solve Marino's problem.

The letter from Padua about this problem – which, when it was received, required an immediate answer since any intervention by Marco might all too easily do more harm than good – also included a copy of the professor of chemistry's recent report to the authorities of the University of Padua, in which he submitted his choice of 'the best chemistry textbook to be used as a guide to my lessons'. The book chosen was Johann Juncker's *Conspectus chemiae theoretico-practicae in forma tabularum repraesentatum*. Giovambattista read Marco's justification of this choice carefully, wincing at the brusque dismissal of Boerhaave whose *Medical Principles* and *Aphorisms on the Recognition and Treatment of Diseases* had been early and valued additions to his own library. Marco conceded that Boerhaave had much to teach physicians yet described him as 'among the most mediocre of chemists' so that, as he put it with his customary lack of tact (though thank goodness naming no names), 'Your Excellencies may very easily realise what is the worth of all those others who are inferior to Boerhaave but yet, in spite of their lack of skill, are generally held to be good chemists.' Giovambattista was less offended by the statement that earlier scholars – Le Fèvre, Lémery the Elder, Glaser, for example – had been familiar with only one or at most two branches of chemistry, and this in a rudimentary way, but nevertheless made a mental note to warn Marco that it is on the whole wise to avoid excessively scathing language when speaking of other men of science, regardless of one's private opinion of them.

However, the last part of Marco's report met with his brother's approval: 'A public professor of chemistry,' he had written, 'has to rely on many authors and of course on himself, chemistry being based not on abstract dreams and arbitrary theories but on an inseparable series of connected facts which, in the hands of a skilful chemist, will multiply themselves daily and thus extend the boundaries of this science, without which the sciences of physics, medicine and pharmacology would remain incomplete. I have had the presumption to present these truths to your Excellencies out of zeal alone, and I beg you to note for the honour of my Chair and of my own obscure name that I shall be using for my lessons the book generally known here as the *Tavole Chimiche* by Juncker, renowned chemist from Halle in Brandenburg and disciple of Stahl, with a commentary by the mathematician Lange of the same university. This work consists of two volumes and has been translated into many languages, including Italian; the only difficulty which my pupils might encounter could be in finding enough copies – a problem unfortunately common here with all good chemistry books. I would therefore be willing to provide a copy of this work to a bookseller if your Excellencies would deign to patronise its printing.'

It should be noted that 'abstract dreams' were something of which in their youth Marco had frequently accused Marino, who had never quite been able to explain that such dreams do not consist only of fantasies about stowing away on a galley bound for the East but are also a way of thinking about problems. 'Conjuring a solution out of things you don't know that you know,' he might have said – except that 'conjuring' was not a word much liked in the family. As it happened, the plan to grow American crops in Cephalonia seemed to Marco to be in itself not much more than a wild dream – always supposing that Marino were able to return to the island in the first place – yet he loyally refrained from making any comment on the subject to Giambattista.

'I have always been more practical than Marino,' was the thought in Marco's mind – which, since Marino was undoubtedly gifted at making things work, might have seemed questionable: possibly, however, this thought was nothing more than a rough and ready means of expressing a sense of impatient protectiveness.

'Marco is completely impractical and has no knowledge whatsoever of the world,' said Giovambattista later in another context.

What Giovambattista had said to Marino was, 'It is an interesting idea but I fear you will very probably be throwing away your money.'

Marino almost answered, 'It's my money,' yet recognised that this statement was more a manifestation of his brother's tendency to be anxious than anything else; in any case, he was feeling pleasantly expansive and at ease within his skin that afternoon – had, under the startled eyes of a servant, sniffed his own armpits before setting out to visit his brother and thought that some faint scent of Stephanie still lingered on his body. He thus replied gently, 'I know. But the more I look into it, the more I think I have a good chance of succeeding. I no longer have a son, you see, Giambattista, and my daughter's dowry is secure in St Petersburg, so if I fail

I can hardly harm anyone but myself.' He added, 'I shall allow five years for the experiment. If at the end of that time I have had no success, then I shall cease trying.'

Money spent on a serious experiment in Cephalonia which, if all goes well, may in the future provide a source of income is certainly better than money frittered away on frivolous pleasures in the French capital. One should, however, foresee all eventualities: common prudence made Giovambattista point out, 'You may well wish to marry again, you may have more sons.'

Marino replied, 'Yes, it is very likely that I shall marry again but no, I shall not have any other sons.'

When the physician reflected on the whole business in the privacy of his bedchamber, it occurred to him that the calm certainty of this last statement was rather odd. He dismissed this thought as irrelevant, however, and devoted a considerable number of nocturnal hours to musing over the more important issue of how best to arrange matters so that Marino might enter Venetian territory with impunity, followed by a morning spent writing a series of carefully worded letters. He never told anyone to whom these had been addressed, although he informed Marco laconically that 'our brother's matter is under control'. There is not much doubt that one of the letters contained an authorisation to draw on his banker in Venice; however, if any money was ever drawn it did not appear in Giovambattista's account book – unless of course it was included under some other innocuous heading.

The thing about a properly kept account book, with vertical lines carefully ruled so that debits and credits may be entered in two separate columns, is that it enables you to see at a glance how much money is coming in and how much being paid out. The recent safely accomplished lying-in of the

Comtesse d'Artois, Giovambattista's princess, had led to a generous entry on the credit side (always a reassuring sight). This may be one of the reasons why the physician was in calm and pleasant mood when he wrote at greater length than usual to Padua, although no doubt the fact that your brothers apply to you for help and advice is also most satisfactory. After referring briefly and discreetly to his efforts on Marino's behalf and commenting slightly less briefly on Marco's tendency to reject intemperately those scholars with whose theories he did not agree, Giovambattista proceeded to deplore a lack of accuracy in nomenclature that had been increasingly irking him.

'There is, I think we must admit, no doubt that there are genders in the plant kingdom as in the animals: Grue was indeed correct in his early apprehension of this arrangement and it has subsequently been more than adequately confirmed by the respected Swede,' he wrote. 'It may thus be perceived without difficulty that the seed of a plant is as it were an *embryo*' (underlined), 'the product of a union of the sexes rather than a partner in such union. Yet in every language the generative fluid of the male animal is also referred to as "seed". There is an obfuscating confusion in the use of this terminology which cannot fail to be inimical to all rational thought on the subject, although – I must confess it – I have not yet been able to discover any suitable alternative word which could be used for either plant or animal in order to afford greater clarity of distinction.'

Marco replied in due course that his brother was no doubt right, but that since it is never in the least easy to change accustomed usages, it might be better simply to accept the lack of logic in this particular case.

It was, as it happened, Turberville Needham who had drawn Giovambattista's attention to the work of Nehemiah Grew on the anatomy of plants, published in England some

226

hundred years earlier: foreign names being sometimes difficult, the physician can perhaps be forgiven his rare spelling
mistake. If he refrained from mentioning to his brother the
rather excessively nuptial language used by Linnaeus to
describe the matings of plants, this was probably because
he did not wish – even in the privacy of his own mind – to
seem critical of so serious a scholar.

'How do you avoid getting pregnant?' had been one of the
earliest of Marino's curious questions.

'Oh, I don't bother too much about it, it doesn't seem to
happen these days.'

Marino noted that qualifying phrase but did not ask her
how many times she had conceived in the past or indeed
what had been the outcome of these pregnancies.

Neither Giovambattista nor Marco had yet thought to ask
the obvious question, namely where exactly in Cephalonia
Marino envisaged cultivating his strange new crops. Neither
Giovambattista nor Marco ever mentioned Giorgio, presumably out of a well-meant desire to spare their brother pain,
not understanding that this consignment of his boy to a state
of unspoken, limbo-like nonexistence hurt Marino more
than he knew how to say. This may be partly why those
silent, midnight conversations where so much could be
spoken of continued to take place; Giorgio was the only
person in whom Marino confided the full extent of his
project.

'It's the marshes of Livadi that I want,' he told his son. 'I
haven't yet said anything about them to anyone else because
I don't dare tempt providence . . . I've often thought about
their emptiness, it's as if they were waiting for someone like
me to come along . . . That sounds quite lunatic, doesn't it,
perhaps you're thinking that your father has lost his wits

although you're too polite to say so. But actually my plan is perfectly sane and what I've been turning in my mind is how best to set about draining them – if you recollect I've probably told you how fertile marshes are. I always meant to take you there one day.' And later tried to explain: 'The truth is, Giorgio, that I'm restless without something to do.' And, *'Tu me manques chaque jour de ma vie'* (this was in French although Marino often found himself speaking to Giorgio in Italian these days). And, 'I have always needed a place that is all my own.'

After he returned with Stephanie to Cephalonia and set up house on the edge of that lonely place, Marino invariably spoke possessively of 'my marsh' even though, legally speaking, he was only the holder of the concession to it. Maybe there is a certain justice in the fact that long after his death the place continued to be known by his name.

18

'CEPHALONIA IS not at all like Paris,' Marino told Stephanie. 'If you came with me it would be a different sort of life . . . In Argostoli people gossip dreadfully.'

'Well, so they do in Paris too,' she commented.

'It's not the same,' he said, yet couldn't quite explain how on a small island everyone knows everyone else's business as a matter of course.

And later: 'Cephalonia is the most beautiful place on earth.' This statement was made in happy, lazy mood in bed one afternoon: Marino, like his brother Marco, found the afternoon hours a perfect time for long, slow delights.

'Tell me what it's like.'

But this he couldn't or wouldn't do. He was smiling: 'Actually the second most beautiful place,' he pronounced after a moment, as he slipped his hand between her legs.

Stephanie had been thinking about the prospect of life on his distant island, attempting coolly to weigh up advantages and disadvantages; naturally enough, when you have been feeling increasingly shaky about what looks like a very uncertain future the resonance of that improbable and solid word 'marriage' tips the scales quite irresistibly. (It is always wise to grasp hold of opportunities when they are offered.) All the same, she was perfectly aware of the disadvantages on his side; it was perhaps with some feeling that generosity deserves generosity that she thus said out loud, in spite of herself, 'Your family won't like it.'

'I know – but they will simply have to get used to it.' ('I have never been sensible,' he had already told her.)

*　　*　　*

'My family don't own me,' is what Marino might have said, had he been able to formulate such an unthinkable, heretical thought.

People invariably gossip. When a little later word went round in certain circles that Marino was actually thinking of marrying his mistress – or, said some, had already married her, although this was not in fact true – Monsieur Pauquet's first thought when he heard of it was, 'What a fool,' and his second thought something like, 'Well, good luck to her – if she can bring it off.' He kept these reflections to himself, however, as also a minute pang which, although he preferred not to examine it too closely, was possibly a faint twinge of envy for someone who dared to defy his family. (He couldn't help feeling that his children had rather hustled him into getting rid of Stephanie before he was quite ready to do so.)

Someone, bolder than most, laughed to take the sting out of his words and said, 'If you give them half a chance they jump at it, it's what they all long to do. She'd only be marrying you for your money, of course – but then you know that, *mon cher*, as well as I do.' To which Marino replied without the ghost of a smile, 'No, not so, she will be marrying me for security.' When this was repeated (that tranquil future tense proving, incidentally, that the gossip was well founded), no one could see any difference at all between money and security; it was generally agreed that the little engineer from St Petersburg was quite clearly a madman.

One of Marino's rude questions had been, 'Have you got any savings hidden away somewhere?' 'Not as much as I'd like,' Stephanie replied with honesty (although 'Mind your own business' would have been perfectly justified). For some reason this touched him, causing him to feel a sudden expansive tenderness for her.

*   *   *

Giovambattista, who had never given rise to gossip, could not help but hear from time to time certain disquieting rumours about Marco's inclinations, discreetly relayed to him by his correspondents in Venice. 'I fear that Marco is rash,' was a private thought that the physician did not choose to share with anyone.

I had better say at once that Marco's offences were political rather than sexual and had to do with what his elder brother thought of as dangerously liberal ideas (part and parcel no doubt of that other foolish freemasonry business). The following year when they met in Padua and the subject came up, Marco was calm but categorical: 'I respect your views but cannot entirely share them, Giambattista. I believe this is a matter on which we must agree to differ.' By then, however, Marino's appalling conduct had caused such a distressing upheaval that Marco's unworldly naïveté seemed in comparison to be of very minor importance. ('*La condotta di Marino*' was a phrase that was to reverberate through family letters for years to come.)

One does not, of course, necessarily agree with one's friends or revered colleagues. Giovambattista had in the past had a lengthy correspondence with Antonio Vallisneri on the subject of the *Taenia cucurbitina*, pointing out in courteous but firm tones that this worm was a single creature and not, as his friend supposed, made up of a number of *ascarides* accidentally linked together to form one compound worm. He cited the observation made by 'that ingenious anatomist, John Hunter' that the living principle exists in the several parts of the body, indebted to the brain and circulation for its subsistence, but that in proportion as animals have less brain and circulation, so the living power has less dependence on them and becomes a more active principle in itself. This, he added, may be seen in both the humble earthworm and the more pernicious *Taenia*.

'The earthworm,' he noted in a subsequent letter, 'is of a much more complicated structure than either of the species of *Taenia* and is as eminent for its reproductive faculty as any reptile. Above all, it is an hermaphrodite; it unites the organs proper to both sexes, and these organs are of the most exquisite structure. The earthworm, though in appearance the lowest of animals, might exhaust the industry of the most sagacious observer who with the steadiness of a philosopher should confine himself to the examination of this one object alone.'

A letter dispatched to Uppsala, couched in elaborately polite Latin, remarked that although no doubt God in His infinite wisdom had seen fit to create creatures whose natural locus of existence is the mammalian gut, *viz.* the tapeworms and roundworms, the fact remains that other creatures are unlikely to survive if ingested alive, the stomach being a most acid environment. The cause to which that harrowing illness named *Colica Lapponum* was attributed in Sweden – frogs spawning in the intestines after tadpoles have been accidentally imbibed – is thus on balance questionable and more evidence should probably be sought. (Giovambattista felt that 'in Sweden' was more tactful than 'by you'. If a patient were to die from this affliction, then an autopsy would surely establish beyond all doubt the absence of any frogs, he mused.)

There are other differences of opinion which may be left unexpressed; Giovambattista had never, for example, shared the religious beliefs of Father Atanasio Peristiano and felt privately that his friend's conversion from Orthodoxy to the Roman church was in some sense a denial of his forefathers, yet had refrained from any discussion of the subject.

Nevertheless, such disagreements, whether voiced or not, do not call in question the fittingness of hierarchy and order.

It is quite another matter to have what is, after all, a fine and just understanding of the way the world is ordered dismissed as a mere 'view' with which a brother many years your junior may cheerfully disagree.

It is a good rule in life not to act hastily: this the physician knew. When he first became aware of Marco's childish and ill-digested ideas, Giovambattista had been visited by the thought that it might be appropriate to put an end to the regular payment made to his brother each autumn. Almost immediately, however, he perceived a meanness in this and regretted the thought; he was also perfectly well aware that such a course of action would be most unlikely to lead Marco to change his views. (In this case, 'views' was the correct word.) He pondered the matter for several nights in a row and finally decided that there was nothing to be done. Shortly afterwards he wrote to his mother in much despondence, complaining of fatigue, pain in the stomach and an inability to digest anything but the plainest food – then, as soon as it was dispatched, regretted this letter too for the anxiety that it would cause at home and rapidly sent off another letter and a parcel containing ribbons and lace for all the female members of the family as well as chocolate for his mother. A week later he wrote again, informing Caterina that an exceptionally fine dinner service of French porcelain, suitable for the newly decorated dining room, was on its way to her, each piece individually packed in straw to avoid breakages; since this porcelain was far too valuable to be sent unaccompanied, he had entrusted the crate to an acquaintance travelling to Zante, from where his mother must arrange for it to be brought to Cephalonia. There is something curiously soothing about sending off expensive presents to one's family.

Nevertheless, 'My brothers have never been orderly,' was a sad truth recognised long since.

Marco, among other things, had never been willing to arrange his library according to any rational system in spite of all the physician's suggestions and was frequently most disorderly in his dress: small holes in the sleeves of his coat, for example, made by acid burns, were not unusual.

While on the subject of dress it may be as well to note an even more regrettable occurrence that had taken place some weeks earlier. A clumsy movement on the part of Giovambattista's servant caused a drop of candle grease to fall on the sleeve of a particularly fine coat of grey-green cut velvet, at which the master raised his hand and slapped the man's face twice, with some force. This – the first time in his life that he had ever hit a servant – seemed instantly so deeply shameful and distressing that Giovambattista felt quite unable to go out that evening and sent another domestic with a note of apology to the colleague at whose house he was expected. You cannot of course apologise to a servant: the best Giovambattista could do was to unlock his medicine chest then summon the man back to his room and say, 'I was much fatigued. There will be no need to speak more of the matter. I believe the use of this unguent will soothe any bruising on your cheek.'

'It is nothing, *Signor Conte*,' said his servant.

All the same, after a fractional hesitation Giovambattista made the man stand facing the light and, stooping slightly, with his own forefinger gently applied the salve to the reddened cheek.

Needless to say, velvet once marked remains marked for ever; no amount of application of a hot iron and brown paper could remove the grease stain and Giovambattista never wore this suit again. These days Giovambattista's dress was invariably the *habit français*, in which coat, waistcoat and breeches are all made from the same material; there is undoubtedly an elegance and chic about this, but it does have the disadvantage that if one of these garments is spoiled the others are unwearable and useless. (The physician generally had two pairs of breeches made for each suit but of course in the present circumstances this did not help at all.) All the same, there is something shocking about the idea of letting exceptionally fine and expensive embroidery go to waste. Reflecting that fashions in Cephalonia are different, Giovambattista consulted his tailor: the coat was transformed into a second waistcoat of slightly less narrow dimensions, the breeches were cleverly let out at the waist and shortened in the leg, a second coat was made of plain velvet of a similar but slightly darker colour, to the cuffs of which the embroidery from the first was somehow miraculously transferred in a sort of elaborate appliqué band (this was the tailor's idea), and the resulting *habit* was presented to Valliano just before he left Paris.

It was always known as 'my uncle Giambattista's suit', was much admired and was in fact what Valliano wore when he was married – not to Sofia – a couple of years later.

'There is no fool like an old fool' was what Giovambattista thought – but refrained from writing to Marco – when Marino quite publicly installed Stephanie in the rooms he had rented for himself. (There would certainly have been a place for Marino in the rue du Faubourg Poissonnière, this goes without saying, yet possibly the elder brother had been secretly relieved when the younger chose to live elsewhere.) A tearful farewell scene with Monsieur Pauquet – the moist eyes in this case being his not hers – and a reasonably generous present had preceded Stephanie's move. 'Did you like him?' asked Marino curiously, to which she answered, 'Well enough.' This sort of brevity is often meant to discourage further questions; however, a little while later Stephanie added, 'He always treated me fairly,' perhaps feeling that Monsieur Pauquet deserved at least this accolade.

Liking does not really come into the sort of transactions of the Monsieur Pauquet variety: if you are treated fairly and courteously, you may count yourself content.

Liking may similarly have little to do with marriage, and 'love' – whatever this may be – is of course quite irrelevant. Desire is only necessary to an extent that allows marital duties to be performed and children to be begotten. Giovambattista invariably treated his wife with exemplary courtesy and fairness, dining with her several times a week, spending an hour in her drawing room almost daily and making sure that she lacked for nothing; it never crossed his mind to wonder whether he liked her or not. What Giovambattista would no doubt have liked was a son, yet when no more children seemed to be forthcoming after the birth of Carlotta he ceased fairly soon to make more than token efforts to beget one. ('I shall not bother you very frequently, *Signora*,' he had told his wife shortly after their marriage, and later, 'Too regular a practice of the generative act cannot fail to have a deleterious effect on the health of both man and woman.') In the absence of any son of his own he had been attempting to foster in Valliano that sense of responsibility which would one day render him a fitting head of the family.

Servants invariably know everything, and it was probably some idly gossiping maid who told Sofia that Valliano had dined more than once with her father and his mistress. Although not yet perceiving in Stephanie any serious threat to her own position, Sofia henceforth became markedly colder towards her cousin;

236

Giovambattista, noticing this without understanding the reason, felt more than a little put out and wondered anxiously whether the girl might not perhaps be as headstrong and unbiddable as her father.

'But how regular is too regular, do you think?' a youthful Marino had once asked Marco when they were discussing this piece of brotherly advice; 'Perhaps more than four times a day,' Marco had offered, whereupon they had both collapsed into fits of helpless laughter.

'*Mais vous êtes tout à fait fou,*' Stephanie declared (though not with disapproval) at Marino's repeated ardours. The same words, as it happened, had come to her lips when he spoke of marriage for the second time; if she did not say them aloud this was simply because the last thing you want to do if you have any sense is blight your own chances.

'My dearest brother,' Marino wrote – then paused, for he found all of a sudden that he couldn't tell Marco about Stephanie: an uncomfortable realisation that he was no longer sure his brother would instantly understand. He shook his pen impatiently, thus causing a little trail of ink blots to scatter diagonally over the paper which with a few penstrokes he rapidly transformed into the pupils of a series of wide, watching eyes, sighed, threw this sheet away and started again with an equally personal though less controversial subject.

'I have a great many ideas which, strange though some of them may seem, I have long wished to examine further,' he wrote. 'I do not recollect whether I have told you much about that prolific moss characteristic of the marshlands of the country in which I dwelt for so many years. On the sound principle of employing what lies to hand, the peasants there make regular use of it for purposes of insulation in the walls and roofs of their wooden cabins; they also, in summer, cut away the wet, dark, fibrous *substratum* that lies beneath it which, as I was told, when dried in the form of bricks serves as a slow-burning kind of fuel. Gio:Batta: believes that this material may be nothing less than layer upon layer of earlier generations of the plant compressed by the passage of time into a state that is somewhere between vegetable and mineral. For all I know he may be right, although the specimens that I had been carrying with me to show him were unfortunately lost in that sad event which took from me the dearest joy of my life. It is at any rate markedly acidic: this I was able to establish in St Petersburg.'

('Is it a sort of earth?' asked Giorgio.
'It's a strange sort,' replied his father, 'for when once you have dried it, you cannot easily wet it again, the water is reluctant to penetrate it.'
'Why?'
'I don't know. My brothers would know though, and one day we shall ask them.')

'Now, my dear Marco,' Marino continued, 'you may very well be wondering why I write to you of all these matters. The answer is simple, as I shall tell you – after first describing to you one more curious property of this moss which I myself discovered. When I raised my Rock from its marsh the advancing season meant that I must necessarily leave it for many months before embarking on the great task of transporting it. The bed on which I caused it to be placed was a layer of the moss, admixed with a certain amount of straw – an ample layer, being six feet in thickness. Yet when in autumn the Rock was lifted once more and placed on my machine, this layer was found to be a mere two inches in thickness, compressed by the immense weight into a substance of great density, both durable and flexible. My interest was aroused as to its penetrability, so that I caused musket balls to be fired at it from different distances, all of which failed to penetrate it to the slightest degree. I could not, I must confess, see immediately to what use this discovery might be put, yet considered it worthy of note. Such experiences, however, have led me in recent months to ponder much to what extent vegetable materials – and more particularly those deriving from marshes – may possess valuable and hitherto unknown qualities that would render them convenient in, for example, the construction of buildings, and whether the marshes of our native land might not hold secrets which the patient hand could persuade them to yield.'

Marco read this long account carefully, smiling slightly at Marino's irrepressible tendency to dream yet nonetheless interested by the content of the dreams. 'My brother is without doubt an intelligent man,' he told Cecilia as he handed her this letter.

It is very likely that Marco did not notice that of late Marino's letters had been becoming progressively less intimate and more formal in their expression.

Certainly statements like 'I am a tiny bit in love' or 'I am hopelessly, wildly and desperately in love' are more fitting from the pen of a carefree twenty-year-old than from that of a fifty-year-old widower and father whose face in repose has a sad set to it and whose hair is turning silver. Certainly too these things are more easily said to a correspondent whom you have seen a couple of months previously and whom – God willing – you will see again before too long than to a brother whom you have not met for more than one and a half decades. Absence and time may turn the smallest of disparities into a substantial fissure: the random vagaries of wind and weather may scatter far and wide the two halves of what was once perceived as a whole.

Yet if the earlier sense of twin-like closeness had metamorphosed into a less demanding kind of fraternal affection, this may also be because Marino had never needed or wanted more than one person to love at a time. (This habit applied to other areas of life as well: 'faddishness' or 'single-mindedness' was what the family called it when he was a child, depending on whether the current object of his interest met with disapprobation or not.) It is indeed perfectly possible that such intensely focused devotion is never fully reciprocated. However this may be, when the weight of his brothers' anger about his marriage made itself felt, Marco's disapproval was what pained Marino most.

It is an old, old axiom that there is always one person who does the kissing while the other simply puts forward his cheek to be kissed. Stephanie told Marino this one day, although she altered the wording of the phrase: '*Il y a toujours un qui baise et l'autre qui tend le cul,*' she declared, suiting the action to the words and giving rise to much laughter and delight.

Later, as they approached Venice, he asked her suddenly, 'Was it only for the security, Stephanie?'

She understood immediately what he meant, thought for a moment, then replied, 'Well, the fact that I like you helped no end.'

For some reason this answer pleased him. While in Venice, having left her to her own devices for a couple of hours one morning, he made a new will.

In the time to come after Marino's death another phrase much used by the family was '*la scellerata avventuriera francese*' – referring to the wickedness of that abominable

240

Frenchwoman who was grasping hold of the property which Marino had bequeathed to her and tenaciously refusing to let go. Logically speaking, one might have thought that in this particular case the wickedness was Marino's for having made such a foolish and irresponsible will in the first place; at any rate everyone (with the exception of Paolo who was by now in Russia and thus too far away to be consulted) agreed with Giambattista that it was out of the question for such a person to own a share of the family lands. A man less well accustomed to rational habits of mind might have spoken of witchcraft or enchantment; what Giovambattista told Marco on one of the many visits to Venice that this disagreeable business necessitated was, 'Your brother Marino was always a *mounákias*' (spoken in chilly, precise tones), which shocked Marco twice over: first because this word was said in Greek and second because it was of a crudity which he had never dreamed of hearing from his brother's lips – 'cunt-besotted' is more or less what it means.

'I wouldn't call you a whore,' Marino decided, not long before he married her, 'you're more of a *hetaira*.' This word puzzled her so that he explained, 'It's a Greek word. What it means is' (a tiny pause as he realised that he didn't quite know what it meant), 'well, what it means is a very high-class whore indeed.'

19

'YOU ARE jealous,' shouted Marino. 'Your problem is that you've never had the faintest inkling of what love and pleasure really are, so you begrudge them to others. You're envious, dear brother, and you needn't delude yourself that any amount of prim posturing can disguise it.'

'It will not, as I am sure you realise, be possible for my wife or my daughter to receive her,' Giovambattista had said coldly.

'Just as well, isn't it, Giambattista, that no one's ever told your wife or your daughter what you really like. I must say, I wouldn't have thought all those furtive little fumblings in back alleys left you in a position to take quite such a superior moral tone.'

This (fired at hazard perhaps) was an appalling thing to say to an elder brother, breaking all recognised conventions of respect and courtesy. It broke at the same time an unspoken fraternal taboo: apart from one conversation in days long past, the younger brothers had always tended to maintain in their minds a loyal silence on the subject of what might or might not be Giambattista's tastes. It was also, of course, wilfully blind to the point at issue.

Impossible to explain the obvious to someone who doesn't want to see it: 'You will bring dishonour on the family,' was the best Giovambattista could manage, not deigning to point out that back alleys (of whatever kind) are one thing and marriage quite another, 'You will make a laughing-stock of yourself. You will shame all of us.'

There are things that are better left unsaid. Marino's temper, however, was by now lost beyond retrieval. 'When it comes to laughing – if you really want the truth – the fact

242

that you apparently managed to beget a daughter in the first place reduced everyone to uncontrollable fits of hilarity. The whole court sniggered when you got married, didn't you know, all Paris was offering bets on whether you'd ever actually succeed in getting it up at all in your wife's bedchamber. And when your daughter was born everyone was naturally bursting with curiosity to see who she'd look like.'

All this, of course, was fabricated on the spur of the moment, but brothers tend to know each other well enough to be aware of what will hurt: Giovambattista had always had a horror of being ridiculed. He now took refuge in the severely medical and remarked in frigidly dispassionate tones, 'You will have a fit of apoplexy if you cannot calm yourself.'

Marino stormed out without saying goodbye.

The fact that Giambattista's daughter bore a striking resemblance to her uncle Marino was unfortunate. Everyone in the family except Marino himself had long since recognised this and laughed about it; Marino had merely thought in passing that Carlotta had the beginnings of what he privately called 'that agreeable, sulky, beddable look'. On a rational level Giovambattista certainly knew that his wife and his brother had met for the first time when Marino arrived in Paris; this, however, did not prevent him from feeling extremely upset.

The elder brother had already started writing to Marco about the whole unsavoury business; indeed, Marino's angry arrival had interrupted the letter. Now he took up his pen once more: 'Your brother has taken leave of his senses,' he wrote, 'the woman is little better than a common drab,' and Marco, reading between the lines and noting that disowning pronoun, understood that there had been a major quarrel.

A flurry of letters crossed Europe. Marino wrote to Marco, 'I am intending to marry her before returning home.' Marco consulted with Cecilia and replied, 'I beg you, my dearest brother, to reconsider your decision. Marriage is a serious matter and there is – as I'm sure you haven't forgotten – your daughter's future to take into account.' Cecilia, who, to tell the truth, had been rather enjoying the excitement caused by Marino's monstrous announcement, wrote to her mother-in-law a tactful letter, as she thought, aimed at trying to gauge what the reaction would be at home; Caterina (whose immediate reaction had been, 'Marco's wife is incurably given to minding other people's business' – beneath which thought possibly lay the feeling that no one but herself was permitted to criticise her sons) wrote back a chatty letter which made no mention of Marino at all but which included a longish and difficult list of silks and trimmings that she wanted sent from Padua.

Without consulting Cecilia Marco wrote again: 'There is of course no reason why you shouldn't take the lady with you to Cephalonia' (envisaging a discreet establishment such as their father had maintained, in the lower end of town, towards the marsh perhaps). But this letter arrived too late to do any good. The marriage had already been solemnised in Marino's apartments in the presence of four witnesses – two servants, an Austrian musician and a French agronomist. A proper Orthodox marriage: the servant of God Marino espousing the servant of God Stephania.

Shocked by the breach with Giovambattista, Marino forced himself to write before leaving Paris: '*Mio caro fratello*' (he couldn't quite manage *carissimo*), 'I spoke hastily and must ask your pardon if in the heat of the moment I have offended . . .' He received no immediate answer; however, after a lapse of time a business-like letter about property and money, making no mention of the marriage, reached him in Venice just as they were about to embark for the island. The appearance at least of some sort of relation was thus maintained – which was perhaps the best one could hope for. All the same, it is painful to set out on a long journey without having said goodbye to your brother.

'If your brother dislikes me so much,' said Stephanie, 'how will your mother react?'

'We'll cross that bridge when we come to it' (firmly intending to stare down Caterina's displeasure).

They forget that I am not ten years old, was what Marino thought as he read another letter forwarded to him in Venice, which he did not choose to mention to Stephanie. 'I cannot but think that what your brother tells me of your intentions is meant as some kind of ill-advised and vulgar jest,' Caterina wrote. 'In such matters, as in all else, you will do well to be guided by Gio:Batta: who has ever had your best interests at heart.' And: 'I do not in all seriousness believe that you would wish yet once again to drag the family name into the gutter, even were this the place in which you yourself saw fit to reside.'

Staring down this sort of thing is easier said than done, although anger may sometimes offer a source of strength. (Neither Caterina nor Giovambattista had apparently considered that a furious, defensive Marino was unlikely to be biddable.)

It was, needless to say, unwise in the first place to have told anyone what he planned to do: an even more foolish mistake to have tried to explain.

'The thing is that I love her,' Marino had said slowly – a strange admission to make to Giambattista.

'That is neither here nor there, as I am sure you will see if you will but reflect a little,' his brother had responded coldly. 'Your attitude is childish. Such a marriage is out of the question, as you very well know. Let us hear no more of this absurd nonsense.'

*   *   *

Philadélphia – brotherly love – is a wonderful Greek word. But there are other words too that possess a different kind of glitter: *philodoxía* for example, which means ambition (or, more literally, 'the love of glory'). There is *philótimo* too, which is one of those untranslatable words and has to do with one's sense of self-worth made manifest, of personal dignity, one's touchy, prickly honour which may so easily be offended. Transgressions against *philótimo* are hard to forgive.

In every life there may be a certain tension between the public and the private, between the areas where ambition may apply – for success, for distinction, for recognition, for the furthering of the family – and the areas that concern no one else, where no glory is sought but only moments of swift, strange happiness. Perhaps if *philótimo* is ineradicable, this is because it grows from the fertile soil where the public and the private selves meet.

However this may be, the feeling that the limits have suddenly been redefined without your consent is extraordinarily distressing. After Marino's final defiant departure from the rue du Faubourg Poissonnière, Giovambattista bled himself twice in an attempt to subdue the inner outrage, his thin hand shaking slightly as he applied the sharp blade to the vein; he withdrew for hours on end into the private cabinet accessible only from his library, apparently calm as he worked on his great opus on fevers yet more than usually irritable at interruption. He could not prevent himself from thinking, 'If I had known how he was going to repay me, I would not have written the appendix for his book, I would not have expended time and trouble and money to enable him to return home free from all fear of prosecution.' The shabbiness of this feeling shamed him though, so that he refrained from writing it to Marco (and indeed tore up the letter he had begun), then snapped at the servant who came to bring him lights.

* * *

If there is such a thing as a collective family *philótimo*, then this must rely for its existence on tacitly shared assumptions. Neither Giovambattista nor Marino had consciously thought in Greek for many years, yet in some secret part of their minds this word with all its ramifications had gone on flourishing, unexamined and undisturbed. It is unthinkable that brothers who have loved each other for a whole lifetime should quarrel irrevocably; nevertheless, the sad truth is that no matter how close the blood bond, brothers remain different people with separate assumptions. 'Honour' and 'family' ought – one would think – to be words whose resonance is so powerful that even the most obstinate of brothers would give way before them. Yet if appeal to such ideas suddenly proves quite useless, this may be because the weight attached to them is in the end as subjective and impossible to communicate as the perception of colour or the taste of water.

Another wretched fact: you cannot protect people who refuse to be protected. Among the things which caused Giovambattista great hurt was the brutal overthrow of a long-accustomed status quo, the challenge to his loving, protective, fraternal authority.

(*Liberté, égalité, fraternité* were words which were later to betoken ugliness and distress: it seemed to the physician that the first two were mere childish delusions, chimeras, while the third had turned so sour that any thought of it was best suspended.)

To his wife he now said, 'My brother has put himself outside the bounds of decent society. There will be no need to speak of this matter again.' At home his authority was unchallenged.

A clear and starry night, Cassiopeia high in the sky. Marino was teaching Stephanie the constellations.

'You can tell the time by the stars if you know how,' he

said. Then after a moment, with a touch of bitter pride, 'I never explained to Marco how to do it, it was always my own secret.'

'Will you tell me?' (It is usually a wise idea to encourage him to speak of the things he is good at.)

'What you need to know is the time that one particular star is at the zenith on one particular day. I chose Vega, which is in the constellation of the Lyre – it's that one, the bright one' (pointing) 'I always used to think it was my own personal star.' He closed his three middle fingers and spread little finger and thumb wide, then held up his hand to the sky. 'Look at the heavens through my fingers: I worked out that this distance, between thumb and little finger, represents two hours, while *this* distance' (index finger and second finger spread wide) 'is half of it, that is to say one hour. You can estimate the half-hours and quarter-hours accordingly. Each day stars arrive at the zenith four minutes earlier, so all you need do is count the days from the one where you knew its time in order to calculate at what hour your star will be at the zenith on this particular night, then measure through your fingers and calculate how many hours from the zenith it is, perform a little subtraction or addition, and there you are. I always faced north as I looked at my star: if it was to the west it had not yet reached the zenith and if it was to the east it had passed it. It's all perfectly simple really – people only think things are magic when they don't understand them.'

He did not tell Stephanie that the only other person to whom he'd taught this childhood skill had been Giorgio, the autumn after Elena died, six months before they set out on the journey west, or that Giorgio's star had been Sirius. He did, however, admit with a wry laugh that he had sometimes put aside his telescope and idly repeated the exercise on lonely starlit winter nights in the marsh: 'I used to think of my brother,' he explained. ('It's not fair,' an eight-year-old

Marco had wailed at the demonstration of fraternal superiority on fragrant summer evenings as they lay illicitly on the
flat roof of an outbuilding accessible from their window,
'why won't you teach me too?')

Memories of things gone for ever, determinedly dismissed
. . . 'Wait,' said Marino and moved to the leeward side of the
deck.

'What are you doing?' (She had never travelled on a ship
before and was feeling a little anxious about everything.)

'Pissing.' He proceeded to do so. 'Remarkably satisfying,'
he said, turning back to her and buttoning his breeches,
'there's a wonderful fittingness about making water into
water, we always used to like it when we were children.'
(This apparently was a happier memory.) He added, asses-
sing the height of the deck rail, 'If you wanted, I could hold
you and you could try it for yourself.'

She laughed. 'No,' she said, 'too many people about, and
anyway far too complicated.'

The complications of Stephanie's undergarments were a
source of delight but also of fascination: seams and darts
and padding and boning and lacing and ribbons and frills. 'If
I hadn't been an engineer I might have liked to be a tailor,' he
told her during one of those slow disrobings that he appeared
to enjoy, 'except of course that my family would never have
approved.' She, finding this matter-of-fact statement discon-
certingly unromantic, did not attempt to follow the train of
thought; had she asked him to explain, he might have said,
'Cutting and structuring cloth to fit,' or, of her corset which
had triggered the thought, 'It is a marvel of clever design – to
fit and mould the curves of the female body, to support
where it should support, to give where it must give, to
withstand tensions and torsions as you bend or raise your
arms . . .'

What he might have said – but didn't – long, long years earlier as he winced under his father's leather strap was, 'I like to see how things work.' Unfortunately, however, the purest and most disinterested scientific curiosity is as nothing when set against the fact that a mother's body – and by extension the garment that shapes it – is forbidden territory once you have passed the age for suckling.

Cassiopeia reclines in the sky in starry ease. Stephanie could of course recline on a chaise-longue, could raise her arms, thanks to the gussets under the sleeves of her shift, and clasp them provocatively behind her head; what she could not easily do when dressed was bend forwards from the waist, this being prevented by the smooth, flat, rigid piece of wood that formed the front part of her corset, pushing her breasts upwards and apart. Marino, who liked undressing women and had noted the slight involuntary sigh that invariably accompanies the removal of the corset, always felt great tenderness for the small red mark left where the wooden bone presses between the breasts, tended indeed to kiss this spot first: a preliminary ritual before other nuzzlings and kissings.

What Marino also liked was to slip his hand under the skirts and petticoats of a seated woman, slide it up her leg to the top of her stocking and beyond, feeling the warm flesh of a bare thigh and then – if she was in a co-operative mood – the warmer, sweeter, damp hairiness. In the past when they were once comparing notes Marco had agreed, declaring cheerfully, 'If women wore drawers it wouldn't be half as much fun.' These days, however, he was more serious and had apparently left off the pursuit of such delights: this Marino had realised even before they met once more in Venice. But on board ship Stephanie was not co-operative. 'Don't, please don't,' she pleaded, 'people will see.' Tension in her clamped thighs, a faint hint of desperation in her voice although she had never much minded who saw what in the past: he suspected with some amusement that she might be trying to behave in the manner she thought suitable for a newly married countess. He desisted.

'Choose a star for yourself,' he told her the following evening (after all, one has to do something to while away the hours).
'Very well,' she said, 'I shall choose that one.'
'An excellent choice, *chère Comtesse*' (he was teasing her), 'because it's called Venus. Only as a matter of fact it's not a star.' She looked puzzled by this. 'It's a planet,' he explained.
'What's the difference?'
'One sort moves – planets – and the other doesn't.'
This might have appeared to make sense except that his time-telling, if she had understood right, depended on the movement of a star. He was not at all put out when she remarked on this. 'Yes, I know,' he said, 'we speak of them moving because it looks as if they move – but they don't, it's the earth that turns.'
He was silent for a little while, then said softly, 'My son liked the night sky.'

'Neptune was the god of the sea,' Giorgio had declared confidently, for he knew such things: there was great delight that the ship they were to travel on was called *Neptunus*. And later that evening, after they had settled their possessions as best they could in the limited space and explored the ship and discovered where they could relieve themselves (Giorgio was getting a little restive and anxious about this, as Marino suddenly realised), father and son wrapped up warmly and gazed at the darkening spring sky, taking turns with the telescope.
'How do you know the earth is revolving when you can't feel it?' asked the boy.
Marino thought about this for a minute, then answered, 'I

don't really. I don't know it of my own knowledge, I take it on trust. Learned men who have devoted lifetimes to a minute study of the celestial bodies tell me it is so and I see no reason to disbelieve them because it's as good an explanation as any for the things we can see.' He added, 'One way of testing whether things are true, Giorgio, is seeing whether they *fit*.'

In their rather cramped cabin Marino and his son were sleeping together for the first time in their lives. It occurred to the father that his son's body fitted perfectly against his own.

'Is there a planet called Neptune?' Giorgio asked before they settled down for the night.

'There ought to be but actually there isn't.'

'Maybe it's because Neptune is a sea god not a sky god.'

Maybe it is because Neptune is a cruel god.

'Allow me to present my new *Contessa*,' was what Marino had said to Marco, no doubt hoping that if a sort of joke could be made of it, then matters might run more smoothly. The fact that this meeting was in Venice rather than in Padua was uncomfortable; Marino had taken it for granted that he and Stephanie would pass a week or two in his brother's house but was given to understand in a letter awaiting him at the inn in which everyone stayed after crossing the mountains that this was not desirable. 'Send me word as soon as you arrive in Venice,' Marco instructed firmly, 'and I shall come to find you there.' Cecilia, who had been dying to meet her husband's wicked brother and the even wickeder mistress-turned-wife, attempted to suggest that there were various things she needed in Venice, yet rapidly recognised that Marco's decision to go alone was final and for once said nothing further.

Stephanie, who had never met Giovambattista and who had understood with a sudden clarity the reason for

Marino's restlessness and upset stomach as they approached Venice, felt apprehensive about meeting this second brother (and was cross with herself for such quailing). She thus dressed carefully when the appointed day arrived and resolved to say as little as possible, no matter what the provocation. As it turned out, Marco was courteous enough, if cool; the conversation between the brothers seemed strangely formal and nothing very personal was discussed. The following day she spent largely by herself while Marino and Marco met again and dined alone together. She never asked what they'd spoken of and he never told her – judging by his moody silence and total lack of any amorous inclination, it was presumably not very satisfactory to him. In spite of this, his stomach seemed to have recovered.

One of the things that Marco had said in front of her, right at the beginning as if he needed to get it over with, was, 'I am afraid I shall be unable to stay for more than a couple of days. My pupils await me . . .' Stephanie felt a rather surprising pang of something almost like protective sympathy (however you look at it, a couple of days after a separation of nearly seventeen years does seem lacking in generosity); Marino let the statement pass without comment. Nevertheless, after an uncomfortably stiff farewell on the Saturday morning two days later (Marino had got up early for this purpose), he suddenly called out 'Marco . . .' in a sharp voice as his brother moved away, then, when Marco turned round, remarked with a sort of neutral, puzzled curiosity, 'I'm quite sure you don't really lecture on Sundays, do you?' At which Marco came back and hugged him long and hard and said, 'Marino, Marino, *fratello mio*, you always were a fool.'

Marino sat up late by himself that night and the next, long after she had gone to bed. It was three days later that he laid his juggling balls aside, announced, 'I'm going to leave you alone again, Stephanie,' and went out to make his will.

20

'I LOVED MY son,' he told her, 'I loved him *entirely*' (there did not seem to be any other way to express it), 'but I never got an erection when I held him close to me.'

Stephanie, not often caught off balance, was shocked by this. 'He was your child, *bon Dieu*, of course you didn't . . .'

Marino continued with the thought: 'Yet it's strange, is it not, to love someone, to love every inch of his body, and still feel no desire.'

'It isn't strange at all' (very firmly: a bit of common sense is probably good for him when he's in this kind of mood). 'It's perfectly natural, anything else would have been most unnatural.'

He was silent for a while, then offered, 'Come to think of it, I never felt that way about my brother either.'

Well, thank heavens for that, thought Stephanie but said nothing.

In Greek there are two different words for love: *eros*, which covers passion and obsessive preoccupation with the loved one and sexual love, and *agape*, which covers calm, deep, abiding, often non-sexual love (naturally the two may overlap). Marino, speaking in French, certainly did not have these words in mind yet was perhaps groping to find a third term, a meaning that would distinguish between the broadly erotic and the more strictly genital; being unaccustomed to thinking about feelings, he had not recognised quite what he was trying to say, namely that all his loves contained a fair dose of *eros*. He did not tell Stephanie about the private farewell to Giorgio: how he had unwrapped his child, laid him naked on

254

the ground in the chilly barn (hastily scrubbed out but still smelling of cows) in which the bodies of those washed ashore awaited burial, then knelt beside him and kissed him slowly all over, from head to toe, with the tenderest brushing of lips. Someone had come into the barn behind him, said something in a language that Marino did not understand, yet he neither turned nor ceased his careful, gentle communion and whoever it was soon went away again.

He did, however, try to tell her about riding with Giorgio wrapped in the folds of his fur-lined cloak on the saddle in front of him when the boy was small: 'I held him close against me because I wanted him not to be afraid, he didn't much like horses . . . and anyway it was cold, I wanted to keep him warm . . .'

Stephanie said, 'Let it be.' It occurred to her for the first time that if his son had been alive he would not have married her. (So his loss was my gain.) 'Let it be,' she said again, 'don't torment yourself.'

One of the reasons Marino had been letting his mind wander through this unfamiliar, halting contemplation of the various manifestations of love was that such ideas somehow helped him not to think the most tormenting thought of all, which in spite of the passage of time continued to lie in wait for him at unwary moments. This thought was a very simple and terrible one: I let him drown, I did not keep him safe. It was also, as it happened, untrue; for although Marino and everyone else always supposed that Giorgio had drowned, the boy's lungs had no water in them when he died – merely the icy cold had been too great for his small body to withstand.

Very naturally, Giovambattista had made a new will after his marriage and had altered it once more after the birth of his daughter. Shortly after Marino left Paris he changed it yet again: the main clauses remained as before but the physician's share in the family property in Cephalonia was now 'to be divided into two equal parts, which I bequeath respectively to my two brothers, Marco and Paolo Carburi'.

The other thing that Giovambattista did, at about the same time, was to get out all Marino's letters – stored in neatly tied, dated bundles, one for each year – and burn them in the fireplace in his library: a repeated brief spluttering flare as the sealing wax melted and caught fire, a careful use of the poker to make sure that no page remained unconsumed by the flames. His servant (who of course knew exactly what had happened) was a little frightened by the calmness with which this incineration was carried out and wondered which medicine might be required later that night; in the end it turned out that none was needed, although before retiring to bed Giovambattista allowed himself the private, controlled comfort of opening the vein in his left arm and bleeding himself rather more copiously than he usually judged prudent.

Domestics invariably know everything and to begin with Giovambattista's personal servant actually knew rather more about Stephanie than his master did; this state of affairs was soon remedied, however, when the physician systematically set himself to find out whatever he could about her past life. It is unlikely that he was already thinking of a lawsuit, so one can only assume that the collecting of information was somehow satisfying for its own sake. Giovambattista also spent quite a lot of effort and a certain amount of money attempting to follow up a hitherto disregarded rumour that his brother had contracted another marriage before leaving Russia – bigamy suddenly seeming just the kind of sordid, messy trouble that Marino would be likely to get into. These attempts were fruitless, however, for the simple reason that the rumours were untrue: a brief and passionate liaison there may have been just after Elena's death, possibly a few rash promises, but certainly no suspicion of any priest or marriage. Paolo, who had set off for Russia just before Marino left Paris, armed with letters of recommendation to General Bezkoy and General Melissino as well of course as to the Chrysosculeo family, reported that their brother was rather favourably viewed in St Petersburg. Giovambattista ceased his searches and felt for a moment almost ashamed at having instituted them (although this feeling was rapidly dismissed: it is, after all, perfectly proper for the head of the family to know whatever is to be known).

Caterina, incidentally, also burnt Marino's letters, but this was only later, after his death: a sense perhaps of a page needing to be turned firmly against all regrets. Marco was subsequently told of Giambattista's remorseless pyre but somehow found himself unable to follow suit: in Padua Marino's letters were thus simply put away in an old chest and stored in the cellar. To his eldest brother Marco wrote, 'There is no doubt that it has all been a most unfortunate business. However, what is done is done and I fear we shall just have to make the best of it.'

'I shall draw you something and you must guess what it is.'

The first drawing seemed to be easy. She laughed. 'It's what you see when a woman lies with her legs wide apart, it's her private parts.' (More than one of her protectors having had a taste for mirrors, the sight was perfectly familiar to her.)

'Wrong. It's a kind of mollusc called a clam.' She looked doubtful. 'Look, I'll rotate it by one hundred and eighty degrees and you'll see.' He did another drawing, this time with the shell in which this creature lived more recognisable. 'I didn't make it up,' he explained, 'I copied it out of a book in my brother's library.'

The next drawing held no traps.

'It's a house,' said Stephanie.

'Quite correct. It's the house that I shall build for us when my marsh bears fruit.'

The house in the *Carburata* seemed smaller to Marino than the way he remembered it, in spite of Giambattista's new rooms built on what had been part of the garden. Their stay there was not comfortable.

'It doesn't matter at all,' he said when Stephanie started bleeding all over the second best sheets with which their bed had been made up. 'They can be washed, it's what servants are for. It will give them all something to talk about – they were going to have a good look at our sheets anyway, of that you can be sure.'

That the servants should inform their mistress was only natural; speculation of a discreet kind as to the childbearing capacities of Marino's new wife had been indulged in by the entire household and Stephanie's figure carefully scrutinised when they arrived. (Servants are always the first to know who is pregnant and who is not, as well as who might be, should be, could be or couldn't be: even Giovambattista's servants had sometimes in the past known more about his life than their master imagined.)

Caterina, whom her son had not seen for a quarter of a century, also seemed smaller, although unfortunately her authority was not commensurately diminished; if anything, the unrelieved black silk of her widow's garb gave her even greater power to inspire dread into the wayward and prodigal. Her hair had turned quite white by now yet her eyesight seemed undimmed by age, that acerbic dark gaze apparently as capable as ever of penetrating the private recesses of her second son's soul. For the first days after their arrival Marino succeeded in avoiding being alone with her. A direct summons, however, could not be disobeyed, so that he found himself standing before her with bowed head, waiting until she had finished what she wished to say. Possibly the fact that he said nothing at all, simply listened to her in silence then kissed her hand politely and left the room, was a source of additional annoyance: 'dumb insolence' is what this had been called when he was a child. Since neither Marino nor his mother spoke of this interview to anyone, whatever was said remained between the two of them.

Marino wondered how his brother Paolo had managed to live here for so many years and determined to complete as rapidly as possible the last formalities concerning the concession to cultivate the marsh.

'Don't pay too much attention,' he told Stephanie, 'we shall leave for Lixouri as soon as we may.'

'It's not even as if she were good looking,' said the family, who had been expecting a voluptuous siren.

'She's not very young, sort of sandy in colouring with a few freckles and crooked teeth and nothing much in the way of breasts – scrawny is the best way to describe her really,' Marco had said in reply to Cecilia's insistent questioning. Stephanie's appearance had confounded him: Marino, as he remembered, had always liked them plump and dark, had in the past held forth rapturously on the charms of really black pubic hair and a corresponding thick, dark tuft in the armpit, and had once even maintained that the faintest hint of a moustache on a woman's upper lip – 'just a sulky little shadow' – promised untold delights. When people act so unpredictably out of character you are forced to recognise that what you thought you knew was perhaps never quite true.

In theory Lixouri could be reached overland from Argostoli, the distance to be covered being only twenty miles or so once one crosses the narrow inlet on which the principal town is situated. This, however, would have involved sure-footed donkeys or mules, an intrepid spirit and possibly an armed guard, for the land here is wild and rocky and there was no road. In practice anyone travelling to Lixouri went by sea, out of the narrow inlet and across the wider bay: this is in any case the shortest route as the gull flies. Among other things, this means that your family from Argostoli are unlikely to drop in for an afternoon visit, even supposing that they wanted to.

Lixouri is certainly even less like Paris than Argostoli. 'In for a penny, in for a pound,' Stephanie said to herself (or something similar).

Luckily Marino was sometimes capable of coming up with unorthodox ideas. 'You might find it more comfortable if you didn't wear a corset,' he suggested when she flagged under the summer heat. (It is one thing to be told that his island is hotter than Paris, quite another thing to experience it for yourself: itching and sweating in tight lacing is perfectly miserable.) 'You don't really need it anyway – you could keep it for when you get dressed to go out.' He applied the same principle to his own wig; 'We are now respectable and *comme il faut*,' he more than once declared when, suitably bewigged and corseted, they visited or were visited by the local families with whom he remained on such terms.

Naturally, it would be far-fetched in the extreme to imagine that Marino's obstinate marriage to a woman who was neither respectable nor beautiful nor even very young had anything whatsoever to do with subsequent political developments in his brother's adopted land. Nevertheless it is also perhaps understandable that later on Giovambattista could not help feeling Marino's insubordination to have marked in some obscure way a sort of turning point or tide after which nothing would ever be the same: an overthrowing of the natural order of things.

The *secession* of a brother (this was what it seemed like) resembles the severance of a limb from the body; you may try to comfort yourself by deciding that the limb was faulty, injured, diseased anyway and that you are better off without it, yet it is by no means easy to attain such stoicism. Giovambattista found the best method of managing this fraternal amputation was a lofty distancing: for years to come in letters or in conversation with Marco he invariably referred to 'your brother', while to Caterina he spoke with bitter sarcasm of '*Signor* Marino'. When business made it necessary for him to write directly to Marino, he began his letters either with no address at all or, on occasion, with a chilly, curt '*Mio fratello*'. He invariably kept copies of these letters – something he had never seen any reason to do before. In them his signature was now preceded by the plain, stern, authoritative words '*Vostro fratello*', without any token of affection.

Giovambattista was perfectly aware that soldiers who survive the loss of a limb frequently suffer great discomfort from its apparently persistent ghostly presence; he should therefore have been unsurprised that the phantom of a brother who has offended goes on haunting the mind in the vulnerable late night moments no matter what efforts are made to dismiss it.

When a brother disgraces himself you cannot help hoping that he will live to regret it.

'Is it not quite wonderful?' Marino asked Stephanie when he first took her to see the marshes of Livadi which, as various signed and sealed documents confirmed, were now entirely his to drain and cultivate.

What Stephanie saw stretching before her was a flat landscape enclosed between sea and hills: beds of tall reeds and clumps of sedges among which glinted pools of stagnant water. A lonely land full of the cries of birds and an unending croaking of frogs. 'It's certainly a very noisy place,' she said carefully, just as he declared, 'It's the most peaceful place on earth.'

261

'Livadi' means pasture or meadow. *'Beurre des prés salées,'* she said reflectively, looking at the sheep grazing on the outskirts of the marsh and probably remembering other green meadows of childhood beside a greyer sea.

'Actually they make cheese, not butter' (in matter-of-fact tones). 'In any case, once I start work they will have to graze their animals elsewhere.'

It did not occur to either of them that the owners of the sheep, having had their flocks brought down to the marsh since time immemorial, might not feel very happy about this.

'I have always been the black sheep in my family,' Marino had told her in Paris. Later this was followed by, 'People like having something to talk about. I dare say they'll get used to the idea before too long,' although whether this statement referred to his marriage or to his strange new plans for the marsh Marino did not specify (Stephanie assumed the former).

'They can like it or they can lump it,' was what he reflected with a private shrug – it being clearly wiser not to voice such a disrespectful thought – when his mother spoke sharply of the offence caused to all decent-minded people by what she called 'your deliberate misalliance'. If you are thoroughly accustomed to the idea of being disapproved of, this somehow has the effect of blunting your sensitivity to differing degrees of disapprobation; having painfully taught himself to disregard what he thought of as 'spiteful tongues' and pay as little attention as possible to what the world might say, Marino was perhaps now not fully able to perceive the extent of the hostility that arose from his sudden and total occupation of the marshland.

However, by the authorities at least Count Marino Carburi was apparently well seen (his past crime having been conveniently overlooked and various documents relating to it

262

mysteriously abstracted from the files). This, of course, was not entirely due to his renown as the author of the great feat in Russia, nor even solely to the fact that he appeared likely to transform – at his own expense – a wasteland into a fertile source of new crops and revenue, but also to some extent resulted from the undoubted prestige of his brothers. For the family name continues to apply even when your family feels that you have disgraced it.

'My brother is a hypocrite,' Marino told Stephanie, referring to the distinguished physician, although he did not choose to explain what this hypocrisy consisted of. 'Most respectable people are,' she could have replied (but didn't). About Marco he said nothing, although as he set about preparing to drain the marsh there was more than one moment when he might easily have seated himself at the table in the candle-lit evening hours, taken pen and paper and explained to Marco the technicalities involved in digging channels – about depths, about non-existent gradients in a land that lies low and flat beside the sea, about the necessity for some kind of pumping system. A love affair turned sour leads to bitter, angry, lonely feelings: what is perceived as the loss of fraternal love and understanding is in some ways worse, since the affections now brutally rent asunder have formed the web in which a whole lifetime has been cradled. Both Marino and Marco told themselves that they were much too busy to write properly at the moment and thus exchanged a couple of brief and impersonal letters only. Neither was very happy with this state of affairs yet neither wrote again for some time. During this period Marco wrote rather more often than usual to Giambattista: doubtless this was a comfort.

Nevertheless, the habit of letter-writing dies hard, which is possibly why Marino also wrote a couple of times to his brother Paolo, recently settled in St Petersburg: it is rather pleasant to be for the first time in a position to offer help and advice and contacts. But of course these two brothers barely knew one another, having only met once, for three short months more than two and a half decades earlier, when the one had been twenty-five and the other fourteen. Paolo was in any case enjoying his new-found freedom from the restraints of wife and family, and presumably reluctant to devote much thought to Cephalonia, so that his replies were tardy and cursory. It did not occur to Marino that perhaps the youngest brother had always been a little envious of his elders' experience of a wider world. However this may be, one way and another this new correspondence very rapidly dwindled to nothing.

In Paris, in spite of another attack of ague, recurrent dyspepsia, low spirits and a general gloomy sense that all was vanity, Giovambattista ordered more paper, completed his monograph on the Nautilus and continued the preliminary draft of the work on fevers. Since classification is the only sound basis of any serious study, it was clearly necessary to include some schematic account of the way the febrile diseases are related to one another; he thus considered long and hard, rejected what he had so far written on the subject, tentatively made a new division into 'Quotidian' and 'Recurrent' and sorted his detailed notes on symptoms, progress, outcome and autopsy findings accordingly. The sorting of notes in a methodical manner is also no doubt a great comfort.

As indeed is the accurate classification of books, scientific collections and curiosities: a pleasure moreover which may be shared. When Giovambattista took up his pen to write to an extremely eminent correspondent seeking assistance in the securing of a remunerative position for Valliano, he opened his letter with an account of the ordering of his own collection (with which he had long been occupied), enquired about the progress of the catalogue of Monsignore's magnificent library and indeed recalled various happy exchanges of books between them, before mentioning Valliano who, as he said, was a serious and sober young man with an abiding love of books. ('I have been like a father to him during the years that he spent in Paris, and so perhaps should be the last to praise him, yet this is a truth the omission of which would do a grave injustice to my nephew.') Such a description might be considered more than generous in view of the fact that Giovambattista had recently told his sister – who had suggested sending her own eldest son to Paris – that Valliano had behaved thoroughly '*pazzamente*', his conduct having been such a source of endless worry that the physician hardly felt able to take on another nephew immediately. But then of course it is natural that the head of the family should wish to see its members well settled in life. Everyone, incidentally, always acknowledged that Giambattista had a consummate talent for the composition of letters of this kind, striking a fine and delicate balance between politeness, social ease and at the same time respect for one whose station in life was superior, yet without the slightest trace of servility. No one was ever in the least surprised that most of his letters sooner or later bore fruit.

Nieces and nephews are often troublesome. At about this period Giovambattista wrote to both Marco and Marino suggesting that it might be a good idea for Sofia to continue her education in Padua. The letter to Marino was brief and included a request that more money should be sent to cover his daughter's expenses: it received an even briefer offhand reply, more or less declaring, 'Do as you see fit,' without any mention at all of money. Marco wrote back at greater length, saying that their niece would naturally be most welcome in Padua but that unfortunately he was not in a position to maintain her for any length of time without financial assistance. The physician subsequently sent an even shorter, colder letter to Marino to which there was no response whatsoever, so that in the end he put his hand into his own purse once more with that strange mixture of anger and unhappiness which he had recently come to interpret as 'growing old'. This was possibly why an increasing need to be 'left in peace' (once again, his own words for the feeling) suddenly made him suggest to his wife that she and Carlotta might accompany Sofia to Italy, regardless of the expense. In due course he thus kissed them all and bade them farewell with courtesy and well-concealed relief.

As a matter of fact much unhappiness had been caused by another painful fall from grace, even before Marino's. When he acquired Linnaeus's work on molluscs entitled *Fundamenta Testaceologiae* Giovambattista had settled down to read it with all the pleasurable anticipation that a new book on an interesting subject invariably brings, then before long frowned slightly, and finally laid aside the volume with the pained sense of betrayal which generally accompanies the discovery that an idol has feet of clay. 'Betrayal' is a strong word, no doubt, yet the physician's chagrin was also strong that a much admired man of science could descend to so vulgar a facetiousness as to name the parts of the clam after the parts of the female pudendum. (The fact that the species illustrated, with all the parts carefully labelled, was given the name *Venus dione* only added insult to injury.) Quite apart from the crudity of the jest – for so he assumed it must be – what upset Giovambattista was the inaccuracy of using the terms *vulva, labia, hymen, mons veneris* and so on for parts of a mollusc that bear no relation to the parts of the female to which these words are properly applied, even if to the untutored eye they may resemble them. What was most

266

distressing of all was the idea that a serious and learned man should permit himself such inaccuracy merely in order to indulge in licentiousness. Perhaps those earlier references to petals as 'bridal beds' had been indicative. Giovambattista spoke to no one of this matter: if a hero disgraces himself, it is surely better to pass over the lapse in silence.

It is scandalous to take no interest in one's own daughter.

'She'll do better with my brothers,' Marino told Stephanie. 'Anyway, she could hardly come here.'

Stephanie, having not yet realised how implacable his brothers might be, felt that Sofia would very likely be the person most hostile to her and thus acquiesced in this view with relief. They were as it happened living a slightly un-orthodox life in an isolated old house (hurriedly patched up to receive them but far from able to claim any elegance) on the edge of the marsh, along with Etienne Bandu, four servants and five soldiers appointed by the Venetian authorities to act as guards. When Etienne Bandu finally arrived, Stephanie wondered whether she should not perhaps put on a corset again and cease to appear in a state of *déshabillé*; Marino, however, pronounced that the Frenchman had certainly seen countless women wearing even less and that in any case he had his mind on other matters right now, so that in the end she didn't bother and the three of them continued comfortably, wigless, coatless and corsetless.

What the servants or soldiers might think was of no importance. Yet the truth of it was that murmurs were to be heard locally – among the ignorant, that is – that a man who could harness the wind to pump water from a marsh was very likely some kind of magician or wizard, so that for a while at least Marino's servants basked in reflected glory and felt almost proud of any eccentricities.

21

NEITHER MARINO nor Giorgio ever saw the bronze horseman placed on the rock: Paolo it was who was present at the unveiling of the statue and basked in a little reflected glory. He thought of writing a letter to Cephalonia about it but in the end didn't. Marino could have told him that one of the things about St Petersburg is that it is a very, very long way from home. Be this as it may, Paolo proved to be an appallingly erratic correspondent and indeed after his mother died ceased writing to anyone.

As a matter of fact it was also Paolo rather than Marino who later got involved in what their elder brother considered the mess of bigamy. However, if we are to be fair, he was more sinned against than sinning: his wife Aretousa, presumably sick of having to live like a widow during the long years that he stayed in Russia, decided to act as if she were one and found a priest not averse to earning a substantial little backhander by marrying her to someone else without enquiring too closely into what had happened to her first husband. Of course, had Caterina been alive Aretousa would never have dared; had Giovambattista not been trapped in Paris following the dreadful overthrow of all legitimate government he would doubtless have set off for Argostoli with as much haste as possible and intervened. In the old days such a thing could never have happened.

The family in Argostoli had received strict instructions that nothing was to be said about Marino's new wife to any of their friends or neighbours. Caterina certainly knew that servants invariably gossip, yet probably felt that as long as no criticism was openly made or dissatisfaction officially expressed, then face would be saved. All the same, when she wrote to her eldest son about various kinds of scandal-provoking behaviour, including most unsuitable riding lessons, she told him, 'It is bitter indeed for a parent in the evening of life to be exposed to gossip and ridicule through a child's lack of judgment. Your brother persists in his obstinacy – doubtless the Frenchwoman, whose comportment in this house was of the most insolent vulgarity, encourages him in actions which, if they were to become widely known, could not fail to make him an object of scorn.' And later: 'I neither know nor seek to know how work in Livadi is progressing.'

Giovambattista wrote that he had been investigating to the best of his ability his brother's marriage ('The years begin to tell on me, my dearest *Signora Madre*, and I have lately been much fatigued'), but that although it had been performed in what he called 'a hasty hole-and-corner manner', he could find no sign of any irregularity: the priest was a *bona fide* priest, the paperwork was in order, there was no evidence at all to show that the woman had been married before.

His mother, either because for once she was more realistic than the physician or – more likely – simply because she was more aware of the way things were in Cephalonia, begged her son to exhaust himself no further with such enquiries: 'Even were we able to disprove the marriage,' she wrote, 'it would now make little difference to the fact that the woman is already known here as the *Contessa Stefania*.'

Marino, not being such a fool as his family liked to think, had actually taken very great care to ensure that the marriage should be entirely in order.

'I think you had better tell me if you ever had a husband,' he had said, in the most matter-of-fact of tones.

'I was never married,' she answered truthfully.

When you are not married you have only yourself and your own wits to rely upon. Sometimes during the leaner periods of life you may be obliged to change your lodgings rather more hastily and more often than you would normally wish. One of the things that Giovambattista uncovered when he set himself to delve into Stephanie's past was the fact that in the days before she made the acquaintance of Monsieur Pauquet she had changed her address four times in the course of a single year: this he was later to use before the courts in Venice as evidence that she was a person quite unfit to inherit his brother's property.

'I had to marry you,' Marino told her in their house by the marsh, 'because you were the only woman I had ever come across in my whole life who could whistle in tune. Considering that most women can't even whistle at all, it seemed imperative not to let you slip through my fingers.'

More than twenty years later, when she was living in Corfu and was almost respectable and wore black lace mittens in the afternoon, Stephanie remembered these words out of the blue and suddenly whistled a few bars of an air he used to like, to the very great surprise of Valliano, who had come, shortly after Giovambattista's death, to see whether they could not finally arrive at some arrangement about the property.

Possession being nine points of the law and Stephanie indubitably the lawful widow of her late husband, Giovambattista's prosecution of her had met with no success. Valliano now hoped to persuade her to surrender her share of the Carburi property in return for a cash payment, preferably spread over several years.

270

'He was always a generous man,' she said composedly and set out her terms.

Valliano assumed that this statement referred to the generosity of Marino's will. 'You drive a hard bargain, Madame.'

'You may take it or leave it, as you wish.'

After Valliano departed ('to think it over'), Stephanie sat at her window and looked out towards the sea and reflected on generosity of spirit and of body.

One of the things that Etienne Bandu told Marino in Paris when they began to speak seriously of indigo was that the person who had first successfully cultivated this crop in America on a commercial scale was a woman. Perhaps because the idea pleased him, this information stuck in Marino's mind so that he later repeated it to Stephanie. 'When I am dead and gone,' he told her, 'you can continue by yourself and grow rich and fat, like she has no doubt done.'

'Is she called Louise?'

This puzzled him. 'No, Elise,' he said. A moment later he understood her train of thought and laughed. 'She isn't French and she doesn't come from Louisiana and she isn't called Caroline but she does come from a place called Carolina,' he explained. 'She's called Elise Piquenez' (this being Bandu's version of Eliza Pinckney).

The Americas were very far away and Stephanie's knowledge of geography shaky; this woman's improbable name, however, caught her fancy so that '*mon nez me pique*' passed into her vocabulary (to denote feelings of lasciviousness).

Neither Marino nor Stephanie had ever had the misfortune to be afflicted by a tapeworm; neither of them, moreover, had read Giovambattista's book on the subject. They were both thus happily unaware that among the many other

271

symptoms of infestation with this parasite described by the physician was 'itching at the nose'.

For the draining of marshes and the cultivation of crops some kind of labour force is required. 'If only I had my Russians,' Marino lamented when, because of the smallness of the population, he found it impossible to recruit an adequate number of men locally; if there was also a general reluctance to be associated with such a hare-brained, new-fangled idea he perhaps did not perceive it. Migrant labourers from the mainland of Greece, from the barren and rocky peninsula of Lakonia, were thus brought in. These were a rough sort of people, as wild as the land whence they came (or so it was said), but being the poorest of the poor travelled in search of work; Marino selected a score or so of those who looked strong and intelligent and settled them into a kind of encampment at the far end of the marsh.

'I didn't know you were so fluent in the vernacular,' commented his brother-in-law, Elia Corafa, who had ridden over from Lixouri where he had relatives (possibly with instructions from Argostoli to report back in detail on the state of affairs prevailing in Livadi).

'I got quite a bit of practice in Russia,' said Marino, without explaining why or how, and continued to give orders to his workmen.

Elia and his wife were beginning to make slightly self-conscious efforts to use the Greek language: this was not, of course, because all those with whom they came into contact could not manage Italian – or at least, in the case of simpler people, a local version of Italian – but rather had to do with a newly dawning sense of Greekness. 'I do not at all agree with what you tell me of your husband's ideas,' Giovambattista wrote firmly to his sister at about this period, but

272

refrained from any of the stern criticism which Marco, for example, would have received, since it is clearly right and proper for a wife's allegiance to be to her husband. A certain amount of money, moreover, was still owed to Maria's husband in lieu of her share of a fifth of the family house, about which matter Elia had been showing remarkable patience.

'One day I shall teach you Greek,' Marino had told his son, 'and then you will always be able to remember the number that is π, or at any rate the beginning of it.'

'How?' asked Giorgio. He knew that π is a Greek letter; he also knew what it denotes in mathematics and that it begins with three, but had never been able to remember what comes after the decimal point.

'*Aeí o Theós o mégas geometreí.* It means "the great God is ever a geometer" – if you remember that and if you count the letters in each word you get the answer to five decimal places: 3.14159,' explained his father. Then after a moment's reflection added, 'The "th" in *Theós* is one letter in Greek, don't forget.'

'I think you'd better learn Italian first,' he told Stephanie.

If a country boy manages to evade parental observation and takes his girl down to a lonely beach late at night, then no one need have the slightest doubt what he is after or be at all surprised if a baby appears nine months later, with or without a hurried wedding in the meantime.

'I shall teach you to swim,' Marino announced; since this was something that clearly could not be done by daylight without setting tongues wagging, he took Stephanie down to the narrow beach one moonlit night.

'But I don't want to learn to swim,' she protested,

although by now she was wearing only her shift and he nothing at all.

'My most respected elder brother has always maintained that salt water is highly beneficial, and especially to the generative parts. Anyway, I like women in wet shifts,' he said, and led her into the sea.

'*Dis donc, ton nez te pique,*' she commented a little while later.

No knowledge of this folly ever reached anyone's ears in Argostoli. This is not to say, however, that it was not indiscreet or that there were no watching eyes concealed in the reed-bed that remained at the edge of the marsh.

'My brothers are not *discreet,*' was a thought which had more than once made itself felt in Giovambattista's mind. Discretion in this context had less to do with sexual peccadilloes and more to do with lack of tact or of what the physician usually thought of as 'judgment' – in other words that fine understanding of the way in which society is ordered. These things are very hard to explain to someone who does not apprehend them instinctively.

'Ioánnis Vaptistís always knows extremely well which side his bread is buttered,' Marino had once remarked to Marco in a fit of youthful rebelliousness against too much fraternal scolding, and although the expression was perhaps a little crude there was doubtless a certain truth in it. What worried Giovambattista many years later – if we may continue the metaphor – was that the butter would certainly be spread increasingly thinly for Marco if he persisted in pursuing perilous and foolish chimeras. He found himself unable to write more than the most general of warnings to Padua when he became aware that his brother's name was on the Inquisition's list of dangerous freethinkers and masons; the fact that these warnings were disregarded and that Marco's next letter spoke only of work in the laboratory made Giovambattista lie awake for a long time wondering what to do, then suffer a terrible nightmare in which he was sleeping on straw in a wretched garret and telling his brothers, 'I can do nothing to help you, can you not see that I am destitute, I can do nothing.'

At this period in his life the physician, far from being destitute, was really rather prosperous – which of course was a source of pride to the whole family; by and large this was a disinterested pride, although naturally enough there is always a vague and unexamined sense that any money earned by one of its members is ultimately in some way family money. This, incidentally, was why everyone couldn't help feeling that Marino was displaying a shocking degree of egotism when he made it perfectly clear that all those thousands of roubles earned in Russia were going to be kept very firmly in his own hands and used entirely for his own purposes.

Possibly, had he wanted to think about it, Giovambattista might have claimed that the flouting of fraternal authority and family and the flouting of accepted social *mores* are in effect the two sides of the same coin; possibly, had he allowed himself to worry about Marino, he might have perceived that the dangers of the sort of freethinking which Marco went in for are really very minor when compared to the dangers incurred through the breaking of long-established conventions of behaviour. For when these are thrown aside the fragile carapace of authority and respect within which the ruling classes have always dwelt ceases to protect.

'One of the reasons why no one in our native land has ever grown anything much on a large scale except for currants and olives is that they have never had enough water to do so,' Marino had said to Giovambattista in Paris, in the days before the breach, when he mentioned for the first time his intention of attempting to secure the right to cultivate the marshlands outside Lixouri. 'This much is obvious. Livadi has plenty of water – if no one has so far ever exploited it properly it is simply because no one has ever had enough imagination to work out how to do so. There is something else too: among the crops I am thinking of are quite a few which require a plentiful supply of water for the processes by which the *prima materia* is turned into a commodity of value.'

There are many advantages in sticking to the tried and true. Not least among the cares which occupied Giovambattista in Paris was the question of the price of currants on the Venetian market in any given year and the profitability or otherwise of the family lands; letters of instruction or queries or requests for detailed accounts were regularly dispatched to Demetrio Stravolemo, who as well as being their cousin served as Giovambattista's principal agent and man of business in Cephalonia (if you have to place your trust in someone to act on your behalf, then it is safest to rely on a member of your own family). Nevertheless, although he would not have dreamed of taking any risks on the land that was their patrimony, the physician told himself that an open mind befits the seeker after scientific truths. There was, moreover, the indisputable fact that Monsieur Linnaeus considered it possible for plants to be trained to adapt to different conditions of climate, so that – as he maintained – rice, tea and cinnamon might one day be grown in his northern lands; the feasibility of this plan was as yet unproven but Marino's ideas were perhaps not entirely unrealistic.

All the same, 'It would be as well to start on a very small scale until you may see whether your efforts meet with success,' he advised his brother, and shortly afterwards suggested that if Monsieur Bandu were in a position to contribute to some of the capital outlay required, this would no doubt be a wise and prudent idea.

Marino agreed, pleasantly enough, with the first proposition but refrained from saying that he was not in the least desirous of any partner in what he thought of possessively as 'my enterprise' and had already agreed on the salary to be paid to Etienne Bandu.

'The other thing about Livadi, Giambattista,' he said as he prepared to leave his brother's library, 'is that it lies beside the sea. If, as I envisage, I were to construct a small mole, it would be possible to load my crops directly on to the ships that will transport them without any need to carry them to Lixouri.'

This, as it happened, turned out to be the last time that Marino had the happy sensation of being approved of, and indeed the last time the brothers parted with a warm embrace. Marino was never aware that the absence of difficulties encountered – in fact the ease with which he was able to arrange for the concession of the marshland – was in large part due to a letter penned by Giovambattista and dispatched to someone most highly placed in Venice just two and a half hours before the younger brother announced to the elder whom he intended to marry. Letters once sent cannot be recalled, they can only be countermanded by a second missive; it seemed to the physician, however, that there was a lack of dignity about such a procedure, or indeed about making public one's differences with one's brother, so that he did nothing further and merely gave a tight, bitter, grim little smile when he subsequently heard that Livadi had been given into Marino's hands.

Later still, when Marino was no longer alive, Giovambattista tried hard to secure a continuation of the concession for Valliano. Caterina naturally supported these attempts in public; any secret relief she may have felt when her eldest son's plan came to nothing was probably simply due to an underlying conviction that Marino's agricultural experiments had always been doomed to failure, that no good could ever come of Livadi. Conceivably the authorities felt the same, or perhaps it was simply that times were unsettled so that they had other priorities; at any rate the marshes of Livadi gradually reverted to their wild state, never to be cultivated again.

Having drained about half of the marsh with a grid of neat parallel channels from which the water was led into four broader and deeper channels and thence pumped into the sea, Marino proceeded to allocate the resulting rectangular *parterres* (this was Stephanie's joking name for them) into four trial areas: one each for cotton, indigo and sugar cane, and one to lie fallow until it was seen which crop did best. Planting began as soon as Bandu arrived; quite apart from the fact that the Frenchman was to supervise cultivation, it was he who brought with him indigo and cotton seed and the slips of sugar cane (not all of which survived the journey).

There are crops which are perennial, as her husband instructed Stephanie, so that, once planted, they will go on yielding for years: vines, for example, or all manner of fruit trees. Others have to be sown afresh each year, like wheat and barley. Others again will live for a limited number of years but may be harvested more than once in the course of a single year – and one of these most interesting crops is indigo: *indaco* was what Marino always called it, even when speaking French, since for some reason he liked this word. 'It's not really an American plant, it originated in India – hence its name,' he told her. 'When the leaves develop a sort of mealy bloom or patina they are ripe and may be cut, after which the plant promptly puts out new shoots. When the harvested leaves are placed in tanks of water this powdery deposit falls to the bottom and forms a bluish sediment which, after the water has been carefully drained off, is collected and hung up in linen bags to dry.'

To Marino's great satisfaction the indigo flourished right from the beginning so that, after the very first season, they found they could harvest it three times a year, whereupon he decided to sow more plants in the fallow *parterre* and establish by experimentation the optimum depth of the water tanks. A small preliminary sample of the blue powder was sent to Venice and was well received.

'Next year I might plant rice,' he told Stephanie. 'I shall have to increase my band of cut-throats,' by which he meant his work force, 'and drain more land. You need not be afraid, there is plenty more money in St Petersburg, I am not planning to make us destitute.'

'I am not afraid,' she answered, although 'I must be going soft in the head,' was what she had said to herself apropos of this remarkable absence of worry. ('I must be mad, I must be sickening for something' is after all an easier thing to think than 'I trust my strange, hairy, obstinate little magician.')

Another thought which had occurred periodically throughout Stephanie's life, namely that if you don't take risks you never get anywhere, surfaced again one night as they lay in bed. Among Marino's other skills was an occasional unnerving ability to read her mind: 'It is envy pure and simple that makes all our neighbours secretly hope I'll fail – not one of them has ever dared take any risks,' he remarked.

'I think you'll succeed,' she said, stroking his thigh and suddenly very much wanting this to be true for reasons quite other than money.

'I think so too,' he declared comfortably.

*   *   *

279

Some magic practices are incomprehensible, no doubt, yet utterly harmless. One evening not long after this conversation Marino took from his pocket his own private pack, laid five playing cards face up on the table and invited Stephanie and Etienne Bandu to select one each. 'Choose your card, whichever one you want . . . All right, now pick it up and turn it over,' he instructed. When they did so they found that both cards bore the words 'Choose Me' on the back. Marino turned over the remaining three cards: on them was written 'Do Not Choose Me'. Stephanie – who had thought of choosing the queen of hearts but had then decided that this was the card he intended her to pick and thus selected the neutral three of clubs – swore that her choice had been freely made and begged him to explain how he did it, but Marino merely laughed.

Cutting Stephanie in half (and then restoring her to whole- ness again, apparently unharmed) would not have mattered so much if the sole audience had been Bandu – a man of few words who was well able to take these eccentricities in his stride. Being cut in half is not something that any lady would consent to, nor is the performance of such a feat something of which any gentleman should feel proud. For Marino to do it with a flourish in front of two neighbours from Lixouri and his own cousin was certainly the height of indiscretion.

'The tadpole eater,' said someone with a shrug and a brief, mirthless laugh.

22

WHEN MARCO was old and ill (and Giovambattista no longer alive to be consulted), he lay in bed in the chamber above the painted ceiling of his lecture room and submitted himself to a long and careful examination by Salvatore Mandruzzato who, although professor of Pharmaceutical Chemistry rather than physician, was the person in whose judgment he felt most trust. 'The remedies are palliative rather than curative,' he told Cecilia when his self-diagnosis was confirmed by this colleague; what he did not bother to tell her was Giambattista's comment in the past on an acquaintance similarly afflicted, namely that *stranguria* – a painful difficulty in urinating – is an ailment to which by the nature of their anatomy males seem especially prone.

Later that evening Marco fell into a doze and dreamed of pissing in the snow beside Marino with wonderful freedom and ease, then when he awoke was unsure whether this had been merely an idle dream or whether perhaps it might not be something remembered from long ago. Since Marino was rarely spoken of, he refrained from telling his wife either of his dream or indeed of the new idea that by dying in the prime of life Marino had been spared the indignities and discomforts of advancing age.

'All the same, it would be a great comfort if my brother were alive,' he murmured.

Assuming that her husband was referring to Giovambattista, Cecilia agreed: 'I too would feel much happier if he were here to advise you.'

To which he answered merely, 'Well, well, never mind, never mind . . .' and shortly afterwards slept again.

'Your uncle is suffering from a pronounced weakness of the legs as well as a most distressing strangury,' wrote Cecilia to Valliano in Cephalonia, 'and is at present confined to his bed, although he remains in reasonably good spirits.' In spite of these ailments it did not occur to Marco to cease teaching; being a great believer in solving problems as simply as possible, he directed that his students be brought upstairs and for almost two months delivered his lectures from his bed, until the university authorities got wind of this un-orthodox situation and put a firm stop to it.

'Giambattista has always been devoted to the teaching of Medicine,' Marco had told Cecilia when at the age of seventy-five – by which time most people have long since retired – the elder brother was appointed to the Chair of Natural Science at Padua once held by his friend Vallisneri. This statement was certainly not untrue, although there is no doubt that devotion is a comfortable-sounding word which obviates the need to give too much thought to less cheerful aspects of life. Marco could not fail to be aware of his brother's anxieties about money but did not choose to mention to his wife the idea that the professorial salary might well have played some part in Giovambattista's desire to continue teaching.

'Devoted,' incidentally, was also the word used equally comfortably by Marco and Cecilia to describe the character of the servant who had remained in Giambattista's employ throughout all those difficult years in France and now in Padua looked after him so carefully.

What is not at all comfortable is the recognition that you are considered unfit to teach and that a substitute is being sought to take your place. Marco swallowed hard and recommended Carlo Bruni ('whose passion for chemistry made him one of the most assiduous followers of my courses last year, moreover throughout the past Christmas holidays I taught him and various other studious young men every day and had them carry out many experiments in the laboratory under my direction'), or alternatively Leon di Emanuele Salom ('an honest man, devoted to chemistry, who could prove to be a good teacher if the government does not object to his Hebrew religion'). Nevertheless, he resigned himself to the inevitable when his suggestions were disregarded and accepted the appointment of Girolamo Melandri, from the university of Pavia, with as good a grace as possible. That Girolamo supported the theories of the Frenchman Lavoisier was undeniable; whether matters were at all improved by the fact that he proceeded fairly promptly to marry Marco's daughter Vittoria was debatable.

'My brother is devoted to his work,' Marino had said to Stephanie in Venice, possibly feeling that some excuse needed to be made for the brevity of Marco's stay.

'What can't be cured must be endured,' Marco told his wife stoically, which was rather the way everyone had felt at the beginning about Marino's marriage to the Frenchwoman – until, that is, they discovered that he had made her his sole heir.

If Marino and Stephanie rarely spoke of France, this was doubtless due in part to that strange sense that places left behind somehow cease to exist: possibly, for different reasons, both found it simpler to live entirely in the present. All the same, although he never questioned her about whether she missed Paris, Marino did suddenly ask one day, 'If I died, would you go back?' Her response was slightly annoyed – 'I haven't the least idea what I should do' – whereupon he found himself saying, 'All my property will come to you' (in spite of the fact that he hadn't intended telling her of his will). In Stephanie's experience intentions are one thing and actions another, yet she felt a curious embarrassment about asking him to put it into writing. 'It's all signed and sealed,' he said, in one of those sudden flashes of understanding, 'you don't have to worry.' He thought of adding, 'My brothers won't like it much . . . I dare say you may have to fight for it a bit,' but in the end didn't.

Had Giovambattista been able to eavesdrop on his brother's thoughts he would have pointed out sternly that liking or not liking had nothing to do with the matter (there would have been more than a touch of disingenuousness here, since of course when the time came he loathed the idea of sharing the family property with a French whore), but that the disinheriting of a sole surviving child contravenes all natural and man-made laws. When the family later discussed Marino's incomprehensible lack of paternal feeling no one ever understood that just as places may be left behind, so people may be too, that for her father Sofia belonged to a different world, a life that was over, a book in a language best forgotten, now painfully and finally closed and put away: or perhaps that she resembled a pale moon whose orbit, without the radiance and the gravitational pull of Giorgio, was becoming ever wider and more elliptic.

Marino had explained about gravity when he and Giorgio were reading *Micromégas* together (Sirius was a star with which the boy was already familiar). Although Madame Louis David Duval believed she had a pretty fair idea of the uses to which Marino put the money he borrowed, it never occurred to her that sometimes when he had a bit of cash in his pocket he went out and bought proper, grown-up books for his son. ('The child's far too young for them,' protested

Elena; 'He likes them,' answered Marino firmly.) *Micromé-gas* was at any rate a great success. 'It's a Greek name,' the father told his son, 'it means *Petit-Grand*.' Giorgio puzzled for a while over Monsieur Voltaire's statement that this is a name eminently suitable for all those who are '*grand*' since – until Marino pointed out that it might also mean 'great' – he took the word at first to mean simply 'tall'.

The idea of interplanetary travel and indeed of life on other planets and stars was naturally a wonderful one and the boy laughed in delight at the thought of a world where people were millions of feet tall and not grown-up until they were four hundred and fifty years old. In due course this led to another groping thought about the relativity of things: 'If everyone around him on Sirius was as big as Micromégas, then he would seem just normal.'

'Quite right,' said Marino.

Madame Duval was, incidentally, perfectly happy to go on taking care of Marino's money for him after he left Russia. In the time to come, however, when Giovambattista, Marco and Stephanie (and later Colonel Schneyder) bombarded her with letter after letter containing contradictory instructions, she became extremely weary of all the trouble that it caused. Doubtless, in spite of the distance between St Petersburg and Venice or Cephalonia, Madame Duval made it her business to keep track of her clients' affairs and their family lawsuits; 'We cannot,' her clerk wrote at her dictation in his neat, regular handwriting, 'as I am sure you will understand, release any of the money or actions belonging to your late brother unless you are all of you in agreement as to the hands into which we should release them.' Nevertheless, as she wrote to Marco, 'We are naturally by now most anxious to close this account as soon as may be practicable.' (A faint note of exasperation was apparent beneath the flowery compliments on Sofia's recent engagement to Monsieur Schneyder.) It was at about this time that Giovambattista told Colonel Schneyder, 'My brother Marco has no experience whatsoever of the world.' However, not even Giovambattista's tactful letter, describing the many expenses which needed to be met on Sofia's behalf, was able to make the widow Duval budge an inch.

'My brother, Count Marino, is capable of making difficulties,' Giovambattista warned the second of his trusted agents in Argostoli (on whom, all the same, since he was not family, the physician had asked his cousin Demetrio to keep an eye) when he wrote a few months after Marino's departure from Paris, requesting that plans be made of all the family property in Cephalonia, with the scale and orientation clearly marked. Great care should be taken to delineate accurately the portions belonging to himself and to Marco. These plans should cover not only the paternal house opposite the church of St Spyridon in the *Carburata* and the houses to either side of it, as well as the gardens attached to them, but also the lands lying along the public highway, the lands at Fussata, and the property recently acquired from Signor Metaxa; it would moreover be useful if a note was made giving details of the crops currently being grown on all the family lands and an estimate of their value. As an afterthought, Giovambattista specified the sum of money which he considered a suitable price to pay for the preparation of the plans, then made a careful copy of this memorandum (as he called it) for his own records.

Among the other documents neatly filed in the pigeonholes of Giovambattista's bureau was a copy of the *convenzione* or agreement which he had demanded that Marino sign in Venice on his way back to the island: under the circumstances this was a fraternal injunction which could not be disobeyed. What the agreement concerned was not only the division of the family property between the four brothers but also the obligations of each brother with regard to the monies borrowed from Solomon and Isaac Treves in order to complete the purchase of the Metaxa house beside the church of the Annunciation. This loan – the first such transaction to which Giovambattista had ever been party – was very naturally the subject of many careful calculations and more than one midnight anxiety; nevertheless, its purpose being the repossession of a property that had once belonged to the family, the physician had finally made up his mind to it. When in due course the plans arrived in Paris and were spread on his library table on a chilly, wet evening, they seemed to bring with them such a fragrance of sea and rock and sun-warmed, resin-scented security that for a while all worries were dispelled.

Before the plans arrived a copy of another letter had to be filed. 'Mio fratello,' he wrote to Marino on a night of even colder, bone-chilling fog at the beginning of February (abbreviated in the copy to M. fr.), 'more than six months have elapsed since your return to Cephalonia, yet I have had no word from you. I am thus obliged to request once more that you send me without delay an account of the sums received by you during the last year from your metà or share in our patrimony. It is most necessary that a model or plan be now made in which our various shares of this property will appear clearly, as defined in the convenzione you signed last July; I have accordingly instructed Signor Spyridon Cuassan to draw up such a plan, the expense of which will be borne by me alone.' Giovambattista felt a certain stern resignation as he wrote these words. He ended austerely, 'I most sincerely desire your well-being and remain, Your brother, Gio:Batta:.'

It is perfectly natural to feel that a brother who obstinately insists on marrying a woman little better (if we are to call things by their proper names) than a prostitute has somehow forfeited the right to be considered a full and equal member of the family. Nevertheless, when Stephanie suggested that it might be wise to study with great care any document which Giovambattista or his representatives wished him to sign, Marino laughed: 'That my cousin and I have never much cared for one another is true enough, but Giambattista won't try to cheat me.' Stephanie's expression still being doubtful, he explained, 'Ioánnis Vaptistís has always been very, very vain and very, very interested in what the world might say of him, which means among other things that his renowned integrity is very, very precious to him.'

Whether or not this was the reason, it is certainly true that in Giovambattista's arrangements Marino's interests continued to be treated with the same scrupulous fairness as those of Marco and Paolo. To Stephanie's slight surprise, Marino sent the required accounts to Paris shortly thereafter, although his response to his brother's next letter – about Sofia's future – was both tardy and cavalier in the extreme.

After a visit to Livadi the following year their cousin reported to Giovambattista that a large amount of money seemed to be being spent but that so far there was little evidence of tangible results; presumably he was unaware of the bags of indigo stored on slatted shelves in a building down by the sea which he had dismissed in his mind as a flimsy-looking structure, its lower courses built of stone but its upper parts apparently made from reeds. He refrained from adding that Marino's reception of him had been so offhand as to border on rudeness.

The other installation which Demetrio had not been shown was the mill in which the first harvest of sugar cane had recently been crushed and the large tank or cistern close at hand in whose water the residue of the canes – *bagasse* was what Bandu called it – was being soaked.

'It is an experiment,' Marino told Stephanie, 'I do not know whether it will work.'

He thought of writing to Marco (who had always appreciated practical things) about this experiment, in which the vegetable fibres were to be soaked in water, rather in the manner that flax is soaked in the production of linen, then compressed under a great weight in order to see whether they would form a dense substance as the Russian moss had done. However, for one reason or another the letter did not get written. Instead he thought in circles about the whole question as he lay in bed at night, then put his arms around Stephanie and confided the rest of the idea: 'If it became dense and I cut it into blocks or bricks just as the Russian peasants cut the *substratum* of their moss for fuel, then one could build the upper storeys of houses from it.'

She reflected and said, 'I'm not sure that I'd really want to live in a house built of reeds.'

'In an earthquake you would. But anyway, it would not be built of reeds, the ground floor would be built of stone, or no, on second thoughts it would have a timber frame . . . If my experiment works, then one day I shall build one and you will see.'

The only danger would be fire, Marino mused; Marco, it occurred to him, would without doubt be the person best able to devise a means of making combustible materials fireproof. Notwithstanding this thought, no letter was dispatched to Padua.

In the normal way of things it is very natural to want to share your ideas, to speak about the things that occupy your mind. It is also understandable that a certain process of selection often applies, whereby some thoughts are shared at length – with one particular friend, for example, or with a brother – in order that others may remain discreetly in the background. This is probably why, at about the same moment that Marino's first sugar cane was being cut in Livadi, Marco sat in his lecture room in Padua and wrote a long and reflective letter to Giambattista in which his mature thoughts about the science of chemistry were expressed (his equally mature thoughts about the brotherhood of man being reserved for other correspondents – or of course for evening conversations with trusted friends).

'A chemist who does nothing but follow theories and whose formation is based on mere reading cannot be an expert in this science, any more than a metaphysician can be an expert watch-maker,' he wrote. 'You may well smile, my dearest brother, for no doubt I have said this before, yet if I repeat myself it is simply because this is a tenet to which I hold firmly: chemistry is not a sedentary science to be studied, learnt, understood, communicated and promoted without the carrying out and demonstration of experiments. To sit and read chemistry books merely, or even to compile them or write commentaries upon them, does not and cannot produce anything but a semblance of knowledge which is detrimental to the real purposes of this science since it substitutes false and useless reasoning for the practical research which is its most valuable constituent: a chemist can be said to be trained only in proportion to the amount of observations and experiments he has carried out. It is well nigh twenty years since I established my laboratory – and a matter of pride to me, I might add, that it has subsequently served as a model for other laboratories in various cities of Italy.'

The physician, who, on balance, also felt rather proud of his brother's laboratory, did not smile as he read this impassioned statement of a creed, nor was he particularly struck by Marco's vehemence in maintaining that what he called 'the chemistry of gases' does not constitute more than a tiny part of the whole science. ('It would be as ridiculous to consider someone to be a chemist who studied only gases as it would be to regard a simple oculist as a surgeon.') Giovambattista understood immediately to whom his brother was referring: he was certainly aware of the 'modern theory' of Lavoisier but tended to trust Marco's judgment on such matters and thus felt that the question of whether or not it is possible to break up water, through heating, into two gases called respectively 'oxygen' and 'hydrogen' was at best unproved.

'I myself have obtained inflammable gas – that is, *hydrogen* – by passing water vapour over carbon and burnt iron in my globe,' explained Marco. 'I have no doubt whatsoever that this gas was produced by the phlogiston contained in the iron. The pharmacist Vincenzo Dandolo, who has been giving public demonstrations in the Fenice theatre supposedly proving the modern theory, has offered a wager of 400 *zecchini* that he is right and I am wrong. The man is misguided. He is in any case so shy and so poor a speaker that I hardly believe he will convince anyone.'

Since the amount wagered was more than twice his brother's annual salary a few doubts crossed Giovambattista's mind, rapidly dismissed. 'Nevertheless, my dearest Marco,' he wrote in reply, 'among the natural phenomena whose explanation must needs occupy the mind of the medical man is the process by which in all animate beings *respiration*' (underlined) 'quickens the tissues of the body. Here Monsieur Lavoisier's ideas might appear to have a certain pertinence.' It is not necessarily easy to disentangle the confusion over where medicine ends and chemistry begins or vice versa. A brief jotting in Giovambattista's notebook, made as his servant shaved him one morning, may have been an attempt in this direction: he divided the page with a vertical line and wrote on one side 'Respiration' and on the other 'Combustion'. However, nothing further came of this idea; the next time he opened his notebook Giovambattista simply turned over the page and made rapid and detailed notes on the means by which typhus and typhoid fevers may be distinguished – a subject of more immediate interest. Since his notebooks were scrupulously filed in chronological order, it did not prove too difficult to find the case notes made long ago in Turin on a servant carefully nursed: 'It was typhus, no doubt about it,' he now said to himself, and mused on how the young and strong and beautiful may sometimes survive such maladies.

Monsieur Lavoisier's death, some years later, was brought about by the sharp blade of the guillotine, at which even Marco was shocked and appalled. Very naturally Giambattista's situation was by then filling everyone's hearts with anxious dread so that a more frequent than usual correspondence was toing and froing between Padua and Cephalonia. As increasingly worrying news arrived from France, Marco took the pen from Cecilia and for once covered the pages of a letter to their sister himself in his firm, black italic hand: '*Mia amatissima sorella*,' he wrote, 'I have been rejoicing – as I never thought to do – that our beloved mother is not alive to see these turbulent times. I must tell you that I have had no word from Gio:Batta: for the last four months, yet trust and hope that, in spite of his indisputable connections with the Court, our brother may be protected by the fact that he remains a citizen of Venice and by the renown attached to his name: for, surrounded as they are on every side by enemies in all the Courts of Europe, those now ruling in Paris will, I believe, be reluctant to offend the Most Serene Republic by harming one of her distinguished sons.' Giovambattista himself – who, having been turned back on his one attempt to leave Paris, was now staying largely within doors – might have been surprised by the perspicacity of this. 'We can do nothing but trust in God and pray. I embrace you with all my heart, Your most affectionate brother, Marco Carburi.' In a postscript he added, 'I beg you to let me know at once if any of you has any news – I shall of course do the same.' The brotherhood of man is one thing: a flesh and blood brother in peril quite another.

As a general rule it is not a bad idea to pay attention to what the world might think of you and to avoid offending people gratuitously. There are sins of omission just as there are sins of commission: Demetrio Stravolemo, who would certainly not himself have harmed his cousin, said nothing at all to anyone when various rumours reached his ears indicating that Marino might conceivably be in danger.

Giorgio was of course aware that he possessed cousins in that strange place called Home, as well as a girl cousin apiece in Paris and in Padua, and had stored in his mind the answers to all sorts of questions as he tried to work out who was related to whom in what degree and thus weave for himself a mesh of belonging. Your father's brothers are your uncles, this is straightforward, but what relation your father's cousins bear to you is far less clear.

'They are something halfway between cousins and uncles, so you could call them by either title,' Marino decided in answer to this problem, then added reflectively, 'I used to tease our cousin Demetrio terribly because of his name.' ('Stravolemo', as he had explained, in Greek means something like 'crook neck' or 'wry neck'.)

Among the other matters which gave rise to a certain amount of gossip in Lixouri – and this time word inevitably reached Argostoli too – was the fact that Marino taught Stephanie to ride astride, having made her put on first the black silk knitted drawers that she wore when she had her period, then for good measure a pair of his own linen drawers on top of them. These latter were rather too large for her, even with the drawstring pulled tight, so that he tied them round her waist with a length of blue ribbon.

'The Russian Empress rides astride, and wears breeches too,' he remarked as he fastened this ribbon with one of the complicated knots he had a talent for.

Although of course Marino's mother and sister and sister-in-law had no means of knowing what kind of underclothes the Frenchwoman wore during these riding lessons ('Better not even *imagine*,' as they murmured darkly to one another), the indelicacy of the whole business seemed just the sort of thing that might have been expected. Caterina wrote to her son remonstrating about it and was angered – but not entirely surprised – when she received no answer at all. It was probably just as well that various delightful essays in persuading Stephanie to put on a pair of his breeches (with nothing underneath) took place in the privacy of the bedchamber.

Some time later Giovambattista, ever thoughtful of what might give pleasure in Cephalonia and more *au fait* with fashions than his family generally realised, dispatched to his sister, sister-in-law and nieces a pair each of what was the very latest mode in Paris in the way of undergarments for females, the lace-trimmed, ribbon-threaded equivalent of the drawers worn by men. Not knowing what these things should properly be called in Italian, he used the semi-Greek word *braka* for them. If the physician sanctioned such daring garments, then they were clearly not unhygienic – although best kept for high days and holy days, pronounced Caterina. Needless to say, Giovambattista would not have been so disrespectful as to send female drawers to his mother: for her there were black silk gloves and chocolate.

'Just grip him firmly with your knees and make him understand that he must do what you want,' said Marino. 'Imagine that he's me.'

Since his horse was a gelding this provoked a certain

amount of hilarity. Stephanie begged, 'Don't make me laugh or I'll fall off.'

'I shall keep you safe, I won't let you fall off.'

In the days that were gone Giorgio had known very well what a gelding was since – apart from anything else – his father had long since explained, when telling him about Caffarelli and Carestini, exactly what sort of operation is performed to give some singers voices of such heavenly beauty. (Reassuringly: 'It's only for people who want to have very special voices.') Subsequently, during another of those rambling and comfortable conversations, this time about horses, Marino told him, 'The Great Peter's horse was called Lisset – but of course she's been dead now for nearly as many years as her master. All the same, Monsieur Falconet wanted the horse in his statue to be as good a portrait of her as possible, for Lisset was a brave mare, Giorgio, who deserved to be honoured. That's why he searched to find a horse of the same blood to serve as model, and in the end Count Orlov offered two from his own stables, Caprice and Diamond. Monsieur Falconet spent weeks making drawings of them.' Giorgio knew that Count Orlov had once been the Empress's special favourite, for Marino had told him this as well.

'How many drawings?'

'I don't know, scores, hundreds probably. He got the stable boys to make them rear for him again and again. Caprice is a mare and Diamond is a gelding – they were both very patient and co-operative.'

The men who were later sent to kill Marino determined among themselves to geld him into the bargain (although this was not part of their commission); this, however, did not happen, for he offered such unexpected resistance and fought so hard that in the end, by some unspoken agreement, they left him intact.

23

BY THE time their brother-in-law's hastily penned letter arrived in France it was the beginning of June. '*Mio carissimo cognato*,' Giovambattista read on a sunlit morning, 'it is my painful duty to give you the saddest of news.' Marco's letter reached him two days later, for Maria's husband had taken advantage of a neighbour's journey to Venice and thus Marco had received the news in Padua weeks earlier and had immediately sat down to write to Giovambattista. 'I have shed many and bitter tears, my dearest brother,' he wrote, which was in fact close to the truth since, after crossing himself from right to left, Marco had laid his head against Cecilia's meagre but kindly bosom and sobbed in desolation. ('God rest his soul,' said Cecilia and stroked her husband's thinning hair.) 'Your loving, grieving brother', he signed himself. Giovambattista did not weep at the news of Marino's death, merely refolded the letter carefully and placed it in his bureau, then gave orders for his horse to be saddled.

In that far-off graveyard the spring flowers had already gone to seed, yet here, in spite of the unseasonable warmth, daisies and ragged robin and yarrow still bloomed. Giovambattista did not see them, noticing little of his surroundings as he rode. It may be, though, that the painful, luxuriant greenness of the rushes plucked at some inner chord; at any rate he told his servant to wait, dismounted, made his way down to the river on foot.

Brown boys swimming, naked and lissom. Older boys here: no longer children. Giovambattista stood quite still, thin and slightly stooping, timeless in time, watching them till at last they became uncomfortable at his silent presence, whereupon they swam over to the opposite bank and from its safety jeered and taunted. He moved away, surfacing abruptly from his memories, pained at the misinterpretation. Yet one boy it seemed had hesitated, had hung back in order to emerge from the water a little way downstream so that they met beyond the bend in the path, hidden from the others by the flowering hawthorn. A naked body, a knowing flaunting of firm, wet flesh: little rivulets of water running down the dark hairs on strong and shapely young legs. A pale body, he now realised, not brown (it is curious how sunlight and memory play tricks on one), only the hands were already dark and work-worn: a stocky body, the legs fractionally too short, the arms muscular. Giovambattista murmured something in Greek. The boy smiled. Simple hopes of money to be earned . . . And on Giovambattista's part there may after all have been a few heartbeats of temptation, although perhaps it was merely the vain, useless longing to be comforted. '*O adelphós mou péthane,*' he said once more in Greek, 'my brother is dead.' The words sounded halting and stiff, their hinges unoiled, the language rusty from disuse: a taste of iron filings in his mouth. Giovambattista turned and walked slowly back along the muddy path to where his servant waited.

He could not sleep that night because of the croaking of the frogs (although the rue du Faubourg Poissonnière is nowhere near the river) and was short-tempered in the morning. His breakfast coffee tasted thin and sour. His joints ached.

The bitterest tears are perhaps those shed for oneself: for the sunlit past that is gone for ever, for sore gums and creaking bones and thinning hair, for the need to urinate more frequently, for a language half-forgotten, for the once supple, supportive bonds of brotherly love that have been strained and broken and are now beyond all repair. For regrets that have come too late; for the finality of loss. These are dry-eyed, inward tears.

Since there is no way to avoid writing of Marino's death, I shall state quite simply what Elia Corafa preferred not to mention in any detail when he wrote announcing the terrible news to his wife's brothers: namely that Marino died as a result of twenty-seven knife wounds, the last of which severed his pulmonary artery. He fought for longer and with greater agility than his assailants would have believed possible, using for weapons whatever he found to hand – a stool, a china ewer. At one point he almost succeeded in wresting the knife from one of his attackers, momentarily disconcerted by the ferocity of his resistance. But in the end of course a naked fifty-three-year-old man, no matter how agile, does not stand a chance against five fully-dressed and armed Lakonian workmen in their twenties; when he finally fell to the floor, fighting with his bare hands, his palms and fingers were lacerated.

Stephanie was stabbed twice, in the thigh and in the ribs. As she fell she somehow cut her head on the edge of the bed, and it was the profuse bleeding from this third wound that probably saved her life: the attackers, seeing her lying huddled in a pool of blood, assumed that she was dead without bothering to check. She was the sole survivor.

Etienne Bandu was in bed with the cook; their throats were cut before either had time to react. The remaining servants died as they slept, each in his or her own blameless bed.

This is what happened in the isolated house on the edge of the marsh on an April night of poignant sweetness.

*   *   *

'They should never have withdrawn the soldiers,' said Giovambattista. 'He should never have remained at Livadi without the soldiers, it was madness, if I had known . . .'

Marco thought sadly, 'He was always a gambler,' but said nothing.

This was in Venice, whither the younger brother had come at once to join the elder when at last he was able to set out from Paris in the September following Marino's death. Their embrace when they met – tearful on Marco's side, tight-lipped on Giovambattista's – was long and hard and was doubtless a comfort to both.

'It was utter folly to remain alone there without guards,' the physician said again.

The reason the Venetian authorities had decided to withdraw the corporal and four men originally detailed to protect the inhabitants of that lonely house was extremely simple. Although his brothers could have told anyone who asked that Marino had never shown the slightest interest in matters of a political nature, the fact that he had spent so many years in Russia was indisputable and the assumption that his sympathies might thus be pro-Russian understandable; thus when in the complicated ebb and flow of Eastern Mediterranean affairs Russia's championing of Orthodox Christian Greeks against their Ottoman overlords became impossible to ignore, someone in Venice had argued that Marino was suspect – an agent in place, perhaps, to encourage the spread of dangerous ideas from the Greek mainland to the Ionian islands.

'If he had never gone to Russia . . .' said Marco. But this was of course a useless train of thought, as Giovambattista pointed out severely.

The word 'serf' is an emotive one, conjuring up visions of a race of high-handed (and high-cheekboned) Russian lords treating with unspeakable cruelty the downtrodden masses. It was André Grasset Saint Sauveur – he of the plump, white, vicious hands, invariably spiteful about the whole family – who later put about the story that Marino had lived too long in Russia, treated his workmen like serfs (stood over them with a whip and no doubt worse, mounted their womenfolk in broad daylight whenever he got the itch), so that it was really hardly surprising they butchered him in the end.

If Caterina wept over her murdered son, no one ever saw it.

They brought Marino back to Argostoli, to the paternal house in the *Carburata*, and laid him on the table in the *salotto*. News travels fast, and a little crowd had collected on the quay to watch as the boat arrived: subdued conversation, horror of course – but also a certain amount of suppressed excitement, an unadmitted wish to see the gory extent of his injuries. There was not much to see; Marino was closely wrapped in a woven blanket which was in any case red so no blood showed. They stood back as the men carried him home.

Thick white candles were hastily fetched from the church of St Spyridon across the road and set up round the table. The blanket was discarded and Caterina had an embroidered linen sheet, once part of her dowry, brought to replace it. Marino's body had already been washed in Lixouri, washed and washed again even as the message was being sent, so that in fact there was no blood now and no more washing needed; his mother, who had not seen her son naked since he was a child, called for water and washed him anyway. In the evening she sent Maria and Paolo's wife away and announced that she would keep vigil by herself.

And what she did was uncover Marino once more and contemplate the son she had borne. Giovambattista, who in days gone by had occasionally had bodies dead from multiple stab wounds under his dissecting knife in the anatomy theatre, would probably have insisted on sitting with his mother had he been present, would have used his authority to dissuade her from such contemplation. In this he would have been wrong: Caterina looked and, with a hand at first tentative then more sure, touched the stocky, hairy, animal body of her stranger son cut down in his prime, traced the dark curls of his hair now almost silver, the line of his cheek and jaw, his slightly thickening waist, his thighs, his feet. His hands scored with cuts: his signet ring that the assailants had not bothered to remove . . . Letters too few and far between sealed with the imprint of this ring throughout the years . . . A defiant changeling conceived in humiliation and anger . . . And the truth is that in the quiet hours of the night she did weep soundless tears at all this ruin and loss, although in the morning when the others came in they found Marino decently swathed in white linen and his mother dry-eyed and composed.

It was not until after the burial that she thought to ask what had happened to Stephanie (her son-in-law had already told her but she had perhaps not been paying attention).

Stephanie remained motionless for a long time after she heard them leave, then crawled over the floor until she found Marino lying in front of the window: the first thing the men had done had been to open the shutters wide to let the light of the full moon shine in, but by now it had set and the room was dark once more. There was a sound of sobbing or gasping somewhere in the background which distressed her since for some reason it seemed vital to preserve the silence; after a little while she realised that the sobs were her own. She lay down beside him, stroked his hair, cradled him in her arms, thought for a moment that she was waiting for morning and wondered why, there being nothing now that morning could bring.

What morning did bring was fresh, sharp sunlight and birdsong in the boundless silence, then finally human footsteps and a voice calling a cheerful greeting in Greek. Stephanie slowly and carefully hauled herself up until she could lean, naked and bloody, on the windowsill. What she meant to shout was '*Assassins!*' but all that came out was an indeterminate croak. Enough, however, to attract attention: before long there were many footsteps hurrying, shocked faces and orders tersely given, after which a litter was brought and she was carried away.

By the time Elia and Valliano arrived from Argostoli Stephanie was lying washed and bandaged (with most of her hair clipped off) in an upstairs room at the house of their nearest neighbour, Elia's father's cousin, whom Marino had always referred to as 'Old Man Corafa'. Valliano asked if he might see her but was told that this was out of the question – impossible anyway for him to speak to her since she was unconscious and at death's door. That more than half the blood with which her hair had been matted came from Marino's breast on which she had laid her head during the night was something no one had realised, just as no one understood that Stephanie was fully conscious but simply found it easiest to lie motionless and speechless. Keeping extremely still is one way of controlling anguish: this Marino could have told her. She did not ask where they had taken him, knowing without needing to be informed that his family would have claimed in death the member who had always seemed to refuse to be appropriated during his life. They never gave me a chance to say goodbye to him, she thought and kept very still indeed.

Marino's wife and his mother had one thing in common: no one ever saw Stephanie shed a single tear.

* * *

Old Man Corafa, a widower, later made her an offer (not, of course, an offer of marriage but a courteous suggestion that if she should wish to remain in his house and under his protection, then perhaps an arrangement could be arrived at which she might consider not unattractive). Stephanie, fully aware that at this point she needed friends rather than enemies, pressed his hand tenderly as she thanked him, declining what she called his 'most generous kindness' with a charm which seemed to her a trifle threadbare but which nevertheless apparently served its purpose well enough: it was he who ensured that the money due for Marino's last indigo crop came to her hands, just as it was he who recommended a clever lawyer and subsequently escorted her to Corfu where he helped her find a place to live. If a few kisses were allowed in return, even – let us be honest – a brief unbuttoning of the breeches and some rather intimate strokings, this was surely only fair.

'I shall never come back to Cephalonia,' Stephanie told Valliano in their only interview (a painful one), and kept her word.

The men who killed Marino were caught the following day as they attempted to leave the island. Had they had the coolness to return to their cabins behind the reeds at the far end of the marsh, having, needless to say, washed thoroughly in the sea before day broke – and naturally to keep very quiet and refrain from appearing suddenly affluent – then perhaps they might have been allowed to depart discreetly after a decent interval, when all the noise had died down. On the other hand, they had of course failed to carry out their commission to the letter: their instructions had been to leave no living witnesses. In any case, being simple men their one thought was to leave as fast as possible with their hard-earned blood money, with the result that they were apprehended and sent to Venice. Whatever they then confessed or did not confess under questioning was neither here nor there; none of them was ever seen or heard of again.

The family preferred to believe that the slaughter had been caused simply by greed for the vast amounts of gold which Marino had been widely held to possess: 'As if he would have kept it all in Livadi,' said Maria in sorrow to her husband. Condolences were deep and sincere from fellow nobles and landowners, particularly from those in the Lixouri area, who agreed that it was a shocking business and that, no doubt about it, robbery could surely have been the only possible motive. Demetrio Stravolemo wore black and remarked to all and sundry that it had been a sad act of rashness in the first place to bring in such desperadoes as the Lakonians (the remainder of whom soon packed up and left), and there the matter ended.

Stephanie was the only person who recollected what he had said about people fearing and hating the things they do not understand; at first she made great efforts to blot his voice out of her mind, then gradually came to realise that there was a comfort in keeping him alive by remembering.

'What about the fact that I do not understand you in the least yet neither fear you nor hate you?' she had asked fairly early on.

'Ah, but you see people who *fit* invariably understand one another, it's a law of nature' (with a lazy and lascivious chuckle). Then, with complete seriousness, 'You have always understood me, as one day I dare say you will admit.'

'I did understand, you were right,' was among the things that she told him when she got a boatman to take her across the water to the burial ground on the morning of the day she left Cephalonia. She also said, 'C'était génial, tu sais,' since he had always been amused by the phrase which was her greatest expression of approbation ('*Ah, mais c'est génial!*').

Caterina sent a trusted servant to question the boatman about what had transpired at her son's grave but was unable to learn much except that the Frenchwoman had knelt in the dust in a most unladylike way and spoken aloud: 'It was in a foreign language,' explained the man, 'so I don't know what she was going on about.'

When Caterina died, four years after Marino, people said that the loss of her second son, borne with such admirable fortitude, had somehow quenched her inner fire, that the last years of her life had been characterised by a new mildness. This is the sort of pious myth with which no one disagrees in public, although no doubt in private her family may have had other ideas; Marco and Cecilia, for example, had been penning increasingly placatory protestations of devotion and respect, so that when the news arrived that these were no longer necessary there may have been a certain relief. Only Giovambattista probably meant every word literally when he wrote to Marco '*Siamo orfani* – we are now orphans.' (This is certainly an easier thing to say than, 'I am old and lonely and the savour has gone out of life.')

The truth is that these were difficult times for the physician. A fixed stipend, however generous it may be, by definition lacks flexibility. 'The recent financial reforms in France have hit me very hard,' Giovambattista wrote to his mother shortly before her death, 'indeed, my income is now worth less than half what it used to be.' And to Maria, regretting that he was at present unable to settle the last outstanding amount owed to Elia, 'I am in debt for the first time in my life.' It is likely that only Marco would have recognised the depth of misery in this cry; nevertheless, the annual sum of money continued to be paid to Marco and letters to Padua were devoted almost exclusively to scientific subjects, as well of course as periodic exhortations to be discreet about matters unspecified. No one, not even Marco, recognised that the relentless pursuit of Stephanie – 'relict of the late Count Marino Carburi, formerly known as the Chevalier Alexandre de Lascaris' as the court documents called her – stemmed no longer so much from anger as from an increasing need not to fail in the protection of the family interests. Certainly no one ever knew anything of the way Marino began to intrude repeatedly into his elder brother's thoughts during that wretched time in Paris as the physician sat in his library, wearing the plain, unadorned black or dark-brown poplin *habits* that these days seemed wiser than silks and velvets and brocades, and contemplated as dispassionately as possible the idea of parting with his books to raise money. Some things are hard to think of. Indeed, as regards Marino, it would probably be more accurate to speak of a vague half-apprehended perception lurking on the periphery of Giovambattista's mind rather than a conscious thought. The content of these tentative mental gropings after what might or might not be an uncomfortable truth is easily enough stated: namely whether perhaps Marino's determination to go his own way – his obstinate refusal to attempt to be like everyone else – had conceivably required a certain measure of courage.

Naturally, no one ever dreamed of questioning anything that Giambattista did. All the same, when he sent his wife and daughter on a long visit to Cephalonia it was assumed that he was intending to retire from his labours and join them in due course. Since almost immediately afterwards news arrived of the troubles that had broken out in Paris in the middle of July, the timing of their arrival was even considered as an example of the physician's far-sightedness; the fact that he himself did not get out in time was surely simply proof of his devotion to duty.

Perhaps some of the savour went out of life for all of them when Marino died. Perhaps the knowledge of his existence, no matter how eccentric or unacceptable his behaviour, was always part of the fitness of things. Paolo and Maria may have felt this less, having lived their lives for the most part in a world where Marino did not figure so very prominently, yet for Giovambattista and Marco – and indeed in a different way for Caterina – the loss of Marino destroyed for ever the completeness of a whole.

Philádelphos is a gentle word, an adjective denoting one who loves his brother. When at long last he was able to leave Paris, accompanied by the faithful companion grown old in his service, it was to Padua rather than to Cephalonia that Giovambattista headed blindly in search of comfort: for perhaps in the end the only place that can be called home is the place where your brother is. An unthinking habit of love and trust . . .

In the final seconds as he bled to death Marino felt that he was gasping, unable to breath properly: a fleeting, confused notion that he must get his head above the water. Then somehow it no longer seemed necessary. Perhaps at the very end what remained was a permeating sense of something known with certainty: 'My brothers will not let me drown.' He ceased to struggle and died lapped in the security of this knowledge.

EPILOGUE

MARINO WAS buried in Argostoli, Giovambattista some years later in Padua – where in due course Marco was laid by his side. With the passage of time their bones disintegrated to nothingness. In the natural course of events one might have expected all memory of the brothers to have faded too: it is, after all, rare to be remembered for more than a couple of generations at most. Yet there are people who take up space in the imagination, who seem to leave behind them a reverberation that continues to be heard. No one in the family ever forgot the brothers. Paolo's grandchildren and great-grandchildren and their descendants went on speaking with awe of the chemist whose laboratory was famed throughout Europe and of the thin, stooping, physician whose distinguished career had been so glorious and whose care for his family so scrupulous. (Perhaps Paolo's son Valliano sometimes thought of that wonderful library in the rue du Faubourg Poissonnière as he struggled to drum the rules of French and Italian grammar into schoolboys whose first language was by now Greek.)

Marino was a darker, more shadowy figure. Although of course the Rock was remembered with great pride, other matters were passed over in tactful silence. Certainly there was a great deal of interest in the money left without an owner when Sofia died childless; almost a hundred years were to pass before one of Valliano's grandsons succeeded in journeying to Russia and claiming it. And perhaps there was always something of a tolerant shrug when the cultivation of the marsh was mentioned. Nevertheless, for many years ragged children continued to suck sweetness from the sugar cane that had gone wild in the empty loneliness of Livadi and the family always knew why this place unofficially bore their name.

Time passed and the Carburi family left the island for Athens, taking their memories with them. The house in the *Carburata* collapsed into a heap of rubble when Argostoli and Lixouri were destroyed in the earthquake of 1953. There is now nothing left in Cephalonia that Marino or Marco or Giovambattista would recognise, unless it is the lie of the land, the scent of the hillsides, the quality of the light. As in any place whose physical history has been violently obliterated, it is hard not to feel an abiding sense of sadness. In the dead-end alley on the outskirts of Lixouri named 'Marino Carburi Street' a few dilapidated old warehouses remain, from one of which a lean tom-cat emerges warily at dusk and disappears into the shadow of the bus without any wheels that has been abandoned there. Yet life indisputably goes on: from somewhere comes the smell of food cooking, the sound of music from a radio, the distant voices of children playing in the square as the light fades, the revving of motor scooters as the young men of Lixouri prepare to meet their girls – and perhaps later on to take them to find some privacy among the reeds of Livadi by Marino's quiet beach.

It all happened so long ago, yet memories live on . . . It may be that those whose lives have come to an untimely end have special need of remembrance. It is more than two hundred years now since Marino, naked and hairy and increasingly slippery with blood, struggled and fought with his bare hands against five men armed with knives, and finally fell. It is more than two hundred years since Giorgio's heart ceased beating in the icy water and his arms slackened their hold on his father's strong, safe, loving body. Their bones have long since crumbled to dust, their graves – at such great distance the one from the other – unmarked and lost. Their souls, I make no doubt, are together. In the Orthodox Church it is customary to hold a memorial service forty days after the death of someone whom you love, on the first anniversary of the death and yearly thereafter if such is your wish: after a long silence the words of the old, old ritual will once more be chanted in a quiet place full of the scent of incense and the flicker of candles: that the servant of God Marino and the servant of God Giorgio may find everlasting peace.

Giovanni Battista Carburi, born in Cephalonia 1722, died in Padua 1804.

Marino Carburi, born in Cephalonia 1729, murdered in Cephalonia 1782.

Marco Carburi, born in Cephalonia 1731, died in Padua 1808.

Maria Corafa, née Carburi, born in Cephalonia 1735, date of death unknown.

Paolo Carburi, born in Cephalonia 1740, died in Zakynthos 1813.

A NOTE ON THE TYPE

The text of this book is set in Linotype Sabon, named after the type founder, Jacques Sabon. It was designed by Jan Tschichold and jointly developed by Linotype, Monotype and Stempel, in response to a need for a typeface to be available in identical form for mechanical hot metal composition and hand composition using foundry type.

Tschichold based his design for Sabon roman on a fount engraved by Garamond, and Sabon italic on a fount by Granjon. It was first used in 1966 and has proved an enduring modern classic.